BLOOD & BONES: DODGE

Blood Fury MC®

Book 10

JEANNE ST. JAMES

———

Photographer: Jean Maureen Woodfin
Cover Artist: Golden Czermak at FuriousFotog
Cover Model: Josh Faust
Editor: Proofreading by the Page
Beta readers: Andi Babcock, Sharon Abrams & Alexandra Swab
Blood Fury MC Logo: Jennifer Edwards

———

Sign up for Jeanne's newsletter: https://www. authorjeannestjames.com
Join her FB readers' group for the inside scoop: https://www.facebook.com/groups/JeannesReviewCrew/

Sign up for my newsletter for insider information, author news, and new releases:
https://www.authorjeannestjames.com/

———

Buy direct from the author here: https://jeannestjamesauthor.com

Character List

BFMC Members:

Trip Davis – *President* – Son of Buck Davis, half-brother to Sig, mother is Tammy, Runs Buck You Recovery

Sig Stevens – *Vice President* – Son of Buck Davis, mother is Silvia, three years younger than Trip, helps run Buck You Recovery

Judge (Judd Scott) – *Sgt at Arms* - Father (Ox) was an Original, owns Justice Bail Bonds

Deacon Edwards – *Treasurer* – Judge's cousin, Skip Tracer/Bounty Hunter at Justice Bail Bonds

Cage (Chris Dietrich) – *Road Captain* – Dutch's youngest son, mechanic at Dutch's Garage

Ozzy (Thomas Oswald) – *Secretary* – *Original* – manages club-owned The Grove Inn.

Rook (Randy Dietrich) – Dutch's oldest son, mechanic at Dutch's Garage

Dutch (David Dietrich) – *Original* – Owns Dutch's Garage, sons: Cage & Rook

Dodge – Manager at Crazy Pete's Bar, did time with Rook in jail

Whip – Mechanic at Dutch's Garage (formerly the prospect named Sparky)
Rev (Mickey Rivers) – Mechanic at Dutch's Garage (formerly the prospect named Mouse)
Shade (Julian Bennett) – Works at Tioga Pet Crematorium (formerly the prospect named Shady)
Easy – Works at Tioga Pet Crematorium
Tater Tot – *Prospect* – Works at Crazy Pete's
Possum – *Prospect* – Works at Crazy Pete's
Castle – *Prospect* – Works at Shelter from the Storm
Scar – *Prospect* – Bouncer at Crazy Pete's
Bones – *Prospect* – Works at Shelter from the Storm

Ol' Ladies:

Stella – *Trip's ol' lady* - Crazy Pete's daughter, owns Crazy Pete's Bar, Liz's sister
Autumn (Red) – *Sig's ol' lady* – Accountant for the club's businesses
Cassidy (Cassie) – *Judge's ol' lady* – Manages Tioga Pet Crematorium
Reese – *Deacon's ol' lady* – Civil law attorney, Reilly's older sister
Jemma – *Cage's ol' lady* – Hospice Nurse, Judge's younger sister
Chelle (Rachelle) – *Shade's ol' lady* – Elementary school librarian
Jet Bryson – *Rook's ol' lady* – Works at Justice Bail Bonds, Adam Bryson's sister
Reilly – *Rev's ol' lady* – Manages Shelter from the Storm, Reese's younger sister
Shay – *Ozzy's ol' lady* – Website designer/graphic artist

Former Originals:

Buck Davis – *President* – Deceased, Trip & Sig's father
Ox – *Sgt at Arms* – Deceased, Judge & Jemma's father
Crazy Pete – *Treasurer* – Deceased, Stella and Liz's father

<u>Others:</u>

Tessa – Trip's younger sister, Cage and Jemma's house mouse
Henry (Ry) – Judge's son
Daisy – Cassie's daughter
Syn Stevens – Sig's half-sister
Saylor – Rev's sister, Judge and Cassie's house mouse
Dyna – Cage's daughter
Josie (Josephine) – Chelle's younger daughter
Maddie (Madison) – Chelle's older daughter
Jude – 12 yro rescued by Shade, Shade & Chelle's adopted son
Liz – Former sweet butt, Crash's ol' lady, Stella's half-sister & Crazy Pete's daughter
Silvia Stevens – Sig's mother, Razor's former ol' lady
Tammy Davis – Trip's mother, Buck's former ol' lady
Bebe Dietrich – Cage & Rook's mother, Dutch's former ol' lady
Clyde Davis – Buck's father, Trip & Sig's grandfather, deceased
Billie/Angel/Amber/Crystal/Brandy – Sweet butts
Max Bryson – *Chief of Police* – Manning Grove PD, Bryson brother
Marc Bryson – *Corporal* – Manning Grove PD, Bryson brother
Matt Bryson – *Officer* – Manning Grove PD, Bryson brother
Adam Bryson – *Officer* – Manning Grove PD, Bryson's cousin, Teddy's husband
Leah Bryson – *Officer* – Manning Grove PD, Marc's wife
Tommy Dunn – *Officer* – Manning Grove PD

Teddy Sullivan – Owner Manes on Main, Adam Bryson's husband
Amanda Bryson – Max's wife, owner Boneyard Bakery
Carly Bryson – Matt's wife, OB/GYN doctor
Levi Bryson – Adopted son of Matt & Carly Bryson (birth mother: Autumn/Red)

Playlist

Songs mentioned in this book:

Get It On - T. Rex
Smells Like Teen Spirit - Nirvana
Creep - Radiohead
Lightning Crashes - Live
Dream On - Aerosmith
Wanted Dead or Alive - Bon Jovi
My Heart is Broken - Evanescence
Ride Like The Wind - Christopher Cross
Wicked Game - Chris Isaak
Fade into You - Mazzy Star

Prologue

RUNNING ON EMPTY

His lungs were on fire.

An invisible knife stabbed him in the ribs.

He lengthened his stride, pushing through the pain and pushing himself harder.

His destination was clear.

Escape.

The further he got away from that house, the further he got away from them, the better his chances were.

His sneakers slapped the concrete as he sprinted down the sidewalk.

"Stop! Police!"

That fucking house. He knew he'd find her there.

"Stop!"

He always found her there.

Stoned and passed out on the floor on a stained, filthy mattress. What used to be light colored fabric was now black and brown. And even dark red in some spots.

"Stop!"

Tonight, her second-hand dress had been pulled up to her waist. Her legs and other places exposed. Places a son shouldn't see on his mother.

"Stop!"

Her eyes were closed, appearing asleep. Her mouth slack. A rubber tube still tied around her arm above her elbow.

"We're only trying to help you!"

Liars.

The cop who shouted that out was now wheezing.

Good. Maybe they'd give up soon.

"Hey, kid, stop running!"

Needles.

Syringes.

Lighters.

Spoons.

Pipes.

Burnt aluminum foil.

Empty plastic bottles. Empty soda cans.

Empty faces.

Empty bodies.

Empty.

Empty.

All fucking empty.

Junkies propped in the corners of the crumbling, dark rooms. Along the hallway. On the stairs. All of them high. Some of them semi-awake, most of them not. Some of them maybe even dead.

He didn't give a shit. She was the only junkie in that house that mattered to him.

He was only there to find the woman who was supposed to be responsible for him.

It wasn't supposed to be the other way around.

He tried to hear his pursuers over his own strained panting and racing heart. To gauge how close they were.

They hadn't given up yet.

Not yet.

He needed to lose them.

He darted left and down a dark alley.

And stopped short.

Shit. He picked the wrong fucking one.

Headlights sliced across the narrow alley. He winced and shielded his eyes when a spotlight hit him directly in the face.

Fuck!

He swiveled his head back and forth, desperate to find an escape.

He wasn't sure if his mom was dead. He never got a chance to check before the house was swarmed with men in uniform. But dead or not, the cops showing up at a crack house was never good.

Them chasing him was even worse.

A closed dumpster was pushed against one brick wall, but even if he climbed on top of it, he still couldn't reach the roof of the two-story building.

He was trapped. With only one way out.

The way he came in.

He gritted his teeth and took off, right toward the cop car blocking the entrance and heading in his direction.

He screamed as loud as he could as he ran directly at it.

His sprinted as fast as he could but the vehicle was faster.

Worse, so much bigger.

Before he could dart out of its path, what felt like a brick wall knocked him off his feet. He fell backwards, his arms windmilling in a failed attempt to catch his balance.

All the air shot from his lungs as he struck the pavement hard. His brain rattled in his skull as it hit, too.

It was over.

Done.

He closed his eyes and surrendered.

His life just like the alley.

A dead end.

THE FINGERS GRIPPING his shoulder dug in deeper. A silent warning not to flee. But if he got the chance, he would.

He didn't want to be here.

Not on that stoop.

Not with those people. Both the ones outside and inside.

One of the two cops flanking him jabbed his finger against the fancy doorbell again.

A few lock clicks were heard, then one side of the double doors opened, cool air from the air conditioning rushed out and a tall, thin blonde woman stood on the other side, looking down her nose at them.

Victoria Collins.

The woman Dodge's mother called Tricky Vickie for whatever reason. Dodge didn't care why, he just knew the woman was his stepmother in name only.

With a pinched face, her gaze skimmed both cops, then dropped to Dodge, standing between them.

Her lips twisted and her eyes narrowed as she slowly raised her gaze from him back to one of the officers. "May I help you?"

"Good afternoon, ma'am. We're looking for Kevin Collins," the filthy pig to his right announced.

Apparently, the invisible lemon she was sucking on became more bitter. "What's this about?" Her words might as well have icicles hanging off each one.

"We're looking for his father, ma'am."

Dodge rolled his eyes. They were at the wrong house, then. The man who lived there never once acted like his father. The asshole who lived on and off with his mother was more of a father to him than the one at this address.

And that didn't say much.

Tricky Vickie wrinkled her nose. "Why?"

"Are you his wife?"

"Of course."

Of fucking course.

"His mother overdosed and is currently in the hospital. When she gets out, she'll need to get clean to get custody of," Cop One tipped his head toward Dodge, "him. Someone needs to take him until she does. Now, *ma'am*, is Kevin Collins at home?"

Her expression turned into what reminded Dodge of a hoodie after someone yanked the hood string tight.

Fucking bitch.

Dodge jerked his shoulder again, trying to get the cop to ease up. He glanced around wondering if he just took off, whether the two fat pigs could catch him.

They were already sweating enough to soak their collars.

"He is, but… We don't want *him.*"

Dodge's attention sliced from the sweaty cops back to his sperm donor's wife.

"Need to speak to Kevin Collins, ma'am," Cop Two said more firmly. Patience must be running thin on the melting cops.

She stared at the cop for a few more seconds, then twisted her head and called back into the house. "Kevin!"

Once again giving his shoulder a little jerk, Dodge could turn enough to look at the big silver Mercedes parked in the driveway and wondered what other kinds of overpriced cars were parked inside the three-car garage.

Cars that probably cost a lot more than a year's worth of rent on their apartment.

"Mom? Who's at the door?" came a teenager's voice from deeper in the house.

Dodge's eyes narrowed. He wondered how old Kevin's *other* son was. The wanted one.

"It's nobody," Kevin's wife called out over her shoulder.

"Can I invite Chad and Preston over to swim?"

"Yes, Kevin, you can."

Kevin. Probably Kevin Jr. Or Kevin the third. Or even Kevin the twenty-fucking-third. He didn't know because he knew nothing about that side of his family tree.

What he did know was only normal kids from normal families got normal names.

Unlike his. When his mother squirted him out in the back of one, he was named Dodge.

He wasn't a Kevin, Chad or Preston.

To the woman standing there and the man who fucked his mother, he was no one.

A completely invisible nobody.

A mistake his sperm donor made over fourteen years ago when he got drunk at a sports bar and fucked someone he shouldn't have. Something Dodge was sure Kevin Collins regretted from the moment he sobered up.

"Kevin, tell your father to come out front," Vickie called out over her shoulder.

"Why?" came a whine.

"Just do it," she hissed. She stepped outside and closed the door behind her.

Probably so Dodge couldn't get a glimpse of the life he was missing.

Dodge's mother most likely targeted Kevin Collins because the man had money. Maybe she thought she'd get a fat monthly paycheck out of him for eighteen years.

She didn't.

Every month he sent the bare minimum. Only what he was forced to, even though he could pay a lot more. Unfortunately, the man could afford the best lawyers and his mother couldn't. She bitched all the time that amount she got from him was a joke. And having Dodge hadn't been worth it.

Joke or not, it was enough for her to pay for her next high. That was if his "adopted" dad or his uncle didn't take it from her first.

Forget that the money was supposed to help support her son.

Forget food or utilities.

Forget new clothes or shoes.

Forget all of that.

The four of them stood in silence in front of the house bigger than his apartment building, his stepmother's toned and tanned arms crossed over her huge fake tits.

When he heard the door opening again, Dodge's heart leapt into his throat, making it hard to breathe.

The man he hadn't seen in years took one look at him, quickly hid his surprise and replaced it with a scowl, stepped out onto the stone stoop and closed the door behind him.

"What is all of this?" His gaze slid from one cop to the other, avoiding Dodge completely. "Did he do something to get arrested? His mother—"

"Is incapable of taking care of him right now. You need to take your son until she's able to do that again."

His mouth dropped open. "What?"

The people in that house must like sucking on lemons.

The two uniformed pigs glanced at each other.

"Told you," Dodge said. *Not* sounding like a little whiny bitch like Kevin Jr.

"It's either that or he goes into the system," Cop One warned, making a point to glance around. At the Mercedes. The large house. The perfectly landscaped yard. "He's yours, right?"

"So the court says," his father muttered.

"Well, then..." Cop Two started, running a hand over his sweat-beaded forehead.

No surprise that Kevin Collins hadn't even acknowledged him. No "Hi, son." No "How are you? Do you need anything?"

Nothing.

"Try his grandmother. She'll probably take him."

Cop One shook his shaved head. "Kid says she's dead."

"How about the man she shacks up with? The biker?" He spit the last two words out like a piece of shit had flown into his mouth.

"Checked the residence and no one was around. And before you suggest him next, the uncle wasn't around, either. Kid said they'd be back, but we can't just leave him there unsupervised. Not without knowing when or *if* they'll return. You're the only one available."

"Then..." Kevin scraped his fingers through his hair, changing it from neatly combed to standing on end. "I guess I need to call my attorney and see what our options are."

Cop Two's eyebrows rose. "Options? How about just letting him inside?"

"Our kids are inside."

Douchebag.

The two cops glanced at each other again, neither hiding their disbelief.

Cop One jerked his chin toward Dodge. "He's your kid, too."

"Only on paper."

Not even that. Dodge had his mother's last name not Kevin's and he wasn't sure if the man's name was officially on his birth certificate.

"He's not your blood?" Cop Two asked, his dark eyes narrowed because he already knew the answer.

"Not by choice."

Cop One blew out a frustrated breath. "Well, sir, right now, your son has no choice, either. If you're not willing to take him, then we'll have to take him back to the station until Child Welfare Services can come get him."

The asshole who knocked up Dodge's mother shrugged. "Okay."

"Just to be clear, that's what you want?" Cop One asked.

The two cops might be surprised but Dodge wasn't. He

never received one card or present from the man during the past fourteen years. Why would he want to act like a parent now?

Especially when Dodge needed a parent the most. Even a shitty one.

"Thank you, officers, for bringing this problem to our attention, but, I'm sorry, we will not be allowing him into our home," the sperm sack said. "I have to do what's best for my family." He turned toward his wife. "Victoria."

She gave her husband a nod and went inside.

Without another word, the man began to follow his wife. The cops stood there in stunned silence.

"Yo, *Daddy*!" Dodge shouted as the cop pulled on his shoulder, trying to turn him in order to leave.

Kevin Collins paused.

Dodge lifted his hand.

Not to say goodbye.

Instead, he pointed his middle finger straight up to the sky.

And sneered.

Chapter One

DODGE FOLLOWED the woman down the steps from his apartment that led into Crazy Pete's storage room and small kitchen area.

Trip hadn't been able to install a full kitchen, so they couldn't serve anything other than finger foods due to the lack of room.

Because of that, they kept it simple. Besides peanuts, chips and pretzels—salty shit to make people drink more— they had a double fryer to make frozen shit, like wings, cheese sticks, chicken fingers and the rest of that kind of crap. The Fury prez had also installed a cooler to store that crap—smaller than the one in the club's bunkhouse—and a commercial microwave to zap the shit out of it.

Not too many customers ordered food unless they were fucking smashed. Or had the munchies. Or didn't care about eating frozen mass-produced garbage thrown into a vat of grease.

Whatever. It still brought in more scratch for the bar. And, in turn, the club.

Besides bringing in some decent tips, Stella paid him a good salary to manage the bar. He deserved every damn penny of it since most of the time he lived and breathed the business twenty-four, seven.

Living upstairs for free was convenient but it also tied him to the business. Thank fuck for the prospects. And some other local help they could now afford to hire.

In the beginning, when Dodge first rolled into town after his last—and he hoped to fuck *final*—stint in county, he, Stella and Trip were working their asses off to take Crazy Pete's from the red into the black.

He loved working for Stella because she was a badass bitch and he had the utmost respect for her. Trip was one lucky motherfucker.

Of course, the Fury prez knew it.

If he had to be tied down to one woman for the rest of his life, a woman like Trip's ol' lady might not be like another prison sentence.

The thirty-something blonde—he couldn't remember her damn name, not that it mattered—he was now following out of the storage area, through the swinging door and back into the bar was not a badass bitch, but annoying as fuck.

Good thing for most of the short time upstairs, his dick had been in her mouth, keeping her fucking quiet. He should have kept it at that, but he had owed her a damn orgasm and the fuck if he was going down on her. If he did, her mouth might have run the whole time and he would've been tempted to smother her with one of his pillows.

That could be bad for business. Most likely him, too.

Once he had gotten her upstairs, he realized his mistake but by then it was too damn late.

He powered through it since he was not a fucking quitter.

He always escorted women out of his apartment to make sure they left. The one time he didn't, he came back upstairs after closing to find her still in his damn bed.

She wasn't there for long. She also never took a trip up those steps again.

Now he only hoped tonight's catch-and-release didn't hang around until last call. Despite what she might think, she was not getting round two.

She wasn't getting any kind of conversation from him, either. With the way the bar was hopping, at least he had a good excuse to ignore her the rest of the night if she stuck around.

As he always did after taking a "break," he checked in with either Stella or one of the prospects to see if there was anything he needed to be aware of.

"Problems?" Dodge asked Possum as he stepped behind the bar and closed the hinged portion behind him. If he didn't, some asshole would think they could come back there and help themselves.

They couldn't and Scar made sure they never made that mistake again.

The lanky, narrow-faced prospect shook his head. "Nope. But some chick's askin' for the manager."

"Fuck." Dodge frowned. Shielding his mouth with his hand, he asked, "Is it a chick I've banged?" just in case the other chick he just banged was nearby and listening.

"Can't keep track of everyone you banged. But if I had to guess, probably."

"Tell me where she is without lookin' at her."

"Ten o'clock."

"Your ten or my ten?"

Possum squinted.

Dodge shook his head. "Just fuckin' point."

The young prospect jerked a thumb over his shoulder. Dodge lifted his gaze in that direction. The bar was so packed, it was impossible to tell who he was indicating.

But before he could ask Possum to point her out again, the woman who he'd taken upstairs was there leaning across the bar, sliding a slip of paper along the shellacked wood toward him.

What the fuck.

"You forgot this, baby," she said in her husky voice. Her tits and that voice were what had caught his attention in the first place. But neither her tits or her voice were worth the annoying shit she said when she hadn't been gagging on his cock.

So, fuck no, he hadn't forgotten to get her number. He glanced down at the paper that included her name, too. He jerked his chin up at her, grabbed the slip of paper, crumpled it up and tossed it in the overflowing trash can under the bar.

Her blue eyes went wide for a split second, then narrowed. "Nice. Can I at least get a rum and Coke?"

Dodge turned to Possum, now busy pouring a draft beer. "She wants a rum and Coke. Start her a tab."

"A—" she sputtered. "After that, you aren't letting me drink for free?"

"You drink for free, it comes outta my pocket." Not true, but she didn't need to know that.

"What we did wasn't worth you buying me a drink?"

He raised an eyebrow. "Want the truth or d'you prefer a lie?"

Her mouth dropped open and, when it snapped shut, she huffed and yanked her purse off the bar. "Well, here's a truth for you, asshole… You sucked. You have a micro-penis and I had to fake an orgasm just to get you to hurry up and finish. Plus, your apartment is trashy. Just like you."

"Yep," was all he said with a grin. He grabbed a clean glass from under the bar and lifted it in the air. "You still wanna open that tab, or no?"

"Fuck you. I'll drink elsewhere instead of this rat trap." She slipped from the stool, shot him a single finger salute and elbowed her way through the customers crowding around the bar.

"Stella don't like it when you chase away customers like that."

"Stella ain't here, now, is she?" The boss-y lady usually went home early now that she was getting huge with Trip's baby planted in her belly. Trip didn't want her working late, being on her feet too long or overworking herself. Dodge didn't blame the Fury prez for putting his boot down but it did put Dodge in a bind some nights when he didn't have that extra set of hands.

"Also don't think she likes you bangin' all the customers with tits."

"Not all of them." He only banged the ones he didn't have to chase. If they came up to him and were clear about their interest, he considered them. But if they played hard to get and pretended they were being coy, then fuck them.

Possum bent over and when he straightened, he had the crumpled slip of paper in his hand. "Can I have this?"

Dodge eyed it and shrugged. "Yeah, but if she agrees to meet up with you, bring a gag."

Possum grinned. "I can gag her with—"

"Tried that." He twisted his head toward the end of the bar closest to the entrance. "Now point out this chick again. This time be fuckin' clear."

Possum scanned the area he had indicated prior, then frowned. "Don't see her anymore. Maybe she's loadin' her gun to shoot your ass. You probably did her wrong."

"Or I did her right and she came back for seconds. But just in case, I'm gonna make sure I stand behind you the rest of the fuckin' night."

The prospect snorted and shook his head.

"Fuck that. You're too fuckin' skinny. Gonna use Tater instead. He's a bigger target and a better shield."

Possum glanced around again. "Can't find her. Maybe she got tired of waitin'."

"Maybe," he muttered. "Ain't gonna sweat it."

"Wait… There she is."

"Where?"

Possum tipped his head toward the other side of Crazy Pete's. "Standin' on the stage."

Dodge's head whipped around toward the low platform. It wasn't huge since the bar didn't have the square footage or the ceiling height to put in a real stage, but it worked. Having bands come in on Friday and Saturday nights, whether local or not, brought in some major scratch.

Sometimes they even had a band popular enough to charge a cover. They tried not to do that too often, since folks in Manning Grove and the surrounding area were cheap as fuck.

Mansfield college kids didn't mind spending the green to see some bands but then, they were spending their mommy and daddy's hard-earned cash.

Dodge hated when bands pulled in the *I'm-not-a-kid-but-I'm-not-an-adult-either* crowd. Shit tended to end up broken. He'd also spent too much time cleaning up puke after those nights. Or trying to find missing pool balls.

Or replacing the dart boards.

Or finding used wraps in the bathroom. One side of his lip curled up. From now on that would be a prospect's job.

The chick stepping off the platform after circling it once and heading to the jukebox, looked to be about that age.

Trouble.

That was what she looked like.

Too young to know better, too old to use being a kid as an excuse.

He'd be surprised if she was even twenty-one.

"Why the fuck did Scar let a teenager in the door?" He

turned to Possum. "Did you serve her? Is she old enough to be in here?"

"She ain't drinkin'," Possum said, "so I didn't card her."

Her back was to him and her head was tipped down as she studied what he assumed was the music selection in the jukebox.

"Pretty fuckin' sure I didn't bang her," Dodge muttered, "'cause that shit right there's jail bait. No pussy's worth doin' time."

She wore black skinny jeans, black clunky, thick-soled boots with the hem of her jeans and the loose laces tucked into the top, and a black see-through knit sweater that looked too big, hung loosely off one shoulder and halfway down her arm. Under that she wore what might be a tight, white wife-beater. Her *what-might-be* black hair, or at least a very dark brown like his, was long, straight and hung almost halfway down her back.

"Maybe she's here to tell you that she's your long-lost daughter."

Dodge's gaze spun back to him. "Ain't that old, you asshole."

"Dunno. You're pretty fuckin' old."

"The fuck I am."

"Got a few grays in your beard and hair."

Dodge frowned and dragged his fingers down his beard. "Fuck you. Grayin' early that's all. Jesus Christ."

"Startin' to look like a grandpappy, that's all."

He tugged his grey knit cap lower over his head to hide those damn early grays. "How old do you fuckin' think I am?"

"Fifty."

Dodge shook his head. "You're such an asshole."

Tater lumbered down the back of the bar to grab a beer bottle from the cooler and popped off the top for a customer.

"Hey, Tater, how old you think grandpa here is?" Possum asked the other prospect.

Tater froze like a deer stunned by high beams, stared at Dodge and then shrugged. "Dunno… uh… Fifty?"

"What the fuck," Dodge grumbled. "Ain't fifty. I'm not even forty. Hell, I *just* turned thirty-five." Yeah, like six months ago, but those fuckers didn't need to know that.

"Damn, that's old," Possum whispered, his eyes wide. A second later, he broke out in laughter. "Just fuckin' with you, old man."

"The only Fury brother you can call 'old man' is Dutch. He's the only one in the geriatric category."

Except for his sex life. The Original was impressive when it came to banging a slew of women. It didn't matter age, race, ethnicity, or anything. Dutch loved it all and somehow snagged it all.

It had all of them scratching their damn heads.

Tater tossed the bottle cap at the piled-high garbage can. Of course, it bounced out and landed on the floor by Dodge's boot. "He said he'd shoot us if we call him that."

"Okay, then make sure you call him that next time you see him. We could use some new prospects. Ones who take out the fuckin' trash and don't miss when they're tossing shit into the garbage. Make sure you pick that up, Tater Twat. You don't and I'll make you get down on the goddamn floor and pick it up with your teeth."

Tater made a face, then leaned over with a groan to pick the cap off the floor. It shouldn't take such a damn effort to bend over.

"Empty the trash soon's you can. Gonna go see what this chick wants."

"Probably to call you Daddy," Possum called out.

Dodge lifted the hinged bar and let it drop back into place. "Forget Dutch shootin' you. Better sleep with one eye open, asshole."

"What the fuck do you think we've been doin' ever since Scar moved into our bunkroom?" Tater Tot called out loud enough for Dodge but not loud enough for Scar to hear him from where the other prospect stood by the front entrance.

"Rumor has it, circle-jerks," he tossed over his shoulder as he worked his way through the crowded tables toward the jukebox, now playing the classic *Get It On* by T. Rex.

Thank fuck Stella left picking the music selection for the jukebox to him.

Even better, now that the new jukebox was digital, he could change shit out all the time depending on his mood. He could block songs, too. Like the ones sounding like hill-billy mating calls.

Too many folks in these parts liked country music and not the good shit, but the stuff that made Dodge want to stab his eardrums. The shit that made hound dogs howl.

"Heard you're lookin' for me."

She continued to scroll through the music selection. Her short fingernails were painted black, reminding him of Billie. Her slender fingers had a few rings encircling them. She had a tiny tattoo on the webbing between her right thumb and index finger and a silver chain bracelet with a pendant hanging from her left wrist.

At first he thought it was a heart, then he realized it was shaped like a guitar pick.

"You need better music," she murmured.

Fuck, for as petite as she was, her voice sounded smoky as fuck. He had a thing for that shit. Like Stella's. The prez's ol' lady had a voice that could give him a raging hard-on if he closed his eyes and just listened. *And* if he let it.

He didn't because he liked breathing too damn much.

"Music in that thing's just fine."

She turned and she might have well have kicked him in the chest.

He forced himself to breath as the soul-piercing dark

brown eyes landed on him. They were accentuated with black eye liner that wasn't overly thick but enough to make her eyes stand out. The rest of her makeup was light, not over-done like Billie's preferred goth look.

She tipped her face up to him, her head slightly tilted. "Are you in charge here?"

"The manager."

"Does that mean you're in charge?"

The sarcasm was too thick to miss. "Exactly what it means."

"I saw on your website that you schedule bands Friday and Saturday nights."

Having Shay do the bar's website had actually helped. He was skeptical at first but was now glad he didn't fight it.

"Yep." He let his gaze slide down her face and beyond, taking his time and not bothering to hide his curiosity.

He was right. Too fucking young. Though, what was behind her eyes said otherwise.

He knew that look. Only too damn well.

He ignored it and continued on.

Even with the peek-a-boo black sweater covering the tank top underneath it—especially because of the tank top being white—he could tell she wasn't wearing a bra. And what was under the cotton was perky and definitely fucking wide awake.

He'd seen a lot of tits and hers looked fresh out of their teens. But didn't mean he couldn't appreciate them.

That made his answering "yeah" get caught in his throat. He cleared it and repeated his response.

"Do you always eye fuck women like that?"

She didn't sound offended but more as if she was emotionally drained. He understood that, too. "Women, sometimes. Jail bait, no."

"I'm far from jail bait."

"Don't care." Did he say that more for himself than her? Fuck him if he did. She looked like trouble he didn't need.

Just then, the song *Smells Like Teen Spirit* by Nirvana began to spew from the speakers throughout Pete's.

Wasn't that the fucking truth?

Christ.

"Neither do I," she said. She glanced around the interior of the bar. "My question is if you book bands and if you need to fill some spots on your calendar."

"For who?"

"For a band."

"No shit. For whose band?"

"Mine."

He blinked. "We don't book teeny-bopper bands."

"Good. Because I hate teeny-bopper bands."

What the fuck was going on? "How old are you?"

Her head tilted to the side. "How old are you?"

Jesus. She might be tiny but her attitude wasn't. He gritted his teeth. "Christ… What kinda band you got?"

"The kind that plays music."

Dodge sucked in a slow breath. "Alrighty, then. You can see yourself out. Scar there by the front door will hold it open for you." *And plant a boot on your ass to help you through it.*

He spun on his own boot and, before he could take a second step, a hand grabbed his arm to stop him. "Wait."

He hesitated but didn't turn around, though he did glance down at the hand clamped onto his arm. Yeah, the tattoo on the webbing was either a W or an M, depending which way he looked at it.

Not that he cared.

"My band is looking for places to play. We need the… Well, you don't even have to pay us, we're willing to play for tips. We don't even have to headline on a Friday or Saturday. We'll take any night while we're in the area."

What the fuck?

Headline? What kind of place did she think Crazy Pete's was?

And tips? What kind of *living-under-a-bridge* "band" did she have?

When he turned to face her again, she quickly dropped her hand and took a step back. He did his best to keep his eyes above her tits where a practically see-through cotton-covered nipple was trying to escape through one of the sweater holes.

What the fuck good was a sweater full of big holes like that? Was it supposed to be stylish? Like her torn jeans?

Her slim black jeans had a few frayed holes he wasn't sure if they were done on purpose or because she couldn't afford to replace them.

Didn't matter since she wasn't his problem.

She was *not* his fucking problem.

"Do you even have real instruments? Or do you beat pots, pans and five-gallon plastic buckets with metal and wooden spoons?"

Her delicate nostrils flared and when they did, he noticed a small gem piercing on one side of her nose. Definitely not a real diamond.

If it was real, she probably would've hocked it by now.

He remembered those times. In the past, he'd been there himself all too often. That's why he didn't mind living above Crazy Pete's and dealing with the long hours managing the bar. He fucking wanted for nothing anymore.

It might not be raining green but his wallet was no longer dry like the desert.

And dealing with the occasional drunk was a lot fucking better than daily dealings with the asshole screws whenever he was living behind razor wire fence.

"We have real instruments," she said through what looked like clenched teeth.

"What kind of music you play?"

"Rock."

"What kind?"

"Whatever fits the place we're playing." Her gaze cut through the bar again. "This seems to be an older crowd—"

"Depends on the night."

Her attention landed back on him. "We can play whatever you want."

"*Whatever* I want?"

She nodded. "We're flexible and know a variety of stuff from the sixties up to current stuff."

Sixties? That was decades before she was shitting in a diaper. "What do you do in this band?"

"Sing."

"That it?"

"That's not enough?"

Dodge stared at her.

She jerked her slender shoulders up in a shrug. "I can play, too."

"Play what?"

Why the fuck did he care what she could play? What the fuck was wrong with him? He needed to point her toward the door and give her a shove in that direction.

"Guitar, bass, keyboard, drums," she lifted one slender shoulder, "Cow bell."

His head jerked back. "Cow bell?"

"Just seeing if you were listening and wanted an actual answer or if you're just being a jerk."

"It was a valid question."

"You should be more interested in the band as a whole. Not just me."

True, but she was the one standing in front of him. "Do you actually play cow bell?"

"Sometimes. Tambourine, too."

"Don't take any skill to play cow bell or tambourine."

"You know from experience?"

No, but he had two good eyes in his damn head and in the past couple of years plenty of bands had played on Crazy Pete's stage. Some better than others.

His brow dropped low. "How long has your band been together?"

Hers dropped low, too. "Does it matter?"

"I got questions. I need answers. You don't wanna answer them, then guess you don't need this gig as much as you think you do."

Her jaw shifted.

She didn't like that.

He didn't care.

"We can play tomorrow night for tips, if you want. Then if you like how we do and want to pay us…"

"Tomorrow's only Wednesday. It's a slow night."

She shrugged. "Then we'll play a set for food. And playing on an off night's a perfect way for you to see how good we are and whether we deserve a busier one."

The girl knew how to hustle, that was for sure. People like her usually were never handed a damn thing in life. They had to pay for everything they had in sweat, blood and tears.

But just feeding a band and not paying them a stage fee sounded like a pretty good deal. Unless they totally fucking sucked and their music was so bad customers bailed.

"Got frozen chicken fingers and fries."

"Is it real chicken?"

"Doubt it. Does your band have a manager?"

"I'm it."

"Are they all over twenty-one?" Legally they only had to be eighteen as long as they weren't served alcohol, but something about this whole thing was making his Spidey-sense tingle.

"We're all over twenty-one." She lifted one dark, perfectly-shaped eyebrow.

Nah, it wasn't a fucking tingle, it was a tornado wreaking havoc in his damn gut.

This chick both fascinated him and worried the fuck out of him. He didn't like that feeling.

He ground his palm back and forth on the back of his neck as he considered her.

She wasn't begging, she hadn't whined about his hesitation, she simply shut her mouth and waited.

He liked that because if she would've kept pushing him, he probably would have escorted her out of Pete's himself. "Tell you what, you wanna play tomorrow night, we'll keep a tab open for you and your band members for the rest of the night once you play a decent set. You suck, deal's off."

"We won't suck."

"Heard that before," he muttered.

"Swear we won't."

"But you'll work for damn food."

"You do what you got to do," she said with a shrug, not embarrassed at all to be in that situation.

While he normally liked that kind of *go-get-'em* attitude, those words coming from her made the tiny hairs on his neck stand. "Just a warnin', no drugs, no prostitutin'. Ain't gonna tolerate that shit. That big, ugly motherfucker you walked past when you entered? He'll toss you and your shit onto the sidewalk with one word from me and he ain't gonna be gentle about it, either. You got that?"

She nodded. "Understood."

"Warn your girlfriends, too."

She frowned up at him. "Girlfriends?"

"Yeah, the rest of your band."

A thin smile appeared on her face. First smile he saw on her. Though it didn't reach her eyes. "I'll let them know."

"We'll throw somethin' up on the website to announce you bein' here, but ain't sure if that'll do any good since it's last minute. You can put out a tip jar, ain't sure if anyone will be that generous around here. Lots of cheap mother-fuckers. What's the name of your band?"

"The Synners."

"The what?"

"The Synners. With a Y." She stepped past him and threw over her shoulder, "We appreciate the opportunity. See you tomorrow night."

"You go on at eight," he called out. "Set up at seven."

She kept walking and tossed a hand above her head in acknowledgement of her hearing him.

He hoped to fuck he didn't regret this.

But so far in life, whenever he figured he'd regret something—like fucking blondie earlier—it turned out he always did.

Every damn time.

One day he'd fucking learn.

Chapter Two

Dodge shook his head and cursed under his breath when he noticed two pigs walking in his direction.

Two pigs that happened to be married.

He sighed.

Since they were both in uniform, he knew they weren't there to drink. Fuck no. They were there on some sort of official business.

That was never good.

The band hadn't started playing yet, in fact—he glanced at his cell phone—they should've been there a half-hour ago.

Maybe they'd end up being a no-show. Though, with what he saw of her attitude, it would surprise him if she backed out and maybe even disappoint him, too.

That couldn't be right. He had no good reason to want to see her again.

None.

But the truth was, her band not showing would be no fucking loss for the bar since it was only a Wednesday night. Now, if it had been a Friday…

"What?" he barked as Marc Bryson stepped up to the bar, followed by his wife Leah.

"Well, hello to you, too, Dodge," Leah said with a smile, not giving a fuck that seeing them made Dodge a cranky motherfucker.

"You comin' in here ain't good for business."

Marc Bryson rested his hands on his duty belt in typical pig style and glanced around. "Why? Almost everyone in here knows us."

"Why you here?" he asked, not caring one fucking bit that the Brysons were known by just about everyone who lived in or around Manning Grove.

"We have a little problem…" Bryson started.

"Usually do when one of you show up. Must be a big problem if you needed your wife to back you up. Too much for you to handle by yourself, *Officer*? She got bigger balls?"

"Hers are pretty damn big," Bryson agreed. "But mine hang a little heavier."

Leah Bryson turned away and pretended to scan the few customers already in the bar. Dodge didn't miss her shoulders shake the slightest bit.

Out of all the Bryson pigs, Leah was the coolest. Probably because she married into the family instead of being born into it. She happened to be damn smoking hot, too.

If Dodge was into that type.

The type that slipped on a pig skin every day for work. The kind that took joy in making someone's life a living hell for simply a *mistake*. Or two.

He had no idea how Rook fell for Jet Bryson.

Okay, he did. Like Leah, Jet was pretty scorching hot for a pig. She had only become hotter once she shed that fucking pig skin for good.

He bet Rook and her had some crazy-assed sex. Jet probably liked it rough and—

Bryson cleared his throat. "Anyway, there's a school bus

blocking the back alley. We can't have that in case of a fire or medical emergency."

"A what?" He must have misunderstood.

"Schooooool buuuuuus," Bryson dragged out. "Guess you rode on one of the short ones."

Dodge dipped his chin and stared at the pig. "You sayin' I'm slow?"

"I'm not saying you are, but I'm thinking you're not too quick."

"Asshole."

Marc Bryson grinned and shrugged. "How did those windows taste?"

"Mark," Leah scolded and whacked her hubby in the arm.

"After you licked them, they tasted pretty damn clean," Dodge told him.

"Anyway, it has to be moved. So, get 'er done." Bryson tapped his finger on the bar in emphasis.

"The sooner the better, Dodge," Leah added with her signature smile. Warm and friendly unless you crossed her, then that taser could be drawn quicker than shit. She'd only smile again once you were flat on your back on the pavement trying not to shit your pants.

"Gotcha, Leah."

Bryson made a face when Dodge called his wife by her first name. Leah tugged on his arm. "We'll swing back in about fifteen. Make sure it's gone."

Dodge didn't respond but watched both pigs leave. Luckily for them, Scar wasn't working the door tonight since it was a typical slow hump day. Instead, it was the prospect's night to sit watch on Hillbilly Hill to keep an eye on what the Shirleys were up to.

The answer was easy. No fucking good.

"Gonna run out back and see what the fuck's goin' on,"

he called out to Micah, his newest bartender. He was a bit young but worked his ass off. "Keep an eye on shit."

Micah gave him a chin lift and continued to dry pint glasses with a dish towel.

Dodge patted his cut to make sure he had his tin and a lighter, then headed toward the rear of Pete's. He accompanied every damn step in that direction with a muttered curse since his fear was confirmed. That chick last night was trouble.

Once he shoved open the rear door, the stinky-ass diesel smell of a school bus definitely blocking the alley filled his nostrils.

Fuckin' son of a bitch.

The bus was painted in black primer and "The Synners" was spray-painted graffiti-style along the side. The windows were all spray-painted black. He guessed for privacy.

He'd seen a couple of converted school buses before, but this one... If the inside looked anything like the outside... He grimaced.

Shaking his head, he pulled a hand-rolled from the metal container he stored them in and tucked it between his lips. With a flick of the Bic, he lit it, sucked in two lungs full of smoke, then slowly blew it out and up into the frigid December air.

He slowly walked along the skoolie that had to be about thirty-five feet long to where one of the custom-made storage compartments under the bus was wide open and two dudes were pulling out what looked like the shit a band would need.

Two dudes. He sucked on his teeth for a second before taking another pull from his cigarette.

Boyfriends of the band members?

He didn't give a shit. He only cared about their rig totally blocking the alley.

"Yo," he said as he walked behind them and stood

watching them pull out guitar cases, pieces of a drum set and whatever else the band needed to play. Neither guy stopped what they were doing, so he said it again, this time a lot louder. "Yo!"

They finished finagling a bass drum out of the tight area and both straightened.

"Yo," one of them answered.

"Hurry up and get that shit unloaded and move the bus. Otherwise, the pigs are gonna get it towed. And," he let his gaze roll over the bus before doing the same to them, "doubtin' you can afford that bill."

"We're planning on it. Just need to finish unloading our shit."

"Well, get it done faster. You were supposed to be set up a half-hour ago."

One nodded and returned to unload more shit. The other, the one with long dark hair pulled back in a short ponytail, put his hands on his hips and faced Dodge. "Are you the manager?"

"In the flesh."

"Thanks for giving us a shot."

"Gonna revoke that shot if you don't hurry the fuck up. The band needs to get set up and warmed up before eight."

The man with shaggy blond hair pulled a microphone stand out of the storage area and glanced at his phone. "Fuck."

Dodge jerked his chin toward the bus. "The girls in there gettin' ready?"

The man lifted his eyes from his phone and frowned. "Yeah. Sure."

Dodge nodded. "'Kay. Get your shit together and then move this hunk of junk."

Ponytail guy squinted at him. "Do you know where we can park it?"

"Around the corner. Fifth Street Church. They got a decent-sized lot and it'll be empty at this time of night."

Dark-haired guy nodded. "Thanks, dude." He went back to helping his shaggy blond-haired friend.

"They good?" Dodge asked.

"They?"

"The group."

The blond's mouth opened, then shut. "Yeah. The best."

"Good." Dodge spun on his heel to head back to the door. "Door's unlocked. Got a cement block there to prop it open. Soon as you're done bringin' your shit in, make sure you close it since it's colder than a witch's tit out here."

"Sure, brother."

Dodge sucked on his teeth again at the "brother," then took another drag on his hand-rolled before pinching out the end and ripping open the door. He put the remainder of the cigarette back in the old mint tin as he strode back down the short hallway to return to work.

With three guys working, the band's equipment was set-up on the low platform in record time. He sent Possum over there to bring them bottled water and offer them a round of drinks on the house since Dodge got caught up flirting with a woman sitting at one of the high-top tables in the billiard area.

That meant he hadn't been able to keep a close eye on what was being set up. But Micah and Possum knew the deal when it came to bands, so he trusted them to let him know if any problems came up.

In the meantime, he had more important things to worry about… like who was tonight's catch-and-release after he listened to the band and rated their performance to see if they were worthy to play a busy night.

Right now, the strawberry-blonde watching her girl-friends play pool seemed to be a good candidate for a trip north to ride his pole. Unlike the little singer with the big attitude, this woman had big enough tits and thick enough thighs to smother him.

One side of his mouth turned up.

He tipped his head toward her empty glass. "Want another beer?"

She shot him a smile that began to get the blood flowing south. "Sure."

He swiped her pint glass from the small round table and gave her a wink. "I'll go grab you one."

After he stepped out from the billiards' area and into the main bar area, he glanced over to the back corner at the stage. The band had better start warming up soon.

He frowned when he saw only the three younger guys on the platform. Two of them being the same ones unloading the equipment. The third was a redhead working behind the drum set, putting the finishing touches on assembling it.

Sure didn't look like a girl group. In fact, it looked the exact opposite. Before he could pivot and head in that direction, a dark figure emerged from the back hallway.

He couldn't tell if it was the lead singer because whoever it was, was wearing a black hoodie. The hood with cat ears was pulled up and over their head, hiding their face.

Had to be her because the person was tiny. Petite.

Her.

Fuck, he never even asked her name.

Didn't matter.

Since she finally showed, he would let her get warmed up while keeping his distance. Right now he was worried that getting too close could be dangerous. Like a moth flying too close to a flame.

Christ. What the fuck was wrong with him?

He continued on his trek across the floor and ducked behind the bar. While he was back there, he flipped the switch to turn on the stage's spotlight. It wasn't anything fancy but it did the job.

The job it was currently doing was lighting up the lead singer as she pushed down the kitty-eared hood, exposing her long dark hair. When she turned her back to the sparse audience, she unzipped the sweatshirt and shrugged out of it, tossing it onto a nearby empty table.

There were a lot of those tonight. Wednesday was typically slow, but with it being between Thanksgiving and Christmas, not too many people were out and about tonight, anyway. Some of their regulars were financially preparing for the holidays. For them, they kept more pennies in their pockets by drinking at home.

When she turned, the spotlight lit her up as she approached the microphone. He forgot to breathe for a second.

His held breath rushed out of him as he raked his gaze from the top of her dark head all the way to her boots. Unlike last night, they weren't heavy biker-type boots with thick, flat rubber soles. The black leather boots she wore tonight went above the knees, had a killer heel and were laced up the front.

And *fuuuuuuuk*…

She might be wearing a bra tonight, but she wasn't wearing much else. Over the black bra was a black, see-through fishnet long-sleeved crop top. The bottom hem ended right under her bra. Her belly was flat. Her bare skin milky white and smooth. He even spotted the glint of a silver ring piercing her navel.

Like last night, she wore *tight-as-fuck* black shredded jeans. Could even be the same pair.

Her eye makeup was darker and heavier. Her eyeliner drawn past the corners and curved upward to make her look more seductive. Bright red lipstick really emphasized her lips under the spotlight. She wore more eyeshadow, too, but he couldn't quite tell the color from where he stood across the interior of Pete's.

What he could see from where he was, was the splash of color sweeping across each high cheekbone. It wasn't heavy-handed but still noticeable.

At least to him.

He couldn't decide if she looked older with tonight's makeup or younger.

The fingers now gripping the microphone were once again encircled by rings. Around her delicate wrist, she wore the same silver bracelet with the guitar pick pendant. A huge silver ornate cross hung low around her neck and almost reached her pierced belly button. He doubted she wore it for religious reasons since the band's name was The Synners. With a fucking Y.

He had a hard time paying attention to the beer he was pouring because his eyes were glued to the indentation of her spine as she twisted and said something to her male bandmates.

He was such a fucking dumbass to think she had an all-girls band.

He mistakenly *assumed* when he knew better to do so. Life had taught him never to assume shit.

He tilted the pint glass to reduce the head on the beer and, once full, began to carry it back toward the pool table area.

He planned on keeping one ear on the band, the other set on tonight's conquest. As long as the strawberry-blonde thought he was paying attention, then...

He grinned.

That grin quickly slid off his face and crashed to the ground at his feet when he stopped dead in his tracks halfway to his destination, almost getting whiplash as his head twisted toward the stage.

And to her.

The chick who he didn't even know her name.

But that fucking voice.

Jesus.

How could a woman so petite have such a smoky, powerful voice that sent a spark shooting down his spine and ignited a fire in his damn balls?

He glanced down at the beer he was in the process of delivering. His gaze lifted to the billiards area where the strawberry-blonde was tucked around the corner and out of view. It sliced back to the stage.

Did he just rethink his whole fucking night?

Because of those damn boots and that spellbinding voice?

Damn. He had already put in some effort to work the blonde. Was he going to let all that energy go to waste?

He glanced down at the beer again. While he stared at it, *her* voice continued to fill his ears. Take over his brain and tighten his balls.

Drown his thoughts.

He scratched the back of his neck as he considered his options.

Fuck. He no longer had options.

It was damn clear he now only had one.

His feet moved in the opposite direction that he wanted them to take and as he stepped past the half-wall and into the area that contained the pool tables, he stopped at the high-top table where—*Christ*, he didn't know her name, either—*blondie* sat. She gave him a flirty smile and a sugges-tive tilt of her head.

The woman before him was the right choice. She was.

She was a little bit older and more experienced in life. And more importantly, most likely more experienced in bed.

She also knew the deal. It was a one-time thing. He doubted she'd expect anything more, the whole reason he zeroed in on her instead of her friends.

He'd become good at reading women and whether they'd end up being clingy afterward or on the same page as him. A page that read mutual satisfaction and nothing more.

He slid the beer in front of her. "On the house."

Her long red fingernail circled the rim of the glass, then playfully scraped over his hand. "Thank you, baby."

"You need anything else, Possum will get it for you."

Her mouth dropped open. "What?"

"Yeah, sorry, gotta work," he muttered, making sure to slap a disappointed expression on his puss.

"But—"

"For you, drinks are on the house resta the night. Look forward to seein' you back here another night."

"Another…" The air hissed from her.

He rapped his knuckles on the table, then twisted on his boot heel to head back out where he could see the stage.

And *her*.

What the actual fuck?

Why?

He just passed on a sure thing for what? A woman who looked like she only stopped wearing a training bra six months ago? A woman who looked like she'd bring nothing but trouble?

Who most likely wouldn't be easily swayed to do anything?

Everything would probably be a struggle with her. A damn challenge.

Was she even worth that challenge?

If he hadn't rolled his cigarettes himself he'd think the last one he smoked was laced with something.

It could be the only reasonable explanation.

Not only did he never get her damn name, he had no idea how old she was. She could be barely eighteen.

Christ.

He glanced back over his shoulder toward the billiards area and sucked on his teeth.

The first song, *Lightning Crashes*, ended and a silent pause filled the air.

That had his attention swinging back to the woman on stage. She had moved the microphone stand next to the keyboard so she could stand while she sang and played at the same time.

The first notes of the next song flowed through the bar and landed dead center in his chest. Her ringed fingers with the dark-painted nails moved slowly and gracefully over the keys.

He couldn't shake the vision of her fingers touching him the same way. Light but confident. Her touch bringing about a response similar to music.

Her dark eyes caught his and held him there. Entranced. Like a fucking witch.

What the fuck was goin' on?

He suddenly recognized the song. It was a slowed-down, more soul-stirring version of *Creep*, originally sung by Radiohead.

A favorite of his.

One that he actually had loaded into the Jukebox. Had she spotted it last night when she was scrolling through the music?

She had told him he needed a better selection, but *Lightning Crashes* was also in the jukebox.

She had paid the fuck attention. She had made note of the music selection. Maybe on purpose.

If the third song was…

Fuck the third song.

His feet moved toward the stage as she continued to sing *Creep* in the same way the actor Tom Ellis sung it in the Netflix series *Lucifer*. A way that had stuck with him ever since he watched that episode in the early morning hours when he was winding down after a long night. A habit he developed to try to catch some *Zzzs*.

He stopped when he realized what he was doing. He pulled in a deep breath through his nostrils and turned away, breaking the connection between them.

This was totally fucked up.

His chest was tight as his heart thumped in his throat.

With his back turned toward the stage, he closed his eyes, simply inhaled the music, that sexy as fuck voice and felt her eyes burning two holes through his thick leather cut, through his shirt and into his skin. Right to the center of his very soul.

What.

The.

Fuck.

He wasn't smoking the rest of that hand-rolled.

He opened his eyes and purposely focused on the bar. His brain ordered his feet to move. Thank fuck they did and he made it through the hinged portion before getting sucked back into her spell. He wished he had a damn way to lock it to ensure he couldn't escape.

A bump against his shoulder made him jump and mentally shake himself. Stella was watching the band—watching *her*—on stage. Just like all the rest of the customers.

Everybody looked as spellbound as he was.

Had been.

When she finished with the Radiohead song, she seamlessly moved into *Dream On* by Aerosmith. Again, her raspy voice giving it a distinct haunting sound.

He went solid to stop the shiver threatening to slice through him.

"Damn. She's good."

His eyes flicked down to the other woman whose voice could do all kinds of things to him. A voice that belonged on a big stage, not one like Crazy's Pete's.

But Stella's couldn't do even close to what the woman's on stage did.

It was Stella's voice on performance-enhancing drugs.

The notes escaping *her* lips wrapped around his heart and kept tugging like it was trying to pull it free from his chest.

He slapped a hand over his heart to stop it from being stolen.

"Where did you find them?"

"Didn't. She found me."

"She? Me?"

He mentally shook himself again. This was not fucking like him and if he didn't act normal, Stella would quickly pick up on something being off with him.

That would not be good. She would hound him to death about it.

"They found us," he explained.

Stella's gaze bounced from Dodge back to the stage. "Well… I just got a call from the band we had booked this Friday. The lead singer has strep and they need to reschedule. Think they'd be willing to fill that spot? I can change the website, if they can do it."

Dodge lifted his gaze over Stella back to the stage where The Synners were jamming out. "They're workin' for food tonight. Thinkin' they need gigs that pay."

Stella turned toward him with her eyes bugged out. "They're doing what?"

Fuck. "Yeah. She asked if they could play tonight for tips. I offered the food. She jumped on it, hoping to get a chance to play on a busier night. Think they're broke as fuck, so I can offer to throw them a little scratch to fill Friday's spot."

"Not a little scratch, Dodge. You have two functioning ears. They're good. Better than we usually have. They do a good variety of covers. Pay them what we normally pay the bands."

"They'd probably take less."

Stella's head snapped back. "I'm pretty sure you heard what I said. Let me remind you that the cash isn't coming out of your pocket. I actually think we should get them on regular rotation."

"Don't think they're from around here."

"And you know this how?"

He didn't, but he never heard of them before so that was a pretty good sign. Especially in a town the size of Manning Grove. "The shitty converted school bus they rolled up in."

The prez's ol' lady frowned. "A converted school bus? Do you think they live in it? All of them?"

"Maybe. Saw it when they unloaded their equipment. Why else would they have something that big? Most local bands have a van. And the more popular ones have a box truck. Never seen one roll up in a fuckin' bus like that. Unless it's the Partridge Family."

Her face twisted. "You watched that?"

He shrugged. "When you're inside you don't got a choice of what you get to watch."

"I'm surprised that didn't cause a riot." Stella wrinkled her nose. "Do you think she's living with those three guys in it? I could see the guys living like that. Most young guys don't give a shit about much, but her?"

He shrugged. "Maybe she gets some kinda benefit outta it."

"What kind of benefit? Men are pigs. The hell if I'm living in tight quarters with three of them."

He cocked an eyebrow at her. "Then good thing Trip ain't messy and that house of yours is big. Especially if you end up with two boys."

"Trip is anal as fuck. You know that."

Dodge grinned. "That I do."

"Unlike you."

"Ain't gonna argue that."

Stella rolled her blue eyes. "Which reminds me, I have to get the exterminator to spray again."

"Least it ain't for crabs."

Stella shot him a look. "Not yet."

"Funny."

"Won't be when you catch them." She turned back to watch the band and Dodge's gaze dropped down to the boss-y lady's belly.

The other night she had taken his hand and pressed it to where Trip's kid was kicking the shit out of her. It freaked him the fuck out that she was baking a whole other person inside her right now.

A whole fucking human being that would one day be walking, talking and maybe even raising hell.

Not maybe. Would be. That was a guarantee if Trip got his way and had boys.

He wondered if they knew what they were having yet. They hadn't said and he wasn't asking.

Whatever it was in her belly they were stuck with. Trip wanted boys but the universe would have to agree with that want.

Stella grabbed a pint glass and filled it with ice and water. With one hand holding her belly like it would drop to the floor at any second, she drank almost half of it. When she finished, she wiped a hand across her mouth and sighed. "They're almost as good as Dirty Deeds."

"Yeah," he murmured. "Almost." Dirty Deeds played at Stella and Trip's wedding when the Dirty Angels MC came up to celebrate with them. Nash was their lead singer and a long-time member of that club.

That band was recording-label worthy.

The Synners was damn close. *She* was good enough; he wasn't so sure about some of her bandmates. With the right musicians backing her…

What the fuck did he fucking care whether she was good enough or not?

Fuckin' motherfucker!

He ground his teeth together.

"All right, I now need to pee and get the hell out of here before Trip starts blowing up my phone. Make them the offer and text me once you know so I can get online and update the schedule."

Dodge nodded but didn't bother to say anything else. Instead, he watched Stella move out from behind the bar and head toward the rear of Crazy Pete's where the bathrooms were.

He did notice she was starting to waddle. Reese did a lot of that toward the end, too. Along with complaining how uncomfortable she was. She finally popped out Deacon's kid about three weeks ago.

For once, he could understand her complaints since she had gotten so big, Dodge thought an alien was going to burst from her belly.

Deke was now in Daddy euphoria. He took to becoming a father like a fish took to water. However, right now their boy could only lay there, cry, shit and suck on Reese's rack. They'd see how much he enjoyed it once Dane got older.

And maybe even got an attitude like Crazy Daze, Judge and Cassie's daughter.

After experiencing Daisy, Dodge decided he was perfectly fine not planting his seed anywhere.

Fuck that, he was good with shooting his swimmers into a wrap, throwing that shit in the garbage and waving goodbye.

Bye, kiddies.

The only way his seed would end up in any woman's belly, was by way of her mouth.

His attention snapped back to the stage and those damn red lips with lyrics coming out of them.

Bon Jovi's *Wanted Dead or Alive.*

She was killing it. In a good way. In the best way possible.

Her voice was fucking amazing.

She now once again stood at the front edge of the platform, the keyboard abandoned. Both hands were wrapped around the microphone clipped into the stand, her eyes closed as she just let that song flow through her.

Jesus fuckin' Christ.

That tiny body soulfully belting out that larger than life sound.

Her hips rocked slowly back and forth as she hung onto the mic. As if she let go, she would just disappear.

Disintegrate into nothing.

But she wasn't nothing. She was something.

And Dodge didn't like how that something made him feel. How she pulled at him just by singing fucking songs.

Magical spells.

Wicked intentions.

But he was right. Every song choice had been picked for a reason. Every song was in that fucking jukebox.

She hadn't spent that much time in front of it last night. Did she have a photographic memory or was it crazy luck?

He couldn't keep listening. He needed to break free of whatever web she had weaved around him.

He forced his gaze from the stage to Micah. "Yo," he called out. As soon as he had the man's attention, he instructed, "Soon as their set's over, take their food order. Everything's on the house. Whatever they want. Sure they're starvin'."

"Where are you going?"

"Need to..." Go roll some new cigarettes. Go down a bottle of Jack in private. Something. Anything but continue to be be-spelled by *her*. The nameless woman in a band named The Synners. "Don't matter what I need to do. Just do what I tell you. Text me when their set's over. I need to talk to them."

Micah stared at him for a few seconds, then nodded.

He needed to get the fuck out of there until she was done.

If they accepted the Friday night gig, he was fucked. But he had no choice but to offer it to them.

Boss-y Lady said so.

If he looked deep enough, he wanted her to come back Friday night, too.

He just pretended not to see it.

It was smarter that way.

Chapter Three

As he made his way down the steps from his apartment, he slipped his cell phone into his back pocket.

Why did every fucking step feel like he was walking into doom?

Or quicksand?

Or through the fiery gates of hell?

If he was smart, he would've let Possum give them the offer for Friday night.

But of course, he was a dumbass. And, of course, he couldn't resist heading down those damn steps to see her again.

Fuck. My. Life.

When he had gone upstairs earlier, he had flushed all of the hand-rolled cigarettes in his tin down the toilet, grabbed the most recent bag of tobacco he'd gotten from the Amish and rolled new ones.

Because he was a dumbass.

"Fuck!" he shouted into the empty storage room, then grimaced.

With a quick glance, he saw the fryers still on and a mess left behind on the tiny counter next to them.

Possum and Micah knew better than to not clean up once the "kitchen" was closed for the night. That might mean the band was still eating.

The first thing he noticed when he shoved open the swinging door and stepped into the bar area was that all of their customers were gone.

So was Micah.

Possum stood behind the bar wiping shit down, putting shit away. Doing the routine that needed to be done before last call. It was only about eleven, but it was dead. There were still three hours to go before closing.

Maybe they'd shut shit down early tonight. No point in keeping Possum here late when there wasn't any business.

His eyes sliced through the empty bar and found the band sitting at one of the larger square tables by the jukebox, heads down and shoving food into their pie-holes. Like a pack of wild coyotes eating a fresh kill.

He wouldn't be surprised if they licked their plates.

He moved around the bar and stopped on the opposite side of Possum. "Hey, go in the back and toss more chicken fingers and fries in the fryer. Also bring out more ketchup and mustard. While you're back there, grab a few bags of munchies for them, too. Get 'em more water. Beer. Whatever they want."

"But—"

Dodge shot Possum a look. "Don't argue. Just do it."

The prospect nodded, tossed the rag he was using into the hamper kept behind the bar for dirty towels and disappeared behind the swinging door.

Dodge took a breath and headed over to where they sat.

Draft beers sat in front of the three guys and since Possum knew better than to serve anyone underage, that was a sign they were older than twenty-one.

A bottle of water and what looked like a glass of Coke sat in front of the lead singer.

Fuck.

His first suspicion might be right. She was underaged. Not jailbait age, but not quite drinking age yet, either. Last night she had said her band was all over twenty-one but she wouldn't be the first one to get caught lying about her age.

"Possum's makin' you more grub," he told them when he reached their table. He wasn't getting his fingers anywhere near their plates or mouths as they scarfed down what little remained of their food.

The guys lifted their eyes but didn't stop eating.

"Thanks, man," the shaggy blond finally said, talking with his mouth full. He wiped his hand off on his jeans and jutted it out toward Dodge, who gave it a quick shake. "Nico." The bass guitarist jerked his chin toward the dark-haired guy with the ponytail who played lead guitar. "Rex. And that's Eddie," he finished, tipping his head toward the redheaded drummer. "And you already met Syn last night."

Syn. He bet it was with a Y like the band name. He also wondered if it was her real name or a stage name and if it was her real name... Why? What mother named their daughter Syn?

He thought of all the ol' ladies of the Originals. Women like them did. Also, mothers who named their kid after a fucking Dodge Dart.

Maybe it was a shortened version of a longer name. Like Syndee or Synder.

His eyes sliced to her. She sat with her back to him, picking at her food, not inhaling it like the others. Though, her plate was practically empty. She could've already hoovered whatever Possum served her.

"Syn," Dodge repeated.

Her spine snapped straight and her head lifted, but she didn't turn to look at him.

"Need a minute with you." When she didn't respond, he asked Nico, "She's in charge, right?"

Nico frowned and glanced at Syn. "Yeah, she's in charge. It's her gig, we're just lucky to back her up."

Wasn't that the fucking truth. "Then I need to speak to her for a minute."

"You can say whatever you need to say here," she finally said. She sounded tired. Her voice a bit raspier now than earlier.

They had ended up playing two sets instead of only one. Her vocal chords were probably tired, too. Since he wasn't a musician—and was told to shut the fuck up the last time he belted out a song—he wasn't sure if that was even possible.

"I could," Dodge started slowly. He tilted his head and stared at the back of hers. "But I won't."

All three guys stopped eating and stared at her, none of them hiding their confusion.

"Just need a minute of your time before Possum brings out more food. Then you can get back to eatin'."

She shoved the plate in front of her away. She picked up her water bottle and took a long swig from it. Long enough that she almost emptied it.

"It's about business," he added. "Got somethin' you might be interested in."

"Money. I'm interested in money."

"Ain't we all," he muttered. "You don't wanna talk now, we can talk later."

He took a step out of the way to save his shins when she abruptly shoved her chair back with a loud scrape along the floor.

When she turned, he could see it on her face. The exhaustion. Not just physical but mental, too.

Both in her eyes and under them.

He tipped his head toward the bar and without waiting, headed in that direction, hoping she'd follow. If she didn't, it was her loss. He wouldn't kiss her ass.

Well, he'd like to, but not in that way.

He ducked behind the bar, grabbed another bottle of water from the cooler and turned.

Amazingly enough, she was coming in his direction.

She was like a magnet in motion and his eyes the steel. He couldn't pull them free as her slender hips rocked and rolled as she moved across the floor. It had to be the high-heeled boots causing it tonight, since last night he hadn't noticed that motion at all.

She had thrown her sweatshirt back on and zipped it closed, so he could no longer see the exposed skin of her belly or her bra through her peek-a-boo fishnet shirt. Or that graceful line of her spine.

The line that his tongue was itching to lick.

Damn shame.

When she stopped across the bar from him, he offered her the now sweating water bottle.

She took it and mumbled a, "Thanks."

"You ain't drinkin' to save your voice or is it 'cause of your age?"

"I'm not drinking because I don't want to drink."

He considered her a moment. "How old are you?"

"How old are you?"

Christ. "We did this last night."

"We did. And my age shouldn't matter."

It shouldn't but it did.

"What should matter is how we play."

"You're better than them," he said.

"Not too many musicians want to travel the country playing in dives and living in a shitty bus."

"No truer words…"

"That means I have to take what I can get." She turned her head slightly, probably to make sure her bandmates couldn't hear her. "They're loyal."

He studied her profile. "Loyalty's important."

"And they let me make all the decisions," she murmured.

"That's important, too. *If* you know what you're doin'."

She turned back to him, her eyes now hard. He'd hit a nerve.

"You don't think I do?"

He was on the fence about that. From managing Crazy Pete's, he knew enough that a well-managed band could be successful and no longer be considered "starving artists." The way her band was eating, they were more than starving. They were desperate.

"That was smart."

Her eyebrows rose and her dark eyes held his. "What was?"

"What you sung up there. 'Specially after you said my song choices sucked."

"I didn't quite say it like that."

"Close enough."

"I guess it was you who filled the jukebox."

"You think?" He didn't bother to hide his sarcasm.

She lifted her shoulders slightly.

"The songs I heard showed me that you're versatile."

"But you didn't stick around to hear them all."

Well, fuck. She noticed he'd disappeared. "Didn't need to. What I did hear proved it."

"Okay?"

"It's good that you can play different crowds."

She made it a point to glance around. "You get different crowds in here?"

He scratched at his eyebrow, deciding it was best to ignore the insult. "Yeah, sometimes. Mansfield U ain't far from here, so sometimes we pull in a younger crowd. The nights we have pool or dart tournaments, we get a mix."

"I need to know this why?"

Jesus. Normally that attitude would be an instant turn-off. But, surprisingly, it wasn't with her. Instead, it made him crave a little spice. "You don't."

She nodded, but quickly hid the disappointment in her eyes. However, he caught it. He had lured her away from her bandmates on the promise of talking business. He needed to get to that before she simply walked away. Then the boss-y lady would be ripping him a new one for not filling Friday night's slot.

"If you want, you can leave your equipment on stage."

Her dark eyebrows pinned together. "Why would we do that? We need it for gigs."

"When's your next one?"

Her lips thinned and she glanced down at the water bottle, where her dark-painted short fingernails had been picking apart the label.

Exactly what he thought. They didn't have a gig scheduled. Just like when she came into Crazy Pete's, they'd probably find some other bar, wander in and speak to the manager. They didn't have a steady schedule.

Maybe she needed someone to manage her band other than her. Someone who had connections.

But that wasn't his problem, his was filling Friday night's spot. The bar always made bank when they had a band. Karaoke night was a profitable night, too. Most people needed to be tipsy to sing on stage. However, most of the singers ended up making his ears bleed. He'd gone as far as putting in ear plugs to survive some wannabe singers.

"A spot opened up on Friday. Wanna fill it?"

"We were good enough," she murmured. Not a question but her tone still held surprise.

"*You* were."

"Can't sing without a band."

"Don't expect you to. You do what you gotta do to get by. Nobody understands that better than me."

She lifted her dark eyes to his. *For fuck's sake,* he felt she could suddenly see shit she shouldn't be seeing. Out of instinct, he pressed a hand to his chest using it as a shield. Like he needed to protect himself.

From her. From whatever she kept pulling from him.

He didn't like that. Not at fucking all.

"You want it?" When she didn't answer right away, he continued, "Unless you have a gig tomorrow night somewhere, then like I said, you can leave your shit on stage. It'll be safe. No one will fuck with it."

Possum kicked open the swinging door to the left of the bar. His hands and forearms were balancing plates piled high with fried shit.

"Only made twenty in tips," she murmured as her eyes followed the prospect and the food.

"Eatin' and drinkin' a shitload more than that."

Her narrowed gaze swung back to him. "You said our tab would be on the house."

"I remember what I said and it is. It'll be on the house Friday night, too. Boss Lady also said to throw you some scratch if you wanna stick around." He made sure to leave off the Y when he used his nickname for Stella.

Her brow furrowed. "Scratch? How much?"

"What do you normally get for your payin' gigs?"

Her eyes narrowed again. "What do you normally pay bands?"

Damn. "A hundred bucks a head."

"For how many sets?"

"No less than two. You wanna play more that's up to you but you still get paid the same."

"Can we set out our tip jar?"

He hesitated since that wasn't normal practice for the bands they booked. "Yeah. But warnin' you, this town's full of cheap motherfuckers."

"Every town is full of cheap motherfuckers."

"That ain't a lie," he murmured. "So, you in? Or do you need to ask them?" He jerked his chin to the table behind her where her three band members were digging into the freshly-delivered hot food.

Possum came back in their direction, carrying empty platters, and bugged his eyes out at Dodge as he passed.

"Still got all your fingers?" Dodge asked the prospect.

Possum grunted and disappeared behind the swinging door.

"All right. You in or out?"

"In. As long as you provide," she lifted one finger, "food." A second one. "Drinks." A third. "Four hundred in cash." And finally her pinky. "We can set out our tip jar."

"Woman, were you born in the mafia or somethin'? You don't fuck around."

She shot him a smile. The first one he'd seen on her tonight. The first real one he'd seen on her at all, even though it didn't even come close to reaching her eyes. "Close enough. Need one more thing…"

Damn. "What?"

"A place for us to park our bus, unless you don't think the church will mind us camping out in their lot."

"Oh, they'll fuckin' mind. Keep it there tonight, don't make a fuckin' mess, and I'll find a spot for it tomorrow night and Friday night, too. Deal?"

She gave him a single nod. "Deal."

"Looks like we have ourselves a deal. Now, go finish eatin'. You want anythin' else, Possum will get it for you."

He turned to head out from behind the bar and back upstairs. And away from temptation. The farther, the better.

"Hey."

Her smoky voice stopped him with his palm planted on the door. He glanced over his shoulder.

"Thanks."

He wondered if that had been painful for her to say. With a grin he hid from her, he shoved the door open and let it swing shut behind him.

"Get them whatever else they want. Soon as they're done, close up and head back to the farm. No point in stayin' open if no one's out there."

"You got it, brother."

That reminded him. Both Possum and Tater had approached him and asked if he knew when they would finally get their full set of patches.

It was time and both had earned them. He'd have to say something to Trip next time he saw the prez.

———

Dodge worked his way back down the dark steps, one hand full with the Jack bottle he'd kicked, the other shoved down his boxers, holding his junk out of habit. At the bottom of the steps, he flipped the switch and the overhead fluorescent lights took a second to flicker on. He was relieved to see the fryers off, the tiny counter cleared and no mess left behind.

As always, Possum did what needed to be done. He definitely deserved his patches. His year of being a recruit had to be up by now.

Dodge was lucky. After he got sprung from Lycoming County Prison, he only had to prospect for six months since he had an "in" with the Fury by Rook sponsoring him. Those six months still sucked but, in the end, was worth it.

At the time, Trip had been desperate for members to fill the ranks of the resurrected MC. While the prez still wanted it to keep growing, he was no longer in such a rush to patch over prospects. He wanted to make sure they fit, were loyal and were hard-working.

He did not want a repeat of what the Originals went through.

But the prospects weren't Dodge's problem right now, grabbing another bottle of Jack was. He might even grab his hidden bottle of Sinatra Select. He also needed to double-check to make sure both the front and rear doors to Crazy Pete's were locked.

Both Possum and Tater were pretty good about locking up before they left, but still… It was hard for Dodge to sleep without checking. A habit he'd picked up inside… Making sure he was secure before closing his eyes.

During his last bid, Rook had his back and he had Rook's. But now he lived alone and during the middle of the night and early morning hours he was by himself. He kept a baseball bat behind the bar and always kept a .40 with one in the chamber up in his apartment. When he wore jeans, he usually kept a knife strapped to his calf.

He'd dodged dying in prison several times over the years. It didn't take much to piss off a fellow inmate. In fact, sometimes it didn't take shit to piss them off.

Prison fucking sucked ass and not in a good way. Your head was on a constant swivel. You had to have eyes in the back of your head and you needed to find someone inside to help watch your back.

He was lucky to have shared a cell with Rook. That motherfucker had been the ultimate asshole inside and the man made it well known he wouldn't hesitate to shank anyone's ass. Or strangle them with a bed sheet. Or drown them in a mop bucket.

Or even "accidentally" electrocute them in the laundry.

He grinned and gave his balls a squeeze as he used his shoulder to shove open the door and head out into the dark bar area. The only light came from the shelves on the wall behind the bar. He headed back there, threw the empty into the recycle bin, and swiped an already opened Jack bottle from the shelf under the bar.

He'd save his Sinatra Select for another night.

He set the bottle on the bar at the end nearest the swinging door so he could pick it up on his way back through.

Working his way around the long wood bar, he used his bare feet to push in some of the stools that weren't aligned neatly. While mindlessly sliding his fingers up and down his dick, he checked the deadbolt and slide locks on the front door.

Locked.

He turned and headed back past the bar toward the rear door, still tugging on his softie. Since he didn't take anyone upstairs tonight, maybe he should fire up Pornhub and—

He jumped and jerked his hand from his boxers, his heart now racing like a wildfire spreading through a forest in a drought. "Christ!"

A figure sat at one of the tables.

In the fucking dark.

Alone.

Slouched in a chair with that fucking cat-eared hood pulled up over her fucking head.

He slapped a hand over his bare chest to shove his heart back into place. "What the fuck! How d'you get back in here?"

Possum was getting his ass royally reamed if he left the back door unlocked.

"I never left." Her words came out sluggish as if she was either drunk or half-asleep. Did she hit the booze after Possum left because he wouldn't serve her for being underage?

"Possum would've put you out."

"I hid in the women's bathroom until after he left."

Dodge blinked and let that sink in. "What? Why the fuck did you do that?"

Silence.

"You've been drinkin' my shit?"

"I don't drink shit. I heard it has a bad aftertaste."

Dodge closed his eyes and pulled air in through his nostrils. Once his heart dropped from ninety miles an hour to about fifty, he opened his eyes again. "Stick to singin'. Comedy ain't your thing."

"You don't know what my *thing* is."

"Okay, whelp…" He pointed toward the back door. "Exit's that way."

"What do you have down your boxers?"

He dropped his arm. "What?"

"You were hanging onto something. Must be important."

He barked out a laugh. "Okay, maybe you are fuckin' funny." He held his thumb and index finger together leaving a slight gap. "Just a little."

"I wasn't being funny."

"Yeah, neither am I when I show you where the back door is." He jerked his chin toward the hallway. "The same way you came in earlier."

She stayed in the chair. He could hardly make out her features with the hood up and wondered if she washed all that shit off her face yet. Or even bothered to change out of what she had worn on stage. He was tempted to peek under the table to see if she was still wearing those damn, smoking hot boots.

He fought that urge. He'd be able to see that soon enough when he escorted her out.

However, she still wasn't moving.

Good thing it was his dick and not pepper spray down his boxers because he'd be tempted to do the same things the screws did to him one day when he refused to return to his cell.

He got sprayed directly in the face. That was a hard lesson learned but one he never forgot. He would choose a taser over pepper spray any day. The shock of a taser was over as soon as the trigger was released. The burn of pepper spray lingered for a long fucking time. And it had only pissed him off even more.

"That Possum guy said you live upstairs." She slipped the hood off her head.

"What does that have to do with you leavin'?"

He moved closer to the table and saw her lick her lips. Not in a seductive way, but more of a nervous gesture.

What the fuck was she nervous about?

He wasn't going to call the cops on her or anything. Even if she'd been drinking his booze and was underage. He wasn't a snitch. He'd seen plenty of times what happened to them inside. Snitches either got dead or a jailhouse C-section.

While doing time, you learned to look the other way. Even smarter, forget anything you saw or heard. "Hear no evil, see no evil, speak no evil" was a way of life inside and a good way to keep breathing. It also helped keep your asshole intact.

"We've been living in the bus… and…"

Yeah, he saw the outside of it, he could imagine what it looked like inside with four people living in it.

"And it doesn't have the same things as a motorhome…"

Was she asking him for another favor? One that was a lot more personal than asking for a shot to play in the bar?

If so, she didn't need to finish. He got it. She didn't need to plead her case. Not that she would.

What he did understand was how it was like to live with a lack of privacy and clean facilities. He understood that only too well. It sucked and made you feel less than human.

For being the only woman living on a damn shitty bus with three twenty-something guys, it had to suck even more.

"All right."

She lifted her eyes but her eyebrows dropped low. "All right?"

"Yeah. All right." He tipped his head toward the back room. "Let's go."

"I just want to be clear… I don't want to have—"

"Yep," he said quickly, cutting her off. "Know what you want. Been there. Let's go."

She pushed her chair back and reached under the table. When she stood, she shrugged the strap of a overfilled backpack over her shoulder.

Had she left and snuck back in before Possum locked up? Gone out to her bus, changed and came back with the stuff she'd need to shower?

He wondered if she'd lost track of all the truck stops she'd showered in. Or the gas stations restrooms she'd used for a sink bath.

Fuck.

He remembered those damn days.

He turned and didn't check to see if she followed him, but by the time he hit the stairs, he felt her right behind him, then heard her soft footsteps as she climbed the steps.

He opened the door to his apartment, waited for her to step inside, then shut the door behind them, not bothering to lock it.

There was no point since she wouldn't be up there long.

He went over to the laundry basket sitting on the floor next to the couch and pulled out a bath towel. "It's clean," he said as he tossed it at her.

"I got one."

"But you don't got anywhere to wash it. I do. So use mine."

She stared at the dark blue towel in her hands for way

too long. When she finally lifted her face, her voice was thick. "Where's your bathroom?"

He understood that, too. A little kindness could go a long fucking way.

"It's hard to miss. This place ain't big."

She glanced around, purposely avoiding his eyes. What she saw was his unmade bed. And the rest of the clothes that were scattered around his place. Along with the overfull garbage and the empties sitting on the coffee table in front of the couch. The overflowing ashtray with half-smoked hand-rolleds and joints. Even the bong sitting by his bed. Also, his sink full of dirty dishes.

At least he hadn't paused a porno on the big screen. Thank fuck for that. Nothing like seeing a larger-than-life freeze frame of a woman's face in the middle of a fake orgasm.

"Ain't much but it's gotta be better than that damn bus."

"Not by much."

Ouch. "Got everythin' you need?"

"Don't need much."

He nodded and studied her, wondering why she wasn't moving toward the bathroom. Maybe she didn't feel comfortable taking a shower with him still in the apartment.

On the other hand, he wasn't sure if he was comfortable leaving her alone up in his place. He might not have a lot of shit, but he was damn sure he had more than her.

He'd left the bottle of Jack on the bar. It was a good excuse to go back down and make himself scarce. He'd just need to have faith she wouldn't steal any of his shit. If she did, hopefully he'd know what was missing before Friday night.

And either take it out of the band's pay or get it back from her.

"Gonna head downstairs. Just come down when you're done." It was best if he didn't stay up there, anyway.

She might be young, but she still tempted him.

Truth was, she was one temptation he didn't need.

Knowing she'd be naked in his shower just feet away…

Yeah, downstairs he needed to go.

She nodded and disappeared into his bathroom.

He nodded and got the fuck out of there.

DODGE SAT on a stool at the bar, his head propped in both hands, the Jack bottle sitting in front of him. A glass with about two fingers worth of whiskey also sitting next to the bottle.

He hadn't touched it.

His mind was upstairs in that shower.

His mind was on that stage.

His mind was on that stupid zippered sweatshirt with the stupid as fuck cat ears.

He wanted to know her story.

Though, he doubted she'd tell it. It was for the best if she didn't, anyway.

She sang tonight, she'd sing again Friday night and then they could drive that piece of shit bus to their next destination.

A pounding on the rear door made him jerk, sit up and twist his head toward the sound. He heard it again, this time accompanied by a faint male voice coming from behind it.

"Jesus fuck," he muttered as the pounding and shouting continued. He shook his head and slid off the stool, his bare feet slapping along the floor as he moved quickly.

He twisted the deadbolt and slid open the two slide locks, both the one at the top and the one at the bottom strategically placed to keep people from kicking in the door. After taking a breath, he yanked it open, ready to ream out whoever it was.

Frigid December air hit him immediately and a shiver ripped through him, his nipples pebbling in protest. When he saw who it was, his urge to pound the person into the ground dissipated and, instead, he jerked his head toward the interior of Crazy Pete's.

After Rex stepped inside, Dodge slammed the door shut behind him, shutting out the cold winter night.

"Looking for Syn. She still in here?"

"You don't know where she is?"

"She said something about finding a place to shower—"

"Yeah. That's where she's at."

"And where is that?"

He studied the man before him. The urge to pound him returned. "Where the fuck d'you think it is?"

"Take me to her."

This asshole thought he could make demands. He was wrong. "No. She probably never gets privacy. Leave her alone for now."

"We're not leaving her here," Rex insisted.

We're? Only one guy stood in front of him in the narrow hallway. Dodge had purposely positioned himself so he blocked Rex from moving farther inside.

"Good for you. Glad you're protectin' her ass. Don't want you leavin' her here, either. She ain't a fuckin' stray cat." Though, she did wear those stupid cat ears. "When she's done, I'll shoo her back to your piece of shit on wheels."

"I'll wait for her."

Someone was confused on who was in charge of the domain they stood in. "She's safe here."

Rex's gaze slid over Dodge's bare chest, his tattoos, his white boxer shorts and his bare legs. Not in a sexual way but more in a sizing Dodge up way. "With you?"

He should be fucking insulted. "Yeah, with me. Never

had to force myself on any woman. Ain't gonna start tonight."

"How do we know that?"

We again. "*You* don't. But just like I trusted her when she told me your band was good, she musta trusted me enough to ask to use my shower."

"I'll wait for her," he grumbled again, his gaze lifting over Dodge's bare shoulder toward the interior of the bar.

"You doin' her?"

A muscle in Rex's clean-shaven jaw twitched.

It had to be the only explanation for Rex being so damn protective. Either that or he was worried about something happening to his meal ticket. Because without her, the band most likely wouldn't even get offered an open bar tab. Maybe at a college bar somewhere where most of the patrons were drunk off their asses and thought Justin Bieber was good music.

Dodge tried again. "*Any* of you doin' her?"

The lead guitarist's muscle twitch rose into his cheek. "None of us are *doing her.* We know better than to fuck up a good thing. We're not stupid and are aware we'd be shit without her. Without her, we'd be working some minimum wage job somewhere dying a little more inside every fucking day. We might not make a lot of money doing what we do—yet—but at least we love what we do. We can go to sleep content and not miserable every fucking night."

He suddenly found a little bit of respect for the man before him. "Money ain't everythin'."

"But it helps."

"Can't argue that. Look, our club owns a motel on the other side of town—"

Rex quickly interrupted. "We're okay. We're used to living in the bus."

Yeah, money ain't everything but it was needed to rent a motel room. He sighed.

He couldn't put them up for free at the motel. He didn't have the power to make that decision. More importantly, he doubted Trip or Ozzy would be happy about being woken up in the middle of the night over some almost-homeless band.

"All right. Go back to your bus. I'll make sure she gets back safely."

Rex stared at him a few more seconds, then his lips flattened out and his expression turned slightly sheepish. "Do you have any extra cases of water?"

Dodge's eyebrows rose.

Rex quickly continued. "We only made twenty-one bucks in tips and that won't even pay for enough diesel to get to a store. Even if it did, when we got there, we'd have nothing left…"

Christ. Was it more important they go to bed content every night? Or with their guts full? He got that working a shitty job sucked but sometimes you had to nut up and be responsible.

Dodge made him squirm a few seconds before he said, "Yeah," and tipped his head toward the end of the hallway. "Come with me."

Rex followed him in the storage area and Dodge pointed to a stack of bottled water. "Take a case now. Will give you another tomorrow when you come in for food. I'll cover your food 'til after you play Friday night, then that's it. And anyway, our food selection sucks."

"Better than nothing," Rex mumbled as he heaved a twenty-four pack into his arms.

True. Something was better than nothing. Trip's words to live by.

Dodge snagged a case of Coke, too, and set it on top of the water in his arms, making Rex dip a little with the weight. "There you go."

He held open the swinging door and followed Rex back to the rear bar entrance.

"Thanks, dude," Rex said as Dodge shivered, standing in only his skivvies and holding the back door open. As soon as the lead guitarist stepped back out into the dark December night, Dodge pulled the door shut and set all three locks again.

He turned and stared down the dark hallway toward the bar's interior. She had to be done with her shower by now.

When he walked back out into the bar area, it was still empty. He shoved his way through the swinging door and hoofed it back up the steps.

Chapter Four

Dodge cautiously opened the door to his apartment and listened.

Last thing he needed was her screaming about him doing something inappropriate. He was not going back inside for some misunderstanding.

Not for her.

Not for anybody.

He hoped like fuck he didn't regret letting her use his shower.

His brow dropped low as he noticed the bathroom door was now wide open, but—*what the actual fuck?*—the light was off.

He turned in a circle, hoping she wasn't hiding somewhere, ready to ambush him and kick him in the nuts.

Or slice his fucking throat.

He should know better. He'd gotten way too comfortable since landing here and lost his fucking edge. He'd gotten into the habit after the first time behind bars to pay sharp attention to his surroundings.

He cautiously peered behind the counter in his galley kitchen to make sure she wasn't hiding by ducking behind it.

He glanced toward the opposite end of the apartment. The windows were closed... Only one other way out existed...

Unless she was hiding under the damn bed. But why the fuck would she do that? Unless she thought she really *was* a cat.

Was she totally whacked? Living in a shitty bus with three guys, she very well might be.

His eyes flicked toward his messy bed.

Son of a bitch.

How'd he miss her backpack sitting by the couch?

And the new lump in his bed.

His fucking bed!

What the actual fuck?

"Just make yourself at home," he grumbled with a shake of his head.

He didn't know the last time he washed his damn sheets, but she still crawled between them and fell asleep. That had to mean that rat trap they were traveling in was definitely worse that his apartment.

That was disturbing.

He opened his mouth to yell her name but as he took a few steps closer he heard it and snapped his trap shut.

Light snoring.

Didn't matter if she was asleep or unconscious. Or even dead. She needed to get the fuck out of his bed and out of his apartment. He'd been more than generous enough with her already without getting anything in return.

So, fuck that shit. He was not getting evicted from his own fucking bed. He'd spent too many years on a metal bunk with only a thin "cushion" to sleep on. On a normal day it wasn't comfortable but it was made worse when he had to hide his commissary shit under it so it wouldn't be stolen.

He stared down at the petite woman wrapped up in his

wrinkled sheets and blanket like a fucking burrito with only her messy dark hair visible.

He went to shake her awake and halfway to grabbing her shoulder, he stopped and considered her again. Curling his fingers into his palm, he straightened and sucked on his teeth as he stared at her.

Fuck it.

He reached down again, this time not to wake her up, but to sweep away the damp strands covering her face.

Her skin was so damn pale. The shadows under her eyes dark. And her lips, now scrubbed free of the red lipstick she had worn on stage, parted slightly.

Fuck, she couldn't be more than eighteen, could she?

Is that why she didn't want to answer when he asked her twice?

Even if she was, it hit him that she needed that bed a lot more than him.

He blew a breath out of his nose, let his fingertips skim over the silky hair spread out over his pillow and straightened again.

He wondered who she had in her life besides those three guys in her band. He wondered why her family would allow her to wander the country in a damn bus like that. Practically starving. Physically exhausted to the point she'd crawl into a stranger's bed.

He shouldn't let her stay.

He would be a fucking dumbass if he did.

Her bandmates would be wondering where she was. They might even call the damn pigs.

His eyes flicked to her backpack. He grabbed it and moved over to the couch to sit down, putting it on his lap and feeling the outside pockets.

He quickly found what he was looking for. Her cell phone.

He hit the side button and saw the power was almost drained. But also that it was locked. Of course.

He got up, took it over to the bed, carefully slid her hand out from under the sheet, noticing she was wearing at least a T-shirt. *Thank fuck.*

He carefully and slowly put her fingertip to the back of her phone to scan her fingerprint, hoping he picked the right finger to unlock it.

He did.

He could be nosy and go through her phone, but he'd be pissed if someone did that to him. Instead, he went straight for the text app, found the string of texts with Rex and saw he had sent a shitload before Dodge let him in downstairs. Not one had been answered by Syn and all unread. No wonder the guitarist ended up pounding on the door.

Dodge sent Rex a text back. *I'm OK. 2 tired. Sleepn here. Talk in AM.*

He hoped that would be enough to settle their worry. He turned the phone to silent and waited a minute.

With him? U sure????

Dodge set his jaw at that response and quickly texted back. *I'm good. C U in AM.*

He shut the phone off and attached it to the charger next to his bed. This way she'd at least have a full charge come morning.

He stared at her for a few seconds more, shook his head and with a frown, settled on his damn couch.

Her soft, steady snoring made his eyelids become heavy. As it pulled him under into Never Never Land, he realized Never Never Land was one place Syn needed to stay no matter how much she intrigued him.

———

SHE GASPED as she free-fell from the sky and crashed hard, flat on her back. Her eyelids popped open and her pounding heart lodged in her throat.

Syn blinked, trying to catch her breath.

She took a few seconds to acclimate herself to where she landed when she dropped out of her dream. Or nightmare. Or whatever the hell it was this time and wherever she was.

Definitely not in the bus. Or surrounded by a trio of snoring, burping, farting men.

Okay, someone was snoring, but in the singular. Not in unison like a pack of geriatric Pugs.

She was also in an actual *real* bed. She hadn't slept in a real one in what might be forever.

She was so damn tired. She had only wanted to lay down for a few minutes and rest her eyes. She'd figured she'd wake up as soon as she heard his feet on the steps. Unfortunately, forgetting he'd been barefoot.

Her mistake.

She wrinkled her nose. She didn't think it was her that had a funky smell. Last night she had scrubbed any stink off from her after sweating on stage.

It all went down the drain in *his* shower.

She sat up and glanced around.

In *his* apartment.

Shit!

She lifted the edge of the blanket and sheet only enough to make sure she was still dressed the same way as when she crawled between them. And apparently, rolled herself up like a beef *taquito*.

But at least there *had* been sheets. Maybe she shouldn't be relieved about that. She dropped them quickly because she did not want to discover where that funk was coming from or if those sheets had any stains.

A deep snore coming from the couch had her head snap

in that direction. She couldn't see his face, but an arm was flopped over the side, his hand resting on the floor, palm up.

She could also see the top of one bare knee, accented with dark fuzz, since his leg was cocked, and the foot from his other leg hanging off the end. Clearly, he was too big for that couch.

No surprise.

Why the hell hadn't he woken her up and kicked her out?

She unwrapped herself from her warm cocoon and the slight chill in the air instantly hit her. With a shiver, she put her bare feet on the floor—relieved she also had on a pair of leggings—shoved the bedding out of the way and stared at her backpack propped in front of the couch.

That wasn't where she put it.

She hurried to get up, trying to be as quiet as possible and moved closer to the man who slept on the couch near her stuff.

That was when she noticed his other hand buried deep within his boxers. The lump where his junk should be, appearing a lot larger than it really was. While she didn't know firsthand how big he actually was, he'd been flopping freely in his boxer shorts last night.

It wasn't some scary monster but it was definitely large enough to be noticeable. Either way, he sure liked to hang onto it for some reason.

Like a damn blankie or something.

The first thing she searched for was the wad of ones and the single five-spot that made up the twenty-one bucks she'd dug out of their tip jar last night, along with some spare change from some cheap-asses. She blew out a breath in relief when the cash was still there. What wasn't, was her phone. It was gone.

She took her backpack away from the bar manager and

placed it on the bed. Her heart began to race in panic as she checked all of the zippered compartments, still trying not to make too much noise. She couldn't find it anywhere.

Shit! She couldn't afford to replace it.

She groaned and sat on the edge of the bed, dropping her head in her hands. What the hell was she going to do without her phone?

She lifted her head again and glanced over at the couch. Did he take it?

Why? Why would he do that?

She was going to have to wake him up and demand her phone back.

Jesus. She didn't want to wake him. She wanted to get the fuck out of there before he was upright and aware.

The way he looked at her…

It twisted up something inside her.

And not in a bad way.

Not in a good way, either.

His dark brown hair, his deep dark brown eyes. The intensity of his stare.

That fucking body.

She swallowed the saliva beginning to pool in her mouth.

She needed to get the hell out of that apartment.

She did not need trouble like him in her life. She tended to step in plenty of shit all on her own.

If she had to, she'd wait until later, once the bar opened, to come back and demand her phone. Because he had to have it. She had tucked it into the side pocket of her backpack after she'd stripped down last night and before climbing into the shower. The shower she stayed in until the water went cold.

It had felt so damn good. While the tiny bathroom wasn't super clean, it was way cleaner than the truck stops they tended to stop at. But that steaming hot water also drained any remaining energy from her.

That was probably why she ended up in his bed.

She didn't even remember climbing into it. She must have turned into some brainless zombie between her full stomach, the hot shower and all the energy they'd put into playing their best to impress, combined with the late hour.

She sighed softly and combed her fingers through her hair. She didn't have a hairdryer and didn't want to dig through his personal belongings to see if he had one, so it ended up drying curlier than normal. Especially after sleeping with it damp.

She pulled socks from her backpack, hoping they were a clean pair, yanked them over her feet, then pulled on her winter pull-on booties she'd bought second-hand and her zippered sweatshirt.

She actually bought that at a consignment shop, too. As soon as she saw the cat ears as part of the hood, she had to have it, even though it wasn't warm enough for the winter months when they were up north.

She'd have to make a run for the bus—hopefully still parked at the church—so she didn't freeze her ass off before getting there. It was time to turn the bus around and head south where they wouldn't end up with frostbite since the heating system in the bus was hit or miss. Mostly miss.

When she turned to grab her backpack, she spotted it. Her damn phone plugged into a charger on the nightstand. She almost collapsed in relief.

While she didn't have her brother's number any more, she still had hope that somehow, some way, one day he'd find her number and call her.

They had lost track of each other years ago. The last time she talked to him was when she was ten. Thirteen damn years ago. During a time in his life when he'd been in and out of jail and even prison.

She had to assume he'd been arrested again after the last time they spoke. Maybe he was even still locked up. Since, back then, he seemed to be barreling down a rocky path of disaster.

But she always hoped he'd straighten out. That was why the last time they spoke, she begged him to come get her. Even cried to the point she could no longer talk.

He had saved her once.

She had hoped he'd save her again.

He said he'd try.

But, instead, he disappeared.

After that, she disappeared, too. She blocked out who she was, where she was and pretended she was someone else, somewhere else.

Anywhere but where she was.

Until it came to the point she could no longer ignore it all. Because it was no longer just her.

She shook her head violently, trying to shake free those clawing, painful thoughts, then ground the heels of her palms into her eye sockets trying to wipe away the visions she couldn't escape.

She couldn't.

She couldn't go back.

But she had to.

Fuck.

The heat of her anger surged from her gut into her throat, burning every inch of the way as it rose.

She let her eyes once again land on the man still passed out asleep on the couch. Still snoring. He was vulnerable right now with the way he slept. His body relaxed, having no idea that she stood just feet away, staring at him.

He hadn't touched her.

He hadn't forced her to put out in exchange for a hot shower or food. He hadn't even asked or suggested it, either.

He let her sleep undisturbed in his own damn bed.

He relegated himself to an uncomfortable couch.

He could've woken her up and kicked her out.

He hadn't.

He could've told her no when she asked if her band could play, even for only tips.

He hadn't.

He could've said no when she asked to use his shower.

He hadn't.

She closed her eyes and simply breathed.

In…

Out…

He didn't have to agree to any of it. But he did. All for her.

Why? She was nobody to him. He probably felt sorry for her. For her situation. A situation he didn't know anything about.

Living in that damn bus, they weren't technically homeless, but might as well be. Most times they relied on the generosity of others. Whether it was spare change, expiring food, or even truckers donating their shower credits.

Generous people like him.

Dodge.

The name on the front of his vest he wore last night.

She recognized that type of vest. What it was. What it meant. They'd played in several biker bars in the past.

Those bars had been rough. Even a bit scary.

Crazy Pete's didn't hold that same vibe. It seemed to be more of a neighborhood bar. A mix of folks.

But he was a biker. His vest screamed it, even if his look didn't.

The young guy, the tall skinny one, working the bar with him was one, too. But his bottom rocker identified him as a prospect. His front name patch said "Possum."

Last night, no one else in that bar wore a "cut." A term

she learned in one of those biker bars when a burly, bearded biker became way too friendly.

Too handsy.

Too demanding.

Rex had taken a fist to the face and Nico ended up with a black eye just to get her the hell out of there.

Another reason she'd never just dump her bandmates. Rex, Nico and Eddie had been the only ones there for her.

If it wasn't for them...

She continued to stare at Dodge, dead asleep.

She needed to get the hell out of his apartment and needed to do it now. She had no idea what time it was, but it didn't matter. It was time to go.

She went back to the bed, unplugged her phone from the charger, grabbed her backpack and turned to leave. She only took a few steps before she saw it.

His cut. Hanging over the back of one of the stools at the tiny kitchen counter. The place where he probably ate since the apartment was too small to have a kitchen table set in addition to the two stools at the counter.

His place was basic. A bed. A couch, a galley kitchen, a bathroom. And, of course, a large screen TV. It wasn't anything fancy, it wasn't even clean. Or even neat.

But it was his domain.

It held his scent. It held him.

A biker. A bar manager. A man who had a little empathy toward her plight, even though he didn't even know or understand it all.

She took the few steps needed to get to his cut and trace her fingers over the large embroidered patches on the back.

Just like the large tattoo she had seen on his bare back, the top rocker said *Blood Fury*. The bottom said *Pennsylvania*. A small square patch to the side consisted of two letters: *MC*. The large center patch was a skull and crossbones with blood dripping out of the empty eye sockets and the mouth.

Blood Fury MC.

She chewed on her bottom lip as she stared it for a few more seconds.

Then she got the fuck out of there as quickly and quietly as she could.

Chapter Five

THE BUS DOOR opened with an ear-splitting, headache-causing creak, making her wince and reminding Syn that they needed a new can of generic brand WD-40. Nico climbed up the steps with a large box in his arms. What peeked out of it looked like food.

Lots of food.

"Where'd that come from?" Rex asked, his brow pulled low.

Syn wanted to know that, too.

Nico tipped his head back toward the open door that was letting in all the cold and the little heat they had out. "I was outside pissing behind a bush and some chick pulled up in a Chevy and dropped off this box."

Rex squeezed behind him to pull the door shut.

"What?" Syn asked. "Just some random chick?"

Nico shrugged and slid the cardboard box onto the small counter. "No. She said she was instructed to drop it off."

Their "kitchen" was a hell of a lot smaller than what Dodge had in his apartment. It was a joke to even call it a kitchen. Not with only two feet of counter space, a tiny single sink with a leaking faucet, a microwave that was about thirty years old and a fire hazard, and a dinged-up mini-fridge plastered with magnets from some of the locations they'd played. A set-up similar usually found in a small motorhome. One from like 1978. Just like the rest of the bus.

Old and outdated.

They had bought it cheap after the elderly man living in it had died. The son just wanted it gone from his property, so he sold it to them for two hundred bucks. They couldn't pass on it. It was better than the four of them living in an old van. Of course, it had needed work and still did, but Syn and the guys did what they could do on their own.

Syn's eyebrows pinned together. "This chick was someone from the church?"

Nico grimaced. "I don't think she belongs to the church."

"Where does she belong?" Eddie asked, coming out of their tiny bathroom, zipping up and shutting the plastic accordion door behind him.

That meant he'd just dropped a deuce in the toilet. They tried not to use it too often since the water tank and waste tank on the bus were small, especially for four adults. Plus, everywhere charged a fee to fill up with water or to empty their tank.

Money they didn't have.

But the fine, if found dumping their waste where they shouldn't, was higher than the fee to do it legally.

One reason Nico went behind a bush at the church where they were parked was to avoid filling the tank so quickly. All the guys pissed outside whenever they could. Sometimes even Syn did, too, if she could find a spot private enough.

Maybe the church had a hose somewhere where they could at least refill the water tank. Though, at night the temps were below freezing and no one left their outdoor faucets on during winter in the north.

"She said most of the stuff came from the local Amish." Nico's words brought her attention back to her bassist.

"What's in there for breakfast?" Eddie asked, elbowing Nico out of the way. He pulled out what looked like a homemade loaf of bread and a tub of something. He continued to pull shit out and groaned, "Holy shit. Homemade strawberry jam. Apple butter. Fresh-fucking-churned butter. Eggs." He lifted something wrapped in white paper and held it above his head as he screamed, "Bacon!" and then hugged the package to his chest with a huge smile of ecstasy on his face.

"Great," Rex said dryly. "Better hope we have enough propane left to cook it."

"If we do, we might not have any left after," Syn said just as dryly as Rex.

"I don't care," Nico said, still excited. "We have a gig tomorrow night. With that four hundred bucks, we can refill the water and propane, and empty the shitter."

He forgot about filling the fuel tank, which was really important. But Syn kept that to herself for now since her mouth watered at the thought of a bacon, egg and toast breakfast. Her stomach also growled in agreement. "Store what you're not using for breakfast that needs to be refrigerated in one of the compartments under the bus. It'll stay cold enough under there."

The bacon wouldn't last long enough to be stored. Between the four of them, a pound would be instantly devoured. It probably wouldn't even make it to their Styrofoam plates.

Eddie stepped up to the box and pulled out two tomatoes and lettuce. "If there's any bacon left over, we can make BLTs later."

"Or we can go eat in the bar. He said he'll feed us tonight and tomorrow, too," Syn said.

Three sets of eyes turned her way and their excitement about the box of food quickly disappeared.

"What did you have to do to get us this? If you had to…" Eddie shook his head and put the veggies back in the box. "I don't want this shit if he forced you to…" He frowned.

"Did he?" Nico asked, running his gaze over her.

Syn rolled her eyes. Even if he did, what the hell could Nico see? She was wrapped up in a couple layers of clothes and had a blanket wrapped around her so she wouldn't freeze to death. The only part of her exposed was her face under her kitty-eared hood.

Rex lifted Syn's double-socked feet to make room on the couch that turned into her bed when pulled out. He sat in the spot where her feet had been and put them back on his lap, resting one hand on her ankle. "Syn…"

She shook her head. "Rex, I didn't have to do shit."

"You stayed in his place last night."

"I fell asleep. That's all. He didn't make me…" She shook her head again. "He didn't." She left it at that.

"Where'd he sleep?"

"On his couch."

Rex's brow dropped low. "He didn't…"

"No. And if he had demanded *quid pro quo* I would've told him to fuck off."

"So, why is he helping us, then?" Eddie asked, suspicion tinging his words.

"Why does anyone help us? Probably because we look like we need it." Her eyes began to burn and she rubbed at them. If she started crying over fucking nothing, she was going to be pissed at herself. This was their current life. She should be used to it by now. Things would get better, wouldn't it? "We live in a shitty bus. We're fucking broke. We have *nothing* but each other. It's obvious we need help."

"We have our talent, too," Nico said. "At least we're not panhandling."

Right. Their talent.

"You do realize that it's because of our talent that we live in this piece of shit, right?" she asked, blinking back the burn.

Life got so damn overwhelming sometimes. She tried to keep moving forward, hoping one day things would fall into place. Hoping they'd catch a break and things would get better.

It wasn't today and it wouldn't be tomorrow, either. But she could hope.

And once she got her future in order, she could go back and fix her past.

Maybe fixing it wasn't the right word.

"After we eat, we need to move this bus so the church doesn't bitch. We also need to get to a laundromat," she murmured.

"We need a damn mechanic," Rex said. "Or to go south."

"We need to play this gig first. He's going to pay us. Then maybe we can see how much it'll be to fix the heater."

"Too much," Rex muttered.

Eddie had been working on trying to get the heater working. So far, he'd had no luck. He was a drummer, not a bus whisperer.

A loud pounding on the bus door had Syn jumping and her head spinning in that direction. Nico's eyes were wide as he stared toward it, too. "Shit. I bet the church wants us to move."

"No shit," Eddie said.

"Churches are supposed to help people," Nico whispered. "All they do is help themselves."

"We don't know what kind of church it is," Syn hissed in a whisper, in case it *was* someone from the church. "Some do help people."

The pounding came again. "Check to see who it is," Syn instructed Eddie.

Eddie shot her a look, then pushed open the door. He quickly backed up the steps as another man followed him inside.

A man much broader than her drummer.

Now wearing that cut over a black leather jacket. He also had a black beanie pulled over his dark hair. A pair of shades covered his brown eyes.

One dark eyebrow lifted above the frame of his mirrored sunglasses. "Just makin' sure Angel dropped off the food."

"She did," Rex said, drawing Dodge's attention.

His eyes zeroed in on where Syn's feet were on Rex's lap. The other eyebrow joined the first one above the frames.

When he slipped the reflective glasses off, both eyebrows had dropped back into place but his gaze remained where Syn laid on the couch.

"Gotta move…" Dodge started.

Syn held her breath as their gazes locked.

"This thing."

"Do you know where we can park it?" Rex asked, his fingers curling possessively around Syn's ankle. "We don't have a car to get us around, so we can't park in some field out in the middle of nowhere."

"Rex," she warned under her breath.

Rex had zero reason to be possessive. None. Protective, yes. Possessive, no. They were like siblings. All of them were. It was why she felt so comfortable living in a damn bus with them. She did not want that to change.

That would fuck everything up.

She jiggled her foot just enough to make a point and he

removed his hand, shooting her a frown. She bugged her eyes out at him.

Dodge took a step further into the bus, interrupting her and Rex's silent conversation.

In an instant, he made the bus feel more crowded than her three bandmates did all together.

"There's a strip mall down at the east end of town. Can park in the Walmart lot."

"Do they have a laundromat there?" They weren't going to get any gigs at all if they stunk like wet, week-old socks.

"Dunno." He glanced around, his lips pursed as he stroked his bearded chin. She had noticed it last night but noticed again that he had a few strands of gray in that beard.

She didn't think he was old enough to be going gray. Before she snuck out in the middle of the night, she noticed a few in his hair, too.

She never answered him when he asked her how old she was. Twice. He never answered her, either.

It didn't matter. He wasn't for her. Not for one night. Not even for an hour.

But she couldn't pull her eyes from his broad shoulders encased in black leather as he took his time inspecting every-thing within his eyesight. What he couldn't see wasn't much different.

A flicker of something unfamiliar started in her gut when his dark eyes landed back on her and pinned her in place. "Why the fuck's it so cold in here?"

She opened her mouth to answer him but Rex muttered, "The heater's a fickle bitch," first.

"You don't got heat." It wasn't a question but more of a growl, his eyes still glued to her.

She was not taking even a second to explore what that grumble had done to her. Hell no. Not one damn second.

Whatever rabbit was trying to escape down that hole needed to be forced back out of it with a boot to the ass.

"Depends," Nico said behind Dodge.

The older man glanced over his shoulder. "Why don't you have heat?"

Syn attempted to clear the tightness in her throat before saying, "He just told you why."

His head tilted when he looked at her again. "Get it fixed."

She swallowed her, *"Thanks for the advice, genius,"* typical response. He'd been nothing but helpful. She did not want to lose their opportunity to make some money tomorrow night—and the promise of more free food—all because she let out her inner smart-ass demon. Instead, she suggested, "Maybe we can if you give us an advance on our gig tomorrow night."

"Yeah, right. I hand over the scratch and you all just ghost." He snapped his fingers in emphasis.

"We won't ghost," she promised.

"And I know that how?"

He didn't. He was right. If she were in his shoes, she wouldn't fork over the money before the gig was over, either.

She shrugged. "Then don't. We'll head to a warmer location after we play Friday night. Then heat won't be an issue."

"Yes it will, because the A/C isn't working right now, either," Eddie revealed, *oh-so-fucking* helpfully.

Syn sighed.

"What works on this fuckin' bus?" Dodge growled again.

"We do."

His dark eyebrows pinned together.

Syn pressed her palm to her chest over the blanket and repeated, "We do. *We* work."

"Ain't what I meant."

She knew what he meant, she simply decided to pretend to misunderstand him.

"Should get a better ride," he had the balls to say next.

"Maybe we'll do that with the four hundred bucks you give us." She raised her brows at him while his lowered once more.

A corner of his eye twitched.

She waited.

His nostrils flared.

She waited some more.

In her peripheral vision, she could see Rex, Nico and Eddie had turned into stone statues.

She moved her feet from Rex's lap, sat up, lifted her chin, still waiting.

Suddenly the deep freeze inside the bus—definitely not from the winter weather outside—thawed once Dodge's muscles loosened. "Look, my club's got a motel. You could get a room there… A coupla rooms…"

"For free?" Nico asked, unable to hide his excitement of actually sleeping in a real bed and having a real shower. With *hot* water. Like she had last night.

Now she felt guilty they didn't get the same.

"Ain't gonna be for free."

"Thanks, but…" Nico didn't bother to hide his disappointment, either.

Syn had enough of the bar manager-biker-whatever dropping orders. "I don't think we can buy a new bus for us to live in *and* pay for a couple of motel rooms all on that four hundred. Do you?"

Dodge ground his hand over his mouth. Not once. Not twice. But three times. When he was done, she saw his jaw had become as tight as one of Eddie's drums. Even under that thick, dark beard. "You got enough fuel to follow me a coupla miles up through town?"

"To where?" Eddie asked, stepping closer. "To the Walmart?"

Dodge shook his head. "Nope. To someone who might be able to help with the heater."

Silence filled the bus.

"It's an old diesel heater," Syn warned him.

"Okay? Don't know shit about them. Might know someone who does."

The idea of the heat being fixed in the bus made excitement push away any suspicion about why the man kept helping them.

Her first instinct was to ask how much that would cost them. That was always the first concern. But he wouldn't know that answer.

And if whoever looked at it told them some outrageous price, they could simply continue to roll down to the Walmart parking lot.

Wasn't the first time they slept outside that retailer, wouldn't be the last.

But she didn't want to get her hopes up too high about the possible heater repair. Too many times her hopes had come crashing down and became crushed into smithereens.

She couldn't live with too many more disappointments. She'd had more than enough for a lifetime already.

She was also tired of scraping along the bottom.

But maybe...

Maybe...

Could things be looking up for them?

She sure as hell hoped so.

Because the way things were right now, the only direction left to go had to be up.

Chapter Six

Dodge glanced in the rearview mirror of his '79 Power Wagon for the hundredth time to make sure the bus was still behind him. And that it didn't take a shit somewhere along Main Street. It was hard to miss the cloud of black smoke billowing from the exhaust pipes.

His restored Dodge 4x4 was probably much older than the skoolie, but then, his beast was in pristine shape and he also didn't have to live in it. Stepping into that bus a half-hour ago, he had to hide his reaction as best as he could. The inside of it was just as bad, if not worse, than the outside.

Besides being messy, it stunk and was cramped as fuck.

Worse, Syn was living in it with three guys.

What. The. Actual. Fuck.

He gritted his teeth when he recalled the way that mother-fucker was touching her.

Like he owned her.

The lead guitarist had told him they weren't fucking. Was that a complete fucking lie?

His jaw shifted with the same force as he shifted his

truck's three-on-the-tree into a lower gear while turning into the garage's lot.

He reminded himself for the countless time that it didn't matter who was fucking her.

None of that mattered.

She wasn't for him.

He glanced over his shoulder to make sure Eddie, the band's drummer, was following him into the parking lot of Dutch's Garage. Dodge didn't bother to call the Original to warn him of their arrival since the bus needed to be moved out of the church lot anyway.

He slipped his truck into one of the empty spots out front and jumped out. He pointed to the other side of the lot, indicating Eddie should park the bus there out of the way.

He didn't wait for them to get out, but went directly inside and was greeted at the shop door by a yapping three-pound, four-legged asshole who was owned by a two-legged, a buck-ninety-pound asshole.

Or maybe it was the other way around.

"Get fuckin' lost, you little fuckin' shit." He shoved the Chihuahua away from him with his boot. He did it gently, even though the little fucker was snarling and snapping. He knew how to solve that problem but...

Yeah, no.

If the dog loved Rook, he had to have some mental issues he couldn't help. Dodge couldn't blame Cujo for being fucked in the head.

"Yo, Cujo!" came from the other end of the garage.

The dog circled Dodge once, then darted past the four car lifts back to his daddy. Barking the whole fucking way, of course. Yapping seemed to propel the little shit forward.

"Will that motherfucker shut the fuck up?" Dutch grumbled, coming around a truck parked in the first bay, a dirty rag in his hand as he wiped the grease from his fingers. "What the fuck d'you want?"

"Hello to you, too," Dodge grumbled. "You greet all your customers like that?"

"You a customer?"

"No."

Dutch shrugged, then grinned.

"Next time you sit your ass down on a stool at my bar, gonna make sure to ask you that same damn question."

"Ain't *your* bar."

"Close enough."

"Not even. Club owns that bar," Dutch grumbled.

"Ain't I part of the damn club?"

Rook appeared out of nowhere, interrupting them. They clasped hands and bumped shoulders. "Asshole," he greeted.

"Asshole," Dodge greeted back with a grin.

"You miss watchin' me take a shit on a stainless steel throne? That why you're here?" his former cellmate asked with a grin.

"Yeah, gettin' a little homesick for the rank stank comin' from your asshole every time you dropped a bomb in our cage."

"He musta got that stinky shit from his momma. 'Cause we gotta air out the shitter for an hour after he's in there. Know he didn't get that from me 'cause my shit don't stink," Dutch announced. "So, you here to toss this asshole's salad or you here on business?"

"Business."

Dutch's eyes narrowed. "Just inspected that truck of yours. Sled's parked in the shed for the season. What the fuck d'you need worked on?"

"A bus."

"A what?"

Dodge cupped his hands around his mouth and yelled,

"Bus! You know, the long metal vehicle that transports snot monkeys?"

Dutch's bushy salt-and-pepper eyebrows stitched tightly together. "What the fuck did you buy a school bus for?"

"I didn't, I—"

The shop door opened and Syn walked in with the cold air following on her heels.

"Shut that damn door before all the heat gets out," Dutch grumbled.

Syn slammed it shut behind her.

She wore her black sweatshirt with the cat-eared hood pulled up over her hair. That wasn't even a fucking winter jacket. Didn't she have anything warmer?

In the distance machine-gun yapping began again.

"Shut up, asshole!" Dutch yelled. He scowled at his oldest son. "That little rat bastard's gonna have to find somewhere else to stay all day. Can't be chasing customers away."

"First of all, *you* chase the damn customers away. You just yelled at one to shut the door. I wouldn't blame her for turnin' around and walkin' the fuck back out. Second, Cujo's been here for like a fuckin' year, in case your old pea brain has forgotten," Rook reminded his father.

"That means you should have him trained by now."

Rook shook his head. He turned his attention back to Dodge. "You need me?"

"Just for a goodnight kiss." Dodge pursed his lips and made kissing noises. "Miss your cuddles, cellie."

Rook barked out a laugh, then turned around and bent over, patting his coverall-covered ass. "Kiss this, fucker."

"Knew you secretly missed me."

Rook shot him the bird and wandered back to the farthest garage bay. The Hell Hound finally shut the fuck up.

"She with you?" Dutch asked.

Dodge turned back to him and tipped his head toward Syn still standing by the door. "Yeah. She's got a band and they all live in a fuckin' bus. It's," *a piece of shit,* "got some issues."

"Like the Partridge Family?" Dutch asked.

"They didn't live in their bus."

"Oh yeah. I woulda done the mom."

"Why don't that surprise me?"

"Total fuckin' MILF." Dutch pursed his lips and stroked his long, bushy beard. He didn't hide his obvious interest as he raked his eyes over Syn from top to toe.

Dodge cleared his throat sharply and Dutch twisted his head back to him with a huge grin and a sparkle in his eye.

Fucker.

The old man moved to the bay door behind Dodge and glanced out into the lot from one of the small windows. "Certainly is a fuckin' bus."

"Yeah, thanks, Captain Obvious," Dodge said dryly.

Dutch shrugged. "We ain't diesel mechanics. That piece of shit probably got a Cummins in it. We don't work on those things. None of us do. Gotta find yourself a bus mechanic, an RV dealer, or someone who knows those types of engines."

"Ain't the engine. They don't got heat." Or apparently air conditioning but getting them heat was the first step.

Dutch scratched the back of his neck. "Sounds like a fuckin' problem. But one I can't solve." His eyes flicked back to Syn as she took a few steps closer to them.

She had pushed down her hood and now her long, dark brown hair spilled free around her shoulders.

Dodge waited for her to say something but she didn't. However, he couldn't miss the disappointment on her face, even though she was trying to mask it. She was failing.

Jesus fuck. "Know someone who can without havin' to take out a fuckin' mortgage?"

Dutch pulled thoughtfully at his beard while his eyes rolled toward the ceiling. When he finally dropped his gaze back to Dodge, he grunted, "Nope."

Dodge shook his head. "Ain't an engine problem, anyway. It has to do with the heating system."

Dutch raised a salt-and-pepper bushy eyebrow. "You know somethin' about buses?"

"Nope."

"Then shut the fuck up."

"Whatever, old man, just tryin' to help."

"Help who? You or me?"

He jerked his head toward Syn. "Them. They're in a tight spot."

Dutch yanked on his beard again and glanced over at Syn. "Her, you mean. Tryin' to wedge your dick down those tight skinny jeans of hers. With your pencil dick, it just might fit."

"You know she can hear you, right?"

"Yep. And so can you." He bobbled his head and said, "I said what I said."

He said what he said? "Christ, you need to stop baggin' youngins. They're rubbin' off on you."

Dutch lifted one eyebrow toward Syn. "Shouldn't be throwin' rocks right now."

"You mean stones."

"You got what I meant."

Dodge sighed. "Can you at least go out and look at their heater? Maybe there's somethin' you or one of your crew can do."

"You gonna make me go out in the cold?"

"Since when did a tough old fuck like you turn into a pussy?" Dodge asked, knowing Dutch wouldn't like it.

The old man grumbled and pushed past Syn, slamming the door behind him.

Dodge's gaze bounced from the door to Syn and he shot her a smile.

Her dark eyes went wide, she blinked, then he could see her mentally shake herself.

Well, fuck. Was it because he smiled at her?

No.

Was it?

"Should I go out with him?" she asked.

"Nope. You got three adult men out there who can show him the issue. Stay in here where it's warm." He moved closer. "Want coffee?"

She nodded. He tipped his head toward the break room behind the office. "Back there."

As he moved past the office door, he peeked his head in. "Hey, Lee."

Reilly lifted her head from whatever she was looking at on the computer and pulled out one of her earbuds. "Hey, Dodge! What are you doing here? I didn't hear you out there."

"Probably 'cause you're jammin' out."

She shook her head. "Podcast."

"About?"

She only smiled.

Dodge shook his head. "Don't wanna know." He tapped the door jamb twice with his palm, then kept moving. Syn was right behind him. He didn't even have to look to know. He *felt* her there.

Like they were connected somehow.

The whole thing with her was fucked. He didn't understand it and wasn't sure he wanted to.

He just knew whatever it was, wasn't on his life's agenda.

He stepped into the tiny break room and over to the coffeemaker. Thank fuck Reilly must have made a fresh pot of caffeinated fuel. He filled two disposable cups and held one out to Syn. "Black?"

"Got used to black."

Of course she did. Coffee was expensive even without all the extras. "Lee keeps the creamer and sugar stocked. Help yourself."

Syn stepped up next to him and began to doctor her coffee. He pressed one hand against his outer thigh and curled the fingers of his other hand tighter around his cup to keep from reaching out.

From making a physical connection.

She was so goddamn close.

A second later, his mouth gaped open a little when she dumped about a pound of sugar into the cup, took a few sips to make more room, then poured in a bunch of French vanilla creamer, filling it to the brim.

The black coffee was now almost white. His teeth hurt just thinking about how sweet it had to be. "Damn," he whispered. "That ain't coffee anymore."

She shrugged, grabbed a tiny straw and gave it a quick stir. Dodge couldn't unglue his eyes from her as she lifted the cup to her lipstick-free lips and took a sip, closing her eyes as she did so.

The simple act of her drinking coffee shouldn't wake up every fucking cell in his body. Shouldn't make his fucking skin prickle like he stuck a fork in an outlet.

But it did.

The way her throat rolled as she swallowed. The pleasure on her face as the coffee hit her taste buds and the warmth hit her gut.

Worse, the low moan that accompanied it all.

Fuuuuuuck meeeeeee.

He had to shake that shit off. This was not him. He had to be smoking too much potent Kush or something. "How old were you when you first started drinkin' coffee?"

Her eyes opened and she took another sip. "How old were *you*?"

Christ. "You ever gonna answer any of my questions?"

"Are you?"

He barked out a laugh, thankful that her stubborn streak pulled him back to reality. With a shake of his head, he turned and leaned back against the counter, studying her. "You ran out of my place early this mornin'."

He was usually a light sleeper so he was surprised when her fleeing his apartment at some crazy hour didn't wake him. Once he did wake up, he actually had a difficult time prying himself from the couch. Parts on him were stiff and sore and not for a good reason.

"I didn't run anywhere." She lifted her coffee cup to her lips and it hovered there. "Sorry I fell asleep in your bed. You should've woken me up and kicked me out as soon as you found me." She leaned back against the opposite wall in the narrow room, cupping her coffee with both hands. Small, like her.

The space in the break room was tight since, from what he understood, it had originally been some sort of storage closet. It was about as long and as narrow as his apartment's kitchen, if that.

With how they stood across from each other, her black combat boots were only a couple inches from his.

Her feet were tiny next to his.

Everything about her was petite.

But not breakable.

Fuck no, he recognized a survivor when he saw one.

It was in her eyes, in her responses, in how she carried herself.

She might be young but she'd already lived a life.

He wanted to know her story.

Who she was, where she came from, what made her the way she was.

He wanted to peel away those layers and get to her core.

He never had that urge before.

He didn't like having that urge now.

He lifted his gaze slowly from her boots and up her skinny jeans, blue this time but with a couple of rips similar to the black pair. Her hips weren't wide or curvy, and her thighs slender. He paused on her shapeless zippered hoodie that hid the top half of her body.

Syn was not his normal menu choice.

Never once had he ordered a salad over a thick fucking steak smothered in A.1. Sauce. Carrots were for rabbits.

He fucked like a rabbit but didn't eat like one.

Still… Right now, he wouldn't mind picking some lettuce out of his teeth.

The zipper on her kitty cat sweatshirt was pulled all the way up hiding whatever she was wearing underneath it.

"You into cats?"

He waited for her "Are *you* into cats?" to come boomeranging back at him and was surprised when she actually gave him an answer. "No. Hate them. They tend to be assholes."

"Then why would you wear a cat sweatshirt?"

"It's not a cat sweatshirt. It's a sweatshirt with cat ears."

This chick… "Guess you can find an argument with everythin'."

She took a long sip of her coffee as she contemplated his words. "Guess I can." She tilted her head. "Look, sorry I slept in your bed last night. I don't even remember climbing in. But there was no reason for you to be relegated to your own couch."

He lifted one eyebrow. "You sayin' I coulda joined you?"

Her mouth gaped open slightly, then snapped shut. "Like I said, you should've woken me up."

"You looked exhausted and after seein' that…" *That hovel on wheels.* "Where you sleep every night… Hell, even before that, I knew you needed that bed last night more than me."

Her torso slowly lifted as she drew in a long, deep breath. She released it just as slowly. "Thank you."

"That had to fuckin' hurt."

"I take it back."

"Too late. No backsies."

Her lips twitched. "No *backsies*?"

"Never heard that before?"

"Not since," she shook her head, "I don't know… since I was ten, maybe?"

"How long ago was that?"

Her eyes narrowed. "Why do you care how old I am? It's like you're obsessed about it."

He just might be. His interest in her scared the fuck out of him. If she was too young that just might help squash it. Or he hoped to fuck it would. "Just curious, is all."

"Why?"

"Don't fuckin' know. The more you avoid the question, the more I wanna know the answer."

"Why?"

He lifted one shoulder, pursed his lips and stared at the coffee cup in his hand for a second. When he lifted his head again, he asked, "Want the truth?"

She nodded, her eyes holding his. It made his heart thump heavily because everything about this, everything about his pull toward her, spooked him. Worse, it was like she could see right through him.

No, not through him. She could see his center. His very core. She could see everything about him.

Where he came from, what he'd been through, maybe even where he was going. Exactly what he wanted to learn about her.

Witchcraft.

Pure fucking witchcraft.

He should lie. Of fucking course, he didn't. Because he was a dumbass. "Cause I'm interested."

"Do you want the truth?" she shot back at him.

He was going to regret this… "Yeah."

"I'm not." She pushed off the wall but didn't move away. "If you're only helping us to get down my pants like that old man said, you're not going to be successful."

She sounded way too confident about that. He normally didn't waste time on challenges like her. But his reaction to her caught him off guard. It was so opposite than it would normally be with someone like her or with one of his typical catch-and-releases. "First, don't let Dutch hear you call him that. Second, you ain't into men?"

"*First*, I heard you call him that. And here you are, standing in front of me, still breathing. *Second*, I might be down on my luck, but I don't *go down* in an attempt to change that fact."

He considered her for a moment. He wasn't insulted that she said that to him. In fact, he respected that answer. "Ain't askin' for that."

"Then why are you helping us?"

"Two reasons… One, in the past, I've been where you're at."

Something flashed behind her eyes. If he was lucky, he'd earned a little bit of her respect. "And two?"

One corner of his mouth lifted slightly. "'Cause I can."

"From what I've seen, you don't have much, either."

Since they were both lobbing truth bombs… "Got a lot more than you, you just can't see everything I have."

Her dark brown eyes narrowed on him. "What do you mean?"

"Material shit don't mean squat without the rest of it."

"Without the rest of what?"

He jerked his head in the direction where the bus was parked, even though they couldn't see it. "Those three guys out there… What are they to you?"

Her brow pulled low. "What do you mean? They're part of my band."

He shook his head. "No. They're more than that."

Anger colored her cheeks and her words. "I'm not fucking any of them."

That was good to hear. Not that it mattered… Because it didn't matter. Fuck no. "Ain't talkin' about sex. What do they mean to you? What are they to you? Their musical skills don't even come close to yours. Tell me why you keep them around."

"I already told you why."

"Go deeper."

"What, are you a goddamn therapist?"

She was getting pissed over something she shouldn't be. He needed to break down that defensive wall she threw up constantly.

To keep people out.

Dumbasses like him.

Or to keep her own baggage hidden.

"Fuck no." Dodge snorted. "Not even close. Let me tell you somethin'… 'Til I landed in this town, in this club, in my brotherhood, something was missin'. Didn't know what. Didn't know why. I was on a path to nowhere. My life also felt... incomplete. Took me a while to realize why that was since I never took the time to figure it out. I was always on the move, tryin' to outrun whatever was chasin' me instead. Whether it was the pigs or my past. Or a pissed off woman." He swallowed another mouthful of coffee, letting his words sink in before continuing.

"Okay?" she prodded.

Her attitude should be a fucking turn-off. But it only made him more determined to continue instead of simply telling her to fuck off and walking away like he normally would. He normally wouldn't waste time or a second thought on someone like her.

But, *for fuck's sake*, his normal reactions were flipped upside down when it came to the woman standing before him.

He plowed forward before he *did* decide she wasn't worth it. "During my last bid in prison, my cellmate Rook—the guy out there with the noisy Chihuahua—invited me here to join the Fury. Things snowballed from there. No longer had a reason to keep runnin', 'cause I found what was missin'."

"A brotherhood?"

"A family." He tipped his head toward open door of the break room and the garage bays. "All those guys out there are my family now. Reilly, the blonde in the office? She's Rev's ol' lady."

While she didn't know who Rev was, it didn't matter since he had a point to make. She seemed smart enough to pick up what he was putting down. *If* she allowed herself to do so. She seemed to prefer to remain closed up and closed off. His words only needed the tiniest crack to wiggle their way in. *If* she let them.

"But even before Rev claimed her, Lee was family." He put his coffee cup down on the counter behind him and straightened. "So, here's the thing… On the outside it might not look like it, but these people mean every-damn-thing to me. Also got a good reason to stay out of the joint now. Besides family, got more than I've ever had. Ain't a bad gig. Unlike your situation right now."

Dutch's *"I said what I said"* landed once more in his brain. Dodge had laid out some truth. It was up to Syn to take his words and either learn from them or discard them.

If she did the second, that was her loss, not his.

"What were you in prison for?"

That wasn't the part he expected her to focus on. "Which time?"

"My brother has lived his whole life in and out of prison, we lost track of—"

Dutch suddenly appeared in the doorway, shaking his head and grumbling, and making her swallow the rest of her words. Of course the old man would interrupt when he was just about to learn something about her.

"Can't fix that fuckin' thing. It's a diesel heater. They need to buy some electric space heaters or somethin' 'til they can find someone to replace that piece of shit with a new, more efficient propane heater."

"We don't have enough propane."

"Sucks to be you." His gaze took a slow stroll down Syn's body again. "But I could get you—"

"No," Dodge said sharply. Both sets of eyes turned his direction. The older pair holding some annoyance at his interference. "Ain't gonna work like that."

"You—"

He cut off the old man again. "No."

Syn frowned and her gaze bounced back and forth between him and Dutch. He could see it in her face, she knew exactly what Dutch was proposing.

An exchange of sex for services from a man old enough to be her grandfather.

That was never going to happen.

He expected Syn to cut Dutch down at the knees for that suggestion, or more like his attempt at that suggestion. So, Dodge was surprised when she simply said, "We also have nowhere to plug in to be able to use electric heaters, even if we had them."

What she wasn't saying was they had no money to buy them, either.

Jesus Christ. He remembered being so down on his luck that every direction you turned cost fucking scratch.

He still wasn't flush, but at least he had the basics. He wasn't freezing his ass off or going to bed with an empty stomach. He drank as much as he wanted. He smoked as much as he wanted, too.

He had more pussy climb those steps to his apartment than he could count. If he wasn't in the mood for randoms, he could get a sweet butt to land in his bed in a pinch. It only took a text.

One thing was for sure, between the club, the bar and the women, he was never fucking lonely. When he needed some alone time, he took his sled out for a long run.

However, the deeper they went into winter, the opportunities to ride were dwindling. He wasn't as die-hard as some of the rest of his Fury brothers. He preferred to keep all of his digits—and, more importantly, his balls—from freezing and cracking off.

Dodge swiped his coffee from the counter, downed the rest of it and tossed the empty cup into a trash can in the corner. "All right, thanks for checkin' it for me. We'll figure somethin' out."

Dutch stroked his beard as he turned his attention from Syn to him. "Will ya?"

Cocky fucker. "Yeah."

"Would let them plug in here, but it ain't gonna be for free and I really don't need that skoolie takin' up all that space in my lot."

"Understood," Dodge grumbled. He couldn't let them plug in at the bar, either, since there wasn't space for them to park. Also, Stella might have a fit about it since commercial electric rates were higher than residential. He could only imagine how much electricity that monster would use.

But he did have another fucking idea.

If his idea panned out, he could grab a couple of heaters down at Walmart and dock the cost from their gig fee.

Or he could be a nice guy and just outright buy them.

He wasn't sure if he wanted to be that generous yet. Or that nice. He had plenty of time to decide.

"Gotta make a call." He wanted privacy to do so, but there was no way he was leaving Syn alone with Dutch. "Head out to the bus. Meet you out there."

Dodge grabbed the box of fresh donuts sitting on the counter from Coffee and Cream and shoved it at Syn. "Here, take this with you. For them. And you."

"Hey, those are——" Dutch began to protest.

"You don't need them," Dodge cut him off and put his hand over Syn's sweatshirt at the small of her back, steering her past the garage owner, the office and back outside.

As soon as she took a few steps toward the bus, Syn slammed on the brakes and turned to face him, breaking their connection. "We'll go park the bus at Walmart." He shook his head, but she continued, "I appreciate everything you've done, but the heaters will have to wait."

He took a step closer and tipped his face down to meet her upturned one. "Lemme make a call, then we'll go from there."

"Why are you doing this?" she whispered. "We're just a band like any other band that's played in your bar."

No, they weren't.

No, *she* wasn't.

There was no "just" about her.

"Already explained why."

"Because you're interested."

He now regretted telling her that. He should've kept that buried deep where it belonged. "We gonna rehash this out here in the goddamn cold?"

She stared up at him, her gaze unwavering. "I don't understand."

"That makes two of us." He tugged his beanie lower on his head to keep from reaching out and touching her again.

Because, *fuck him*, he wanted to smooth away the wariness on her face. "Go," he ordered softly. "Go wait in the bus."

She continued to stand there, not moving to do what he ordered. He knew exactly why.

I'm just as fuckin' confused as you, woman. Believe me.

She nodded as if he'd said that out loud. Her response made his heart seize for a second, thinking he might have actually slipped and let that out into the universe.

Without another word, she turned and headed toward the bus.

He blew out a breath and forced his muscles to loosen, then strode a few yards away from the bus to where he knew no one would overhear him. He turned his back to both the skoolie and the shop, found the number he needed, then pushed Send.

Hoping like fuck that everything he was doing for her or even trying to do wouldn't come back to bite him in the ass. His dumb ass.

"Yeah," came the gruff answer on the second ring.

"Got a band here that's got an old skoolie with no heat. They need a place to plug in 'til after they play at Pete's tomorrow night."

The other end of the phone was silent.

"Stella wanted me to hire them. To fill in for a band that cancelled." That might give his request some weight with the Fury prez.

"Got campgrounds for that, brother," Trip said.

Not as easy of a solution as it sounded. "They can't afford a campground." Among other things.

More silence.

He knew Trip wouldn't like outsiders staying at the farm. Dodge didn't blame him but he was hoping for an exception. Even if the prez said no, then at least Dodge gave it a shot.

He'd just need to work harder to find a damn solution.

Even though it wasn't his problem.

They weren't his problem.

She wasn't his problem.

For fuck's sake.

He kept making her his problem.

"We've all been there," Dodge reminded him, keeping his voice low. "Every single fuckin' one of us."

"Right," Trip murmured. "You know how I feel about outsiders bein' on the farm."

"Yeah."

After a long-assed pause, Trip asked, "Stella meet them?"

"She saw them play." She never actually stayed long enough last night to meet the band. Usually, the only time she took the time to speak to a band was when she was deciding whether to book them or not.

She had a good ear because apparently her ex had been a musician. Dodge didn't know a lot about her past, but he did know that much.

"Give me a few. I'll text you back."

"Hey," Dodge called out before the Fury prez hung up.

Trip grunted.

"It might be for tomorrow night, too. Not sure if they'll hit the road right after they're done playin' Friday night or if they'll head out Saturday mornin'."

The phone not only went silent this time, but dark. Dodge stared at it for a few seconds then tapped the edge of it against his beanie-covered forehead as he considered what his next move would be to help them if Trip said no.

Their options were getting slimmer with every minute that passed.

He dropped the hand holding his phone and stared at the piece of shit skoolie across the lot.

Why the fuck did he even care enough to help them?

Why was he even getting involved in something that had nothing to do with him?

His answer rounded the back of the bus.

Jesus fuck.

He'd never been a slave to pussy.

Not once.

Even worse, he hadn't even fucked her. If he was smart, he shouldn't plan on it, either.

Especially since the woman had a difficult time listening.

I said what I said.

Dutch's words were one more thing he needed to scrape out of his melon.

"Told you to wait in the fuckin' bus," he called out.

When his cell phone dinged, he read the long, very Trip-like message that popped up on his screen.

Tell them they need to be out no later than Saturday morning. No Exceptions. No nosing around. I hear they're being nosy, I'm towing that fucker off the property. With or without them in it.

Dodge grinned at his phone. That man would do it, too. He did not fuck around when it came to keeping everyone in the Fury safe. What happened in the Fury stayed within the Fury.

Especially with some of the activities they'd been involved in the past with the Shirleys. Activities they might once again get involved with in the near future since the mountain clan seemed to be infesting Hillbilly Hill again.

Another text came in.

Church tonight. 8. Be there.

Chapter Seven

Syn couldn't pull her eyes from Dodge as his long legs ate up the distance between them.

"Told you to stay in the bus," he growled.

He was a bossy motherfucker. She was proud of herself when she managed to keep that observation to herself.

Today, her filter wasn't broken. That was a good thing since they were kind of at his mercy right now.

No, not kind of, they were. They were stuck.

She hated that helpless feeling. Of not being able to solve their own problems. Of not being able to provide for her "family."

Because no matter how he rubbed her the wrong way, he was right.

Everything he said in that break room was true. Rex, Eddie and Nico were her family. But she didn't need him to tell her that. She'd known it for a long time.

They loved music as much as she did. They needed it as much as she did.

Music to her was like oxygen to someone else.

She would die without it.

Right now, it was the only thing that was hers that she had full control over.

Because everything else? She didn't.

Her fucking life was a wreck. She was treading as fast as she could to try to keep her head above water. Every once in a while, that water got so rough, so choppy, she ended up swallowing a mouthful and choking.

Like now.

She made the wrong decision to stay north. She should've told Eddie to point the bus south after that last paying gig in Williamsport. Before that, they had found a dive bar to play at in Scranton.

Unfortunately, the bar owner there stiffed them out of the money he agreed to pay them. When Syn went to collect it after they were done loading up their equipment, the owner said he needed to grab cash from the safe in his office and she was to follow him.

Her first instinct was to refuse, but they needed the money and the fucker said he'd only give it to her. When she heard that, the hairs on the back of her neck rose and her stomach twisted.

She'd dealt with men like him before.

Too many times to count.

Men who thought they held all the power over the "weaker" fucking sex.

They wielded their misogyny like a sword.

While the bar owner held the cash tightly in his paw, he said her "gig" wasn't done yet. With a smile that made bile rise up Syn's throat, the motherfucker demanded she get on her knees.

Instead, she kneed him.

He ended up on his own knee caps—which she should've broken—not her, and she got the hell out of there while he howled in pain and rage.

The guys wanted to go back in and teach him a lesson.

Unfortunately, none of them had the skills to fight. It also didn't help that a couple of the owner's friends rushed out of the bar and began to chase her.

She sprinted back to the bus, almost breaking an ankle in the high-heeled boots she wore on stage. As soon as she sprinted up the steps, she screamed at Eddie to get them the fuck out of there. He floored it and left the two men in a cloud of black diesel exhaust, coughing up a lung.

Unfortunately, their promised two hundred bucks was left behind, too. The only thing they drove away with was some balled-up gum wrappers, some peanut shells, three quarters and a handful of pennies from their tip jar.

Never let them see you cry.

Never let them see you cry.

Never—

"It's too cold for you to be standin' out here in only that goddamn sweatshirt."

Keep your shit together, Syn. He doesn't have to help you. "It isn't much warmer inside the bus, either."

"Gonna solve that problem." The man had confidence seeping from his pores.

In one way she found it appealing, even sexy as hell, but in another way, worrying, since it didn't take much for confidence to tip over into arrogance. "How?"

"Get in my truck and you'll find out."

She glanced back over her shoulder at the bus. "What about them?"

"We'll be back shortly."

"They're not going to like me leaving with you."

"You think I give a fuck about that? They want heat?"

He was currently riding that edge of being over-bearing. Even a borderline dick.

"Show me how much you want this money, girl. You aren't getting what you want until I get what I want."

Her heart had been stuck in her throat when she

insisted, *"We played two sets. Just like you wanted. Pay me what you owe us."*

"First, you're going to play one more. On your knees."

She squeezed her eyes shut and somehow managed to get out a, "Yes."

When a finger was tucked under her chin and her face lifted, she opened her eyes, quickly hiding the anger that always followed her panic.

"What the fuck?" he whispered, his eyebrows pulled together.

She shook her head. It hadn't been the only time that something like that happened but it was the most recent and, for some reason, she couldn't shake it.

"We only have twenty-one bucks," she reminded him. "And we need to get fuel."

"There's a station a coupla blocks west of here. Tell them to go put fuel in the tank and then meet us back here."

"How long are we going to be? They're going to ask." She wasn't sure if they would or wouldn't, but he didn't need to know that.

"Hopefully not long. Got shit to do today other than to keep rescuin' a buncha strays."

She jerked her head and his hand fell away.

Without another word or flipping him off—something she struggled not to do—she spun on her heels and headed back to the bus before she lost that fight.

"Gonna be waitin' in my truck," she heard him call out.

She pressed her lips together to keep from telling him off and kept walking.

———

SYN GLANCED at the passenger side mirror to make sure the bus was still behind them as Dodge led the way to a destination unknown.

She hated leaving the control in his hands.

She hated having to rely on his help.

You have no choice right now. Take the help when you can get it. Especially when you aren't expected to pay for it with your dignity.

The interior of the truck cab was silent except for the road and engine noise. The Dodge pickup was old but in really good condition. Perfect, actually. He took care of it. Unlike his apartment.

At the big name store, he had purchased two compact ceramic heaters that alone ended up lightening his chained wallet by a hundred bucks. That total didn't include the personal items she needed. Items he told her to grab, as well.

She didn't argue with him about it or hide the economy-sized box of tampons she picked up along with a big bottle of shampoo and a bulk pack of toilet paper.

He stared at that stuff at the register but said nothing.

Since he didn't, she grabbed a roll of mint Lifesavers, a Hershey bar and a four-pack of AA batteries from the racks along the check-out lane and tossed those onto the belt, too.

After a quick glance at the additions, he still said nothing.

So, she grabbed the latest issue of Rolling Stone magazine and threw it on top.

He snagged that and said, "You either use the toilet paper or the magazine to wipe your ass. Choose."

The magazine went back on the rack.

She hid her grin by turning her head away. She didn't quite like his bossiness but it could be entertaining if she didn't let it annoy her.

He hadn't tried anything on the way to Walmart and kept a large gap between them on the bench seat on the return trip. They had swung back to the garage to pick up the skoolie.

Now they were pulling onto some long farm lane not far outside of town.

"You live above the bar, so who lives here?" she asked as they passed a farmhouse that looked well-maintained. From the style of it, she guessed it had to be built in the late 1800s.

Not her taste but somebody loved it enough to keep it in tip-top shape.

"Our club's president and his ol' lady."

A huge barn appeared before them. It didn't look like a typical barn, though. Huge windows were at the top but nothing below. There weren't any fences for livestock or even any animals.

A long storage shed with several garage doors sat to their left and a few smaller ones dotted the area nearby, along with a large covered pavilion to the left of the barn. Beyond that were fields, and trees beyond those fields. On the other side of a line of bare trees to their left, sat a row of homes. Newer, unlike the farmhouse, and not as large. If it wasn't winter, she might not have noticed them right away.

The lane they were following did branch off to those houses so they had to be part of the same property.

"What is this place?"

"Home to the Blood Fury," he said.

She glanced around again. "I don't get it. Does everyone live here?"

"Mostly. A few of us don't."

"There aren't a lot of houses over there. How big is your club?"

"Ain't big but some of my brothers live in a bunkhouse behind The Barn." He tipped his head toward the long building to their right. "There's a coupla apartments on the second floor around back, too."

"How many of you are there?"

He slowed to a stop near the end of the long shed, put the column shifter into neutral and stomped on the pedal for the parking brake. He twisted his torso toward her. "Thirteen fully-patched. Five prospects, two of those about to get patched-in."

"What's a normal-sized club?"

"Ain't nothin' normal about any MC. We're all different. Got different by-laws, rules, limits. They all do their own thing, includin' us. Our club ain't been around that long. It's still growin'."

"Who started it?"

He pursed his lips for a second and she figured he wasn't going to answer, but he finally did. "The Originals started it way back in the day, but they also destroyed it. Trip, our president, rebuilt the club from the ground up after his father was responsible for causin' that destruction."

"The president destroyed his own club? Something he built?"

"He wasn't the only one," he muttered and glanced over his shoulder and through the back window of the pickup's cab at her band's bus. "Stay here a sec. Gonna give your guys some instructions. Stay in the warmth."

He opened the driver's door, climbed out, then leaned back inside. "Just a word of advice… You guys are here 'cause of our prez's generosity. My advice is don't wander around, don't be nosy, don't ask questions. Especially about the club. I gave you too much already."

He had hardly given her anything at all.

He slammed the door shut. She turned on the bench seat and stared at him through the large rear window as he approached the bus and disappeared inside.

A few seconds later, he and Eddie were standing outside the skoolie and Dodge was pointing at a field beyond the barn.

He wanted them to park in a field? How would that give them the electricity needed for the heaters?

She watched Eddie's head bob up and down in agreement with whatever Dodge told him. A smile crossed her drummer's freckled face and he held out his fist for a fist bump.

Syn rolled her lips inward as Dodge stared at Eddie's fist for a split second, shook his head in the same way someone would roll their eyes and took long strides back to his truck. He yanked open his door, climbed inside and slammed it shut, cutting off the rush of December air into the cab.

Syn's attention was drawn to the bus passing them and heading toward the field. She gritted her teeth as she watched the vehicle bounce and roll over the rough terrain. If that off-road trip broke the suspension, or anything else, they were thoroughly screwed. They might as well hitchhike south from there with their instruments strapped to their backs.

When she turned back to Dodge, her heart skipped a beat, then raced. He'd been watching her.

He also didn't bother to hide it when she caught him.

What she saw in his eyes scared her and not because she was worried that he'd hurt her but because she was worried it was the exact opposite.

He admitted to her he was interested.

Right now, that was very fucking obvious. Suddenly, the truck cab got a whole lot smaller.

The heat she was feeling was no longer coming from the vents.

She cleared her throat. "Where are they going? Parking in a field—"

"Ain't parkin' in a field."

"Then—"

"They're goin' out there to dump the waste tank."

She slowly closed her gaping mouth. "Isn't that illegal?"

His head tipped slightly to the side. "Does it look like I give a fuck if it is?"

No, it didn't.

"You want it emptied?"

Hell yes. She nodded, unable to pull her eyes from him to check where the bus ended up. Hopefully, the guys had it all under control.

"After they're done with that, they're gonna park it next to the shed. There's water and an electrical hook-up you can use. Any other questions?"

"Is it the right amperage?"

"Yep."

"How do you know?"

"'Cause it was installed for one of my brothers and his baby girl."

"They lived in an RV?"

"Somethin' similar."

Syn couldn't rip her eyes from his throat as his Adam's apple rolled when he swallowed.

Without dropping his gaze from her, he reached into his cut that had been lying on the seat between them. When she asked earlier why he wasn't wearing it, he said they didn't wear their cuts inside of a vehicle. Or, if they did, they wore them with their colors inside out.

He didn't explain the reasoning behind it and she decided not to ask. But now, he pulled out a tin and a lighter from an inner pocket, popped it open and tucked what looked like a joint between his lips.

He rolled down the window a crack and lit it.

Immediately she knew it wasn't pot, but tobacco. He turned his head away from her only for the seconds it took to blow the smoke out of the narrow opening. His dark brown eyes scanned the field, then came back to her.

"Later, gonna get one of the… uh… girls to bring out another box of food."

"Girls?" Why did he hesitate like that?

"Yeah, like Angel did. Got a meetin' in The Barn tonight. After that, if you guys wanna grab hot food at

Pete's, I can fit two of you in my truck. Can get Possum or Tater to bring you back here after you eat. Yeah?"

"Possum or Tater?" she repeated.

"You met Possum last night. Tater's another prospect. They live here in the bunkhouse, so whoever's comin' back here first will haul your asses back. Sound good?"

It sounded fucking awesome and she wanted to once again ask why he was going out of his way to help them. It didn't make sense that he was doing all of this just because he was simply "interested." Especially since, so far, he had kept his hands to himself or hadn't used his helping them as blackmail to get something more than she was willing to give.

"What about the other two?"

He took a long drag off his cigarette and blew it out of the crack again. Some of the smoke got trapped inside and swirled around them like a mystical cloud. He rested his hand holding the lit hand-rolled cigarette on the top of the truck's steering wheel, then his rich baritone voice filled the cab again. "Can find someone at the meetin' to bring them over to the bar since everybody's gonna be there. Shade or Ozzy maybe since they don't live here on site."

The last part he said more to himself than her since she had no idea who she was talking about anyway.

Out of the corner of her eye, she saw the bus approaching.

"Stay in the truck and stay warm while they get shit hooked up. Gonna go show them where to park."

Within seconds she was once again alone with the heat still blasting.

She chewed on her bottom lip and watched him direct Eddie where to park. The dark-haired man with the dark eyes and the deliciously rich voice then stood there with his hands on his narrow hips as he supervised her bandmates while they worked to get everything hooked up.

She didn't follow his order and wait for him to return this time. Instead, she climbed out of the truck and headed over to where they'd be parked for the next couple of nights.

When she joined them, there were two things she couldn't ignore. The smiles on the guys' faces because they knew they wouldn't be cold or hungry tonight and...

Dodge.

After a few more seconds, he grumbled, "Will come get you later." With a departing chin lift, he was gone.

Watching his truck head back out the same way they drove in, she suddenly felt a sense of loss and really fucking alone.

And that was just plain crazy.

———

"Just wanna throw a few words out there about what's goin' on up on Hillbilly Hill. Thought about just sendin' a group text but since we suspended club runs for the season —unless there's a freak day where we get lucky and it's warm enough—we ain't all in one spot often. I get we all got busy lives and our families are growin', but we need to remain connected and informed. Long story short, this is why I called a meetin'." Trip stood on the crate he normally used during church so he could be seen and heard.

Also like normal, Sig stood on the ground to his right, Judge to the left. Jury, Judge's American Bulldog, sat on her haunches and leaned into the Grumpy Green Giant's leg as the enforcer rubbed her ears.

From where Dodge propped himself against one of the pool tables, he could see the dog's eyelids drooping heavily and figured she might be half-asleep. Since he heard no ferocious, ear-piercing yapping, Rook must not have Cujo with him tonight. Normally the little shit tried to take on both Jury and Justice, Deke's bully, like he could kick their asses.

He couldn't.

But the little asshole would die trying.

"So yeah, even though the shitty weather's finally here, those motherfuckers seem to be preparin' to settle back on that mountain. Scar, Bones and Castle are still takin' turns headin' up there to keep an eye on how things are progressin'. Just wanna make everyone aware to keep your sight balls and listenin' flaps open."

"We need to keep ahead of those hillbilly goat fuckers," Sig added.

"What are we gonna do about it? Sit on our fuckin' hands 'til they start shit with us all over again?" Deacon asked.

Trip ripped his black baseball cap off his head, scraped his fingers through his hair and slapped it back on. Even though Dodge wasn't close, he could see their prez's jaw popping. It didn't take much.

"I don't wanna wait to deal with those fuckers this time. They probably think we called in the fuckin' feds and they'll be out for revenge," Deke continued. "Got my son to worry about now. Cassie and Stella are pregnant. Dyna's vulnerable as fuck. Daisy's left unprotected all day at school. So is Jude. What and who we have at risk is higher now than ever."

"Know that. But we also don't know if the feds are watchin' those motherfuckers," Judge responded to his cousin. "Yeah, we need to protect our women and children, but we also gotta go about it in a way we all ain't fucked up the ass. And you know what I mean by that. If we all get locked up, then who's gonna protect them?"

All of the men in that barn knew the women could protect themselves, but Dodge got what Judge was saying. Getting busted for going in and recklessly wiping out the clan would not only break up the club and brotherhood, but would break up families.

"Jet can't ask the chief for any details on the feds after…" Rook shook his head. "After we all know what fuckin' went down. But whenever she's around her family she keeps an ear open for anything new. The Shirleys ain't a topic of conversation at the Bryson get-togethers. The head pig knows any talk on those goat fuckers will get back to us and he's tryin' to avoid that war we thought we were goin' to have before the feds stepped in."

"We talked about tippin' off the feds," Rev said, "They'd probably like to know that those roaches are scurryin' up that mountain again."

Trip dropped his head and scratched the back of his neck. "Like Judge said, they might already know and that could make it more risky for us."

"Ain't into helpin' any pigs, feds or otherwise. Not for somethin' we can handle ourselves," Ozzy said next to him.

"Agreed," Rook said. "Fuck those fuckin' pigs."

"Just don't want those pigs fuckin' us. Somethin' they'd do in a hot second if they got the chance," Judge responded. "Right now, if one of the prospects get caught up there, it's only trespassin'."

"Could pick them off as they return," Shade suggested. "Right now, it's just the men and they're returnin' slowly. Probably to test the waters."

"Once again, it'll eventually come down to what to do with their women and children," Trip reminded them, "even if we start pickin' off their men one at a time. You know once the Shirley men get shit ready, their women and spawn will be returnin', too."

"Fuck those breeders and snot monkeys," Sig barked. "They're a threat to our family, then we're a threat to theirs."

A few "yeahs" rose around Dodge. He didn't have an ol' lady or kids like most of his brothers but he agreed with Sig.

Especially after one of those inbred cunts almost blew off his head with a shotgun when they went to save Dyna. That wasn't the only time the Shirley clan tried to kill Dodge. He still had a scar on his arm from where a bullet grazed him as they were heading back down the mountain after getting Cage's baby girl back.

They were lucky none of them were seriously hurt that day or ended up dead.

Fuck those motherfuckers.

"All right, basically tonight was for a quick update and a warnin'. Prospects will continue to monitor the situation and report back. Gonna tell them if they can get any of those men up there alone they got permission to do what they gotta do. After that, Shade," Trip jerked his head toward the long-haired man, "and Easy can do what they do best."

Turn trash into ash.

"We still need more fuckin' prospects," Ozzy said. "We need numbers on our side."

"And like dealin' with the Shirleys, that ain't an easy fix," Trip reminded the motel manager.

"Speakin' of prospects," Dodge called out, "ain't it time to vote on Possum and Tater gettin' their patches?"

"Probably is," Trip answered with a nod. "Since we're all here right now let's get it over with and vote. As you all know, the vote needs to be unanimous." He scanned the small group of their brothers. "Anyone got objections? If so, shout out now or forever hold your fuckin' bitchin'."

"Still need them at Pete's, though," Dodge reminded him. "But they've been askin' about it. They've been doin' a good job at the bar and Stella can confirm that."

Trip nodded. "As I can since I'm there more than most of you, except for Dodge. They've been loyal. Work their asses off. Not one of them has caused any fuckin' drama. Unlike Scar."

"As much as Scar has pissed me off," Rook said. "I recognize the fact a man with no soul will be an asset when it comes to dealin' with shit like the Shirleys."

"He's also a good bouncer," Ozzy said, since he witnessed Scar in action in that capacity recently.

"When his ugly mug ain't scarin' off some of the fuckin' customers," Dodge added. "But yeah, he's good at escortin' out the fuckwads when I need him to."

"Okay, forget Scar for now. We only got Possum and Tater to decide on. No objections?"

Trip's answer from the group was silence.

He nodded. "All in favor?"

A loud shout went up from the group.

"All opposed?"

Again silence.

"It's fuckin' unanimous," Trip announced and glanced over at Deacon. "Get their patches together. We'll surprise them Sunday night."

"What about their name patches?" Deke asked.

"They can get those after they decide what they want their new names to be. Doubt either will keep their prospect name. But nobody say shit to them 'til we meet and present them with a full set of patches. In fact, let's have a little fun with them and when we call them out on Sunday, they'll think the worst." Trip grinned. "Maybe one of them will shit their pants. Especially if Judge is standin' there with the Punisher in his hand." He turned to his half-brother. "Sig, get the sweet butts to get two rooms in the bunkhouse prepped for them, too. Tell them to keep their traps shut about why, though."

Sig nodded as he took a long drag on his hand-rolled cigarette.

"Before I forget... The sisterhood's already plannin' the

annual Christmas party. Once again, we'll do it Christmas Eve so Cassie and Judge can take Daisy over to her sister's on Christmas. Plus, that'll free up whoever wants to spend the holiday with blood. Like Jet. I'm sure the Brysons can't wait for you to sit at their table and break bread with them, Rook." He snorted, then clapped sharply once. "'Kay. Anything else need to be discussed? Openin' up the floor to suggestions, problems, grievances since the officers are headin' upstairs to continue to discuss the Shirley issue once we're done down here."

"We airin' grievances," Easy asked nearby, "like Festivus?"

Dutch grabbed his crotch and shook it. "Gotta pole you can gather around for that."

Cage feigned a loud gagging sound, causing a few of Dodge's brothers to laugh.

"All right," Trip called out, the impatience clear in his tone. "If nobody's got anythin' important to say…"

"I do. Gonna repeat this 'cause we can't fuckin' repeat this enough. Eyes and ears open at all times. Keep vigilant. Now's not the time to get sloppy," Judge warned. "No one wants to go up that mountain again to retrieve someone we love, kid or otherwise. So, think about that."

After a few mumbled agreements, Trip announced, "Normally at this point, I'd shout out our motto, but fuck that, since I'm workin' on a new one. Gonna run it by the exec committee first. Decided since we ain't the Originals, we need to put that old one to bed. By the time the Originals were done, that motto no longer meant what it should."

Dodge didn't think the old one was bad, but he understood why Trip didn't like it. Trip, Sig, Judge, Rook and Cage had all lived through the Original's destruction of their parents' club. He felt the motto *For one, for all, for our brothers, we live and die!* was tainted since it ended up meaning jack to any of them.

In the end, the Originals had zero loyalty to each other. Most of them had turned on each other. Once things began to unravel, it only took a couple of weeks to destroy a brotherhood that took years to build.

Dodge had to hand it to Trip, the prez was doing his damnedest to prevent that cluster-fuck from ever happening again.

Right now, the Fury was solid, but there was no guarantee it would remain that way. The best preventative would be to cut out any signs of rot within the club before it spread. By any means necessary. Just like they needed to do with the Shirleys.

It took a village to raise kids, it also took one to protect them.

Dodge was a part of that village. He'd do whatever was asked of him when it came down to it.

Because the people in that village were now his family even if they weren't blood.

Chapter Eight

She was warm, her stomach full and they had a paying gig tomorrow night. One she knew she'd walk away from with actual cash in her hand this time.

Those things might not be much to anyone else, but to Syn, they were huge.

Things were looking up. They just needed to keep heading in that direction and not take a nose-dive again.

She put another quarter in the digital jukebox and scrolled through the music until she found a song she hadn't heard in a while and was surprised to find it in the selection. *My Heart is Broken.*

Of course, it was a song she couldn't pull off singing the way Evanescence originally did, but she could do it some justice when she put her own spin on it. She envied the band's talent and could only dream to be that good one day.

Putting her own style to the covers she sang was something she liked to do. She hardly sang her own originals because in the places they played, bars like Crazy Pete's and the like, the patrons usually didn't want to hear anything unfamiliar. They preferred to hear music they recognized.

That didn't mean she didn't occasionally write her own songs. Nico and Rex sometimes wrote some cool lyrics, too. But they normally didn't have anywhere to practice it all together as a band unless they did it acapella in the bus while they traveled. That wasn't nearly the same as practicing with the accompanying music.

When they were lucky, a bar owner or manager would allow them to set up early, before the bar was open to the public. That was when they could work on their original songs, but that opportunity was rare.

Right now, the most important thing was getting people to tip them more than pocket change. To do that they had to play songs the patrons wanted to hear. Sometimes they were even reduced to taking requests.

Syn grimaced as she continued to scroll through the list of songs, searching for another selection.

For some reason, requests rubbed her the wrong way. It made her feel like they were circus monkeys performing on demand instead of real musicians. There wasn't much she could control in her life but what The Synners performed was one of them. Requests took that creative control away.

Maybe she was being petty but she didn't give a shit.

She didn't have much in life, but her voice was one asset that belonged to her. It was why she took care of it. She didn't drink, didn't smoke, and tried to rest it when she could.

Dodge hadn't said much to her or Rex on the drive to Pete's. But once they arrived and he parked in the rear, he told them once again the tab was on the house and nothing on the menu or behind the bar was off limits.

Syn had a feeling he worded it that way for a reason.

Dodge would most likely be behind the bar. If she wanted him, she had a hard time believing he'd turn her down.

That shouldn't get her blood flowing.

It did.

Eddie and Nico had hitched a ride with a man named Shade. He only dropped them off around back, then quickly drove away. The Subaru station wagon he drove did not fit him. But like Dodge, she could see the long-haired man straddling a Harley.

With Rex in the truck, Syn had been forced to sit in the middle of the bench seat and tried to ignore how close Dodge's hand was to her hip and thigh when he wasn't shifting. She failed because, for most of the trip, she couldn't take her eyes from his long fingers donned with a few bulky silver rings. Worse, she couldn't stop thinking about how they would feel sliding along her skin.

And other places.

Those thoughts were dangerous.

She normally wasn't into one-night stands. Living on the road, it was difficult to make a connection with anyone, even someone she might be interested in.

Dodge had said he was "interested."

And, surprisingly, she was more comfortable around him in a short amount of time than most men she came across. Maybe it had to do with the fact he'd left her undisturbed last night as she slept in his bed.

Should she be surprised? No. In a perfect world, she shouldn't. But in actuality, this world was twisted and dark and there'd been too many situations that solidified her distrust for men. Especially strangers.

When she put The Synners together and they began touring, it took a little while for her to trust Eddie, Nico and Rex, too. It took weeks before she could close her eyes at night and not worry about whether she had put herself into a bad situation by living in a bus with three men.

It also took a while before she didn't wake up every time one of them got up in the night or made a noise.

For her, trust did not come automatically. Just like respect, it had to be earned.

Dodge was quickly earning both.

"Want the truth?" he had asked and then answered with, *"'Cause I'm interested."*

At the time, she had told him that she wasn't.

That turned out to be a damn lie.

Sitting with the guys while the young bartender named Micah kept bringing out food for them, she had purposely chosen the chair at the table where her back would be to the bar. Otherwise, she would have a difficult time not staring at the bar manager the whole time.

He had to be at least ten years older than her, if the few grays in his beard and hair were any indication. He was curious about her age, too, since he asked twice.

She knew she appeared younger than she was. Being petite all over didn't help that. Some bar owners had accused her of using a fake ID when they demanded to see it before booking them. Even though she wasn't underaged, she always assured them that she wouldn't drink and get their establishment in trouble.

She found another song, selected it and then turned to head back to their table.

"We're going to go shoot some pool," Rex announced as he stood. Since he was almost six feet tall, he towered over her. "Want to play doubles?"

Rex was a pro at pool and sometimes they relied on him to bet on games so they'd have some extra cash for fuel or food.

On the flip side, Syn sucked at pool.

She shook her head and raised both eyebrows. "Maybe you can find someone other than us to beat tonight."

Rex stared at her briefly, then nodded. "Yeah, you're right. We could use some extra money." He glanced around.

"Not too many people in here tonight, though. And both tables in their billiards area are empty. Maybe tomorrow night we can get here early and I can play a couple of games before our first set."

"Just don't piss anyone off," Syn warned. "We don't want anyone screaming that you're cheating and the manager kicks us out before we get to play and get paid."

"I don't cheat," Rex stated firmly.

"We know that, but you know how people get when you take their money."

"Hell yeah, that one time in that biker bar, we almost didn't get out of there alive. Thank fuck we had the equipment already loaded and ready to go," Nico reminded them.

That was another ugly night and a close call. Apparently, bikers don't like losing a game of Eight-ball or their money. Even worse when it's both.

Lesson learned.

"Tomorrow pick wisely," Syn warned Rex.

He nodded. "I could use some practice with these two tonight first. It's also hard to bet when you don't have anything to bet with."

"But you've got that down pat," Nico said, squeezing Rex's shoulder.

"Unless they ask to see the cash first," Eddie threw in there.

True. No one wanted to bet against someone with empty pockets.

"Are you coming with us or staying at the table?" Nico asked her.

"Go. I might wander over to watch in a little bit." She glanced around quickly. "I'm not sure when we'll have a ride back to the bus."

"I'm thinking it's going to be a while yet. If you want, I can go ask him?" Eddie volunteered.

Syn shook her head. "No, I'm in no rush to get back to the cramped bus. Plus, I'm sure you guys will want another round of food and drinks."

"Just one?" Rex joked with a wink. "I'm sure we'll eat your share, too. But, seriously, Syn, eat as much as you can. We don't know the next time..."

Her guitarist didn't have to finish his thought.

There had been stretches of days where they'd had to share a single value meal from a fast food restaurant. Or stop at a grocery store to pick up packs of Ramen noodles. Just to put something in their growling guts.

"I will," she assured them.

The guys disappeared into a side room toward the front of the bar, and out of her sightline, to play pool. With her fingers curled around the back of an empty chair, she stared at the low platform the business considered a stage.

She wasn't in the mood to sing tonight. She wanted to keep her voice rested for tomorrow night's gig, but her fingers were itching to do something she recently hadn't had a lot of opportunity to do.

Instead of taking a seat at the table now covered in dirty dishes and empty glasses and mugs, she dug out the remaining two quarters from her pocket, dropped them into the jukebox and quickly selected a half dozen more songs from various artists.

She headed over to where their equipment was still setup and weaved her way around it and to Eddie's drum set.

They might not have a lot, but what they did have was quality. If anything would happen to their instruments, they'd have a hard time replacing them right now.

Dodge had assured her their stuff was safe in his bar. She had to trust him on that.

She leaned down, dug out Eddie's sticks from where he normally tucked them out of sight and settled on the stool behind the drum set.

She closed her eyes, took a few seconds to absorb the music coming from the speakers, then lifted the sticks and began to play along. She wasn't nearly as good as Eddie but she loved playing the drums.

When the song ended, her eyes were still closed as the next one began. She had picked these songs for a reason. They were songs she could play the drums to without much effort. She'd never pick a song from a band like Rush because some drummers, like Neil Peart, would make her skills sound worse than amateurish.

But tonight, it didn't matter since she was playing strictly for pleasure. No pressure. No one to impress. It was simply for her.

To take her into her own little world, the one she lived for. Music.

Without it, she was nothing.

With it, each song gave her what she needed. A sense of peace, the warmth of love and a slice of happiness. Even if only until the last note faded away.

When the current song finished, she licked her dry lips. She should've brought a bottle of water on stage with her.

She opened her eyes and quickly blinked in surprise.

She followed the hand holding a sweating water bottle up to the person who was offering it.

Was she imagining him? She thought about water and he just appeared with what she desired?

She blanked out her thoughts just in case he could read them.

She collected both drum sticks in one hand and took the already opened bottle from him. "Thank you."

"Mean what you say." His voice reminded her of the music she loved so much.

The timbre, the cadence, the pitch. The way it swirled around her almost like a warm hug.

"I meant it. I appreciate it. Just like I appreciate everything else you've done for us."

"You don't gotta play tonight."

She lifted her eyes to meet his dark ones. "I'm not playing for anyone but myself."

He stared at her for far too long, then finally gave a single nod. "Let me know if you need anythin' else."

As he turned, she said, "I do."

He stopped, facing away from her, and waited.

"I was hoping…"

After a few seconds, he turned to face her again. "Hopin'?"

"To use your shower again."

Again, he stared at her. For the first time ever, she wished she could read a man's mind. Especially since his face was unreadable.

She knew she was pushing his generosity by asking. But with the low propane tank, they didn't have enough for long showers. *Hell*, not even enough for short ones.

If he allowed her to use his again, that would mean the guys could probably squeak out enough hot water for theirs.

After filling the fuel tank once they got paid tomorrow night, the propane tank would be next on the list. Twenty dollars in diesel had hardly moved the needle.

"Once you're done playin' and you're ready, come see me. I'll be behind the bar."

"Nothin' behind the bar's off limits."

He began to turn away again but paused, his brow wrinkling. He drove his hand deep into the front pocket of his jeans and pulled out a fistful of what looked like quarters. "Put out your hands."

It wasn't a request, but an order.

Did he normally carry around that many quarters? Odd.

She tucked the sticks between her thighs and extended her cupped hands. He dropped the quarters into them.

When he was done, he curled her fingers around the change and said in a low voice, "Keep playin'."

Holy shit.

The touch of their hands made a weird energy prickle along her skin.

She tensed to avoid the shiver that threatened to slide down her spine and perk her nipples. It must not have worked since his graze dropped to her chest.

"Nice T-shirt," was the last thing he said over his shoulder as he headed back to his job and she rose to go put more quarters in the jukebox.

She had picked the shirt because it was clean, not because of what was printed on the front. The black tee had a huge white graphic of a hand giving the finger.

She pressed her lips together at the statement her shirt made loud and clear. Then she used every damn quarter he gave her and played Eddie's drums until she no longer had energy left to play.

While she did so, she didn't hide her smile.

She also didn't give a shit who saw it.

———

"You see her come back down yet?" Dodge asked Micah an hour after Syn had finished playing the drums.

When she had approached him ready to use his shower, her hair had been damp from sweat. Her cheeks flushed from exertion. Her eyes held a spark that caught and held his attention.

Even though she looked exhausted from how intensely she played for almost two hours straight, her body still vibrated. Almost as if she herself had been plugged into an amplifier.

Tonight, he had caught himself several times stopping in the middle of whatever he was doing to just stare across the bar. At the dark-haired woman giving that drum set her all. Pouring her heart and soul into every beat of the sticks against the drums or cymbals. Every stomp of her foot on the pedal of the bass drum or Hi-Hat.

Even from across the room he could see she mustered up every ounce of energy she had to put it all into her playing.

Her band, her music, wasn't just a way to make money, but for her, a way of life.

Fucking witchcraft.

There was no other excuse for him to be so fucking mesmerized by the tiny, powder keg of a woman who kept herself guarded.

Closed-off.

When she finally came to stand in front of him with her pale skin still covered with a light sheen of sweat and dark half-moons under eyes, she didn't have to say a word.

He automatically dug into his pocket and pulled out his apartment key, holding it out to her. "Here. You saw where I pulled out the clean towel from last time."

She snagged the key from his fingers and fisted it like she was afraid he might change his mind. "You didn't put away your laundry yet?"

"It's waitin' on you."

She blinked. "You really want me to put away your underwear?"

His lips twitched. "It ain't like you didn't see me in them."

"Men hide shit in their underwear drawer."

"Ain't gonna lie, you might be surprised by what's in mine. Just don't dig too deep."

The corners of her lips curved up the slightest bit. Almost a smile. Nothing like the one she wore while on stage beating the fuck out of those drums like she was beating back demons.

"You could probably put a hurtin' on somebody the way you wield those sticks."

"Not *probably*," was all she answered.

He grinned at picturing her drumming a beatdown on some asshole who deserved it.

He wanted to continue talking to her because somewhere below the surface, below the armor she wore, was her true personality. She hid it for some reason.

It also seemed like it took an effort for her to make small talk. It didn't come naturally for her.

Dodge had always been able to talk to anyone. That skill made him a good manager and bartender. More importantly, it helped save his ass while he was in prison. *Hell*, even out of it.

Maybe she only opened up when she was on stage doing what she loved most. Because with what he saw last night, and again tonight, it was clear her love for music was strong.

He wondered if she had the same amount of passion for anything else.

He also wondered who hurt her.

Because someone did.

He didn't know how, when or why, but with the years he spent on his own, in prison, bartending, and even being part of the Fury, he'd learn to recognize the signs.

Even when someone did their best to hide it.

He reminded himself for the hundredth time, she wasn't his problem. Her band wasn't, either.

After tomorrow night, they'd be gone.

They'd continue on the path struggling musicians made, hoping for that lucky break. The one that only came to a select few. Syn and her band would only be able to live that life for so long before it took its toll.

But he wasn't saying any of that to her because she'd

shut him out like a cell door slamming shut. That closed door had protected him from the dangers of people wishing him harm. Other inmates in his case.

While her door was invisible, it still protected her from other people, too.

Not his fuckin' problem.

"She who?" Micah's question pulled him from his drifting thoughts. "I thought you no longer left them upstairs alone."

"She ain't up there for that."

"What's she up there for, then?"

Dodge rolled his damn eyes so hard he probably broke a blood vessel. "Christ. Never mind."

He opened the hinged portion of the bar and took a sweeping glance to make sure she hadn't slipped back downstairs without him knowing. He strode over to where the rest of her band were sitting at the table after finishing off more plates full of fried foods.

"You seen Syn?" he asked them.

"No, she didn't go up to use your shower?" Nico asked, his tone concerned.

"Yeah, just wanted to make sure I didn't miss her comin' back down."

"We haven't seen her. Should we go up and check on her?" Rex asked with a furrowed brow.

"I got it." He spun on his boot heel, but stopped mid-turn. "Told Possum as soon as he's done with what he's doin' he can head back to the farm and you can catch a ride with him."

"What about Syn?"

"She can hitch a ride with Tater if she ain't done before Possum is."

He didn't wait for a response from any of them—mostly because he didn't give a fuck what they thought about what he just said—and headed back toward the bar area and through the swinging door to the left of it.

He took the steps two at a time and, at the top, found his apartment door locked.

Fuckin' fuck.

If she was asleep in his bed again…

No matter what, tonight he was not sleeping on his fucking couch.

He didn't even bother to pound on the door in case she was still in the shower. It was just easier for him to jog back down the stairs and find the spare set of keys for the bar where he had hidden them in the storage area. This time when he headed back up, it was a little slower than the first time.

Okay, a lot slower, because, *fuck him*, he wasn't in shape enough to be running up and down stairs.

He unlocked the door, shoved it open and stopped.

She was nowhere in sight. Not even in his bed. Not on his couch. Not raiding his fridge.

He couldn't hear the shower running, either.

It was way too quiet for his liking.

He instinctively glanced at the back windows to make sure she didn't jump since that was the only other way out of the apartment. Thank fuck all the windows were still shut tight.

He headed over to the bathroom door, leaned closer and listened.

Nothing.

"Syn."

Still nothing.

His heart began to pound.

The door was open a crack, probably to release the steam when she showered since the exhaust fan was broken in his tiny bathroom. He always had to shower with the door wide open so he didn't suffocate.

He put his eye to the opening and peeked in.

He felt like such a fucking creeper, but he was more concerned than anything.

He saw a thin arm hanging out of the side of the tub and peeking out from behind the shower curtain.

For fuck's sake, she didn't slice her wrists or anything crazy like that, did she?

He shoved the door open and stopped when he heard it.

Her soft snoring.

Again.

What the fuck?

She was asleep? In the damn tub?

He yanked the curtain back and yelled, "Syn!"

She jerked awake and sat straight up. The water splashed his jeans and boots and sloshed over the side, soaking his bathroom floor.

"What," she murmured sluggishly, confused. As she blinked herself awake, he saw her thick, black eyelashes were clumped together from the water. Or the thick humidity. Since she must have been simmering in the tub like a pot of Amish chicken corn soup.

What was not sluggish was his blood as it rushed from his damn brain south to his dick.

She was slick with the soapy water.

And naked.

In his fucking bathtub.

Thank fuck she was alive, but now he wanted to kill her for scaring the fuck out of him.

He quickly turned away, left the tiny room and slammed the door behind him.

He suddenly needed more than one door between them.

Not even two would be enough.

He needed at least two towns, two counties, two states. *Hell,* an ocean between them might do it.

"Why were you in here?" he heard her yell, now no longer sounding sluggish but a bit panicked.

She wasn't the only one.

Jesus Christ.

"Why were you in here?" she shrieked again through the closed door.

He tried to shove aside the vision that was now seared into his brain.

Syn completely fucking naked.

Looking more delicate and breakable without her clothes.

Everything about her milky white except for the shock of wet, dark ropey strands of hair, wide dark eyes and… the dark patch of hair he could barely see under the water.

But her tits…

Small, but perfect, with her nipples puckered.

Shit. "You never came the fuck back down. Got worried."

"But why were you in *here*?"

"'Cause I thought…" *Fuck. 'Cause I thought you fuckin' hurt yourself. Or passed out. Or…*

He yanked the wool beanie off his head because he was beginning to sweat and scraped his fingers through his hair. "I didn't see shit."

Fuck! He saw *everything.*

Silence came from the other side of the door.

Then water splashing.

Cursing.

Stomping.

More mumbled cursing.

A few seconds later, the door whipped open and she stepped out with only a towel wrapped around her. She hadn't taken the time to dry off because her hair was still dripping wet and the exposed skin he could see was still shiny.

He quickly dropped his beanie in front of his hard-on and, since his kitchen was right next to the bathroom, he moved to the other side of the small island counter. He already felt like a goddamn pervert and the last thing he needed was her noticing his reaction to seeing her naked.

She would close up like a fucking clam.

"Nice," she said when her eyes flicked to his erection. She jerked the towel tighter around her.

He grimaced, then threw his beanie on the counter. "Didn't mean to…"

"Didn't mean to, but you did."

"It's my fuckin' apartment."

"And I'll get out of it. Thank you for letting me use the shower."

"You weren't takin' a fuckin' shower."

"I cleaned it before I used it, by the way. You're welcome."

"You're welcome, too, by the way, for all the shit I've done for you," he said sharply. "Get dressed and come back down. Possum will take you back to your bus soon. You're welcome for that, too." He swiped his beanie from the counter and tugged it over his head. "You got five."

She closed her eyes and released a long sigh. "Sorry."

"Me, too. Get plenty of women without havin' to be a creepy peeper."

Her eyes opened and she nodded.

"Trip wants your band and that bus off the farm by Saturday mornin'. Make sure that happens."

She nodded again.

"It's for the best," he added.

"I agree."

As he turned, he noticed his laundry basket on the couch.

It was empty.

His eyes sliced over to his dresser. All the drawers were shut, but something sat on top.

Against his warning, she had dug deep.

He had to assume that was on purpose.

He turned away to hide his grin and went back downstairs.

Maybe she wasn't such a skittish little kitten after all and only hiding her inner lioness.

After all, wasn't it a lioness who was always the leader of her pride?

If so, he wouldn't mind feeling those claws raking along his skin.

Chapter Nine

THEY PARKED the bus down at the church and walked to Crazy Pete's. They drove over early so the guys could grab some food and drinks first. And with any luck, Rex could bet on and win a few games of pool before they headed up on stage at eight.

Syn wouldn't eat until after they played since she had a hard time singing with a full stomach. It bogged her down and made her sleepy.

But now they were finishing up their second set, after taking a fifteen minute break between them, to grab water and dry off some sweat.

Rex also had an extra sixty bucks in his wallet. Unfortunately, after winning three games in a row and taking his competition's money, no one else wanted to play him. That stream of income quickly dried up.

But, *hey*, sixty bucks was sixty more than they had. With that and the four hundred they'd get at the end of the night, they'd be able to fuel up the bus, fill the propane and head out on their search for their next gig.

Hopefully somewhere warmer.

They had to trudge through about an inch of snow

between the church's parking lot and the rear of Crazy Pete's. Wearing her high heel boots, she had to hang onto Nico the whole way so she wouldn't fall and break anything. Like her neck.

She should've just worn her combat boots, but she dressed the way she did on stage to encourage more tips.

Tonight, she had worn her lace-up, black, above-the-knee boots with the three-inch heels paired with a pair of black, fake leather leggings that clung like a second skin. She wore a black lacy push-up bra under a loose white top that had a draping V neckline that exposed most of it.

She didn't give a shit about looking sexy or attracting men, she only cared about making enough money for them to survive.

She had also given herself smoky eyes and bright red lips. Had hair-sprayed her hair into a "freshly fucked" look, even though that was far from the truth. It had been so long since she welcomed a man's touch that her body forgot what it was like to want it.

If she was being honest with herself, she had forgotten until she met the man behind the bar currently hustling to serve a packed house.

His touches, even as brief as they'd been, seemed to awaken every nerve ending under her skin. When he stared at her with those intense dark brown eyes, heat licked along every part of her.

He was dangerous.

Even though he hadn't done anything inappropriate.

He didn't enter the bathroom last night because he wanted to force himself on her, but had come in to check on her. He had no evil intentions when he burst into the tiny room, instead, he said he'd been worried.

She believed him.

His genuine concern made him even more attractive.

Safe. That was how she felt around him. Besides with

her band members, she didn't remember ever feeling this safe with anyone of the opposite sex.

Well, at least not in a very long time. Before she discovered she couldn't trust any man until he proved himself to be trustworthy.

Unfortunately, too many had proved otherwise.

They only had two more songs for this last set.

She was tired, hungry and thirsty.

She finished up their version of Christopher Cross's *Ride like the Wind*. They slowed it down a few notches from the original and gave it a more soulful sound. It usually went over better for an older crowd versus a college bar packed with barely twenty-one-year-olds who had no clue who Christopher Cross was.

They transitioned right into their last song for the night, her unique version of *Wicked Game* by Chris Isaak. One of her favorites.

She loved a variety of music and, because of that, The Synners played a wide selection, but some songs simply stuck with her. When they did, they put it into their rotation as long as she could pull off the vocals. Or at least get away with putting her twist on it enough so that it sounded good.

When the last note drifted off and nothing but the noise of the bar patrons surrounded them, Rex took the time to announce once more who they were and thanked them for coming out to see them. He always thanked them for their generous tips, even when that wasn't true.

It was a passive-aggressive way to try to get some of the audience to dig a little deeper. Sometimes it worked, sometimes it failed.

She turned as the applause began and gave her guys a smile. She received a smile and a return nod from Nico and a tip of the head from Eddie.

Rex was looking past her. Toward the bar. His face a mask.

A burst of heat rolled through her because she knew exactly who he was staring at.

She cleared her throat, called out, "Hey," to get their attention. "One more." She wasn't surprised when confusion filled their faces. "For me."

She told them the name of the song, then stepped back in front of the microphone stand, wrapping her ringed fingers around the mic.

Then she found what—or who—Rex was staring at. Since the platform wasn't high, at first it was difficult seeing him through the crowd as he worked the back side of the bar. But he was there. She quickly zeroed in on him like a moth drawn to a flame.

When she began to sing *Fade into You* by Mazzy Star, suddenly no one stood between them. No one existed but the two of them in that bar. In that time. In that space.

It was at that very fucking moment she knew how her night would end.

He would be giving her more than the four hundred dollars he owed them.

And she would be taking everything else he was willing to give.

———

Nico slammed the hatch closed to the compartment under the bus where they stored their equipment.

Once again, their bellies were full. She was no longer hungry or thirsty thanks to Dodge's generosity, but she was now past the point of tired.

Her ass was dragging.

She glanced at her cell phone. It was already one in the morning and too late to hit the road. The best thing to do would be take the skoolie back to the Fury's farm, plug in for the night and leave once the sun rose.

But her night wasn't over yet.

One hour remained before the bar's last call. Though, by the time they were done stuffing their faces and packing away their stuff, the crowd had thinned to just a handful of people.

Plus, it started snowing again a couple of hours ago, which might have made customers scurry home earlier than normal. With her eyes closed, she tipped up her face and let some of the large flakes slowly falling from the sky land on her. She stuck out her tongue and caught a few of the frozen crystals but they quickly melted away.

"You ready?" Rex asked.

She opened her eyes and saw him perched on the bottom step of the open bus door.

They were waiting on her.

"Take the bus back to the farm."

"That was already the plan," he said with a frown. "Wait…" His eyes narrowed. "Do you mean without you?"

She nodded as more cold, crystalized flakes fell on her cheeks and quickly melted. She shivered and her words turned into white cloudy puffs. "I'll get a ride back with one of the prospects."

"Syn."

"I'll be okay."

"I don't like this," Rex said.

"You don't have to."

"We need to be off the farm in the morning."

"We will," she promised.

He stared at her and she stared back. Finally, he shook his head. "We'll keep our phones on."

She appreciated that he worried about her and she always worried when one of the guys went off with some random woman they met at one of their gigs.

In truth, women could be just as dangerous as men. Whether with false accusations or with violence. The world was full of unstable people who would simply hurt another person for no valid reason.

She had lost faith in humanity a long damn time ago.

"Call if you need us to come back and get you," he insisted.

"Thanks, Rex."

"Anything for you, Syn."

She quickly turned away since she didn't want him to see how those words affected her.

It made all of this worthwhile.

The struggle.

The persistence.

The hope.

Her little patchwork family.

Unfortunately, her family was missing a member. An important one. Maybe not to the guys but to her.

She couldn't let that darkness swallow her. Not tonight.

Tonight, she was going to do something for herself. Not for anyone else.

She yanked the rear door to Crazy Pete's open, kicked the block that kept them from becoming locked outside out of the way, took a brief pitstop in the women's room, then headed back into the now eerily quiet bar.

No music was even playing on the jukebox.

The stragglers seemed to be gone.

And only two men remained behind the bar. Neither of them were Dodge.

Shit.

She headed over to them.

"We thought you left," the prospect named Tater said.

"No, not yet."

"Need somethin' else?" he asked.

Yes, your boss. "Can I get a bottle of water?" They already loaded up another case that Micah had carried out to their bus when they started packing away their equipment.

With a nod, Tater dug into a cooler, twisted the cap off and placed the bottle in front of her. "That it?"

"Need to speak to the manager."

"He didn't pay you?"

He did. He had given the money to Nico before they broke down their equipment and removed it from the stage. "Yes, but I wanted to see if he'd put us on the schedule again."

That wasn't quite true. While tonight the tips had actually been decent, they were not sticking around northern Pennsylvania. She wouldn't mind returning when the weather turned milder but that wasn't the reason she needed to speak to Dodge.

Actually, she didn't want to speak to him at all. What she wanted had nothing to do with talking.

When she used his shower earlier and changed into more comfortable clothes—jeans, her combat boots and her last clean shirt—he hadn't come upstairs at all. She also made sure she didn't fall asleep. In his bed, tub or even on his damn floor.

He had kept his distance, so maybe she had mistaken the silent conversation they had from across the bar while she sang the Mazzy Star song directly to him.

Maybe she should have made it clearer.

Too late now.

Her heart skipped a beat when the swinging door to the left of the bar opened and the man himself stepped out.

His eyes immediately fell on her and without breaking their locked gazes, asked, "Customers gone?"

"Yeah," one of the guys answered.

"Then you two can go."

"We're not done—"

"I got it. Go."

Silence swirled around them for a couple of heartbeats, then three sets of eyes burned her.

After a visible shift of his jaw, he said, "Go hang by the pool tables. Be over to play that game of pool I promised you as soon as I lock up."

He did what?

When she let her gaze slide over to the other two men, it was like someone had pushed a switch and they began to scramble.

Probably to get while the getting was good.

Or to keep from pissing off their boss.

Maybe both.

She snagged her water bottle off the bar and headed over to the billiards room, having zero interest in knocking balls into pockets but plenty of interest in knocking balls and boots.

She slowly circled one table, grabbing the pool balls left scattered across the green felt and rolling them hard enough to bounce off the rails and crack into each other. A couple of them actually dropped into pockets.

With the furious beat of her heart and the rush of blood in her ears, her body hummed like she'd grabbed a live wire.

She hoped she didn't regret this.

Please don't let me regret this.

If she was smart, she would scrap this idea and hitch a ride back to the farm with Tater. That was what she should do.

Yes, this was a stupid idea.

It didn't matter that she hadn't allowed anyone to touch her in so long. It didn't matter that she craved the kind of touch…

The kind of touch that was wanted and welcomed. A touch that could set her skin on fire.

Since she felt safe with Dodge, if she didn't take the opportunity to do it with him, she had no idea when and with whom she'd want to do it again.

The number of guys she'd had sex with, by choice, she could count on one hand.

In truth, with only three fingers.

Three men in the past five years since turning eighteen. And with those three men, only once each. Out of those three times, one was awkward, painful and an experience she never wanted repeated. The other two were… okay.

That was the best way to describe it. Just okay.

With the way Dodge moved, with the way he carried himself, she hoped he would be better than "just okay." She hoped it would be memorable and he'd be able to satisfy the urge that pulled at her when she saw him or heard his voice.

She grabbed a cue stick that was leaning in the corner of the billiards area and tucked it back in the rack on the wall where it belonged. She went over and collected another one to do the same.

His, "Don't gotta do that," made her jump and her heart skip a beat.

She rubbed her palms down her outer thighs, wiping the clamminess off and onto her jeans. Slowly, she turned to see him standing at the opening of the two half-walls that separated the area where she stood and the main part of the bar.

"I don't want to play pool," she forced up her constricted throat.

"Me, neither."

Then why was he just standing there?

"What do you want, Syn?"

He just answered his own question. That was exactly what she wanted, what some people considered a sin.

She took a sip of her water, trying to swallow down the lump that had wedged in her throat. The lump that prevented her from simply coming out and saying what she wanted.

Most times, she could be as outspoken as him.

Just not this time and not about this.

Her weakness was dealing with men when it came to sex. It was one reason, among others, why she hadn't had much. But she reminded herself it was only sex. Nothing more. Nothing less. People did it all the time. She was making a bigger deal out of it than she should.

Nothing ventured, nothing gained. Right?

"This ain't happenin' 'til you tell me how old you are. Tellin' you now, if you don't answer this time, gonna call Tater back to come pick up your ass and drop you off at that rat trap on wheels you call a home."

Truthfully, that may be for the best.

"Know that's not what you want."

He was so damn confident. She was torn about whether it annoyed her or if she was envious. She lifted her chin. "What do I want?"

"Same as me."

"You could be right; you could be wrong." She mentally groaned at her stupid non-answer. Why was she putting this off? She wanted him and he was obviously willing to oblige.

Was she purposely trying to tank this opportunity?

Unlike her, he probably had plenty of sex and didn't need to work hard to get someone to have it with him.

"I ain't wrong. Also ain't gonna play games. Never needed to, ain't gonna start. So, if you wanna play games, and I ain't talkin' about pool, then let me text Tater." He pulled his cell phone from his back pocket.

Before he could finish typing out a message, she moved.

She stopped when she was toe-to-toe with him and put her hand on his phone, blocking him from sending it. "Don't," she whispered, tipping her face up to his.

One of his dark eyebrows rose. "Don't what?"

"Don't call him back."

"Need him to take you back to your bus."

"I don't want to go back to the bus."

"Then what do you want, Syn? Need to hear it. Loudly. Clearly. No fuckin' games."

She tucked her bottom lip between her teeth, inhaled a deep breath, then slowly released both. "You."

He gave his head a little shake. "Me what?"

He wanted it loudly and clearly. "I want you."

He drove his fingers along the side of her head and into her hair, using it to tip her face up even higher. "You know what else I need."

The deep, demanding timbre of his voice caused her to fight a shiver. "A condom?"

His jaw tensed, his fingers slipped from her hair and he took a step back, lifting his phone again.

"Twenty-three," she spouted out before she fucked this whole thing up.

He stared at her for a few seconds while her heartbeat thumped in her ears. She wasn't underaged, but was she still too young for him? Even just for sex? Maybe he preferred an older, more experienced woman.

Something she was not.

Had she experienced a lot in her twenty-three years? Yes. But she didn't have the same confidence about sex like she did other things.

Like music.

Making love should be like making music. The passion and connection should come from one's soul. But she knew what they were about to do—or so she hoped—had nothing to do with the act of making love. What she wanted from him would only be a physical connection and not an emotional one.

Afterward, there would be no expectations of anything more. It would just be about the "here and now." But she needed him to be willing and for her to stop trying to sabotage this opportunity.

Otherwise, yes, he should text Tater and have the prospect take her "home."

She didn't want that.

She wanted him. The man standing before her, now not saying a word and his expression unreadable.

She didn't fuck up, did she?

Her breath seized as he surged forward and his much larger body almost plowed her over. But somehow with his hand once again threaded through her hair and the other one on her hip, he kept from knocking her to the ground. He drove her backward until her ass hit the pool table behind her.

He said nothing. But then, nothing more needed to be said.

Nothing *could* be said, either, since their mouths were too busy when he took hers. His tongue tangled with hers and invaded her mouth, his weight pressed her into the end of the pool table and his thick hard-on was unmistakable.

Heat surged through her like a rogue wave. That heat pooled between her legs and made her pussy pulse so intensely she almost broke the kiss in surprise.

Holy shit.

She twisted her fingers into the thermal shirt he wore under his cut. Not to hold him there or push him away, but to keep herself upright because her legs had quickly turned to rubber with how he kissed.

This man knew what the fuck he was doing.

She only knew she didn't want him to stop.

She was so much smaller and with him now pressed against her, she felt completely engulfed. Like he could easily swallow her up and make her disappear.

For a little while, she'd be okay with that.

To help her forget some of the things that constantly weighed on her. The things that attempted to pull her under.

Put aside, even temporarily, what she was working toward. Why she was struggling so hard to be successful.

To take this moment—these moments—for herself and no one else.

For some crazy reason she wanted this man—the one now gripping her hair almost painfully, the one kissing her to the point where she wanted to simply surrender—more than any man she'd ever met before.

While that shouldn't surprise her, how her body reacted to him did.

A groan rose from deep inside her and it had nowhere else to go but get caught in his mouth as he deepened the kiss, tilting his head even more. The hand on her hip moving up to unzip her sweatshirt and slide under her shirt.

She was braless since most of the time she only wore one on stage and only when it was part of her "outfit." In truth, her breasts weren't large enough to need one. And she hated those torture devices anyway.

The second his fingers grazed over her nipple, her back instinctively arched, pushing her breast deeper into his palm. She slapped her other hand over his, squeezing it, showing him what she wanted, what she needed.

He followed her lead and, even better, he circled the very tip of her nipple, like rolling a tiny pebble under the pad of his thumb.

Around and around.

Roll, roll, roll.

Holy shit, whispered through her mind.

Her clit seemed to be directly attached to her nipple and everything he did felt like he was doing the same to her down there. When he wasn't.

Not yet.

Please.

Oh, please.

When he squeezed and kneaded her breast, then moved

to the other, she was unable to stop another groan from filling his mouth.

Then one more.

Her body was on fire. She was the tinder and he the match.

When he combined her moan with one of his own, wetness slipped from her and trickled along her heated skin. She needed her jeans off. She needed to feel his skin against hers.

She might die if she didn't get that. And soon.

Please.

Oh, please.

She didn't want to waste time on kissing, but she also didn't want him to stop. She'd never been kissed like this before, as if he was trying to consume her.

But he did stop. He separated their mouths and pressed his forehead to hers, panting out a shaky, "Witchcraft."

Witchcraft? What did he mean?

She didn't get a chance to ask because he stepped back, yanked her around like she was no more than the weight of a feather, grabbed a fistful of her hair and jerked her head to the side, planting his lips on her neck.

How could something so simple stoke the flames already licking at her into a roaring wildfire?

Keeping a hold of her hair, he worked the button on her jeans free and slid down the zipper, his fingers grazing along her heated skin as he did so, pulling another moan from her.

Then he was there... Touching her slick and swollen flesh, which pulsed with every beat of her heart.

An unexpected shudder overtook her. Simply from his touch. From his finger circling her clit, him sucking on the side of her neck. From the weight of his erection now pressed into her back.

Even though her jeans were tight and he didn't have a

lot of room, he managed to work his middle finger inside her.

"Goddamn witchcraft," he murmured against her skin.

She never wanted someone inside her so badly.

Not once.

So, yes, he was right. It was witchcraft.

She closed her eyes to concentrate on what he was doing. With his hand, his mouth.

She wanted…

She needed…

"Let go," he growled against her skin.

She shook her head slightly.

"Let fuckin' go."

"I… can't." She wanted to. Not once had she simply let herself go.

"You can. Stop holdin' back." His growled demand caused more goosebumps to break out along her skin.

Let him take you where you want to go.

Let him.

Trust him. He knows what he's doing.

Even though he didn't have a lot of room to work, his middle finger slid easily in and out of her. Over and over.

He released her hair, grabbed her breast, this time over her shirt, and twisted her aching nipple through the cotton.

Putting his mouth to her ear, he licked the outer shell, grabbed her lobe between his teeth and lightly bit down.

"Let go." His gruff demand and his warm breath sweeping over her ear caused another shudder.

Let go.

Let go.

Let go.

She finally did. She let go.

A little cry escaped her as the ripples radiated from her pussy and his finger all the way up to her breasts, which now felt swollen and heavy.

He slipped his finger free, worked his hand from her snug jeans and, once again, spun her around.

Without a word, he caught her eyes with his, slowly lifted his hand and tucked his middle finger into his mouth, sucking it clean.

Her pussy pulsed intensely again. Simply from that sight.

"Jeans off." His order low and growly. "Now. Before I rip them off."

She couldn't afford to lose a pair of jeans. She scrambled to toe off her combat boots and wiggle out of her jeans and thong, throwing them onto the pool table behind her.

Not caring about the bright lights. Not caring if anyone would walk in on them.

Not caring that she was the only one half-naked between the two of them. While she had been doing that, he'd pulled out a large wallet from his back pocket, dug out a condom and tucked it between his teeth as he unbuckled his belt, unfastened his jeans and shoved them down just enough to pull out his cock.

Not once had his eyes left her as he stroked it a couple of times.

As if he'd changed his mind, he suddenly threw the wrapped condom on the pool table next to her, grabbed her waist and planted her bare ass on the edge of the table.

Digging his thumbs into her thighs, he spread them, saying, "Need to taste more of that."

Those words and the way he said them sent sparks of fire crackling through her. No one. Not one of the three men she'd been with had put their mouth on her down there.

Not one.

Both fear and excitement made her tense as he dropped to his knees before her, pushing her legs open even wider.

Fuck. He was looking at her.

Really looking.

What could he see?

What would he discover?

Naked from the waist down, sitting on the edge of the pool table, she felt exposed, vulnerable.

But her worry quickly fled and her muscles loosened a touch when he said nothing and, instead, he planted his face between her legs.

The scratch of his beard along the skin of her inner thighs and the scrape of the wiry hairs along her sensitive folds had her closing her eyes in anticipation.

Just. Let. Go.

As soon as his mouth touched her down there, her hips jerked. Not from shock, but from pleasure. And when he sucked on her clit, she couldn't bite back a cry.

The man knew how to use his mouth. And not just for kissing.

He sucked on each fold, then scraped them with his teeth, making her flinch but not in discomfort. His tongue divided and conquered her. He sucked her clit, then flicked at it, driving two fingers inside her.

One thick finger had been one thing, but two…

It had been so long. Living in the bus with no privacy, she didn't even have a chance to pleasure herself.

Any sexual desires were kept stifled and buried.

Tonight, Dodge was lifting the flood gates and releasing all those pent-up desires she'd been beating back forever.

Years.

Let. Go.

She was trying to get out of her head and do just that, when he paused.

"For fuck's sake, you're so fuckin' tight. Don't tell me you're a virgin."

That accusation should be laughable but right now, she wasn't finding it funny. "Keep going," she moaned, reached down and wrapping one hand around the back of his head and one around the back of his neck, lifting her hips slightly in encouragement. "Don't stop."

"Tell me you ain't a virgin," he insisted more loudly.

"I'm not. *Please.*" She was far, far, *far* from a virgin. Couldn't he tell? Couldn't he see that life had left a mark on her? Had changed her? Maybe he didn't notice and she worried about it for nothing.

Only once in her life had she begged for anything. But if he didn't continue, she'd be reduced to begging him.

She wanted to let go.

She needed for him to help her.

If anyone could do it, it would be him.

It had to be him.

It wasn't much longer before it *was* him.

As he took her over the edge a second time, the orgasm was even more intense than the first. She drove her fingers into his neck as her hips shot up.

The first one had been good. The second even better.

Would there be a third?

Could there be a third?

She sure as hell hoped so.

Chapter Ten

Dodge pushed to his feet and swiped a hand down his mouth and beard.

For fuck's sake, she said she wasn't a virgin but she was a lot tighter than he ever expected.

She was so goddamn young, too. Older than he first thought, but still…

For a split moment, he considered stopping things right where they were before taking it any further. She'd already had two orgasms; he'd be the only one missing out.

Well, not quite.

He had enjoyed every second of making her "let go." And as soon as he sucked her tang off his middle finger after the first orgasm, he knew he had to have more.

But was only satisfying her enough to satisfy him? If he searched deep enough and didn't fucking lie to himself, no.

Her cheeks were flushed, her eyes unfocused and she blinked up at him slowly as he towered over her. He couldn't deny he wanted her naked. Or that he wanted her in his bed. But he had no patience right now to wait for either of those things to happen.

So, fuck reconsidering.

He wanted her. She wanted him. Enough fucking said.

Her, "Please," came out thick and sluggish, almost as if she was drunk. He knew for a fact she hadn't drank a damn thing tonight. Not even one drop of alcohol. Why? Because he paid attention to that, something he normally didn't care about unless a potential fuck was buzzed enough not to make a good decision. And sloppy drunks were not only unattractive, but a huge no-go for him.

He needed to get it in his fat head that she wouldn't be any different than any of the other women he'd had in his recent past. He had sex with plenty of women for mutual satisfaction and nothing more. He'd always made it clear before taking them upstairs. They could agree or he'd walk away.

What consenting adults did was between those participants. No one else.

Syn was definitely an adult. *Thank fuck.*

Another whispered, "Please," proved she was consenting. No risk of second thoughts on her part. But on his? Would there be afterwards?

He usually never had regrets as long as the woman was willing and wasn't annoying as fuck, even for the short amount of time he spent with her. Syn wasn't annoying but she *was* frustrating.

"Dodge."

His name snapped him out of his thoughts. He snagged the wrap off the pool table and ripped it open before rolling it down his uncomfortably hard dick that was throbbing like it had its own heart. At the same time his balls screamed at him about needing relief and to "fuck off" with any second thoughts.

The woman now lying back on the pool table should only be only that. Relief. Nothing more.

Just another catch-and-release.

Remember, not a goddamn thing more, dumbass. She should be no different than any of the rest of them.

Her dark eyes, her parted lipstick-free lips, the long, dark hair spilled around her. Her nipples trying to punch through her cotton shirt. The smooth, ivory skin of her bare legs, that patch of dark hair he wanted to bury his face in again… Why was it all so damn mesmerizing?

Addicting.

Soul sucking.

Why was he letting her fuck with his head? Even if she wasn't doing it on purpose, it was still happening.

He grabbed her arm and yanked her off the table.

He should pull the wrap off his dick, tell her to get dressed and walk away while he still could.

Of fucking course, that wasn't what he did.

Fuck no. Because he was a dumbass speeding down Dumbass Lane at a hundred miles an hour in a cage with a loose wheel about to fall off.

He spun her around again, bent her over the pool table and with one hand planted on her back to hold her in place, he shoved his jeans down further.

It was better this way. To not look at her. To prevent himself from falling into whatever spell she was conjuring, even if she wasn't aware of it.

Continuing down this road was dangerous.

So damn dangerous.

But, *Jesus fuck*, her ass. Two perfect handfuls, so pale they couldn't have seen the light of day in years. One sharp smack of his palm would leave a red mark behind on that perfect skin.

He was tempted, so fucking tempted, but managed to refrain, unsure whether she'd be into that or not. She seemed to be obstinate enough that if he spanked her ass, even play-fully, she might try to give him a black eye in return.

With one hand, he spread those cheeks, with the other, he slid the head of his dick through her crease and planted it right where it needed to be. Right where it would only take one small thrust to be inside her.

Was she holding her breath in anticipation like he was?

He worried that he'd hurt her. He wasn't huge, but she had been so much tighter than expected. He was average length, but girth-wise... He hadn't gotten any complaints. Because of that, he'd fight his urge to go balls to the walls like he normally did. Instead, he'd take it slow, take his time, let her get used to—

"Fuck!" he shouted in surprise when she slammed her ass back and impaled herself before he could stop her.

Fuuuuuck. Her inner walls clenched and unclenched as if trying to milk the cum all the way from his brains through his balls.

He gritted his teeth and held still, waiting for her body to stretch around him, letting her get comfortable. She was a hot, tight sheath still slick from her previous orgasms and he struggled not to just start pumping like a dog mounting a bitch in heat.

Because, *for fuck's sake*, he wanted to.

He wanted to drive fast and deep to chase the same euphoria she felt after she came. Twice.

He wanted to give her time, but the more she pulsed around him, the less he was able to resist.

"Don't just stand there." Her complaint came out in a combination hiss-moan. An irritated plea.

Okay, then...

For once, he was trying to be considerate, but, *screw it*, if she wanted him to rail her, he was willing to accommodate her.

Maybe a fuck more than willing.

He dug his fingers into her narrow hips and gave her

exactly what she wanted. So much so, her body slammed forward with each thrust in and out of her slick heat.

His fingers itched to mark that perfectly unblemished skin. To leave a reminder behind. He closed his eyes, dropped his head and breathed through that urge.

When he got his shit together, he opened his eyes again and saw she now had both hands planted on the green felt of the pool table and her back was arched. So was her neck, causing all her long, dark brown hair to sweep across her back like a cape.

He couldn't see her face, or if her eyes were opened or closed. He couldn't see if she was enjoying this as much as he was.

Maybe taking her from behind had been a mistake.

But the whole reason he did so was to protect himself. To prevent himself from being sucked up into her vortex and being unable to escape.

She just needed to be a fuck. That was it. A fuck who was hitting the road after tonight and he'd never see her again.

It was a perfect scenario.

He gathered the strands of her hair and wrapped them around his left hand. Using the silky rope, he tugged, twisting her head to the side, enough to expose the delicate line of her neck.

Folding himself over her, he continued to drive into her tight, hot channel that squeezed and released his length like the fingers of a fist. Over and over.

It was fucking insane. If she continued to do that, it wouldn't be long before he blew his load. And if that happened, it would be too soon.

Because, *fuck him*, he wanted to feel her come around his dick. He wanted to feel the same intensity that he had around his fingers.

He traced his tongue up the side of her neck, turning it into a path of gooseflesh, and sucked at the tender spot behind her ear. He released her right hip and circled his fingers around her stretched throat, only using enough pressure to gauge her response.

He squeezed slightly and her groan vibrated against his palm.

Fuck yeah.

He squeezed her throat a little tighter and, at the same time, she did the same around his dick. He'd like to explore her reaction a little more, to take it even further, but he was playing with fire.

Not with her. But with himself.

He loosened his grip, slid his hand up her slender throat to cup her chin, using it to keep her head arched back, and pushed his thumb into her mouth. She tightened her lips around it and sucked hard.

Fuuuuck. He wasn't expecting that, either.

His hips stuttered to a stop because he had no choice but to pause.

He needed a second. Or two.

Or, *fuck him,* five.

With him holding her up by her chin, she could remove one hand from the table. Reaching around to grab his bare ass cheek, she dug her nails into his flesh. The pain she inflicted encouraged him to continue on their path of pleasure.

When he began to move again, her arm wasn't long enough to keep a good hold and her nails dragged over his flexing ass cheek, marking him like he had wanted to mark her.

Damn.

He smiled against her neck and still fisting her hair, he shoved her cheek against the table, pinning her there, plunging his thumb in and out of her mouth at the same pace he was plunging his dick into her pussy.

The longer he went, the rougher he got, and he heard not one complaint. She didn't stop him, either. Instead, her muscles loosened as each stroke hit the end of her. He was no longer worried about being gentle.

"Yes," she released on a ragged breath around his thumb, then bit him, driving her teeth into his flesh. Not hard enough to break the skin, but hard enough to make his hips stutter once more.

Damn. He was not expecting any of this from her. Not even close. Was this really happening or was he imagining it? Was his mind still fucking with him by molding her into a woman he craved?

Was what he was experiencing a fantasy? Or was she truly that woman?

Could she be that woman?

At first he was worried that she might be a virgin, but now…

Now he wondered what she was into.

Wondered how far she was willing to go.

Her bus and her band weren't leaving until the morning, so if she was willing, they had plenty of time yet to discover how much their likes and needs meshed. To see if she was into the same things he was.

He normally didn't take the time to explore any of that with the women he took upstairs. Mostly because those were quick hookups. He was usually working and didn't have time to play. He simply scratched an itch and went back to work.

When the occasional right woman crossed his path, he'd see if she was willing to hang around after closing so they'd have more time. But even then, he never allowed them to remain in his bed for more than a couple of hours.

Letting them stay might give them the wrong idea.

Even so, out of those few women, even less liked everything he did.

He wasn't super kinky, but he wasn't quite vanilla, either. He considered himself the perfect flavor.

Vanilla spice.

While vanilla was okay for most nights, a pinch of spice could take it up a notch.

When he wanted anything more than a pinch, he sought out Billie, the sadist sweet butt. When he was in the mood, she could put a hurting on him that took a few days to recover from. Due to that, he could only deal with Billie in small doses.

But it wasn't Billie he was sliding in and out of right now.

It was Syn who reached back and wrapped her fingers around the back of his neck.

It was Syn who dug her nails into his flesh there, too.

It was Syn who made him hiss as she dragged those nails along his skin, no doubt leaving marks behind this time. Possibly even drawing blood.

"Want me to stop?" he asked. To be sure. To make sure this was exactly what she wanted.

For fuck's sake, tell me no.

"No," she groaned in her husky way. In that tempting voice that had sucked him in right from the moment he heard it. "Fuck me."

She didn't have to tell him twice. He hadn't planned on stopping unless she told him to, but she gave him the green light to continue.

The harder he fucked her, the deeper her nails dug into his skin. She scraped them through his beard, down his throat.

Not Billie-type torture, but definitely a turn-on.

She continued to claw at him in encouragement and the

only thing keeping his arms from being ripped up was his long-sleeved thermal shirt.

Thank fuck her nails weren't super long or sharply pointed like some of the sweet butts. Otherwise, he might end up looking like he tangled with a feral cat.

Though, he had no doubt Syn was a little on the feral side. Especially when he'd seen how wary she'd been with him at first. She seemed to be cautious around people she didn't know. Or maybe it was just men in general.

While nothing was wrong with that, he wondered what caused it. A reason always existed. Whether it was the way she was raised or because of shit she'd experienced.

He hoped like fuck it was the first and not the second.

Right now, that shouldn't be his concern. In fact, it shouldn't be his concern at all. She wasn't sticking around.

Instead, he needed to concentrate on getting her to climax because he was quickly catapulting in that direction himself.

"Tell me what you need," he whispered in her ear.

She gave her head a little shake, at least as much as she could with his grip on her hair and her cheek pressed into the green felt.

"Tell me," he demanded because he was quickly sprinting toward his own finish line and he didn't want her to forfeit the race. When she still didn't answer, he growled her name. "Syn."

"I… don't know. Just… Just keep going."

That wasn't possible. If he continued on the way he was, she wouldn't get to the end along with him.

She had put some trust in him for them to be doing this in the first place and he didn't want her to regret doing so. He didn't want her to be disappointed.

He paused.

Why he would even care about that? Normally, he'd give

it half a thought, especially if the woman already came, but with Syn...

Goddamn witchcraft.

Pulling shit from him that he wasn't prepared for.

Like actually fucking *caring*.

What. The. Fuck.

"Come or don't. Don't give a fuck." *Lie.*

"I don't know," she said again, sounding frustrated herself. "I..."

She what?

With another growl, he pulled out and took a half-step back. Using the fistful of her hair, he jerked her to her feet. "Asked what you needed, can't give me a fuckin' answer. If you can't tell me what you need to get you there, then I'm gonna take what I want and forget about you."

Again, a fucking lie.

He grabbed her around the waist, lifted her enough to plant her ass on the edge of the table again, just like when he'd eaten her out, and stepped between her legs, forcing them wider.

"Legs around my waist," he ordered, shoving his jeans down a little further. As soon as she complied, he speared her with his dick.

Her cheeks were flushed, her eyes half-lidded and her fingernails dug once again dug firmly into his ass, to the point that it felt like she was slicing open his skin. It also made his dick flex deep inside her.

There was no fucking way he was going to tell her to lighten up because he didn't want that. Anything she was willing to give him, he was going to take it all.

If she wanted to draw blood, he'd let her.

If she wanted to chain him up and ride him until he was shooting nothing but dust, he'd be onboard with that, too.

He only drew the line with certain things, but he doubted she'd ever cross that line. She didn't seem experienced enough to know even half of the shit he'd done in his past. His sex life had been an interesting journey and he rarely said no to trying new things.

It's also why he tended to hone in on more experienced women and those women were usually on the older side. It might not always be that way, but he'd found it to be the majority.

Shade had the right idea when claiming Chelle as his ol' lady. For the first time ever, Dodge had actually been a little jealous of one of his brothers. Especially after watching the video of him and Chelle getting it on in the back of her Subaru. It might not have been kinky but it had been hot as fuck.

That was the moment he realized that having sex with someone you actually had a connection with could make the experience so much fucking better. At this point he wasn't looking for that kind of connection, but once he decided he was done playing the field, then maybe he wouldn't mind "settling down" or at least some sort of version of it.

At only thirty-five he was in no rush to find what most of his brothers had found. Most only settled down once they found "the one." The woman who fit them perfectly.

However, a couple of them, like Trip and Judge, had thought they found "the one" previously and it ended up being a complete fucking disaster. A problem he wanted to avoid. What Trip dealt with when it came to his first wife—the reason he ended up doing time—and also the bullshit Judge dealt with with his first wife and with missing out on his son, Ry, growing up.

But again, why the fuck was his brain even processing this shit right now?

Syn wasn't "the one." She was just "the one right now."

Keep it simple, stupid.

He needed to get the fuck out of his head and get Syn to where she needed to go. This way he could quickly follow.

Now that she was facing him, he wanted to taste those tits. The ones he fantasized about early this morning during his "wind down" time before trying to catch some *zzz*'s. Tiny but tempting, especially after seeing them wet while she was in the tub.

He shoved her shirt up, exposing them, clamped his lips around one of her nipples and sucked as hard as he could. With a whimper and an arch of her back, her nails once again sank into his ass, but with both hands this time.

Moving his mouth to her other tit, he released her shirt and wedged his hand between their slapping bodies to touch where they were connected, where he drove in and out of her. He found her slick nub.

He knew what she needed even if she didn't.

She was going to come, *goddamn it.* He'd make sure of it.

He pounded her as hard as he could in that position, using his fingers to play with her clit. Using his mouth to play with her nipples, to suck on the soft flesh, to scrape his teeth over the very peaks, to flick those hard tips with his tongue.

The more he worked her, the louder she became. Goddamn music to his ears. Even more addictive than the way she sung on stage. Because in this instance, she was singing for him. Each note told him he was doing what she needed.

When she tensed everywhere, even her fingers clamping down on his ass, he gritted his teeth and kept going, knowing she was close. She was right there.

She just needed the slightest shove.

Her slight gasp turning into a low moan and the way she clamped down around his dick told him she finally crossed that finish line.

Thank fuck.

He shoved his face into her neck and grunted as he came, his hips twitching almost as much as his dick as he emptied inside her. Even after her ripples subsided, his muscles relaxed and he could breathe with only a slight pant, he stayed right where he was for a few moments more.

She didn't tell him to move or try to push him off, she continued to clasp his ass, almost as if she wanted to keep him there, too. To keep that connection. Like she didn't want this to be over yet.

It wasn't over. They still had the rest of the night and early morning.

In all the time he'd been the manager of Crazy Pete's, he never once fucked anyone on one of the pool tables. After tonight, he'd never be able to look at the one where they'd fucked and not think of Syn.

He couldn't remember most of the women he'd been with in the past few years. He couldn't remember names or faces. But he already knew he wouldn't be able to forget her.

He ignored the gut feeling that fucking her might have been a huge mistake.

Not because it sucked, because it didn't.

Not because he'd forget her within a day or two, because he wouldn't.

That realization made him move.

He circled his fingers around the root of his dick to hold the full wrap in place as he pulled out. After removing the wrap, he knotted the end and tossed it in the garbage can in the corner of the billiards area. As he did so, she hopped off the pool table and the light hit the wet sheen of her skin along the top of her inner thighs. Her reaction to his attention. Her arousal.

His nostrils flared.

Sometimes he didn't learn from mistakes or listen to his gut. Especially when he walked right into shit even knowing it was a bad idea.

Dumbass, that was what he was. And he was about to prove it.

She turned away, breaking their locked gazes to gather her clothes. "Can you give me a ride back to the bus?"

That ass was still perfectly white and he wanted to add some color to it. "No." He yanked his jeans and boxers up over his hips but didn't bother to fasten them.

Her head snapped up as she held the balled up clothes to her lower belly, covering the dark patch of hair, hiding the result of her orgasms. "I'll have to call—"

He shook his head. "No."

Yeah, he was going to regret tonight. But not for the reason he normally did.

"Rex," she finished weakly.

"Ain't callin' your boy."

Her eyebrows pinned together. "How am I supposed to get back?"

"You ain't. And don't bother to put that shit back on, just gonna end up takin' it back off. Ain't done with you yet."

Those dark eyebrows launched up her forehead. "What if I'm done with you?"

He tilted his head and stared at her. "Are you?"

"I should be."

Believe me, woman, I feel that answer to my very fuckin' core. "Got a comfortable bed upstairs that you've already tested out like Goldilocks. Bonus, I even changed the sheets."

"I'm no Goldilocks."

That was for fucking sure.

"And clean sheets are always a bonus, but... If sex can be like this, I don't plan on sleeping in that bed or keeping those sheets clean. Do you?"

If sex can be like this... "You musta been fuckin' the wrong people."

"I can tell you none of them made me come three times."

Hearing that, one corner of his lips twitched with a little bit of cockiness. Just a little.

He'd bet none of them made her come even once. She had probably fucked boys who were pretending to be men, because assholes like that only cared about one thing…

Themselves.

He wasn't going to analyze the fact he'd only ever cared about himself, too. But at least he did his best to make a woman orgasm. If she didn't, it wasn't for a lack of trying on his part.

So, yeah, he cared about himself, but he wasn't totally fucking selfish.

"I'm standing here half-naked," she reminded him, shaking his thoughts loose.

"Not for long," he said, snagging her boots off the floor and shoving them toward her. "Hang onto these."

She automatically took them in one hand while she held onto her jeans and thong with the other.

Before she could realize what he was about, he bent his knees and picked her up into his arms. She probably weighed the same as Justice.

"I don't need you to carry me," she complained as he began to hoof it across the bar.

"Know you don't. Doin' it anyway."

"Why?"

"'Cause I can and I wanna. That good enough?"

"Not really."

"Too fuckin' bad."

"You're an asshole."

He smiled. "You bet I am."

She wrapped one arm around his neck and hung onto her clothes and boots with the other. Her thumb rubbed back and forth over what had to be a long welt on his neck. "I didn't mean to scratch you up like that."

"Yeah, you did."

She tipped her face up to him as he pushed through the swinging door. "You don't mind?"

"Fuck no," he answered as he took the stairs up to his apartment.

When he reached the top landing, he managed to get his keys out of his pocket, open the door and shut it behind them, all without dropping her.

He walked straight over to the bed and dumped her on it.

Mission accomplished.

Without waiting to see if she finished getting naked, he turned and headed to his kitchenette, shucked out of his cut, draping it over the back of one of the stools at the counter.

"You use that last night?"

Her question made him turn. She sat cross-legged in the middle of his bed, staring at his nightstand.

"Nope."

What sat on top of it was what she had dug out of his underwear drawer. His blue Best Friend Jelly Pocket Sleeve that was not only ribbed on the inside, it had massaging beads. It truly was his "best friend."

"This morning," he confessed.

Beside it lay a half-empty tube of lube. He made a mental note to get more.

She had to have seen it earlier when she came upstairs to shower. Not that he cared. If he did, he would've hidden it in his drawer.

He had left it out because he'd actually planned to use it again tonight. But it turned out to be unneeded because the fantasy he'd played in his head while stroking himself to orgasm this morning, was now in his bed.

And after what he'd already experienced with her, neither of them would be needing the lube, either.

"No shame, huh?" she asked, picking up the tube of

lube, reading the label and then tossing it back onto the nightstand.

"Not even the slightest."

"You saw me naked last night."

"Yeah, thanks for the assistance."

She rolled her lips inward for a second. "Glad I could be of help."

"How 'bout that? You said the same thing to me this mornin'." Actually, she didn't. In this morning's fantasy, she didn't speak much at all. Just like in real life.

"You thought I was young."

"But I knew you were legal."

"Does that make a difference when it comes to your fantasies?" she asked, the amusement disappearing from her eyes.

"Fuck yeah, it does. I'd kick my own fuckin' ass if I started whackin' off to someone underage."

"How about whacking off to unsuspecting adults?"

"Would you have known if I hadn't told you?"

She lifted and dropped one slender shoulder. "No."

"Then there you go. No harm, no foul."

"But now I know."

"You sure as fuck do. Gotta piss. Be naked by the time I come back out."

"Are you always this bossy?"

He thought of Billie. When they hooked up there was only one boss. It wasn't him. "Not always."

He was done with this Q and A session. He turned and strode to the bathroom.

Once inside, he paused in front of the sink and glanced in the small mirror above it.

Red welts crisscrossed his neck. He twisted his head back and forth, then lifted his chin to see them on the back, the sides and his throat. He ran a finger over one of the deeper scratches and saw it had bled slightly.

He grinned and murmured, "Damn, you little hellcat."

Yep, this whole thing was a mistake because now he wanted to be the person to try and tame her. Then teach her how great sex could be.

He just might have to put both her and her band on a regular rotation.

That sounded like a fucking plan he could live with.

Now he just needed her to get onboard, too.

He still had a few hours left to convince her.

Chapter Eleven

SYN HAD both hands planted on his chest, using her arms for support, as she slowly lifted and lowered herself on his cock.

It was a nice cock. She hadn't seen a lot of them, but from what she'd seen, whether in person or in pictures and videos, his was right up there with one of the nicest.

He also seemed to be proud of it. Like it was blue ribbon award-winning or something.

The wide black leather cuff that now circled her left wrist was the only thing she currently wore. She had snatched it from the top of his dresser when she crawled off the bed earlier to finish getting undressed. Like he demanded.

She had to wrap the cuff around her wrist twice before securing it. Even then it was looser than she liked to wear her own similar cuffs since her wrist was much narrower than his.

He had spotted it on her almost immediately, of course, but had said nothing. Instead, as he'd stalked toward the bed, he had been stripping down, too.

Everything else was quickly forgotten as she studied him

once he began to shed his clothes, exposing himself in bits and pieces.

She enjoyed that show a lot better than if he'd simply stepped out of the bathroom fully naked already. This way, as he exposed each part of his body, she had a moment to appreciate the area he uncovered before moving on to the next.

Now she understood the appeal of a striptease. And how anticipation ramped up desire.

Tonight was the first time she'd ever been on top. She had started on the bottom, with him taking his time to enter her, letting her body slowly adjust to his width. Then, after no more than a few pumps of his hips, he'd suddenly rolled over, taking her with him and she ended up where she was now. With his cock deep, *deep* inside her. At first, it was a little uncomfortable, but this position became an instant favorite.

Maybe not with every man, but with this one? Hell yes.

Once he was on the bottom, he no longer moved his hips the way he did so well. He let her set the pace, let her take the time to explore different moves and angles. Amazingly enough, he'd kept his instructions to himself instead of ordering her on what to do.

But the whole time, he watched her, his intense, dark brown eyes sliding over her body, pausing on her breasts, her belly, and what he could see of her pussy swallowing his cock. When he slowly worked his way back up, he once again inspected every inch he could see before locking gazes with her.

At one point, she had hidden her reaction from him since her face, her expressions, were completely exposed. Normally, she tended to hide her emotions. She had learned early on that getting emotional, showing anyone your weakness, could make you more vulnerable. Becoming emotional over something you couldn't control, also did no good. Sometimes, it even made things worse.

But he wasn't having any of that. With a frown, he had grabbed her chin, pulled it down and warned, "Don't hide anythin' from me."

The only order he gave her since joining her in bed had turned the blood in her veins to lava. With a pointed look, he also noticed how hearing that demand had puckered her nipples so tightly, they ached.

Not just with discomfort but for his attention.

For some reason, he wasn't giving them any. He wasn't moving at all. All he did was watch as she discovered what she liked, and what she didn't, while she was on top.

She found that really hot, too. A man like him handing over control during sex to her.

She understood why. He had recognized what little experience she had in the sex department without her having to admit it out loud.

The other three men she had chosen to have sex with had taken the reins when they got together. But not one had asked what she needed from them to orgasm, unlike the man currently beneath her had downstairs.

One asked if she had come and when she told him no, he didn't make the effort to make sure she did.

Dodge had made the effort.

He was bossy as fuck but also surprisingly unselfish.

She also realized, by seeing the slightly protruding tendons in his scratched-up neck and a muscle jumping in his jaw, simply lying on his back and letting her fuck him at her own pace, that giving her the lead was costing him.

The knowledge of holding that power over him was also a turn-on. However, that power could quickly change. If he wanted to take it back, she couldn't stop him.

She paused, sat up straighter and held out both her hands.

Without even the slightest hesitation and as if he could read her mind, he placed his much larger hands in hers, interlinking their fingers. She lifted his right hand to her throat and wrapped his fingers around it. The other she lifted to her breast and after placing it there, she leaned forward, planted her hands on his heaving, tattooed chest again and caught his eyes with hers.

When she smiled at him, an answering smile slowly crept across his face.

It should be illegal to be that gorgeous. She normally didn't consider men to be beautiful. To her, he was.

His dark hair with a few strands of gray and on the longer side but not long enough to reach his shoulders. The thick, but neatly trimmed, dark beard also had a few gray hairs. Those skilled, bitable lips. His broad nose and slightly darker skin tone, not ghost-white like hers, that suggested he was not completely from European descent.

And a smile, when directed at her, could dampen her panties along with make her heart beat a little faster. Especially if it was accompanied with an expression that clearly said he was having very dirty thoughts.

She'd never been so sexually in tune with herself until the moment she met him. In the beginning, she didn't understand it and her body's response had been annoying. Her surprising reaction to him affected every part of her. From the top of her head all the way to her toes.

At first, she was uncomfortable with the way he made her feel. Tonight, she embraced it and understood it a little better. She also looked forward to their remaining hours together to learn why she never experienced this with anyone else.

Only with him.

At the back of her mind, she worried that no one else would ever make her feel this way again. It would only be him.

As strange and as unexpected as it was.

Even so, he couldn't be the only one. Impossible. He just happened to be the first to build the fire, to stoke the flames from the cold ash that filled the gaping hole inside her.

Dark, cold, empty.

A future that looked dim no matter how much she wanted to change it, how hard she tried to do the same.

But not only did Dodge heat her in new ways, he also gave her a sliver of hope. Deep down that bothered her, because it made no sense.

When she'd walked into Crazy Pete's on Tuesday night, she had been drowning in despair, feeling hopeless that nothing would ever get better, that things would never change. The second he agreed to let them play, a spark of hope ignited.

But that all could be nothing more than landing a gig, right?

Or was it something else?

Had it been more about the man than the money?

If it was, did it even matter? She wasn't looking for a savior, whether he was one or not.

Anyway, they weren't sticking around. They needed to hit the road and search for some gigs in warmer states. She had no time to explore these unfamiliar feelings.

She had no inclination to, either. It could only mean trouble. She did not need to add this man to her pile of life's obstacles.

She never had anything handed to her in life. She'd torn every damn nail along the way as she scrambled to climb. Not even to the top, she'd simply be happy to reach a safe and secure level. One she could use for a break before continuing on her attempt to rise. Somehow, she always tumbled back down to the base of that never-ending mountain. Where once again she'd have to dust herself back off and try again.

She was working on it the best way she could by using the only skills she had. Her voice, her ear for music and her natural ability to put her own twist on familiar songs so they sounded new.

She was doing it all for herself. For Rex, Nico and Eddie, too.

But none of them were in this room tonight. It was only her and Dodge.

And right now, she didn't think he was appreciating the way she lazily rode him.

He wasn't bothering to hide his struggle to not take over. In fact, she was prepared for him to twist his body again, taking her with him so he was back on top and in control.

For now, she wanted to keep things the way they were.

Instead of increasing her pace, Syn decided to ramp things up between them in a different way. Since he didn't seem to mind the scratches on his neck, she raked her short nails down his chest and over both of his nipples, not bothering to be gentle at all. The skin along her path rose and became red as she went, turning his torso into a piece of abstract art. Or a map full of roads with dead ends.

His stomach hollowed slightly when she dragged her nails down it, then followed the line of black hair that connected his navel to his cock. Once she reached the spot where they were connected, she tentatively touched him there before following the same path back up to his chest.

She planted both palms over his nipples, leaned over, giving him her weight, and whispered one word into his ear. "Tighter."

She made it an order, not a request, and she wondered how he would react to being told what to do by someone half his weight and size.

Inside her, his cock flexed first, then his fingers clamped tighter around the delicate column of her throat. She had to trust him enough to know just how much pressure to use.

No surprise that he knew the perfect amount.

Not enough to cut off her breathing, but enough to feel the restraint and the control he held within his fingers. How vulnerable she made herself by encouraging him to grip a place where, if he squeezed hard enough, he could easily end her life. Or at least change it in a debilitating way.

By encouraging him with that order, she quickly learned she handed him even more power.

Putting that power, and also that risk, in his large hand made every nerve flare along the surface of her skin. Like a fast-moving wildfire in hurricane-force winds.

She might be tired from a long, energy-draining night, but every inch of her was alive and wide awake. Every one of her senses, too, and all of them added to the experience.

His smoky scent, the feel of his fingers on her nipple as he twisted, the sound of the grunt he released as she began to fuck him harder and faster, the salty taste on the tip of her tongue as she drew it from his ear along the visible beating pulse to the hollow of his throat. She sucked his skin there and then took his mouth.

She gave him back the same. The scent of her arousal, the taste of her tongue against his, the touch of her lips, the moan that escaped her and got trapped within his mouth.

When she opened her eyes while they still kissed, she saw his were open, too. Darkness drawing her in, sucking her into a spinning vortex, trapping her within whatever power he held over her.

The intense heat of it all turned her bones to ash, her flesh to liquid. As her muscles melted and she loosened even more, he kept one hand on her throat as they continued to kiss but slid the other from her breast down her ribs, across her hip to her ass.

Then in a flash, he was twisting, flipping her over and driving his much heavier weight into her, burying her into the soft mattress, taking her in full unapologetic strokes, powering up and into her. Spearing her over and over with his cock.

The scrape of her teeth across his bottom lip prompted him to snag hers between his teeth and bite down until she whimpered and the metallic taste of blood hit her tongue.

Everything on her began to pulse in time to his rhythm. Her heart had expanded so much that it was no longer contained in her chest and now encased her completely.

Everywhere he touched, inside and out, thumped intensely. Whether that touch was from his eyes, his mouth, his fingers or his cock. Or simply the drag of his skin across hers.

He ended the kiss, their breaths blending as both of them panted. The shadow that crossed behind his eyes caught her off guard and sent a shiver slithering down her spine.

Dangerous. So damn dangerous.

He wanted control she might not be willing to give him. But she had a feeling he wouldn't ask for it. He would just take it. Like it belonged to him.

He was its rightful owner.

The control he gave her while she was on top now a fleeting memory. Soon to be forgotten and never achieved again.

He more than wanted her.

He wanted to *own* her.

She felt that in every pulsing cell, in every ragged breath, in every rapid heartbeat. The feeling became stronger with every passing second, with every thrust of his hips. Until it began to overpower her, overwhelm her.

Scare the fuck out of her.

Not because he would hurt her. She had no fear of that.

But because he would turn her into a slave to his desires.

She shouldn't let him have that. She should stop whatever was happening.

But she couldn't.

Whatever it was about him that drew her was like injecting heroin directly into her vein. He was giving her a high that might never be enough, a euphoria she'd want to keep chasing. An unbreakable addiction.

She avoided drugs and didn't drink alcohol for that very reason. Addiction could be hereditary and she feared falling into the same trap her mother did.

Except tonight she willingly stepped into it, completely unaware sex could be similar.

It couldn't be just the sex, it had to be the man she was having it with. Because she'd had sex before. Just not like this.

The oxygen fled her lungs when he put his lips to her ear and demanded in a low growl, "Want you to come when I tell you to."

Was that even possible, to come on command? Could his words push her to the point of orgasm?

No way. Impossible.

That would not only take physical control, but mental. A simple mind over matter.

"Hands above your head, cross your wrists."

When she lifted her arms and did what he demanded, he immediately clamped his free hand over them, holding them together, pinning them to the mattress, restraining her.

With his weight on her, his fingers around her throat, her hands "bound" by his, she was...

Trapped.

Fully under his control.

She felt no panic, no fear, but a sense of unexpected calmness swept through her.

She didn't fight that control. She welcomed it.

The weight of the world that dragged her down suddenly disappeared. She'd take that relief for now, even if it didn't last.

Of course, it would only be temporary, she was leaving in a few hours and didn't know when, or if, she'd ever return.

She'd let herself have this for now. Let him have it, too.

"Come for me," filled her ears. "Now."

For fuck's sake, that voice, that demand. The tone that told her she had no option other than to obey.

With a strength she didn't know she had, her hips shot up and slammed into him, driving him deeper than he'd ever been, even when she had been on top.

She jerked one of her hands free from its prison and sliced her nails across his chest, deep enough to draw blood.

He twitched in reaction, including his cock still driving relentlessly deep inside her. His fist tightened even more around her throat, now constricting her breathing enough for her to start becoming light-headed.

But she could still speak.

She could still say no.

Tell him to stop.

She didn't want to.

His words had started the avalanche, his actions made it speed out of control. Sliding, sliding, sliding, picking up speed and gaining momentum, until that avalanche hit bottom and exploded around them both.

He drove into her one more time, everything on him tightening, including where he held her, the pressure increasing on her neck, the wrist he still had pinned.

She should panic, she *would* panic if it wasn't him.

And that was so fucked up.

Was she losing her damn mind?

Why would she like this?

She shouldn't.

She shouldn't.

But, *holy fuck*, she did.

Chapter Twelve

His eyes were closed and a deep-seated satisfaction he'd never experienced before saturated his bones. It soaked all the way to his very center, including his brain matter.

He'd done some crazy shit before and sex with Syn hadn't been crazy at all. But it had stirred something inside him that had apparently been lurking. Waiting to show itself when the right woman came along.

Now *that* was the crazy part.

Normally, pussy didn't make him lose his mind. With Syn, it wasn't about the sex at all and it wasn't the reason making him question his actions or reactions.

They just fucked for the third time and he doubted there would be a fourth before she extracted herself from his bed and his life, and moved on to a warmer location.

Did he want a fourth time? Fuck yes.

Could he muster up enough strength? In the time they had left, probably not. He was normally pretty good about bouncing back, but he still had his limits and he wasn't going to start something he couldn't finish. That would be a major blow to his ego.

She must have thought he'd fallen asleep because it was

the first time in the last few hours where she'd touched him when they weren't having sex.

Her fingers brushed over his messy hair and a portion of his beard and he knew exactly why. She touched him where the few strands of gray could be found. Once again, reminding them both, she was young, he was not.

Dodge wasn't *old* like Dutch but he was older than her.

Twenty-fucking-three.

Practically a baby.

When he was twenty-three, he thought he knew how the world worked. Believed he was so damn knowledgeable. That false thinking made him nothing but arrogant.

That cockiness also caused him to lose his freedom.

Both then and several times afterward.

He now knew he didn't know jack at that age. Because if he had known what he knew now, he might have made different—and hopefully better—decisions along the way.

But then, most people, if they could go back, would probably do the same.

With experience came knowledge. Good, bad and even useless.

Life could kick you in the fucking balls when you least expected it and you either learned from it and never repeated that mistake again, or you repeated it over and over until you finally got a fucking clue. That message usually delivered by a two-by-four cracked across the forehead.

Or you ended up six feet under because you were too stupid or stubborn to learn.

Dodge had known some of those types of people, too. His so-called "stepfather" and uncle were two perfect examples of skin bags filled with useless wind who were too stupid to live.

The world's collective IQ did not lessen when those two disappeared. It might have even risen a bit.

He had a feeling that Syn's life experience had been fast-tracked.

Maybe not when it came to sex, but everywhere else. His gut told him she'd walked barefooted along a path full of broken glass and dangerous drop-offs.

However, she was also a survivor.

When the very tip of her finger lightly traced along the seam of his lips, he opened them and bit it lightly.

Her hand jerked away in surprise and she face-planted into his side as her body shook.

With laughter?

He opened his eyes and raised his head to witness it.

"Syn," he murmured, wanting to see what she was hiding.

When she lifted her face, any possible laughter was already wiped away. That was if it had even existed in the first place and he hadn't imagined it.

"I've discovered something tonight," she said, her brown eyes just as soft as her voice. They held his. He could get lost in the deep well of those fucking eyes.

He pushed that fucked-up thought away and became concerned she hadn't slept at all. The half-circles under her eyes were now the darkest he'd seen on her yet. He blamed himself for that since he couldn't get enough of her and wanted to take advantage of the limited time he'd have her in his bed.

Hopefully she'd catch up on some sleep once she and the band hit the road. "What?"

"I like sex."

Out of all the things she could've said, he hadn't been expecting that. He'd actually expected some snark.

He didn't bother to hide the twitch of his lips. However, he didn't want to laugh or grin outright if she wasn't kidding. "You only figured that out tonight?"

"Is it pathetic to answer that question with a yes?"

Shit.

It was, but not for the reason she might think. So, he answered with, "Fuck no. More like surprisin', maybe even disappointin', more than pathetic. Unless you've had a lot of it, then sorry for your shitty luck. If your experiences have been limited, then I guess it ain't a surprise." Everything pointed to the second scenario rather than the first. "Just in case you didn't pick up on it, I like sex, too."

"I don't think that was in question."

He liked this softer side of her and wondered how long it would last. It seemed her first instinct was to always hide her feelings. To wear armor to protect herself.

He understood that all too well. But he was pleased she was dropping that armor with him. "Not even for a second?"

"No." She slid the finger he had nipped down his chin and scratched-up throat, circled the hollow of his neck, then traced a few of the deeper scratches decorating his chest.

Total fucking hellcat.

He liked it. Scratches would heal and be forgotten but how he got those scratches would remain seared into his brain.

Most sex he'd had with randoms was forgettable.

He'd never forget tonight.

Disturbing but true.

"It reminds me of music."

He frowned and dipped his chin to see her better. "What does?"

"Sex. The rhythm, the beats, the same loss of self-awareness because you get so caught up in it. I could get completely absorbed in it like I do when I'm singing. I could get lost in it but also feel grounded at the same time. I don't know how else to explain it. Maybe it's because music and sex use both the mind and body. It seems great sex is more than physical, it's mental, too."

Her words caught him off guard. He usually didn't have a conversation with the women he fucked, at least nothing as deep as their current one. Usually when he talked to women, he kept it on the surface and shallow. Most times he just let them ramble on and he occasionally grunted, pretending he was listening.

But this woman… Syn was deeper than he ever expected.

Again, a good indication she'd lived a harder life than a twenty-three-year-old ever should.

"I'm only saying that because the way I feel after spending hours on stage is how I feel after having sex with you."

"Guessin' that's a good thing?" He sure as fuck hoped it was.

Christ, again, he never cared about any of this kind of shit before. Why the fuck now?

"I lose myself in my music, just like I lost myself while having sex with you."

Okay, he was going to assume that *was* a good thing. "That bother you?"

"No. The only difference was that all of my senses were heightened during sex. Usually I block everything else out but the music when I sing. I can get hyper-focused."

"But it depends on the song, right?"

She considered that. "That's true. There are some songs I don't enjoy singing as much as others. It's one reason I hate taking requests. I'm not a DJ or a jukebox, or even a machine. Then there are songs I absolutely hate and never sing at all."

"Same with men, then. You connect with a song the same way you connect with a man. Or woman. Dependin' what you're into."

"I never had sex with a woman."

He would love to watch if she ever decided to try it. His dick actually attempted to revive at that mental image.

Down, boy. Don't start somethin' you can't finish. This has been a good experience for her so far, let's not fuckin' ruin it.

He managed to get back on track. "If it's good, sex can be like gettin' high 'cause of the endorphins the body produces. Is that the way you feel when you're on stage?"

Did he knock the sense out of himself while knocking the bottom out of her? When the fuck did he turn into some kind of doctor or therapist or something?

"Sometimes. Sometimes it feels like the music takes over. I'm no longer me, but I've become part of the music itself. That probably sounds… weird."

"Ain't weird, but interestin'. I like how you gave yourself up to me the same way you give yourself to your music. That right there is…"

This conversation had headed into unfamiliar territory. When the fuck did he ever talk about feelings with anyone?

Never, that was when.

Even as a bartender, when customers rambled on about their problems, he only listened with half an ear. If they were lucky.

He normally didn't give a fuck if Jimmy-John's wife, Betty-Jo, was leaving his ass and he was crying in his damn beer. He handed them a cocktail napkin for their tears, a bowl of peanuts and advice that was short and sweet. *"There's plenty of other pussy out there, go find another snatch. No woman was worth cryin' over. Nut up and go nut in someone else."*

Simple? Fuck yeah.

Effective? He didn't give a fuck if it was or wasn't.

"Is?" she prodded with one of her dark eyebrows raised, drawing his attention back to her.

"Is a huge fuckin' compliment. But it ain't just me. It's you, too. Allowin' yourself to let go and give yourself to me like that."

"That doesn't happen all the time?"

Fuck no, it didn't. Her not knowing that was proof she hadn't had a lot of sexual partners.

That said, when he normally had sex, it rarely was an "experience." It was only two bodies slapping together until the ultimate goal was achieved. That was it.

That wasn't what happened with Syn.

He should actually be freaked the fuck out about that.

He was heading in that direction, so he needed to abandon this line of conversation. He could do it in one of two ways. Kick her the fuck out of his bed and apartment, or change the topic.

He didn't want to do his normal go-to for scraping off a woman—at least, not yet—so he went with the second option. "Where you from?"

She frowned, most likely from the sudden topic change. Instantly, he saw her walls slide back up and lock into place. *Fuck.*

"Nowhere. You saw I live in a bus."

She wasn't born in that fucking bus, though. "No home base?"

"That's home."

For fuck's sake, she was back to being difficult. Maybe he could chip away at that wall. "Where'd you grow up?"

She hesitated. "I was born in West Virginia."

"You grew up there?"

"Yes."

"Your parents still there? Family?"

She hesitated again. "No."

She went from Chatty Cathy to one word answers. Frustrating as fuck.

"Nothin' left for you in West Virginia, then?" Her longer hesitation this time made him tip his head up again and really look at her. "Nothin' left for you there? No family? Nothin'?"

Before he could ask more questions, she came up with a way to divert him off their current path of conversation by using his own tactic. "How about you? How did you end up in an MC? Did you always live in this town?"

He normally didn't talk about his past or his personal business, especially to women who landed in his bed. But maybe if he answered some of her questions, she'd answer more of his. It was worth a shot.

"Fuck no. Only came here because I did time in a county prison not far from here and my cellmate at the time convinced me to join a club that was just startin' out. Rook. From the garage, remember?"

"So, you weren't raised around bikers or anything? You became one not knowing anything about the life?"

Sort of. "Knew about the life. In truth, growin' up, I wasn't a big fan of bikers."

"Really? Why?"

"Because of the shit my so-called 'stepdad' put my mother through. My uncle, my mom's brother, was a total dick, too."

"They were both bikers?"

He did not miss when she relaxed against him and was back to talking more, now that she wasn't the focus. Imagine that.

"Yeah. They belonged to the same club and both of them used her. Only used our place as a crash pad when they weren't on the road doin' whatever the fuck they were doin'. No good, mostly. Only time those assholes showed up was when they were outta scratch. Or when Smokey wanted an easy lay. Funny how those motherfuckers magically appear around the same time my mother got her monthly checks. Then, a few days later, they'd hop on their sleds and disappear again for long stretches. Sometimes months at a time. One time, we didn't see them for a whole year straight." Dodge had hoped neither would show back up.

Unfortunately, they did. It was hard to kill roaches. Though, eventually someone must have been successful. Dodge wished he could buy whoever took those fuckers out a beer. Or two. *Hell*, a whole damn case.

"Was your mom upset they'd desert her like that? They'd take her money and run? And not stick around to help out or anything?"

"The only fuckin' thing she fussed about was that they took her damn scratch. That was it." Couldn't buy drugs if you didn't have the green to pay for it. Instead, she had to score her smack in other ways.

"Well, of course. Then she didn't have money for food and rent, right? To help take care of you?"

"Had nothin' to do with takin' care of me. Ended up raisin' myself, mostly. It had to do with her drug habit."

Syn shifted until she could see his face, planting her forearm on his chest and leaning into it. Why did the talk of his mother's addiction make her perk up like that?

That night so fucking long ago, the night he found her in that crack house and ran from the pigs, she somehow survived that overdose. How? He had no fucking clue. Maybe at the time she was indestructible as a roach, too. Like her brother, Breaker, and that useless fuckhead who wanted him to call him Dad for whatever fucking reason.

Dodge had no idea why since the fucker had the paternal instinct of a flea. It was probably just a ploy to stay in good with his mother. And maybe even his uncle.

Dodge didn't know, he also didn't fucking care.

After that night, she cleaned up her act for a while. The main reason was she did some jail time, rehab and then had to live in half-way house where she was forced to stay clean.

The other reason was while she had been hospitalized, they found out she was pregnant.

Fucking pregnant.

How that baby survived, he had no fucking idea. He also

never got to meet the kid since his mother gave it up for adoption at birth. For once she did something smart and unselfish. Though, he guessed she might have been pressured to do it.

"What was she doing?"

What?

Fuck.

"Anythin' cheap and everythin' she could get her hands on."

Once she was done baking that kid and was free of the half-way house for good, she slipped right back into her old ways. She refused to talk about the baby. Dodge didn't know if it was a boy or a girl, nothing.

He only hoped the kid had a better life wherever they ended up. Someone who actually cared and made the kid feel loved and wanted.

"What happened to her?"

"Five years ago, while I was doin' a short stint in county, got notification that she was found dead after being raped and assaulted in a crack house."

Another fucking crack house. The only thing that surprised him at the time was that she'd survived that long. He thought she'd eventually die of an overdose but he'd been wrong.

His lip curled up as he remembered the moment he found out. A screw had told him through the solid locked door of his cell.

She must have had his information on her somewhere. He wouldn't have been surprised if she'd had his name and number tattooed onto her in case she turned up dead.

He cared as much about her dying as she had cared about him while she was living.

But then, nobody mattered to Sandra Duke. Not Dodge. Not the baby she gave up. Because if they mattered, she would've stayed clean and kept that kid. Not to mention, took care of the one she already had.

The one she forgot time and time again.

"Holy shit."

Her whisper drew him from thoughts that could quickly send him down a dark and dangerous path. One he worked hard to stay off. "Let's just say, it wasn't a shock. The only thing that surprised me was that it hadn't happened sooner. If she wasn't gonna get clean for her kids, who the fuck was she gonna get clean for? Certainly not her damn self."

"But she raised you, right? Even though she was an addict?"

"Barely. When all you do is focus on where your next high's comin' from, you forget to focus on your kid. Sometimes you even forget you have one."

During her time served and also her time in recovery, he'd been thrown into a temporary foster care. Surprisingly, his uncle came and got him two months later. Most likely to try to collect the checks. Breaker had taken Dodge to some scummy apartment, stuck around for a few days, then left him there alone to raise himself.

So, Dodge did that. He finished raising himself.

He stole for scratch. He stole for food. He forged any checks that came in the second they landed in the mail slot so Breaker and Smokey couldn't steal them. Those included the child support payments forwarded to that apartment.

Dodge did whatever he had to do to survive.

What he did not do was go back to Kevin Collins.

He did not need that motherfucker. He might not have much but he had his fucking pride.

Dodge basically turned feral and ran wild while learning how to stay off the pigs' radar as best as he could. He also learned to talk his way out of a lot of situations and use his age as an excuse. He was "too young" to know better.

He only kept going to school for the free breakfasts and

lunches. For the showers when the water in the apartment was shut off. For warmth when the heat was turned off, too. And, of course, for the girls.

By sweet talking some of his female classmates, he learned quickly they'd let him climb in their windows at night and sleep in their bed. Even better, they'd let him do other things, too.

Somehow he managed to make it to graduation without getting thrown in juvie or getting evicted from the apartment housing. Though, he barely earned his diploma. But the diploma he earned with all Ds looked exactly the same as the class Valedictorian's.

Same certificate, just a different name. So, who was the real smart one in that case?

He only saw Breaker and Smokey when they occasionally rolled back into town. And when they did, he made himself scarce.

Then about ten years ago, he never heard from either of them again. He'd heard rumors here and there that the club they belonged to, the Shadow Warriors, had been decimated.

Unlike the Fury, the story going around was that MC's demise came from the outside instead of within. His best guess was a rival club must have had it out for them and decided it was easier if they no longer existed.

Dodge did not shed a tear over that news.

In fact, he drank a few shots to celebrate. It could've been more than a few.

What it did not do was leave him with a desire to join an MC. Not full of motherfucking useless pieces of shit like his uncle and Smokey.

Not until the Fury offered him a place to land and a promise of something solid.

"Sorry," she said. "Not everyone should be a parent."

No truer words. But, *fuck*, now he regretted starting this

whole damn conversation. He did not want to relive the past.

At least the effort to get her to open up worked, even though it also returned him to a time he wanted to forget.

He dropped his gaze from where he'd been staring at the ceiling to the woman now laying across his chest, her chin propped on her forearm as she stared at him with eyes that sucked him in like quicksand. They could easily pull him under, making it impossible to escape.

"There should be a list of requirements or a parenting test before you're ever allowed to have children. My birth mother had a similar story to yours. She actually drank herself to death. Feeding her addiction was more important to her than her kids, too."

Christ almighty. Some people needed to be spayed and neutered like pets. "She die recently?"

"No."

"What about your pop?"

"No one knew who he was. I don't even think she did."

Damn.

"After I…"

After she what?

Why the fuck was he so goddamn invested in her story? Why was he hanging on her every damn word?

Was her pussy laced with some sort of drug?

She gave her head a little shake like she was trying to shake free of something, then finally said, "Because alcoholism can be genetic, I rarely drink. I don't want to ever end up like her. Where you prioritize alcohol or drugs over taking care of your…"

"Your?"

"Responsibilities."

"What happened to you after that?"

She shook her head. "Nothing."

"You weren't living with her then?"

"No. I never really lived with her."

It was rare that a child was removed from their mother's care. No matter how rotten that care was.

"It's why…"

After a few silent moments, he wanted to yell, "It's why what?"

She shook her head again. "Nothing."

"Ain't nothin'. Finish what you were gonna say." He might have said that a little more forcefully than he should have. He didn't want her slamming her walls up again. But her hesitation was driving him fucking crazy.

Finally, she repeated, "That's why I don't drink much or do drugs."

Bullshit. That wasn't what she was going to say. But he let it go. Everyone had secrets.

So did Syn.

Did he want to know hers? Fuck yeah.

Did he want to share all of his? Fuck no.

"Did family raise you, instead?" His certainly didn't.

"No. Right after I was born, my brother smuggled me out of our trailer and gave me to another family."

Wait. Hold the fuck up. "He did fuckin' what? What d'you mean he gave you to another family?"

"He was trying to save me."

"From what?"

"A horrible life. A screwed up childhood. Like I said, my mom was a drunk—like drink until she blacked out kind— and though my brother didn't tell me everything, once I got older, I could understand why he did what he did."

If Syn's mother was anything like Dodge's, he could understand it, too. Now he was thankful as fuck that his mother gave up her second child.

Syn's situation sounded similar.

Too fucking similar.

However, it had to be worse for a girl growing up in that

kind of environment than a boy. Especially if strange men were coming in and out of their house. Or in her case, trailer. Something that might happen if the mother was desperate for scratch to feed her addiction. Like Dodge, Syn would've been left unprotected while her mother was passed out drunk or high.

Syn probably wouldn't have escaped unscathed.

Her brother had to be a lot older than her to make that kind of decision.

Hell, would he have done the same if his mother had brought the baby home? Or would he have ended up raising the kid just like Reese did with Reilly?

He knew it would've been tougher to survive if he had another mouth to feed and body to clothe. Someone else to be responsible for when he could hardly be responsible for himself.

He could even see his mother selling the baby in exchange for whatever her drug of choice was for that week.

Just the thought turned his fucking stomach.

Were people so desperate for their next high they'd sell their own children?

Of course they would. Sometimes humanity wasn't so humane. Sick motherfuckers.

"And did he save you by doin' that?" He hoped like fuck she had ended up in a better situation.

"That's… debatable."

That wasn't the answer he wanted to hear. Probably one that her brother wouldn't want to hear, either. "Where's he now?"

"My brother? No idea. He was in and out of prison a lot. We lost track of each other a few years back."

A few years back? She was only twenty-three. "When's the last time you seen him?"

She jerked one shoulder. "He approached me one day when he was still a teen and I was really little. I had no clue who he was until he told me after I thought he was trying to abduct me. Stranger danger and all that shit. Funny how most times it's not strangers you have to worry about."

"Yeah, it's people you know. The people who are supposed to protect you are sometimes the worst." They were two examples of that.

Hell, his whole club was full of good examples.

Her eyes squeezed shut for a few seconds, making him trace his fingers along her jawline.

While he waited for her to continue talking, he studied her throat. It was sexy as fuck. Both with the sultry sound that came out of it while on stage or while he was fucking her. It was even sexier with his fingers wrapped around it.

His blood rushed south and his dick actually started to perk up. Maybe he could muster up a fourth time without embarrassing himself. By the time they were done talking, maybe he'd be all revved up and ready to go and he wouldn't have to be worried about a failure to launch.

The only problem was the topic they were on wasn't as sexy as the woman who was speaking.

"He promised that he'd keep checking in on me when he could. I was in kindergarten at the time and out on the playground. A teacher saw him and chased him away. I saw him a couple more times after that, here and there, for only very short amounts of time. Then he'd go missing for a while. One day he brought me a prepaid cell phone and told me to hide it from my parents. He was afraid they'd take it away. Occasionally he would call or text it. Then one day it just… stopped. I never heard from him again. I don't know what happened. I called him and texted him until the minutes ran out."

"Maybe he lost his phone or it got destroyed and didn't have your number memorized." Or something bad happened to him.

"Yeah, maybe," she murmured.

"He never showed back up at your school?"

"No. My parents—my adoptive parents—began to homeschool me after we had to move."

"So, he had no idea where you went, either," Dodge murmured.

"No, I texted him our new address. Our phones were our only connection. Without that line of communication, we had nothing." She licked her bottom lip leaving a wet sheen behind. "I really want to find him again but I have no idea where else to look. I think I've exhausted all avenues." Her brow furrowed.

"Google?"

"Tried that. I know he went to juvie and then jail a few times before we lost touch. Whenever he got arrested, he always called me as soon as he got back out. I even tried to search online inmate records. No luck."

"You travel enough; you ask around when you do? It's a long shot, but you never know, you could end up bein' lucky. Someone out there, somewhere could know him."

"The problem is, I only have his first name. That makes it more difficult."

"You don't have the same last name? Was it changed when you were adopted?"

She sighed softly. "I'm not sure what's on my birth certificate since I don't have it. I have no idea what hospital I was born at, either. As for an official adoption… When you're taken from your drunk mother and given illegally to another family by another kid, you don't come with any paperwork like a social security number or birth certificate."

It was almost like buying a baby on the black market. Dodge wondered how old her brother had been at the time to make that decision and what steps he took to make sure the family he gave her to was worthy of taking care of her and providing for her. How did he know he wasn't putting her into a worse situation than the one with her real mother?

Most likely, he didn't.

That had to be scary as fuck.

"Nobody but your brother was checkin' on you? Makin' sure you were good?"

"No. If I had been adopted through an agency…" Her eyes shut again and remained shut. "I kept hoping Sig would come back and get me."

Hold the fuck up. Who the fuck did she just say? Was he that fucking tired he was hearing things? He had to have misunderstood her, right? "Say again? Who did you say?"

Her eyes opened and she frowned at him. "My brother. That's who we were just talking about."

No shit, but… "What'd you say his name was?"

Her frown deepened. "Sig."

Oh fuck.

The chances of them being one and the same were slim, but definitely not zero.

Motherfuckin' fuck.

Chapter Thirteen

As SOON AS the mattress shifted, Dodge's eyes flashed open. The apartment was still dark and it had to be too early for the sun to have risen since no light was peeking through the blinds. That meant they might have gotten an hour of sleep at the most after he managed to work up the energy to fuck her a fourth time.

While he didn't say it out loud, he was proud of himself for his performance. It wasn't fast and furious, but more relaxed and lazy and definitely satisfying for both of them. But it was no surprise that they both passed out shortly afterward.

Now, Syn was no longer using him as a body pillow. As the mattress moved again, he turned his head to see her trying to sneak off the bed.

Even as tired as he was, his reflexes were still sharp enough to snake out his hand and snag her wrist in time to stop her. "Where you goin'?"

"Gotta go." She lifted her cell phone and turned the lit screen toward him. He could see a text bubble but not what it said. "They're out there waiting for me."

They were what? "Right now?"

She nodded.

What the fuck.

He tilted his head and could faintly hear the diesel engine's exhaust rumbling outside. "You call them to come get you?" When she didn't answer fast enough, he asked, "Text them?"

She nodded.

"Why so fuckin' early?"

"It's time for us to go. You wanted us off the farm by morning."

He didn't want them off the farm, Trip did, but... *Damn.* Already? It was too fucking early.

"Please thank your president for letting us hook up there. And thanks for the heaters."

Thanks for the heaters.

Damn.

He glanced at the wrist he held. The one his leather cuff encircled. He opened his mouth to ask for it back, then snapped it shut. For some crazy reason, he wanted her to keep it.

Maybe she wanted to keep it, too. As a memento. To remember him. To remember this night.

Maybe. Or with the way she'd been trying to sneak out, maybe she was simply a thief.

If that was true, though, she had plenty of opportunity to take other shit every time she'd been alone in his apartment taking a shower while he was downstairs. He hadn't noticed anything missing.

Even if she did take anything, she probably needed it more than him. In truth, there was nothing in his apartment he couldn't live without.

Maybe his gun. But he had that secured in a lock box and that was hidden on the bottom of his dresser.

When she gave her arm a little tug, he reluctantly released her. She immediately moved through the dark to his dresser where she had stacked her neatly-folded clothes.

Her skin was so damn pale her naked body almost glowed in the dark.

A ghost who was ghosting him.

She turned her back to the bed and tugged on her clothes, jammed her feet into her boots and then shrugged on her cat-eared sweatshirt.

He gritted his teeth. She needed a real damn winter coat. Not that fucking hoodie. Too bad he didn't have any warm coats in the lost-and-found downstairs.

Fuck, he was not ready for her to go. Not yet.

"Hey," he called out as she bent over to lace up her boots.

When she was done, she straightened and turned back toward the bed. Now she wasn't as easy to see since her sweatshirt was black and so were her jeans and boots. No longer a ghost but a shadow that blended into the darkness. If she pulled her hood up, she'd simply disappear.

Just like she was trying to do.

If he hadn't woken up, she would have left without saying another word to him. That shouldn't bother him as much as it did.

"Been thinkin'," he continued.

She paused.

"Thinkin' I'd like to get your band on a regular rotation. Got a few bands already that play once a month. We could do the same for The Synners. You up for that?"

Did that sound like a desperate attempt to keep her from disappearing completely?

It really wasn't. The truth was, they were a better band than they'd had in a while. And none of the lead singers of their regular bookings were even close to being as good as Syn.

"We need to head south."

For fuck's sake, it wasn't just about the band. "Yeah, get that. Maybe once it warms up a bit. Or you get better heat." Or we find out that Sig is actually your brother.

He had kept that possibility to himself since he wasn't sure what to do with that information yet.

It took a bit after she mentioned her brother's name for his mind to stop spinning. The only reason it did was because of that fourth round of sex. A record for him and definitely a record for her.

Once exhaustion took over and dragged him under, his brain had finally shut off. Now he was awake, even though it was way too soon, he needed to seriously consider that possibility.

He should tell her.

But he was on the fence. He owed his loyalty to Sig first. His loyalty to his club and his brothers would always remain at the top of his list. It was why he had no problem getting the club colors inked onto his back permanently.

Proof of his loyalty. Proof that he finally belonged some-where with people who actually fucking cared about him. Loyalty ran both directions.

While she wanted to find her brother, did her brother want to find her? Or did he disappear out of her life for good reason?

Dodge couldn't imagine what that reason could be. But it was Sig and…

Yeah, enough said.

If she had mentioned any of his brothers other than Sig, then he might be approaching this possible situation differ-ently. Besides the little she told him, Dodge didn't know the complete story, or even the backstory.

It would be smart to run this possibility by the VP first and it would also be the right thing to do. Then, it would be up to Sig to figure out the next step *if* it turned out they were siblings.

Syn had been an infant when her brother took her from their mother and handed her off to, Dodge assumed, people who were not family. Because of that, he guessed her brother hadn't told her everything.

But Dodge really wanted her number. Not only selfishly for himself, but so he could give it to Sig, this way the VP could be the one to reach out.

Sig wasn't a popular name, but there had to be more than one out there in the world. It could just be coincidence that his brother and hers happened to have the same name.

His gut instinct was telling him otherwise, but he told his gut to shut the fuck up. He would let his brain handle it, instead. Probably a mistake but he'd made a shitload of mistakes in his life. What was one more?

Though, this one might be a big one. If she was Sig's sister and Sig found out Dodge fucked her… *Hell*, fucked her on the pool table in Pete's…

Yeah. He wasn't sure how that would go over. Although, he had a pretty good idea.

One step off a crumbling cliff at a time. Go to Sig, ask him about Syn, then…

Deal with it from there.

It might end up being nothing.

Or it might end up being a fucking problem. Especially with Sig's trigger temper.

He should probably run it by Trip first. Or at least have Trip with him since they were half-brothers. *Hell*, maybe even Red nearby. Just in case…

"Maybe once it warms up," Syn finally said, bringing him back to their conversation.

He grabbed his cell phone off the nightstand and pressed the power button to wake it up. "Give me your number. Gonna check the schedule and let you know what spots I got open after March."

She glanced down at the phone in her hand for a

second, like she had forgotten she was holding it, then glanced up. What she didn't do was rattle off her number.

Fuck. Here she was getting difficult again.

Was she afraid he'd stalk her? Or harass her or something?

He sighed.

He got plenty of pussy, he didn't need to chase it. Even someone like Syn.

But if she wasn't comfortable, he'd have to respect that and also accept it. Even if it did aggravate him a bit.

He leaned over the side of the bed, snagged his discarded jeans off the floor and pulled out his wallet.

"Will give you mine, then." He dug out a business card for the bar. "You can call me when you guys are ready to head back to this area. I'll make a spot for you."

She eyed the card that he extended toward her held between his two fingers like it might bite. They just spent the last few hours naked, sweating and swapping fluids and suddenly she was suspicious of him?

He shifted until he was sitting up and leaning against the headboard.

If she wanted it, she was going to have to come to him. Otherwise, fuck her. He wasn't begging. He'd already done more for her than most women who landed in his bed.

He gave her band a chance when he didn't have to. She also told him shit that he was damn sure she didn't freely share. More importantly, he shared shit with her he never talked about.

If she didn't trust him after all of that, then that was her issue, not his.

Even so, he didn't understand the sudden turn-around. But then, when had he ever understood women? He should know better than to even try because it never worked out well for him.

They continued to stare at each other through the dark.

He was not dropping his hand until she approached him and took the card. "Ain't gonna bite."

Did her lips curl slightly?

Huh. "Unless you want me to."

Fuck yeah, they did.

She finally unstuck herself from where she'd been standing and moved closer. She snagged the card from his fingers and glanced at it. "You had your personal cell phone number printed on the card?"

"Yeah, 'cause I'm the manager and I don't give those out like candy. Plus, now that Stella's pregnant, don't want anyone buggin' her. Neither does her ol' man."

She began to flip the card over and over within her fingers.

She wasn't turning and running so that was a good sign. Maybe she'd seriously consider coming back to play.

Not just on stage. But with him.

He rarely did repeat business with the women he took upstairs, but for some reason, tonight with Syn wasn't enough. Like her band, he'd like to put her in regular rotation, too. A first for him.

If she was down for that.

"Stella. She's the owner?"

"Half. The other half's officially owned by the club. Well, now that she's legally married to the prez, guessin' unofficially the club owns the whole thing."

Her dark eyebrows knitted together. "What if they get divorced?"

He snorted. "They ain't gettin' divorced." They were a forever type of couple. Just like the tattoos they had on their ring fingers.

"No one plans on getting divorced. But it happens."

"True. If that happens, then I don't fuckin' know. Ain't my worry as long as I got scratch comin' in, a roof over my head, a real bed to sleep in and my door can be unlocked from both sides."

That last part was the most important. This time he was doing his fucking best to hold onto his freedom.

She flicked the business card with her fingernail. "So… If we come back… Is it only for the band to play?"

"Think you know that answer. You didn't need to ask it."

"If I didn't need to ask it, I wouldn't have asked it," she said with a touch of attitude.

One he was tempted to change with a palm on those ghost-white cheeks.

With the way his bed had turned into a revolving door, he rarely had a chance to play like that. Would she like it, or knee him in the nuts for it?

He stifled his grin and the urge to grab his dick. Even with how many times they fucked throughout the night, he still was left wanting.

For more. Of her. The woman who tucked his business card into her back pocket and then hit his gaze with hers, holding it. Almost as if she had read his dirty-assed mind.

Even in the limited light, her eyes held a gleam that made him brace for what she was about to say next. "You're expecting me to come play, too? With you?"

Well, damn. "Anythin' wrong with that arrangement?" He saw no problem with it but he needed her to be willing, too. He'd also love to take things further than he had. Push her limits a bit. See what would make her squirm.

His dead dick actually perked up a little at that thought.

"Is that the only reason you want to book my band again?"

"What d'you think?"

"I'd like an answer, that's what I think."

Fuck. That attitude. It both aggravated him and also made him want her even more. "Why you askin' questions you already know the answers to?"

"Because I'm not going to assume anything. Assuming shit can screw you over. I don't like to be screwed over. Just as I'm sure you don't, either."

Point taken.

He took a deep inhale and blew out any remaining annoyance with it. "No, it ain't only 'cause I want you in my bed. Though, ain't gonna lie about that. Bookin' your band's also good business. The sex would be a bonus. I think if we get you comin' in once a month or so, then the locals will spread the word on how good you guys are. I could see you bringin' in a good crowd on a regular basis."

Her chin rose slightly. Again, that fucking attitude that made his fingers curl just like they would around her throat. "We'd want a stage fee plus a percentage."

She wanted a what? "A percentage of what?"

"Of the cover charge if you have one. If not, then a percentage of the bar take."

She practically begged him to let them play for tips the other night. Now she was making demands?

Get the fuck outta here.

"Gonna tell you this again. *You're* good but I ain't sure your band's that good for you to be actin' like some shark-like negotiator." When she opened her mouth, he continued. "Before you try to serve me another helpin' of that attitude, think about what I just said."

The woman had pipes on her, but her band was mediocre. Not horrible, but not top-notch, either. The talent was definitely not equally distributed throughout that band.

Her band would be considered good, possibly even great in this area. However, if they tried to book a gig at some big venue like a club in New York or L.A.?

Dodge doubted it would be happening until she scraped off the rest of them. Now, if she had the right musicians standing behind her...

"And *you're* not in the music industry, so I'm not sure why you'd think you're an expert."

"How 'bout the fact that I've been listenin' to music all my life? Good fuckin' music. Also, I've booked a lot of fuckin' bands to play on that stage downstairs. Is it Madison Square Garden? Fuck no. But I know what the fuck I heard when you played both nights. If it wasn't for you, I wouldn't have invited your guys back to play last night. That's the hard truth whether you wanna hear it or not. I don't hire garage bands, Syn. And hate to tell you, without you, that's what they are."

She opened her mouth and he braced for a hailstorm. But at this point, he was now ready to fight since someone needed an attitude adjustment and if he couldn't do that the way he'd like, he'd do it with his words.

He was trying to help her out and she had the balls to make demands.

What the actual fuck.

She should be thanking him, not giving him fucking heartburn.

She sucked on her teeth, but kept that chin raised. She also stared him down.

Oh yeah. Maybe it was good she wasn't sticking around. While she flipped his switch in a good way, it wouldn't take much more to switch it in the other direction.

"I'll think about it."

He casually shrugged, pretending he didn't give a fuck whether she did or she didn't.

"You do that. You got my offer and my number. Do with it what you will."

She nodded, even though it looked like that gesture took more effort than it should. "Well, it's been..." Her words drifted off and she dropped her gaze from him to the floor.

He knew exactly why she broke eye contact. That submissive action got his blood pumping all over again.

She had fire in her but knew when to back off.

He liked that.

A controllable flame.

As if she was an oil lantern and he adjusted the wick. He wanted to be the only one to make her burn hot.

The thought of anyone else touching her to make her burn like that…

He clenched his teeth.

He shouldn't have thoughts like this about her. It just didn't make any fucking sense.

As he waited for her to finish her thought, his heartbeat counted off the seconds.

When she finally did, he was more disappointed than he should be. "Gotta go," she mumbled and turned to head to the door.

Without any hesitation, she yanked it open, stepped out onto the landing and shut the door quietly behind her.

That soft click went through him like a gunshot.

Yeah, for now her leaving was for the best. He needed to figure things out, including why he was having these urges and thoughts about her.

More importantly, figure out if her brother was his brother, too.

Christ, why did that make his asshole pucker?

He got up and wandered naked over to the windows, using his fingers to separate the blinds only enough so he could peer out but not be spotted. She appeared from the rear door of Crazy Pete's. But instead of rushing to the bus, she paused in the alley and her head, covered with the cat-eared hood, tipped down.

His heart began to thump in his chest as he waited to see what she did next.

Did she forget something?

Why was she standing out there in the freezing cold in that goddamn sweatshirt not moving?

A few heartbeats later, she lifted her head, glanced over her shoulder and up at his windows.

Fuck.

He held his breath as she continued to stare up at him. He knew she couldn't see him but it still made his pounding heart skip a beat.

Then she moved.

All the air he'd been holding rushed from him as she hurried to the waiting skoolie and disappeared inside.

Not even a minute later, black smoke bellowed from the rear of the bus as whoever was driving hit the accelerator and the piece of shit moved forward.

Heading out of Manning Grove and taking Syn with it.

Chapter Fourteen

As soon as Dodge opened the door to The Barn, the music hit him. Above that, he could hear the shouts of his brothers drinking, playing darts, pool and just fucking around with each other.

Smoke, both of the tobacco variety and the good shit, hovered in the air.

No ol' ladies, sweet butts or prospects were in sight since none were allowed in the clubhouse during a church meeting.

As he drove his Power Wagon down the farm's lane, his eyes had automatically bounced to where The Synners' skoolie had been parked.

Of course, the spot was empty.

She was gone.

For the hundredth time over the past two days, he told himself that was for the best.

In a way, he was glad she didn't give him her number because he would've been tempted to call or text her every time he thought of her.

Possibly to even tell her to come back.

That alone was fucking ridiculous. She was aggravating and stubborn. Not to mention, way too fucking young.

Also for the hundredth time since early Saturday morning, he reminded himself that he preferred women his age. Sometimes, even older.

Shade had it right hooking up with Chelle who was eleven years older than him. The man was happy as fuck. Well, as happy as the man could be.

Even so...

Dodge couldn't get her out of his head. He never should've fucked her. It only made things worse for him. Only burrowed her more deeply under his damn skin.

Maybe he just needed to flay off his skin, scrape her clean, and find someone else to concentrate on. Get his mind focused on something or someone else.

Anyone but her.

He could even get in a session with Billie. A session where she'd push him hard enough that he'd actually consider using his safe word. He'd never had to use it before, but maybe that would make his brain switch gears.

Do a whole reset.

He could do that later after the meeting and after he talked to Sig.

That was his other issue. What if by some crazy act of fate, the Fury's VP was actually the same Sig she mentioned?

How many people in the world had that name? Probably very few. And what were the odds that the Sig he knew was the same person as her brother?

With his fucking luck, the odds were damn good.

He headed directly to the bar and ducked behind it to grab the tequila and poured himself a double. On second thought... He tipped the bottle again and made it a triple.

He'd need it to talk to Sig.

But first, they had club business to discuss, along with patching in Tater and Possum.

The two prospects weren't around even though they were given the night off from Crazy Pete's since he had Micah and Scar working the bar. Most likely one of the officers had told them to go back in the bunkhouse with the excuse that prospects weren't allowed to participate in club meetings.

This way they could be surprised.

Trip sidled up to Deacon. "You got their patches?"

The club's treasurer nodded. "Yeah, under the bar. I can hand them to you when you're ready."

Trip clapped his hands sharply together once. His signature signal for everyone to pay attention.

When that didn't work, Judge bellowed out a, "Yo, fucknuts, pay attention. Your prez is about to speak."

That worked more effectively to quiet everyone's running mouth and get their attention turned toward Trip, who stepped up onto his "box" to raise him above the rest of them.

Dodge moved from behind the bar and shrugged out of his cut for a second to remove his leather jacket. A fire was roaring in the center fireplace and The Barn was warm as fuck.

He tossed his jacket on the end of the bar and slipped his colors back on since he felt naked without them. As soon as he turned, a hand grabbed his arm.

That hand, which belonged to Sig, tugged the neckline of his thermal shirt away from his neck. "Fuck, brother. You get into a fight with a fuckin' cat? Those are some hellacious claw marks."

Shit. "Somethin' like that," he muttered. He had no way to cover the scratches that still marked up his neck. Not without using women's makeup and fuck if he was doing that. Excuses were easier.

Dodge jerked free, pulling his neckline back in place and tugging it up a little higher.

With a knowing grin, Sig then spotted Dodge's exposed forearms, where he had his sleeves pushed up to his elbows. He yanked them back down until they covered him to his wrists.

"You never had to fight one off like that before," Sig said with his brow drawn low. "Also didn't know you were into that."

Dodge shot him a pointed look. "We all got our thing."

Sig grinned and his brown eyes lit up. "That we do, brother."

The irony of this conversation was not fucking lost on Dodge and he was thankful as fuck when Trip did his single clap again. "Don't make me get the fuckin' gavel. 'Cause if I gotta climb those fuckin' steps, I ain't gonna hit it on the bar to get your fuckin' attention, I'm gonna clock you in the head with it, instead."

"Or you could use The Punisher," Judge suggested, the corners of his eyes crinkled. "It's a bit closer. Actually, I don't mind doin' it for you, Prez. I've been practicin' Whac-A-Mole with Daze."

"You teachin' her to take over from you and be our first female enforcer?" Cage shouted out from the back of the pack with a snicker.

Hell, that question was a good way to get everyone to shut the fuck up.

"A female enforcer?" Dutch grumped near Dodge. "That ain't ever happenin'."

"Never say never, old man," Rook said, wearing a smirk. "Jet would be a good one."

"Women got their place in this club, and it ain't as an officer," Dutch said next.

"Not even as a member, either. Ain't that in the by-laws?" Deacon asked.

Trip shook his head. "As an officer yourself, you should fuckin' know what's in the by-laws."

"Well, it ain't like I walk around with a copy in my fuckin' back pocket."

"Alrighty," Trip shouted, rubbing at his forehead. "Enough of this shit. Dutch is right, so drop it. If women want a club, they can start their own."

"The fuck they are," Shade growled. He probably felt strongly about that idea since he had three women in his household he had to worry about.

"Not *our* women. Other women," Trip clarified and then lifted a hand. "And what I just fuckin' said does not hit our women's ears. You get me?"

"Yeah, Trip don't wanna be beaten to death with The Punisher durin' the night," Easy said on a laugh. "Stella would make a great prez. Don't tell her she can't do or be somethin', cause knowin' her, she'd probably purposely do it to prove otherwise."

That was for damn sure. Having an Original's blood surging through her veins, Stella was truly Trip's queen and could easily step into his place. But Dodge was keeping that shit to himself. He might be a dumbass, but he wasn't that much of a damn dumbass.

"Stel's got enough on her plate. Nobody plant that fuckin' seed."

"Like you planted yours?" Deacon asked on a half-snort.

Trip yanked his black baseball cap off his head, scraped his fingers through his hair, then slammed it back on. A gesture he tended to do when his temper was flaring.

That also was a signal for everyone to get back to business before he lost his shit.

"Someone go get those two fuckers," the prez ordered. "They should be included in tonight's club business. We'll hand them their patches and get that over with first."

Whip quickly slipped through the door between The Barn and the bunkhouse to retrieve the two prospects.

"All the sweet butts here?" Trip asked nobody in particular.

"Yeah," Sig answered. "In the kitchen gettin' shit prepared for the celebration after."

Trip nodded. "All right, everyone shut the fuck up, then. They got no fuckin' clue that we all voted already, so when I tell them, let's get them goin' and pucker their assholes a bit first."

Even if the vote had gone the opposite way, Dodge would've still wanted to keep them on at Crazy Pete's. They both did a good job at the bar and good help was hard to find. Now that they would be patched over, he'd have to talk to Stella about what to offer them salary-wise.

As prospects, they were free labor. They got a roof over their head, a place to lay that head and food and booze to fill their bellies. If they needed extra scratch, they had to earn that elsewhere. Working at Pete's, they at least earned tips. It wouldn't be enough for them to live on if everything else wasn't already handed to them.

They might be treated like slave-labor but their basics were covered by the club. Anything above that was for them to figure out.

Even Dutch made them work off any repairs or service needed to their sleds.

Being a prospect usually sucked ass. As a prospect, Dodge had it easy and he was well aware of that fact. He only had to do half the time as the newer prospects and he'd been lucky to fall into the position of manager at Crazy Pete's since it was a solid fucking job. One that didn't need a formal education.

Other than the occasional required training by the Liquor Control Board, he just needed to be good with people and have common sense. Two skills a lot of people lacked.

If he hadn't learned that in prison, he learned it by dealing with customers. Though, people made him scratch his fucking head every damn day. He also wondered how they functioned in life.

The complete room went silent as soon as the rear door opened again with Whip leading the way. Tater and Possum followed slowly. As much as Dodge worked with them, he could recognize the worry on their faces, even though they were doing their damnedest to hide it.

Dodge pinned his lips together to keep from grinning. Trip didn't need to fuck with them, their assholes were already puckered.

"Tater Twat and Pus Sack, get your asses up here front and center," Judge bellowed, pointing to a spot in front of where Trip stood on the box. He also now had The Punisher in his hand and was thwapping it against his palm. That sound alone should make all of their assholes pucker. Especially Cage's.

Cage's blanket party was a day none of them would ever forget and also made them all think twice before doing something stupid.

Like fucking a brother's sister on a pool table.

At least his excuse was that he didn't know who she was. And some of the blame landed on Sig, since never once had he mentioned he had a fucking sister. Or half-sister. Whatever.

Ignorance should be a valid excuse in this situation. One he hoped Sig would accept if he and Syn were actually related.

They all had secrets but that particular one was huge. Dodge also couldn't understand why Sig would keep Syn a secret.

His only hope was that those two didn't share even one drop of blood.

For fuck's sake, let that be the fucking case…

As the prospects approached, a few of Dodge's brothers backed away cautiously from where Trip and Judge stood, playing their part in squeezing the prospects' assholes even tighter. Both Tater and Possum shot a glance toward Dodge and he quickly put a grim expression on his face and shook his head in a way that read "Sorry, can't help you. You two are on your own." Both sets of eyes widened and both men quickly glanced at each other. They were also deathly pale.

Dodge hoped like fuck someone was secretly recording this.

"We know you've been buggin' Dodge about gettin' patched in. Lemme first say, you shouldn't have been buggin' anyone about that. You got me?"

Both prospects, now standing side-by-side in front of Trip both nodded in unison. The two were so damn opposite. Tater was of average height but very round and Possum was taller and lean. Not as skinny as Bones but damn close. They kind of reminded Dodge of Laurel and Hardy. Not that those two young bikers would know who the fuck they were.

"Should we make 'em get on their knees to get what's comin' to them?" Judge asked, still striking his palm with the stained club. Everyone assumed those stains were made from Originals' blood. Or strangers' blood.

Either way, someone's blood.

Even from where Dodge stood, he could see both of them became an even whiter shade of pale. At least they weren't green. Trip would be pissed if one of them projectile-puked on him.

"Should make them lick my fuckin' boots first for what they did," Trip said.

"What did—" Possum started.

Judge cut him off with merely a glare and a very loud slap of The Punisher against his huge palm.

Dodge covered his mouth to cover his reaction when he swore he heard Possum swallow all the way from where he stood.

When Tater began to sink to his knees, Trip barked at him, "No. You stand and take what's comin' to you like a fuckin' man. We ain't pussies here. Only men become Fury members. Remember that."

Tater locked his knees, though Dodge saw him sway a bit.

Trip held out his hand towards Judge as if he wanted The Punisher. Instead, Deacon leaned over the bar and put two Blood Fury top rockers in his hand. How the fuck Deke was keeping a straight face, Dodge had no idea. He was only glad that he was standing behind the prospects instead of in front of them. Otherwise, he might have lost it and gave it all away.

"Now," Trip continued, while holding the patches out in front of him with both hands palms up like he was holding a sacrifice. "You men or pussies?"

"Men!" both prospects shouted, finally getting a clue on what was happening.

"Worthy of wearin' the Blood Fury colors?"

"Fuck yeah!" both shouted again.

"Bet you're ready to get out of that fuckin' bunkroom."

"Hell yeah," Tater yelled.

They both hated sharing a room with Scar and vice versa. No way would Dodge want to close his fucking eyes in a dark room when Scar was just feet away. If Scar was his cellmate, Dodge probably never would have slept.

"You know what wearin' these colors on your backs mean, right? I don't gotta go over how important these patches are, right?"

"Fuck no!" both shouted, color now back in their faces

and no longer scared about dying. Their pucker factor was now down to zero.

Dodge grinned.

"We all voted the other night and as you know, it's gotta be unanimous. And lucky for you two, it was."

Both nodded as Trip handed them their top rockers. Deacon came around the bar with the bottom rockers and the smaller square "MC" patches, saying, "Gonna get those prospect patches removed this week and replaced with your permanent ones."

Trip picked up again from there. "The only thing left to do is pick your road name. I'm sure as fuck that you two have spent the last fuckin' year thinkin' about that. And I'm also sure neither of you wanna keep the name we gave you. So, let's hear them." He glanced at Tater first.

"Dozer."

Dozer?

Just like Dodge, Trip lifted an eyebrow at that, shook his head, then glanced over at Possum.

"Woody."

A variety of noises came from the brothers surrounding Dodge. He'd had the same reaction as them, except his was a muttered, "Christ."

"You look like a fuckin' tater tot and you look like a fuckin' tampon. But you want Dozer and Woody?" Trip shrugged and shook his head again.

Next to him, Judge snorted and dropped his head, also shaking it.

"Can kinda understand the Dozer name," Ozzy said on a laugh. "Since he's about as fast as one."

"And as big as one, too," Dutch added on a huff.

"Where'd you get Woody from?" Trip asked the former prospect.

"Name's Elwood. Figured Woody would work."

"I got a woody…" Deacon started, grabbing his crotch with a sly grin.

"That one might not be so smart," Trip told Possum. "It's almost the same as pickin' Pecker Head." His head twisted toward Sig. "Remember that name for a future prospect."

Sig gave his brother a thumbs up.

"It's a name I was called my whole life," Possum explained. "Well, 'til I became a prospect."

"Now's the perfect time to change it," Trip suggested.

"Don't wanna change it."

Trip's eyebrows shot up. "Okay, then fuck it. Possum is now officially Woody." He shook his head again. "Good fuckin' luck with that around here."

"We got access to the sweet butts now, right?" Dozer, formerly known as Tater Tot, asked with his eyes all lit the fuck up.

Christ. The first thing Dozer wanted to do was bust a fucking nut. Dodge couldn't blame him since the man tended to strike out when trying to pick up randoms at Pete's. It wasn't only the fact he was shaped like a potato, but it also had to do with him not having anywhere to bang them. Most women weren't into having sex in a bunkbed where anyone could walk in and watch. And would.

Now he'd have his own room and the sweet butts wouldn't turn him down. Well, they could but knew better. Being available to any of the brothers was part of the "job requirement" of being a sweet butt.

If they didn't like it, they could find a new job.

"Yeah, full access just like you have in the kitchen," Judge said, smirking. "But I'm sure you'll be inside them less than the fridge."

"All right. We got more important shit to discuss than… *Dozer* bulldozin' one of the sweet butts." Trip made a face and faked a shudder. "Let's get to it so we can get to partyin' 'stead of pukin'.'"

Ozzy snorted and slapped Dozer in the chest. "Now I ain't gonna get that image outta my fuckin' head." He faked a gag.

"I'm so ready to fuckin' party!" Woody yelled, pumping a fist into the air and ignoring everyone else.

Trip's eyebrows rose and Woody quickly controlled his excitement. "All right. Next order of business... Took me forever, but finally came up with a motto that belongs to us. Not the Originals, *us*. 'Cause even though a lot of us might have that Original blood in us... We. Are. Not. Them!" The last four words were shouted. "And I wanna make sure we never become them, either."

A roar rose up in The Barn and some boot stomping accompanied it. Trip being so fucking passionate about the club made everyone else's blood start pumping, too. The Fury brotherhood would not exist without him.

He continued, "Wanna know what you think about it since, like I said, it belongs to us. All of us. You don't like it, speak up. 'Cause if no one objects, it's gonna be official. We'll move the sign above the front door and hang it on the wall inside here. I'll get a sign with the new motto to replace it. Yeah?"

A bunch of "Fuck yeahs!" circled the room, including one from Dodge.

He had thanked Rook before for inviting him into this brotherhood, but after tonight he was going to thank him again. Also Trip. He owed both of those men since they'd tossed a life preserver to save him from sinking. His last bid inside had been the roughest one to date and he'd been thankful for Rook having his fucking back.

If he hadn't, Dodge might have ended up doing life since, a couple of times, he'd been close to shanking some motherfuckers. More than a couple.

So, yeah, he owed Rook. He also owed the man shouting out their new proposed motto.

From the ashes we rise,
For our brothers we live and die!

At the end, Trip pumped his fist in the air and everyone once again hooted and hollered. Once it quieted down, he asked, "Anyone opposed to that? Anyone got anything better?"

Of course, nobody did.

It wasn't the motto that made their brotherhood, it was the men he stood among.

Dodge's gaze circled the group. Family. All were now his fucking family. And, like it should be, they'd die for each other. Unlike the Originals who, in the end, did each other dirty.

"Let's do this again. You all know how this works." Trip shouted, "From the ashes we rise…"

Everyone yelled in unison, "For our brothers we live and die!" also raising their fists into the air.

Another loud "Fuck yeah!" was shouted out from somewhere behind Dodge. More stomping of boots and pounding of chests erupted around him, causing a chill to run through him.

"Haven't we already risen from those ashes, though?" Whip asked.

Trip found him in the crowd. "You never stop risin'. 'Cause the moment you do, is the exact fuckin' moment you begin to fall."

"So, I guess that's settled," Deke began. "I'll get the Amish to make up a sign and install it above the door."

Trip nodded and turned back to the rest of them. "Now, in other fuckin' news…" He handed the floor over to Judge.

"Speakin' of risin', as you all know, the Shirleys are definitely tryin' to rise out of their own sludge. The activity up there's increasin' every fuckin' day. These past coupla days the clan had a crew up there doin' a shitload of repairs on the remaining structures. Seems like they're in a rush to move back in before winter hits hard. This is a problem we're keepin' a close eye on."

"What are we gonna do about it?" Cage asked, his tone as sharp as a blade.

"Like I said the other night, we don't fuckin' know what the feds are doin' yet. Right now it's a wait and see," Trip answered.

"Anybody spot any federal pigs lurkin' around?" Easy asked.

"No, but that don't mean they ain't lurkin'," Judge answered. "They ain't gonna be settin' up a lawn chair at the bottom of Hillbilly Hill to monitor those inbred mother-fuckers."

"So, we're just gonna wait and let them return instead of takin' them out as they come in?" Rook asked, just as sharply as Cage. There wasn't a lot Rook gave a shit about but his niece, Dyna, was one of them. "They'd be easier to deal with in small batches than a whole fuckin' clan at one shot."

"Agreed, but *again*," Trip sighed, "if the feds are watchin' them and we go up there, guess who's also gonna get caught up in their fuckin' net? Us. We want that? I don't. I gotta life outside of concrete walls and razor wire that I kinda like. We also don't wanna land on their radar. Last thing we want is them keepin' track of us. That could get messy for those times we need to stay under that same damn radar. You catchin' what I'm puttin' down? What if we need to take care of business and agents start sittin' on the crematorium 'cause of suspicious activity? Then what? We're fucked. We gotta be smart about how this is gonna be handled. Nobody wants to wipe those fuckers out more than me."

"Sig and Cage," Shade reminded the prez. Dodge doubted Trip needed that reminder. None of them did.

Trip continued, "Look, when Red was taken, she was taken from all of us. Same with Dyna. Dyna is *our* child, not just Cage and Jemma's. Just like Daisy, Jude, Ry, Chelle's girls, now Dane and soon my own son are all of ours. It's our duty to protect and love every fuckin' child no matter whose fuckin' loins they came from. I've said this before, but gonna say it again, your child is my child. Mine will be yours. We raise these kids together. And if we do it well, they'll be the next generation of Fury. I want them to be better than us. I wanna be proud of them. Sure you do, too."

Silence descended over the group because no one was going to argue any of that. Anyone who did didn't belong as part of the Fury. The family connection was strong within the brotherhood. Just like Trip strived for and just like it should be.

Without the Fury, Dodge wouldn't have shit. He'd be back doing the same old, same old and none of that "same old" had been any good.

He'd been on a straight path to nowheresville.

"Yeah so, Trip's right. We need to remain smart and also vigilant. We said it before and we'll repeat it as much as we need to. We can't get sloppy and we also need to expect some backlash from them," Judge added. "Those mother-fuckers are too fuckin' stupid to know when to quit."

"I mean, we could let them strike first and if the feds don't come outta the woodwork, then we know they're not payin' attention," Rev suggested.

"It's a risk either way. Either we finally get that war we thought was comin' 'til the feds stepped in or we end up casualties of the feds," Trip told them. "We gotta protect ourselves from the Shirleys but we also gotta protect ourselves from the feds. Two sides of the same damn coin."

"All of those hillbilly goat fuckers," Sig said, "need to die a slow fuckin' torturous death."

"By chokin' on their own severed dicks," Easy said with a smirk. "That was badass, Sig. But I still got nightmares about that. Sometimes I wake up in the middle of the night just to make sure my dick's still attached."

Dodge was pretty sure they all did. Those who didn't witness it firsthand, heard about it in great detail. Definitely the stuff of nightmares.

"If they strike first and the feds don't show themselves, that means we can do what we need to do how we need to do it," Shade spoke up in the deliberate way he normally talked, picking each word carefully.

The longer he lived with Chelle, the faster his speech became but it was still slower than normal. Dodge had no idea why being with Chelle made a difference, but it was an obvious change. Maybe it had to do with his ol' lady being a school librarian.

Dodge didn't know or care because either way, it wasn't his business. Shade probably had the most secrets out of all his brothers and that was okay with him. He was just glad that the quiet, but deadly, man with the long, curly hair was on their side. The man had crazy-ass knife skills that all the rest of them envied.

"Still risky but a risk we might have to take," Trip answered.

"Say we wipe out all the mouth breathers up there? Then what? It's possible they'll just keep comin' 'cause their goal is to breed and increase their numbers. When the fuck will it all end? Will we never be able to live in peace?" Cage asked. "Will our families never be safe? Are we always gonna have to fuckin' worry about our most vulnerable? Our women and children?"

"Best bet would be to blow up that fuckin' mountain so

there's nothin' left for them to go back to," Sig growled. "Then they'd have no choice but to move the fuck on."

"Yeah, easy, right?" Trip's question was sharp with sarcasm. "Simply get our hands on enough ammonium nitrate to blow that motherfuckin' hill to smithereens. Even purchasin' a small amount of explosives will get law enforcement sittin' up and takin' notice. And, anyway, we'd need more than the amount used to blow open a hole large enough for a tunnel through the side of a mountain. One, we could never afford it, and two, nobody here knows how to handle that shit. It ain't like just lightin' a fuckin' fuse. So, let's get back to reality and think of a real solution."

"If we burn it down, they'll just rebuild. If we kill them all, they'll just breed more elsewhere and possibly return to that mountain. So, is there any real solution?" Deacon asked.

Trip dropped his head and rubbed at his forehead under the brim of his ball cap.

Dodge got it. It had to be frustrating as all fuck to try to keep everyone safe. Trip was doing his best to protect his "family" from a crazy motherfucking clan of inbreds who were too stupid to know not to go back to the scene of their previous crime.

Dodge hated to think about it, but having the feds handle them might be the best bet. But if the Shirleys ended up laying low for a while and not doing anything illegal, not giving the feds a reason to haul them off that mountain again, then what?

They were a threat to the Fury no matter what.

Dodge did not want to be in Trip's boots. No way, no how. No one else did, either. They all relied on the man to lead them and to make the right decisions.

Now that Stella was knocked up, it had to have created more pressure on the man.

The whole issue with the Shirleys all stemmed back to

Sig finding Red on that mountain in the condition she was found. Would any of them have done anything different? Probably not. Sig saved Red's life and saved Levi's life, too. In turn, Red saved Sig's life.

Sig had been on a path to destruction. Trip had been desperate to help his brother and had been failing. Who would've thought Sig's savior would come running naked and pregnant down a mountain?

Nobody in their right fucking mind.

Fate.

That was what it was. No other way to put it.

They found each other at the right damn moment.

If Syn was Sig's sister, did fate drop her in Dodge's path? Or was it merely coincidence?

As soon as this meeting was over, he was pulling Sig and Trip aside. *After* he drank more tequila and before Sig disappeared like he tended to do. He was never away from Red for too long.

Though, tonight he might not head up to his apartment right away since once the patch party started the ol' ladies, the prospects and the sweet butts could join in.

"Anyhow, the point of this discussion was to tell you the officers are open to any and all ideas." Trip shot a quick glance at Sig. "Except blowin' up a mountain." He scanned the group again. "We need *reasonable* ideas. This was also a reminder to keep your eyes and ears open. You'll probably get sick of us tellin' you that, but it is what the fuck it is. I'd rather you get sick of us than end up dead or back in a concrete fuckin' box. You all get that?"

Muttered "yeahs" circled Dodge.

"You report back anythin' to me, Judge or Sig. Even if you're not sure if it's important. Right now, I'm leanin' toward lettin' them strike first on our territory like we tried before. Before those damn feds stepped in. We thought that would be the end of it, we shoulda known better."

"Stupid is as stupid does," Judge said.

"Yeah, they got a dozen brain cells they share amongst them and even less teeth. We gotta assume they'll never learn that fuckin' with us will end up fuckin' them harder in the end."

"It's a lesson we need to teach them," Cage said. "They touch me and mine again..." Dutch's youngest son shook his head.

"Then they're gonna deal with Dad, me and Jet, too. They ain't touchin' Jemma or Dyna again," Rook promised. "If I gotta go back inside, then I'm goin' back inside."

Dutch, who was standing behind his oldest son, whacked Rook in the head. "We wear these colors for a fuckin' reason. We all gotta stick together, asshole. You start doin' vigilante shit and the same shit that happened to the Originals will happen to this club."

"Agreed," Trip said. "We all gotta be on the same fuckin' page and can't be goin' off on a tangent on our own. That could break down the very foundation of this club just as quickly as backstabbin' and the rest of the bullshit the Originals ended up doin'." He took a deep breath and finished up with, "All right, enough of this heavy shit, it's time to fuckin' party. Brothers, message your women. Whip, let anyone in the bunkhouse know they can join us. Somebody get the music crankin', the beer and booze flowin' and I need a fuckin' hit of some quality-assed Kush." He stepped off his box and glanced around. "Who's got some?"

The prez disappeared behind a couple of Dodge's brothers, but Dodge needed to corral him at the same time as Sig.

Dodge ducked behind the bar again, grabbed the tequila bottle and didn't even bother with a glass this time. *Fuck that.* He tipped the bottle to his lips and let that shit slide down his throat and warm his gut, hoping it bolstered him enough for a conversation he wasn't looking forward to.

Drinking tequila straight in that amount was a bit rough, but he had a feeling the conversation he was about to have would be even rougher.

He saw Sig standing next to Trip, passing a bong back and forth.

Good, maybe that would mellow the Temper Twins out a touch.

He took another long swallow of the Jose Cuervo, whacked his fist against his chest while it pooled in his gut, then slammed the bottle on the bar.

Let's fuckin' do this.

He moved around the end of the bar and stepped up to the half-brothers. Trip offered him the bong and Dodge accepted it without hesitation.

A bit of Kush on top of the booze wouldn't hurt, either.

Once he let the smoke roll from his mouth, he said, "Gotta run somethin' past you, brother."

"Who?" Trip asked with a frown.

"Sig. But need you to stick around, too."

Sig's frown suddenly matched Trip's. "Somethin' to do with the Shirleys?"

Dodge shook his head. "No."

The VP's frown turned into a scowl. "Red?"

Dodge shook his head again. Maybe doing this right now wasn't the best time since he had those fucking scratches marking up his neck. Sig might put two and two together.

It also might trigger his temper. It was more than ugly when Sig lost his shit on Vernon Shirley, the now very dead former clan leader. It was the work of a man who had been pushed past sanity.

Trip had a habit of touching Stella when he needed to bring his anger down a few notches. Maybe it worked the same way with Sig and Red.

"Red comin' down to join us?"

Instantly, it was like someone pushed a button on the man, Sig spine snapped straight and every muscle tensed. "Why?"

Shit. "Just wonderin'."

"She need to be a part of whatever you're runnin' past me?"

"Nah." He just needed to get this the fuck over with.

He could be worried for nothing.

Or he could have every reason to worry.

Shit could go either way.

It was the not knowing that bothered him.

Chapter Fifteen

DODGE PULLED a hand-rolled from his cut, lit it and once he took a deep inhale to fill his lungs, he slowly let the smoke slide back out while he asked, "You got a sister?"

If he thought Sig was tense before, he just watched the man turn to concrete. The VP's eyes narrowed. "Say again?"

Jesus. "You got a sister?" Dodge asked again, louder this time. Crazy enough, Trip, who had also gone stiff, echoed the same damn question at the same damn time, so it ended up in stereo.

Sig's dark eyes flicked to his half-brother for a second, then settled back on Dodge. "What the fuck you talkin' about?"

"You know, a fuckin' sister. A siblin' that mighta came outta Silvia's snatch. You should know what a fuckin' sister is," Trip growled.

Better Trip be an asshole to Sig than Dodge. Because he'd been tempted to say something similar.

"Maybe Red and Stella should be a part of this conversation," Dodge suggested, hoping neither man exploded like the aluminum nitrate Trip said they'd need to blow up Hill-billy Hill.

Sig shook his head and glanced around. He then tipped his head toward the stairs leading up to the executive meeting room. "Upstairs."

Hell, since the man didn't instantly deny having a sister, maybe it was for the best they take it somewhere more private. Especially since The Barn was getting loud and rowdy and would only get worse as the night went on.

If Sig would've said no, the discussion would've been over in an instant, Dodge would be free and clear, and they all could concentrate on getting shit-faced.

Dodge was already heading in that direction with the tequila and pot, but he still had a ways to go until he hit the level of shit-faced. He hardly drank when he worked the bar at Pete's, but when it came to down time, he liked to let loose.

Right now, nothing was loose. Not on him, Sig or Trip.

"Yeah, upstairs," Trip said, ripping off his baseball cap and slamming it back on, clearly agitated.

Dodge nodded and headed in that direction. He rarely climbed those steps since he wasn't an officer and had no reason to go up there. The few times he had was when he took a sweet butt or a smokin' hot hang-around up there for a bit of fun during a pig roast or party.

Or, *hell*, just any night that ended in a Y and he happened to be at the farm instead of Pete's when the clubhouse was swarming with available and agreeable pussy.

As he ascended the steps, he had a flashback of him, Ozzy and Easy running a train on some chick who came up from Harrisburg thinking it would be fun to party with an MC. They decided to give her the full experience.

Afterward, Ozzy said the difference between them and the Originals was the Originals wouldn't have stopped if she tried to back out. Luckily, she didn't change her mind and loved every fucking second of it.

It had been a good night.

Tonight might not be such a good fucking night.

He'd find out soon enough.

As soon as the three of them stepped into the loft, Trip shut the door and turned, planting his hands on his hips.

Sig was now standing next to the long table with his hands on his hips also, but with his head tipped down as he stared at the center carving of the Fury's insignia. When his brother said nothing, Trip asked Dodge, "Why you askin' if Sig has a sister?"

"The band that parked here on the farm? The band who played Pete's Wednesday and Friday nights? Where it was parked he mighta missed the name spray-painted on the side."

"He mighta but I didn't. Said The Synners."

Dodge nodded, keeping one eye on Sig as he talked to Trip, whose eyebrows rose.

"That bus had Sig's sister on it?"

"Can't answer that 'til I know if Sig has a fuckin' sister." At this point, he could pretty much guess. Now he just needed to find out what his sister's name was.

Though, he was sure he knew that already, too.

From the corner of his eye, Dodge saw Sig turn. "Who gave you those fuckin' scratches?"

Ah, fuck. Maybe it was best to tell a half-truth right about now. "A chick I hooked up with Friday night."

Sig's eyes narrowed on his neck. "She fightin' you off or was she just that into it?"

Dodge fought the instinct to cover his neck with his hand. "Ain't into forcin' women, Sig. Would think by now you know me better than that."

"Don't know what the fuck you're into," Sig grumbled.

"He don't need to force anyone, brother," Trip assured

him. "Watched him many a night at Pete's workin' it and I can tell you he don't gotta work that hard."

Dodge wanted to get this shit over with and wasn't sure why Sig was hesitating and drawing this out. He pulled his cell out of his back pocket, hit the power button and pulled up his most recent pictures. Three were of Syn on stage. "This her?"

If Syn would've caught him taking those photos, he would've just told her he took them of all the bands that played at Pete's for promotional purposes. The only issue was, all three photos were only of her. None of her bandmates made it into the frame.

On purpose.

Sig came over and snagged the phone from Dodge's fingers. He squinted at each photo, swiping back and forth between the three.

"Don't swipe too far," Dodge warned him.

Sig's head lifted and he glared at Dodge. "You better not got naked photos of my sister on here."

"Ain't no naked pics of Syn." Thank fuck there weren't.

"So, I'm guessin' that's her?" Trip asked, confiscating the phone from Sig and glancing through the photos.

"Ain't seen her since she was little, so can't be sure."

"Christ, brother, shouldn't be difficult to figure out. She told me she had a brother named Sig. What are the odds that there are another set of siblin's out there with the same damn names?" Dodge asked, beginning to get annoyed. "You got a sister named Syn?"

"Yeah."

Well, fuck.

"Fuck," Sig echoed Dodge's thoughts, drawing his fingers down his beard. That was when Dodge noticed how tight the man's jaw was. "Wasn't that band broke as fuck?"

"Yeah," Dodge answered. "They don't got shit. They didn't even have fuckin' heat 'til I helped them out." Maybe pointing that out would help soften the blow of him fucking Sig's sister. Who also happened to be twelve years younger than him.

Though, that shouldn't matter since Sig out of everyone was into women on the younger side. Like *young*. If he had the fucking nerve to point out how much younger Syn was compared to Dodge, then he'd have to remind the VP that his own ol' lady was seven years younger than him.

Sig narrowed his eyes on him. "Ain't she livin' on that bus with a bunch of guys?"

"Three."

Sig snagged Dodge's cell phone back from his brother, looked at the pictures once more and then handed it back to Dodge. "Why you got pics of her?"

Dodge's eyes sliced to Trip and back. The prez was smart enough to sort truth from lies, but he was going to have to risk it in this situation. He was not telling Sig that he had quickly become obsessed with his baby sister.

He might be a dumbass but he was smart enough to know better than to confess that.

"To..." *Nope, try again.* "For this. To see if you recognized her. She didn't have a clue what your last name was, which was fuckin' strange for siblin's. She definitely didn't know you were a part of the Fury or here in Manning Grove. And anyway, that fuckin' bus was parked a few hundred yards from your apartment, Sig."

"Lost track of her," he growled. "And you shoulda told me before that fuckin' bus drove away yesterday."

"Don't fuckin' blame me for losin' track of your own sister. Or not payin' attention to the huge fuckin' name painted on the side of a damn bus like a fuckin' billboard."

"We lost track of each other," the man snarled, practically baring his teeth.

Dodge lifted his palms. "Look, no point in fightin' about

it. You're right, shoulda texted you and asked." But at the time he had a naked Syn in his bed.

"Agreed," Trip said. "Can't turn back time, so we gotta figure out where to go from here. And how to contact her. You wanna reconnect with her, right?"

Instead of answering Trip's question, Sig asked, "You got her number?"

Shit. Dodge braced. "No."

"What the fuck?" Sig exploded.

For fuck's sake, this was going exactly how he expected. "I asked and she wouldn't give it to me."

"Why? She gave you those fuckin' scratches but wouldn't give you her number? Must be a reason for that."

He ignored the scratches question because he was not confirming that shit. Not now with how Sig's temper was simmering. Maybe not ever. What he and Syn had done in his bed—and on the pool table—was not the man's fucking business. Just like the shit Sig had done with women before he found Red was really none of his.

"Let's just say she likes to be difficult... like you. So, it makes sense you two are related. But I gave her my number since she refused to give me hers."

"Maybe she didn't want a repeat performance. You must not've left a good impression." Trip smirked.

Dodge ignored that, too.

That smirk quickly disappeared. "Okay, let's get back to the immediate issue here and not Dodge's performance or the possibility that it was Sig's sister who left those scratches." One of Trip's eyebrows lifted. "'Cause I'm gonna assume that if it was her, they were left before you figured out who she was."

He nodded, even though he wasn't sure if knowing would've made a difference.

He wanted Syn before and he still wanted Syn now. Sig being her brother hadn't changed that one fucking bit.

Trip turned toward Sig and the two half-brothers stared at each other for a few seconds. Dodge could feel the tension ramping up between them.

Those two men *were* aluminum fucking nitrate and both highly explosive.

Maybe he should duck under the heavy wood table and take cover from any fallout.

"You never once told me, your fuckin' brother, that you have a sister. Not fuckin' once, Sig. Not once in the last three fuckin' years. Kinda an important fact to reveal, don'cha think?" Both eyebrows were now hiked up so high they were hidden under his ball cap.

"Nobody's business," Sig muttered.

"Nobody's fuckin' business?" Trip bellowed. He tilted his head and stared at Sig with flared nostrils, not looking any kind of happy. Of course he wouldn't. The prez was big on family. It was why he hunted down Sig and made him VP when the man didn't deserve it at the time. When he was nothing but a derailed train. "Wanna explain that? To me, your fuckin' *brother*?"

"She ain't *your* sister and, like I said, lost track of her."

"She's family," Trip yelled at him.

"She ain't *your* family," Sig yelled back. "She don't share a goddamn drop of blood with you. She don't even got Fury blood in her."

"Bullshit. Close enough. She's Silvia's daughter and she's *your* sister. That makes her *my* sister, too. Blood or not."

Both men had squared off with fingers curled into loose fists. It wouldn't take much for those fists to tighten and begin swinging. If that happened, Dodge wasn't getting in the middle of that shit. They could beat the fuck out of each other for all he cared. Maybe it was what they needed.

And, anyway, their women would make them regret getting into a brawl with each other. That alone would cause more pain and discomfort for the two men than an actual fight. Both women would be pissed and disappointed. Stella leaning more towards pissed, Red more towards disappointed.

Dodge knew for a fact Sig did not want to disappoint his ol' lady. Maybe they needed to be reminded of that. That might cool them both down a few degrees.

"Stel and Red are gonna have your nuts in their fists," Dodge squeezed his hand in the air like he was trying to crack a nut barehanded, "if you two start wailin' on each other with yours."

Both men stared at each other for a few more tense seconds, then they both nodded.

Thank fuck. One crisis diverted.

"Red know about her?"

He nodded stiffly. "Yeah. Red knows everythin'. Don't hide shit from her, even if it's ugly."

"Just tell me why you kept this a secret from us, then." Trip shook his head. "From me. You told Red, but you couldn't tell me." He did not hide his disappointment.

Trip had come from a shitty family like most of them. He strived to do better, be better, than the last generation and pass that mindset on to the next generation to continue to improve. It was one of a few reasons Dodge held a lot of respect for Trip. While he had his faults, they were outweighed by the good.

"She's supposed to be livin' a good fuckin' life. Figured it would be better without me in it."

Sig's confession suddenly made Dodge think of his own sibling, who had been given away in hopes to give him or her a better chance at life.

Dodge got it. He did. But…

"You're wrong, Sig," he said reluctantly, knowing it might cause another wave of anger. Even so, the VP needed to hear it. "She said she wished her brother had come back for her."

Sig's head twitched and he stared at Dodge, his face now a mask of nothing. A complete fucking blank. A whole shit-load of stuff moved behind the man's eyes but none of it reached his expression.

What Dodge said must've cut him deep. It wasn't his intent, but he wanted Sig to know that the man was worth something to his sister, whether he thought he was or not. No matter how fucked up Sig was, or what kind of train wreck he'd been before Trip dragged him back onto the tracks.

"Why'd she need me to come back for her?"

Yeah, he was trying to hide it, but the hurt and regret was apparent.

To anyone outside the club, Sig could seem like a highly disturbed, very volatile man. His Fury family knew the truth. They knew it because of how he was with Red.

His feelings for his ol' lady were intense and hard to ignore.

Not one of his Fury brothers wanted to be in Sig's shoes —or his head—but they wanted the same love the man had for his soulmate. They all considered themselves lucky as fuck when they found something even remotely close.

Dodge hoped to find the same if he ever decided to settle down. He'd never say never because he'd witnessed his brothers fall for their women one at a time like dominoes. None of them had been looking for an ol' lady.

Trip was the exception. However, Dodge was still behind bars when the prez found his queen and he didn't witness the tumultuous shit the couple went through before their jagged edges smoothed out and their pieces finally fit together perfectly. He'd only heard about it.

"Sorry, brother, got no fuckin' clue why she needed you other than you bein' her blood. Didn't get her whole life story since we had limited time together. Doubt that she would've told me anyway since most of that time, her mouth was only open when she was singin' on stage. Let's just say she ain't no social butterfly. And she certainly wasn't spillin' secrets." *Just like you, brother.*

"But you're wearin' her scratches, ain't you?" Sig asked, his tone turning sharp. Even dangerous. "She did that to you, didn't she? You said I should know you well enough. Brother, I do. Know you don't have deep convos with the chicks you normally bang. Also know you don't have deep conversations with chicks you don't bang. You had to have one with her long enough to find out what her brother's name was."

"Was helpin' the band out. They're down and out."

"Or were you helpin' out yourself?"

Dodge pulled in a breath. "Low blow, Sig."

"Callin' it as I see it. Now, gonna ask you and I expect the fuckin' truth. You bang my sister?"

Fuck. The truth was, Dodge knew it would come out sooner or later. Especially if Syn ever rolled back into Manning Grove. "When's the last time you did anythin' for her? Besides smugglin' her out of your trailer and givin' her to another family, what the fuck have you done for her?" Dodge lifted a palm. "Oh, wait, you bought her a cell phone, then stopped callin' and textin'."

Sig scowled. "She told you that?"

"Yeah."

"That before or after she gave you those fuckin' scratches?"

"You can ask her that, along with why she needed you."

"Can't ask her if I don't have a way to fuckin' contact her, asshole."

"And if we hadn't gotten to the point of us actually talkin', you never would've known where the fuck she was, *asshole.* Maybe you should thank me for these goddamn scratches. Now you know your fuckin' sister's alive, at least. Not to mention, interested in findin' you, her asshole of a brother. Maybe it *would* be better for her if she didn't fuckin' know where you were."

"Christ!" Trip shouted. "Enough. You're both in the fuckin' wrong here. The difference is, Sig, you knew you had a sister and kept it from us, while Dodge had… a… discussion with her that involved… scratchin' some itches." He grimaced as he rubbed a hand down his beard. "Sure it wouldn't have gotten that far if he'd known Syn was your sister."

"Think he would've kicked her out of his bed as soon as he knew?" Sig asked, each word like bubbling lava. "As soon as she said my name, did you tell her where I was?"

"No, 'cause I wanted to run it by you first. My brothers are priority over some—" He blew out a breath, glad he stopped himself before he slipped. "Woman. And I didn't want to assume you were her brother. Figured it was smarter to talk to you first. Now I'm fuckin' regrettin' it. Just the same as you are for never callin' her or textin' her." This time he managed to leave the "asshole" off. Barely.

"My fuckin' phone got lost durin' one of the times I went inside. Never saw it again. Didn't have that number memorized. Or any fuckin' number. When I got out, I went to the address of the family who had taken her in. They were gone. She was no longer in the same school. Figured at the time, it was for the best 'cause I was fuckin' wired out on drugs and drinkin' so much I was blacked out more than I was conscious. So, now you fuckin' know why I lost track of her. So fuck you," he snarled. "Shouldn't have to explain this to anyone but her. Now I might not even get that fuckin' chance, you motherfuckin' asshole."

He was right. The only person he really needed to explain it to was his sister. Sig didn't owe anyone else an explanation. "I said I tried to get her number."

"You shouldn't have let her fuckin' leave!" Sig screamed, his face now blood red.

The door burst open and Autumn rushed in, her face pale as a ghost. Her wide hazel eyes landed on Sig. She rushed over to him and cupped his face in her hands, pulling his head down so their eyes met. "What's going on?" When Sig said nothing, Red insisted, "Sig, tell me what's going on. I heard you downstairs over all the other noise."

The blood and heat drained from Sig's face enough so it went back to its normal color as he stared at his ol' lady. But his chest still heaved and a muscle in his cheek was popping from clenching his teeth so hard.

Without releasing his face, she glanced over at Trip. "What's going on? Someone tell me!"

Her panic was rising. Like Sig, she dealt with bad PTSD from the shit she went through. If she went into some sort of panic attack or shut down completely like she sometimes did, it would only spin Sig out of control even more.

Thank fuck through his haze of fury, Sig noticed it, too. He squeezed his eyes shut for a moment. When he opened them, he hauled Red against him, encircling her tightly within his arms. His cheek pressed against her fiery red hair and he simply breathed for another moment.

Second by second, he visibly relaxed. But it was Trip who spoke.

"Syn was in town. Dodge didn't know who she was to him, so he let her leave. We don't have any way to get in touch with her right now to tell her Sig is here."

Red nodded a silent thanks to Trip but remained clinging to her ol' man.

Dodge watched in amazement as their breathing synchronized. He had no doubt so did their heartbeats. It was wild and he wouldn't believe it unless he saw it himself.

Red turned her head towards Dodge. "You didn't know?"

"I wasn't sure… 'Til now. My fuckin' mistake."

"No, he fucked her and didn't want me to know."

"That's not why, Sig. If I knew she was your sister and was worried about that, why the fuck would I ask you if she was your sister? I would've just let her leave and not said a fuckin' word. Christ. I'm so done with this shit. You want me to say I fucked up?" Dodge jerked his shoulders up. "Then fine, I fucked up. My fault. I'll take all the fuckin' blame. But what I won't do is apologize for fuckin' your sister 'cause I didn't know she was your sister at the time. And if you don't believe that, then… fuck you."

Trip closed his eyes and released a loud sigh.

"She's a fuckin' kid."

"She's far from a fuckin' kid, Sig. That's how *you* see her 'cause you lost track of her when she was little. But she's twenty-fuckin'-three years old and only two years younger than Red when you met her. Last time I checked, she's legally an adult and old enough to decide whose bed she lands in."

"Okay," Trip cut-in quickly. "Can we avoid the talk of beds and… and what happens in beds right now?"

"What if it was Tessa?" Sig asked him.

"Do you think Tessa's a virgin and ain't fuckin'?" Trip shot back. "I'm not a damn fool and neither are you."

"So, you'd have no problem with Dodge fuckin' Tessa?"

Dodge watched the struggle cross Trip's face, but somehow the man managed to get out, "He would have to approach me first and get my approval, but… This ain't the same thing."

"Close enough," Sig grumbled.

"Honey, you can't fault the man when he didn't know."

Finally a voice of fucking reason. Dodge was right. Red should've been involved in this conversation from the start. It might have kept the explosions to a minimum.

Sig's nostrils flared as he stared down at Red. After what looked like unspoken words were exchanged between them, the VP finally nodded.

However, when he said, "But now he does," Dodge knew exactly what that meant.

And that wasn't going to fly with Dodge.

If anything happened between him and Syn in the future, it would be up to Syn. Not Sig.

If Sig had a problem with it, then he could take it up with Syn. But for a brother who hadn't been in his sister's life for over a decade, he had no right to try to control her.

Dodge doubted Syn would allow that, anyway. He smothered his grin at the thought of Sig trying.

Thank fuck Sig and Trip inherited their temper from their father and Syn did not come from Buck's loins.

"Asked her to come back and I'd put her band on regular rotation at Pete's. Let's hope she jumps on that. Know they're headed south for milder weather since that piece of shit on wheels is exactly that, a piece of shit. It's one thing to use it to haul a band from one place to another. It's another for all of them to be livin' in it."

"You were in it?" Sig asked.

Dodge nodded. "Yeah. Ain't ideal."

"Well, guess now we wait and hope to fuck she contacts Dodge," Trip announced, sounding like he was done with this conversation for now.

Right. There was nothing they could do until The Synners either came back to town or Syn contacted him. "Might not be 'til spring," he warned them. Though, he hoped to fuck she didn't wait that long.

"It's better than nothin'," Trip said on a sigh. He pulled his baseball cap off and rubbed his furrowed forehead.

"They good?" Sig asked Dodge.

It seemed like the level of his irritation had dropped from a one hundred to about a ten. Thank fuck for Red.

"Truth? She's one of the best I've heard, brother. The band, not so much. With the right manager she could go far, but I told her she'd have to scrape off the rest of them."

"Would she?"

"At where they're at now? No. Those three guys are loyal as fuck to her. And besides that piece of shit skoolie they travel and live in, that's all she got."

"What the fuck," Sig muttered. "Gave her to a family who I thought would give her a better fuckin' life. Now she's livin' in a tin can with three men struggling to make it."

Dodge wanted to ask him how well he knew that family or how much research he'd done on them before handing over an infant, but he knew that'd go over like a lead fucking balloon. A balloon that might crush him.

He'd like to avoid riling Sig back up if possible.

"Yeah, don't know the details about that family. She didn't share them, but thinkin' your good deed mighta backfired."

Sig closed his eyes and turned away. "Shoulda worked harder to track her down."

"When?" Trip asked sharply. "When the fuck were you outta prison long enough to help her?"

Sig turned around and snarled, "These last three fuckin' years. I figured she was off livin' a good fuckin' life and didn't need a goddamn fuck-up like me fuckin' up her life for her."

Trip tilted his head and studied his brother for a long moment. "That shoulda been her choice to make, Sig," he finally said a little more softly. He scratched the back of his neck. "All right. For now, there's nothin' more we can do 'til she contacts Dodge."

"We can do online searches to see if the name of the band shows up on any venue websites."

All three sets of eyeballs landed on Red.

Trip closed his eyes and shook his head. "We're dumb motherfuckers. That's all I'm gonna say besides thank fuck for our women who are smarter than us."

Dodge barked out a laugh. "Then I'm in big fuckin'

trouble since I don't got a woman to give me that extra brainpower. Guess I'm just gonna remain stupid as fuck."

Sig's lips twitched as he pulled Red into him again and pressed his lips to her temple. "So fuckin' smart, baby. Don't know how you can stand bein' around a bunch of dumb fucks like us."

She shrugged and smiled up at him. "It's a struggle but we manage." She rubbed his wiry jawline.

"We ain't worthy," Sig murmured.

"You are, just in other ways." She smirked slightly. "Now, the atmosphere is way too heavy up here. Let's go downstairs and take part in celebrating two more newly-patched members. Two more toward your goal, Trip."

"That they are. It also makes room for more prospects."

"Just gotta find some," Sig added, releasing Red but interlocking their hands instead.

Trip nodded and headed toward the door. He paused before opening it with his hand on the knob. He glanced over his shoulder at his brother. "We'll find her. Once we do, we'll take care of her."

After Sig nodded, Trip opened the door and disappeared through it.

He turned toward Dodge. "Gonna talk later."

Red tugged gently on his cut. "Not tonight." She glanced at Dodge.

He gave her an appreciative chin lift in return.

She turned toward the door, tugging Sig behind her. "Let's go. I'm missing out on all the gossip and also cuddling with Dane and Dyna."

"Can't have that," Sig grumbled as they disappeared.

Dodge waited for their footsteps to fade off, then he followed.

He'd be pulling out the bar's laptop tonight after he got back to his apartment and hopping on Google.

He only hoped the next few bars or pubs The Synners

played at had a website like the one Ozzy's ol' lady, Shay, had created for Crazy Pete's. Most dives didn't.

Dodge was afraid those were the only kind of places The Synners would be able to beg for a spot.

And only for fucking tips.

Trip's words once again filled his head. *"We'll find her. Once we do, we'll take care of her."*

Dodge snorted. Syn probably didn't want to be taken care of.

In the end, she might not have a choice.

To Trip, family was family.

Period.

Chapter Sixteen

Syn tossed and turned on the couch that converted into a pull-out bed.

Normally, she was restless because the "bed" sucked. That wasn't the case tonight. Or this morning. Or whatever time it was.

The guys' snores filled the skoolie. Rex was asleep in his bunk above the driver's seat. Eddie and Nico were sharing the room and queen-sized bed in the rear. Sometimes they forced Rex to switch out with them because they got sick of sleeping together.

Syn offered to take a turn sharing but none of the guys would let her. There weren't too many people she trusted, but those three were at the top. Actually, the list was so short it had only included them.

Until recently.

Her gut instinct indicated she could trust Dodge.

And if she ever found her brother, she hoped she could trust Sig. Unfortunately, she had no idea what he was like. The last time she talked to him was right before…

Right before things changed.

She took a deep inhale and squeezed her eyes shut. Not

to forget, but to remember why she was working so hard, why she kept trudging on even when it felt like she was getting nowhere.

Why she kept walking on a treadmill that never stopped moving.

She'd keep at it until she couldn't keep at it anymore.

She'd fight until she was dead and buried.

She'd never give up.

She hoped if she ever found Sig, he'd be able to help her in some way.

She only hoped he wasn't a disappointment. She'd had too many of those already.

She never got rid of the phone he gave her. It was still buried somewhere at the bottom of her duffle bag. It hadn't been charged in years and was outdated. Even so, she couldn't get rid of it.

It might be useless, but to her, it was the only thread left that connected her and her brother. If she threw it away, she'd have nothing left of that connection. All hope would be gone. So, she clung onto it like she clung to her hope.

She wasn't too proud to ask him for help. Not when it came to the help she needed and the reason she needed it. If he couldn't, she had no idea what her next step would be.

She had exhausted everything else to the point where she felt powerless and helpless.

She didn't want to think about it. She couldn't think about it. Otherwise, she'd be sucked into a dark hole and she'd have a hard time climbing back out.

Her thumb rubbed mindlessly back and forth over the screen of her current cell phone. She had brought it to bed with her since she'd thought of Dodge one too many times tonight. Each time she'd been tempted to text him.

It was a bad idea.

He offered them a regular gig. That might not be a big deal to any other band, but for them it could mean a regular influx of money. Well, at least once a month or however many times he wanted to put The Synners on the schedule.

It might not be enough to live on or even enough to put away for what she needed, but it would be better than nothing.

Tonight, they'd been desperate enough to find a park, set up their equipment and play an "open-air" concert without any amplifiers or even any power. That meant they relied on the strength of her voice, Eddie's drum playing, and their acoustic guitars to draw a crowd.

The size of the crowd ended up being disappointing but they did manage to get enough money in their tip jar to grab a hot meal and top off the fuel tank.

Of course, that was before the cops showed up and threatened to arrest them if they didn't shut down their concert because of a lack of permission and a permit. Apparently, they had considered what The Synners were doing the same as panhandling.

What-fucking-ever.

If she knew that giving up her dreams and getting a regular job would help achieve what she needed to, then she'd do it. However, it hadn't worked in the past since she didn't have any marketable skills other than her musical talent. So, she had to hope one day those talents would pay off.

She only wished it was one day soon. Before it was too late.

She stopped sliding her thumb over the smooth screen and pulled her phone from under the blanket. Holding it in front of her face, she hit the side button to light it up and squinted as the bright light hit her eyes.

As soon as Rex had driven the skoolie away from Crazy Pete's last Saturday morning, she had plugged both the direct number for the bar and also Dodge's cell phone number into her phone. Then she tucked the card away in her backpack, just in case something happened to her phone.

She glanced at the time. It was late, but that wasn't the reason she shouldn't text him. It was because she couldn't stop thinking about him.

She couldn't stop thinking about what he did to her on the pool table. Or in his bed.

When she closed her eyes, she saw his face.

When she closed her eyes, she felt his touch.

When she closed her eyes, she remembered his scent.

His voice.

The taste of his tongue against hers.

The pressure of his lips against hers.

How her body quivered under his.

She couldn't stop thinking about him no matter how hard she tried.

It both disturbed her and pissed her off, too.

She had one night with him.

One.

One night should mean nothing. People had one-night-stands all the time. *Hell*, how many "quickies" had she walked in on in the restrooms and back storage areas of places The Synners had played? Personally, she didn't do quickies or one-night-stands, but other people did and she doubted they obsessed over the person they fucked.

To them it was a transaction, not a purchase.

Maybe her unexpected obsession was due to her weary brain not functioning properly.

Her finger hovered over the app for her contacts.

She should leave him alone and forget about him.

She should forget about him. She didn't need a distraction.

She didn't.

Don't do it. Don't, Syn.

By contacting him, you hand him power.

He'll know he's in your thoughts. He'll know you can't stop thinking about him.

She laid the phone on her chest until the screen went dark.

Staring up at the bus roof, she listened to the snoring and released a long, frustrated groan.

She snatched up the phone and the screen lit up again.

Before she could stop herself, she jabbed her contacts app, opened it and found his number. She quickly typed out a text and hit send before she was tempted to stop herself.

Her message was simple. *Thank u 4 givn us a chance.*

She quickly followed it up with, *Thank u 4 the heaters.*

"Fuck," she whispered, turned the screen off and slammed the phone face down on her chest.

It *was* late. He probably wouldn't get those messages until morning, anyway.

She should turn the power off on her phone. To conserve the battery. To resist texting him anything else.

Suddenly, her eyes went wide and her pulse raced.

He now had her phone number.

Oh shit. That was a huge mistake.

Or was it even a mistake at all?

DODGE STARED at his phone as he peeled his fingers from around his hard-on. The two texts that came in covered Syn's photo. The one he happened to be staring at while he did a little self-help stress relief.

Should he feel guilty for using her picture? Probably.

Did he? Fuck no.

Last call downstairs had been over an hour ago. Micah and the newly-named Dozer had finished closing and the bar was now empty. Everything was quiet. It had been the perfect time to relax and wind down so he could fall asleep.

He didn't want to think about how many times he pulled

out his phone while working tonight and glanced at one of her photos. He also didn't want to think about how many times he'd done that since last Saturday.

Too many to count.

The problem was, he couldn't get her out of his head enough to even consider fucking anyone else.

She was living in his goddamn head rent-free. He should evict her.

But her text proved he was also living in hers.

His mouth pulled up on one side and he scratched his beard while considering her texts again. Did she even realize by texting him, he now had her number?

Did she do that on purpose?

At least Sig had a way to contact her now. Dodge hadn't seen the man since last Sunday but the VP kept texting him to ask if Dodge heard from his sister.

Like Dodge wouldn't tell him if he had. He wouldn't do that to Sig or Syn.

But first he needed to give Syn a heads up. That would only be smart, right?

Of course. It also gave him the perfect excuse to hear her sultry voice in his ear again. *If* she picked up the phone instead of being difficult and sending him directly to voicemail.

She was probably someone who hated phone calls and preferred texts. Too fucking bad.

He hit the phone icon in her text and was shocked as fuck when the call connected. A whispered, "Hey," filled his ear.

Best goddamn "hey" he'd ever heard. It filled him with shit he never felt before and certainly didn't want to identify.

It also caused his erection to flex and remind him that it had been rudely forgotten.

Christ. He only slept with her one night. His reaction to her was not normal.

None of this was.

"Don't gotta thank me again."

"I don't. But one of the heaters just kicked on and it reminded me of you."

He cleared the late-night rough from his throat. "Should I be insulted that you're only rememberin' me for a heater instead of anythin' else?"

"It got me warm, so it reminded me of you."

Could he hear an actual smile in her throaty voice? Or was he imagining it?

Either way, her confession made him grin. "Gonna take it as a compliment then."

There was a pause and he could hear her soft breathing. However, he could also hear someone snoring. That reminded him she was sharing a tight space with three fucking men right now.

He was as thrilled about that as Sig had been.

"Why'd you call me?" she whispered, most likely not to wake up her bandmates.

"Wanted to hear your voice in my ear. Like your heaters, it makes me warm." He stared up at the ceiling and shoved his hand down his boxers again, cupping his balls and giving them a slight squeeze. "Where are you?"

"In bed."

Dodge barked out a laugh since she was back to being difficult. "You know what I meant."

"In Virginia."

Every time she acted like a brat he got the urge to spank her, but he wasn't sure she'd be into it. One thing he *was* sure of was that he'd like to find out. He hoped he got that opportunity. "How soon can you get back here?"

Another hesitation, then, "I scored us a gig in Richmond. If I can't find any more around here after that, we're continuing south."

That wasn't going to work. "When's your gig?"

"Tomorrow night."

"After your gig, you need to come back north." He made sure his tone didn't make it sound like a suggestion. This wasn't going to turn into a debate.

More silence answered him.

After a few moments he pulled his phone away to make sure she hadn't hung up. He pressed the phone back to his ear and, if he listened hard enough, he could hear the snoring again. "Got somethin' better to give you than those heaters."

A soft snort filled his ear.

"Not that." He slid his fingers up and down his hard length. He thumbed a slick drop of precum off the tip. "Okay, ain't gonna lie... Maybe that, too. But no, it ain't my carrot I'm danglin' for you to come back." *To me and my bed,* he added silently.

"I hate carrots."

"You might not hate this one."

"How about you just tell me instead of playing this game."

"Ain't playin' no game, Syn. I don't fuckin' play games. Games are for boys. Been a long time since I've been a boy."

"Then tell me about this golden carrot."

It was far from golden. In fact, it was tarnished and dented. "Your brother."

Silence filled the hundreds of miles between them, then a whispered, "Sig?"

"Yeah. Well, I didn't actually find him. More like figured out who he was... Or is." He pursed his lips for a second. "He's my brother, too."

"What?" burst from her. Probably loud enough to wake her bandmates.

Dodge winced at what might be a mistaken assumption. "Club brother," he corrected quickly.

"He's... How long has he been your club brother?"

"About three years or so." Suddenly the phone sounded muffled and he couldn't figure out what she was doing. "Syn?" No answer. "Yo. Syn!"

What the fuck?

The background noise changed. He could actually hear traffic through the phone now. "Syn!" he shouted.

"I'm here," she hissed. "I had to step outside. I'm trying not to freak out."

"'Cause you're excited?"

"No, because you knew my brother and didn't say shit to me when I mentioned him."

"I wasn't sure—"

"How many fucking people have that first name?" she yelled into the phone.

If her yelling at him didn't make his palm itch, he didn't know what would. He kept his tone level when he answered, "Don't know that answer but it has to be more than one."

She growled. It wasn't supposed to be sexy, but, *fuck him*, it was. "He was right there in Manning Grove and we left?"

Fuck. So much for him expecting her to be happy to find her brother. But then he should've known she wasn't a typical ray of sunshine. Her personality reminded him more of a stormy winter night than a clear summer day.

"Let me explain somethin' to you before I fuckin' regret tellin' you where your brother is... Listen carefully. My first loyalty's to my brotherhood. Had no fuckin' clue that my brother's the same as yours. You didn't know his fuckin' last name and I wasn't assumin' shit. So, I wanted to ask him first to be certain. If you don't think that's reasonable..." He sucked on his teeth and pulled his hand from his boxers since he had lost his hard-on. "You know what? Don't give a fuck if you think that was reasonable or not. Didn't want to give you false hope if they weren't one and the same. I asked for your fuckin' number, you were the one who refused to give it to me."

"Why the hell didn't you tell me that's why you wanted it?"

"'Cause it wasn't the only reason. It might've been part of the reason but not the whole fuckin' thing."

Air hissed out of her. "What was the rest?"

"You're bein' difficult again 'cause you know the fuckin' reasons. Shouldn't have to spell it out for you."

"Because you want to fuck me again."

He wasn't going to deny that. "And what's the other?"

"You really want us to play at Pete's again?" That question came out more softly. "I figured that was just an excuse."

"Yeah, Syn, I do. I think it would be good for The Synners and also for the bar."

When she blew out a breath, it filled his ear, taking him back for a second to last Friday night and early Saturday morning.

His dick twitched as he remembered how hot and tight and how into it she'd been. He wished she was back in his bed right now. His fist was a poor substitution. Once he got off the phone with her, he might have to dig his jelly sleeve back out.

He cleared his throat. "Want you to come back." It wasn't a suggestion but it wasn't quite a demand. Not yet, anyway.

"What did my brother say?"

Fuck, he said a lot of shit. "He was pissed I didn't get your number."

"He wants to reconnect?"

He could hear the hope clinging to her words. "Yeah, Syn, he wants to reconnect. Said he lost track of you one of the times he went inside and his phone got lost. He didn't have your number memorized."

A weird but muffled sound came through the phone.

"I'm sure he kicked his own ass a few times for losin'

your number. More importantly, for losin' track of you. He said he went back to your family's house to find you but you were gone."

"I told you we moved. We moved…" Her voice had become strained and thick.

Dodge squeezed both his eyes shut and the phone tighter within his fingers when he heard it.

A muffled hiccup-sob.

For fuck's sake, was she going to lose it?

"You should be happy, not cryin', baby," he said more softly, hoping she'd pull herself together. "This is a good thing, I thought. Yeah?"

She cleared her throat and he heard a sniffle. "I don't know what I'm feeling. I… I'm sort of relieved but I'm…"

He waited. When she hesitated too long, he prodded, "You're?"

"Scared."

Scared? His brow dropped low. "Why the fuck would you be scared?"

"Because I…" After another frustrating hesitation, all the words began to tumble out. "I need his help and I'm afraid he won't help me. Or that he won't be able to help me."

Dodge sat straight up in bed. "What the fuck do you need help with?" And why didn't she ask him when she was in his fucking bed? When she didn't answer, he shouted, "Help for what, Syn?"

"It's… It's a family matter."

Dodge raked his fingers through his messy hair. "You don't trust me," he said flatly.

"It's not that. I… don't know you well enough to burden you with this shit."

"You don't *know* him, either, Syn," he reminded her. "You said he dropped you off with what I assume were strangers as a baby and you only talked on the phone and saw each other a few times when you were younger."

"I know…"

"That doesn't mean you're close. Would you even recognize him if you saw him?"

"I don't know."

"Would he recognize you?"

"I don't know."

"If you needed help you could've come to me."

"Why?"

Dodge closed his eyes and slowly drew air in through his nose. That was a valid question. Why?

Why the fuck would he put himself out for a woman he hardly knew?

Why would she even think he'd help her. She was right, she didn't know him. Spending what amounted to a few hours together didn't make someone an ally. Someone she could go to for help.

She had three men living in that tin can with her. Why didn't she get them to help her with whatever problem she had?

Or had she and they hadn't been able to do shit?

If not, what the fuck was this "problem." Was it so big that Sig wouldn't be able to do shit, either?

"Tell me what this problem is."

"I… can't." Her broken whisper made his heart thump in his throat.

"Why?" When she didn't answer, he said, "You could. You just don't wanna." He did not hide his disappointment in his tone. "Why, Syn?" he demanded more firmly.

"Because I can't," she screamed into the phone, making him pull his away from his ear slightly.

"But you'll tell Sig."

"Yes."

"A man you know about as much as you do me."

"He's my brother. We're family."

"Just 'cause someone is blood doesn't mean they'll feel obligated to help. Look at your mother. Look at mine. Blood don't mean shit, Syn. You *know* that."

"I have to go."

"Syn…"

"We'll head north right after our gig. We need the money to fill up the tank and for food."

"I can send you money."

"You don't have to do that."

"You're right. I don't. But I want to."

Again silence. "I don't want to owe you anything."

"You won't owe me shit."

"You say that now, but I know how it works."

Christ. So goddamn difficult. "Fine. You call me if you need money. I can take it out of the band's fee the next time you play Pete's."

"Okay," she breathed in what sounded like resignation.

"Want me to give Sig your number? Want him to call you?"

"Can you give me his instead?"

"Gonna text it to you." He wondered if he should warn her about her brother's issues. Maybe it was best for her to find out on her own. He didn't want any of that stopping her from coming back north. "Gonna tell him to wait to hear from you first. But I gotta tell him you're headin' back this way. He's gonna want to know that for sure."

He waited for her to insist she wasn't coming back north. When she didn't, he felt relieved.

"Dodge…"

"Yeah?" She didn't have to thank him, he heard it in her silence. "Don't worry about it. Only wanna help."

"I don't know why…"

"Sometimes we don't need to know why, Syn. No point in askin'. Just accept it. All right, stay safe. You got my number." He hoped that piece of shit got them back to Pennsylvania in one piece. Luckily, they hadn't gotten too far.

"Okay."

"See you soon."

His phone went dead silent. He pulled it away from his ear and saw she had hung up.

A text popped up a couple of seconds later.

Thankn u anyway, whether u want it or not. Just accept it.

He grinned at his own words being thrown back at him.

He was going to find out why she needed help whether she wanted that or not. Whatever her issue was, Sig didn't need to handle it alone. He had a whole brotherhood behind him.

That brotherhood also would stand behind Syn.

She just didn't know how powerful a brotherhood that stuck together could be.

But she would.

He had no doubt about that.

Chapter Seventeen

As soon as Rex parked the bus next to the shed on the MC's farm, he was there. Pounding on the bus's folding door and making it sound as though he was going to bust open that door with impatience.

Rex glanced over his shoulder with raised eyebrows at Syn and she simply nodded. Her lead guitarist rolled his eyes and jerked on the lever harder than he needed to, opening the two halves of the door and letting a rush of cold air in.

The second they were open wide enough for Dodge to squeeze through, he did so. When he climbed up the steps, he once again made the skoolie feel smaller than it already did. He gave a stiff chin lift to Rex, then his dark eyes immediately landed on her and raked her from head to toe. Almost as if he was checking to make sure she was in one piece.

She almost didn't arrive that way. The more north they traveled, the worse the snow had become. There had to be at least six inches already covering the farm lane.

The tires on the bus were total shit—dry rotted in some spots and bald in others—and should be replaced. Unfortunately, that wouldn't happen any time soon. It was another good reason to keep heading south.

But here they were again. In snow and ice country. On a farm belonging to a motorcycle club. A farm her *brother* lived on.

It was crazy. Over a week ago, they'd been in such close proximity and didn't even know it.

She ended up not calling him, but she did text him to give him an idea when they'd arrive and told him that they'd talk once they were face to face. She needed to see him when she talked to him.

Honestly, she just needed to see him. She needed to see *who* he was and wanted to know how he ended up here. She was just glad he was no longer in prison and hoped he'd turned his life around enough that he wouldn't ever go back.

While Syn couldn't wait to see him, Dodge had been right. She hardly knew Sig. Just because they were biologically related also didn't mean they'd get along.

In contrast to her limited text conversation with Sig, Dodge had called her every night, usually after closing down the bar and once he was alone in his apartment. He texted her several times during the day. They didn't talk about anything deep. He didn't hound her about her "problem," either, but she could hear it in his voice.

He wanted to know. He was also a little salty that she wouldn't tell him.

She almost did. Several times.

She wanted to relieve the burden she'd been keeping buried and carrying alone for so long. But she wanted to talk to her brother first because she hadn't told anyone her secret.

Not even Rex, Nico or Eddie.

If, for some reason, they overheard her telling Dodge, they might be upset she didn't want to share it with them. Maybe even disappointed.

They also might tell her that traveling around in a damn bus trying to make money wasn't smart and might even suggest breaking up the band and encourage her to go get some minimum wage job that wouldn't help.

Minimum wage was called that for a reason. It only gave you enough to afford the minimum, if even that. And she needed a lot more than the minimum to solve her problem. Or at least attempt to solve it.

She'd been at a loss for a long time. A complete and utter loss.

She thought things would change once she turned eighteen.

She was wrong.

So very wrong.

She thought it would be a magical age. She'd officially become an "adult" and would get the power back that she had lost years before as a teen.

She found out the hard way that wasn't true.

She quickly discovered she was just as helpless at eighteen as she had been at twelve, thirteen, fourteen and every year after that. Why? Because she had no money.

Becoming labeled as an adult didn't do shit. Having money did.

The saying was true: Money talked.

The only good thing about turning old enough was that she could leave.

The only bad thing was, what she had to leave behind.

She'd been torn.

Now she hoped her brother would help her recover what had been stolen from her.

Not her innocence. That could never be recovered.

But the one thing she valued most in life.

Her secret.

The secret she'd kept shoved so far deep and never discussed because if she did, it would break her heart into a million little shards and she was afraid she'd never be able to recover from that.

She needed to remain strong and determined. Also focused.

On her music. On making a name for the band. On her goals. And in turn, making money.

No matter how hard things got, she never gave up. Not once.

Dodge's deep and delicious voice filled her ears, bringing her back to the skoolie. She focused once again on him. On his larger than life presence. On the man that had twisted things inside her. Who made her question almost everything.

Who made her drop her guard.

He'd been watching her with his own eyes guarded. He didn't like what he'd seen cross her face. He didn't like being kept in the dark.

But he didn't need to like it. It was her burden, not his.

A warmth swirled through her as she did the same to him, checking him out from the top of his knit cap covered head all the way to his biker boots still coated with a dusting of snow.

When she lifted her gaze again and their eyes locked once more, he tipped his head toward the door to his left. "Outside."

Her heart began to thump heavily in her chest for two reasons. The man standing before her and the man she was about to meet. A brother but still a stranger. When Sig shouldn't be.

When she took the few steps to close the gap between them, Dodge kept his eyes locked on her while he ordered, "Go ahead and hook up the bus to the utilities again. You won't be goin' anywhere for a while."

He did not wait for a response from any of the guys, instead he turned on his boot heel and headed back outside into the cold.

As she passed Rex in the driver's seat, she nodded. "Hook up for now. I don't know how long we'll be here."

"We should go with you," Nico said behind her.

"No, it'll be fine. I need to talk to my brother first and figure out some things. Then we can make a new plan."

"Syn…" Rex said, turning her name into a warning.

"I'll be fine. I'll see if I can score us some more food, too. Sit tight and I'll be back as soon as I can."

"We don't know these fucking people," Rex insisted.

Syn paused on the bottom step. "You're right." She stepped out into late night chill. She was surprised Dodge had even been waiting at the farm and not working the bar since it was a Saturday night.

The bus door closed tightly behind her and in the dark, she saw the man, also dressed in almost all black, standing off to the side. Waiting.

Big, heavy snowflakes fell around them, landing on his leather-clad shoulders, on his black beanie and getting caught in his beard.

In a blur, his hand snaked out of the dark, wrapped around her throat and he twisted them both until her back was pressed against the side of the bus. His chest and hips pinned hers, trapping her.

His other hand drove into her hair, using a tight grip to tip her head back, arching the very same throat he held onto, and he took her mouth. Their lips and tongues colliding.

Right there. Out in the December night, with snow falling around them and her bandmates just feet away. Her brother who knew where… He could be standing in the shadows, watching them.

But she didn't care who saw them. Apparently, neither did Dodge.

The much larger man claimed her mouth, stealing her breath, stirring her very soul.

His thumb rubbed up and down her pulse in her neck. He had to feel it pounding. With her need for him.

One night.

That was all it took for her to want more.

Why him?

She groaned as he deepened the kiss, continuing to take her mouth like he owned it.

She gripped the wrist of the hand wrapped around her throat, but did nothing to attempt to free it. She only held on to keep herself on her feet. To keep her rubbery legs from giving out.

She wasn't afraid to admit she liked his hand there. She liked the power it gave him. More than she ever thought she would.

A quiet strength. A possessive touch. A promise of what might come.

Everything on her began to throb, to pulse, to race. Every cell in her body screamed for his touch.

Her groan mixed with his when his erection pressed hard against her belly. He tilted his hips just enough to make sure she didn't miss it.

An impossible feat. Unfortunately, it only made her want him more.

Now was not the time or place for that.

She twisted her head to break the kiss since he had told the guys to hook up the bus. They could step out at any second and see them like this.

To witness their "leader" letting someone else take control. To them it may be a sign of weakness or they might misconstrue the situation. Think what Dodge was doing wasn't welcomed.

When it was far, far from that.

No matter what, she didn't want to create more tension between Dodge and Rex. Or even between him with Nico and Eddie.

They were more her big brothers than Sig was.

His fingers tightened the slightest bit on her throat as she caught her breath and tried to slow her spinning thoughts.

When she turned her face back to him, she tried to tell him that they should move away from the bus. However, nothing but a ragged rush of air came out when she saw his face in the limited light coming from light over the shed door.

His head was tipped down. In the pocket of darkness where they stood, she couldn't read his eyes, but she could feel them.

Hot. Intense. Even possessive.

Both a thrill and fear shot through her.

Her breathing shallowed, the deafening beat of her heart filled her ears.

She knew right then and there he wanted to own her.

Not only have sex with her, but truly take her as his own.

But that made no sense.

Who in their right mind allowed that? Did anyone hand over their power to someone else willingly?

And why did she want to give him that? Give herself to him?

Again, that made no sense. It was crazy.

They only had one night together. One damn night!

Was she finally cracking apart and watching her pieces scatter?

He cupped her jaw and dragged his thumb over her bottom lip swollen from his kiss.

"Why do I want you so damn much?" he murmured, sounding annoyed.

With her? With himself? She didn't know. But what she did know was she had asked herself the same damn question.

"You're all I've been able to think about."

His confession surprised her. It was the same for her but

she wouldn't admit it out loud. To do so, would give him that power she wasn't ready to hand over.

In contrast, by him doing so, he showed her that he wasn't afraid of doing the same. He wasn't worried about handing any power over to her, otherwise, he would've kept that information to himself.

She needed to stop standing outside the bus in the cold and go meet with her brother. That was the true reason why they had turned the bus around and headed back north. Not to question her damn sanity over a man.

"What you said…" she started.

"It's true." The guttural sound of his voice swirled around her the same as the falling snow.

She shook her head. "About us not going anywhere for a while. We need to find more gigs, Dodge. We can't stay long." Her voice had become huskier than normal. Her nipples were painfully peaked from both the cold and from him being still pressed against her. "This is our livelihood."

He released her throat, his fingertips slowly dragging across her skin as he did so, causing her to swallow hard. Making her want to tell him to not let go.

To keep holding on so she wouldn't fall apart.

"You can play tomorrow night at Pete's."

"You don't have another band booked?"

"Normally don't book Sundays, but—"

"We'll take what we can get," she quickly told him, relieved for another chance to put a little cash in their pockets. "My plan will be to head back out Monday morning, then."

Dodge shot her a look that, even in the dark, clearly said, "We'll see."

Yes, they'd see.

The only thing that might change that decision would be what happened between her and Sig. Whether her brother could help her or not. Or even be willing.

If not, there was definitely no reason to stay. And, anyway, she had to think of her guys. Them staying or leaving wasn't all about her. That decision affected the men inside the bus, too.

A shiver shook her violently.

He brushed his knuckles down her cold cheek and grabbed the front of her cat-eared zippered hoodie, giving it a gentle tug. "This goddamn sweatshirt. Gonna ask the sisterhood if they got a coat you can borrow."

"The sisterhood?"

"Yeah, the ol' ladies."

"Ol' ladies are… the wives?"

"Same shit."

From a legal standpoint, Syn doubted it was. "I won't need a coat if we head south."

"We'll see," he said out loud this time.

He grabbed her hand, interlocking their fingers, and tugged her away from the bus. "You nervous?" he asked as he pretty much dragged her through the snow like a sleigh horse toward the big barn-like structure.

Instead of taking her toward the front door, they walked along the side and around back where he released her hand. He jerked his chin toward the metal staircase that was barely covered in snow because the steps were like grates.

She raised her gaze to the lit landing above them and noticed two solid doors and two large picture windows. The blinds were closed on both, but slivers of light still peeked through.

"Head up," he said.

"Where are we going?"

"To meet your brother. He and Red are waitin'."

"Red?"

"His ol' lady. Go." He gave her a gentle nudge.

She climbed the steps, very aware he was following closely on her heels. When she got to the top and glanced over her shoulder, he jerked his head to the door on the right. She stepped over to it and hesitated, another shiver shooting through her. This time from both the winter chill and nervousness.

As she stared at the door, her heart skipped a beat, then began to thump. She had waited for this for a long time.

What if they were mistaken and this Sig wasn't her brother? Would this end up being another disappointment added to the already long list of them?

"Are you sure it's him?" she whispered, doing her best to keep her teeth from chattering.

"Yeah, baby, it's him." Dodge's chest pressed to her back when he leaned past her and pounded on the door with the heel of his palm. Just like how her heart pounded every time he called her "baby." No man had ever called her that before and it not feel insulting or condescending.

Within a few seconds, the door flung open and she squinted when the light hit her eyes. She could only see a male silhouette before her.

When the man stepped back, the interior light made her brother appear and she lost her breath.

Dodge hadn't been wrong. This Sig was her Sig.

Holy shit.

Dodge bumped her back with his chest again and she automatically took another step forward into the warmth and out of the snow. He followed her inside, though she didn't leave him much room to close the door behind them.

"Brother," Dodge greeted in a gravelly rumble.

Sig didn't answer him, instead he stared at her. His eyes were dark and troubled as he inspected her from head to toe, just like Dodge had done. His brow dipped low, making his forehead crease. When he was done, he glanced past her to Dodge and his jaw shifted before his eyes landed back on her.

"Syn," escaped his mouth.

Hearing his voice brought back the memories of their brief conversations on the phone. Though the tone sounded richer and more mature than it had back then.

She nodded, not sure what to do. Hug him?

What she didn't want to do was collapse into a blubbering mess at his feet. But the relief that flooded her suddenly made her eyes sting. She quickly rubbed at them and took a deep, shaky breath.

The broad hand planted on her back gently urged her forward. Even after she took another step closer to the brother she hadn't seen in at least a decade, Dodge kept his hand at the small of her back.

Again, possessive. Maybe even a bit protective.

Sig noticed, too, and his nostrils flared.

She studied his face. He looked both the way she remembered him and different at the same time.

Older for sure, but showing evidence life hadn't been so easy for him, either.

"Hi, Syn, I'm Autumn."

Syn flinched. She'd been so caught up in staring at the man in front of her, she hadn't even noticed the redhead off to the side. She had no idea who this woman was.

She looked very young, maybe a couple of years older than Syn. Possibly mid- to late-twenties. But her hazel eyes held something behind them that Syn recognized.

Like Syn's brother, Autumn had also seen and experienced things that had left a mark.

Dodge's low voice filled her ear. "That's your brother's ol' lady."

"I thought you said her name was Red," she mumbled out of the side of her mouth.

Autumn's smile widened. "That's what everyone around here calls me. You can call me that or Autumn. I answer to either." She took a step closer. "I'm so glad to finally meet you."

"You knew about me?"

She nodded. "Yes. Your brother and I keep nothing hidden between us. No matter what it is."

No matter what it is.

Syn found that statement curious, but that wasn't why she was here.

Once again, Sig lifted his eyes to look at Dodge over Syn's shoulder. "There a reason you're still standin' there?"

The hand on her back tensed. "Yep. She wants me here."

She did?

"This ain't your business," Sig said harshly.

"You might not think so," Dodge answered, his voice as strained as when Nico over-tightened one of his guitar strings.

Shit.

"You fuck my sister and now you think she's your property?" Sig asked, his tone as sharp as a blade and just as threatening.

"Property?" Syn echoed.

"That ain't it, brother."

Sig's chin rose. "Then what is it, *brother*?"

"Want me to leave?"

The murmured question made her twist her head and look up at him. Did she? Sig might be blood but Dodge was the only one she really knew in that apartment. His presence comforted her. She shook her head and turned back to Sig. "I want him to stay." Not just *want*, but *need*.

His hand on her back anchored her. If he left, she might feel like she was getting pulled out to sea caught in a riptide.

Dodge had also mentioned something about helping her with her "problem." If he was capable of that, she wanted him to stick around and hear everything. She was going to say it once and once only.

"Would you like me to leave?" Red asked. "I can head downstairs or next door while you two talk."

"Think it's best you stay, too," Dodge told her.

A silent message must have been shared between Red and Dodge because after a second Red nodded and stepped closer to Sig. As if she was preparing for something.

"Maybe we should sit down," Red said softly. "Are you hungry? Thirsty?"

She was, but now wasn't the time to put anything in her stomach. Not yet. Not while her stomach was twisting and turning.

Before anyone could move toward the sectional couch, Sig's words stopped them, causing everyone to freeze in place. "You fuckin' disappeared."

Syn sucked in a breath. "*I* disappeared? Every time you went inside, *you* disappeared."

She didn't miss when his fingers curled into fists and his body went wired. She reminded herself again that he might be her brother but she really didn't know him.

Not at all.

And that was all his fault. Maybe if he hadn't been in and out of prison so damn much, he wouldn't have lost his phone and her number.

"And when I got out, you had fuckin' disappeared."

"That wasn't my choice, Sig. I had no choice but to move with the people you left me with."

"You mean your parents?" he growled, his fingers now curling and uncurling at his side.

Dodge had warned her he had a short fuse that Sig had inherited from his biological father. She was already seeing evidence of it and they'd hardly begun to speak.

"If that's what you want to call them. I wouldn't."

Sig jerked and that made Syn flinch again. It also made Dodge's hand on her back press harder. Her brother spun and strode away, clearly agitated.

He stopped by the counter of the small galley kitchen, keeping his back to them. He planted his hands on his hips and dropped his head.

Autumn didn't move but instead watched him from where she stood. She seemed to know it was best to just let him work out whatever he was working out.

When he finally turned again, she saw it.

Guilt.

Both in his expression and it hung thick in the air, making it hard to breathe.

For both of them.

This wasn't going to be a joyful family reunion, but a painful one.

Once they got past that, they could work on healing, then moving past it. Hopefully to the point where they could build a relationship.

She wanted that. He was the only real family she had.

In truth, she needed him. Not just for his help, though that was important. But she longed to have a brother. A real brother. To share things with, to go to when she needed help, to get his support. And in turn, she could be there for him for the same reasons.

But if he wasn't willing…

It wasn't just guilt that ravaged his face, it was anger, too. His voice was raw when he claimed, "Besides Red, you're the only good deed I ever did. Now you're shittin' all over it."

That was harsh but true. Only because he didn't know everything.

Not yet.

He might feel differently once he did.

"Do you think I don't appreciate you getting me away from her? But you just left me with some random family, Sig." Her voice cracked and she shook her head.

Dodge's hand slid from her back to her hip and he stepped up next to her, pulling her against his side.

Not just supporting her but also a clear message he was protecting what was his.

That gesture made Sig's lip pull up into a snarl. "Better than goin' into the system."

"But was it?"

"She woulda *sold* you, Syn. First your virginity and then you. And she wouldn't have waited until you were older but while you were a goddamn baby. Told you that. Maybe you didn't believe me 'cause you were too fuckin' young to truly understand it. But she didn't give a fuck about you. She didn't give a fuck about anythin' but her next fix. Her next bottle. The next fuckin' man who would pay her for lettin' him stick his dick in her cunt." He slapped a hand on his forehead and began to pace from the edge of the kitchen counter to the edge of the hallway and back. "They were already eyeballin' you when you were days fuckin' old, Syn. Days!" he screamed. "What kinda sick motherfuckers are attracted to newborns? To any fuckin' babies at all? For fuck's sake!"

Both the volume and the unrestrained fury of his rant made Syn wince and she saw Autumn's face beginning to twist as did her hands that were clasped in front of her. The young redhead also had her bottom lip clamped between her teeth. Syn wouldn't be surprised if she was tasting blood.

This conversation was affecting her. Deeply.

Hell, it was affecting them all. Dodge seemed to be the only steady ship in the stormy sea.

Before Syn could respond, Sig stopped short in his pacing and growled, "Shoulda just left you there to rot, then, and just saved myself."

"Sig," Red whispered sharply as she moved close enough to clamp a hand around his forearm, squeezing it. Sig dropped his eyes to her hand and Syn could see him visibly take a breath. Then another. It took a minute or two, but he didn't sound as angry when he finally continued. "Did the best I could, Syn."

She closed her eyes for a second. She shouldn't say it, but she needed to. She needed to finally have a chance to get it out. Until she did, they wouldn't be able to clear the turbulent air between them. "You could have taken me with you."

She would have taken a step back if Dodge wasn't holding onto her so tightly when Sig yelled, "Are you fuckin' kiddin' me? A fucked in the head thirteen-year-old and an infant livin' on the damn streets? That wouldn't have been too fuckin' smart."

"If he'd done that, so many things coulda went wrong, Syn. At that age, he did what he thought was best. For you. He thought he was controllin' the narrative. Doin' damage control," Dodge said, his voice too calm, too level, like he had to work at it.

She closed her eyes again and let oxygen fill her lungs, slowly and completely. With her eyes closed, she said, "I know. But the problem was the family he gave me to wasn't what they seemed." She opened her eyes and found Sig's. "You didn't save me. By giving me to them you only delayed the inevitable. You sacrificed me without even realizing it."

Chapter Eighteen

THE AIR in that small apartment became so thick and weighed so heavily on her chest, Syn had a difficult time taking a breath.

Sig needed to know. He needed to know everything.

Well, maybe not everything. At least the most important parts.

"You wanna fuckin' explain that?" Sig growled, breaking free of Autumn's grip and taking long strides toward Syn.

Dodge's fingers tightened on her hip and he grumbled a warning, "Yo, brother."

Sig's dark eyes landed on the man next to her. "You don't belong here."

"The fuck I don't."

"Just 'cause you fucked her once don't mean you got a say in shit. Or that you'll get to do it again."

Dodge stiffened against her. "That ain't up to you."

"Sig, stop it," Autumn hissed and moved to stand behind him. "You're not making this easy for anyone. Syn's an adult and can make her own decisions. What she feels for Dodge, if anything, isn't your business."

"The fuck it ain't," Sig said.

"No," Syn said, shaking her head. "It isn't. That's not why I'm here."

"If you don't want me to act like your brother, then why the fuck *are* you here?"

"I'm here because I want you in my life but I also… need you. And, yes, I want you to act like my brother, but not my father. There's a difference."

"Tell me what the fuck happened and why what I did was such a goddamn mistake." Sig insisted. He pressed fingers to his temple and winced like he had a bad headache.

"Before I get to that, I want to be upfront that I'm asking for your help. I'm hoping that you can help me because I have nowhere else to turn and I'm… desperate. But the reason I need this help is more important than what happened to me. Though, in truth, it's tied together."

"What kind of assistance do you need?" Autumn asked calmly. "We'll do whatever we can."

Syn believed her. She directed her answer toward her brother's ol' lady instead of him. Being a woman, she might understand why she was so desperate. "I need an attorney."

"An attorney?" Sig asked, his brow pulled low.

"A defense attorney?" Dodge asked from beside her.

She shook her head. "No. Not for defense."

"Why the fuck do you need an attorney?" Sig asked, scowling. "Just fuckin' say what the fuck's goin' on, goddamn it."

She blew out a breath. Telling them this, unburying the deep hurt and sharp pain, would be like pulling the rope on a bucket from the bottom of a well. Attempting to lift that full bucket to the surface without tipping it along the way. She had dropped that bucket to the very bottom a long time ago and left it there because every time she tried to pull it up, it tipped and slipped and she got nothing but an empty bucket when it finally reached the top.

She hoped like hell she now would have help getting that full bucket to the surface with hardly spilling a drop.

Even so, her head began to spin and her stomach churned at what she was about to reveal. "To help me get my daughter."

"What the fuck?" Sig growled and Dodge whispered at the same time.

"What daughter? You ain't old enough to have a daughter!" Sig shouted.

That wasn't true. "I have a—"

"Who the fuck has her? How old is she? Why the fuck does someone else got her? Why the fuck ain't she with you?"

"Sig! Give her a chance to answer your questions one at a time instead of bombarding her with them all at once," Autumn scolded, once again holding onto him. "This has to be hard on her."

Dodge's hand moved from her hip, slid up her back, under her hair and those long, warm fingers curled around the back of her neck. For some odd reason, his touch gave her strength. "The problem is, I need a *good* attorney, but I can't afford even a bad one. I can't afford a retainer at all."

"Who has her? The father?" While Dodge's questions were asked calmly, they still held an edge.

Syn shook her head. "The people Sig gave me to. They have her and won't give her to me. I just want her back. That's all I want. I don't care about everything or anything else."

"What do you mean 'everything or anything else?'" Dodge asked, using the grip on her neck to turn her toward him. His dark brown eyes narrowed on her.

He had read between the lines but she didn't want to get pulled into that gaping space between. She needed to stay steady and stick to those critical lines.

So, she ignored that question. That wasn't the important

part. Getting Maya back was. "They took guardianship of her after she was born and now won't even let me see her anymore. They're afraid I'll snatch her. Just take her and run."

"She's your baby girl. Of course you would," Dodge grumbled.

"Yes, I would. She's mine. I'm the one who carried her for nine months. After hours and hours of labor, they finally had to do a C-Section." Because of her age, her hips had been too narrow and they'd had no other choice. She slapped a hand to her chest. "*I* went through that, not them. As soon as she was born, they petitioned the courts for guardianship saying that I couldn't give her what she needed, using my age as an excuse. They claimed I couldn't take care of her because I couldn't even take care of myself. My only option has been to get a lawyer and fight them. It doesn't matter how old I am, I'm her," Syn's voice broke but she forced out the rest, "mother. I should be her guardian, not them. She belongs to me. She belongs *with* me."

Don't fucking break down right now, Syn.

She had no idea what those people were doing to Maya. She had no idea if her daughter was safe. The last time she tried to see her, they told Syn they had a restraining order against her and would have her arrested if she ever tried to see Maya again or even stepped on their property.

She couldn't even snag her while Maya was in school because they were homeschooling her, just like they ended up doing with Syn.

What good would it do Maya if Syn ended up in jail? She figured her only choice would be to fight it in court but to do so, she needed legal representation. *Good* legal representation. The kind she couldn't afford.

"Did you try looking for someone to do it pro bono?" Autumn asked.

"I've had no luck with that. Those people lie. They lie

about everything. Even to the point where they've told law enforcement I'm not Maya's mother and that I have mental issues and refuse to take my meds. I'm not even on any meds. But that's how they got a permanent restraining order against me. They say I'm trying to steal Maya so I can hurt her. That I was jealous of the new baby they *adopted*." A bitter laugh escaped her. "They didn't even adopt her. They might have even lied about the guardianship, too. I don't know that for sure, but they told others I was adopted and I never was. They had fake papers made up to show the school and whoever else asked. All of it was fake. Everything."

Sig, appearing about to pop like a shaken two-liter bottle of soda, turned to Autumn. "Reese next door right now?"

The redhead nodded, still wide-eyed and looking a bit shell-shocked.

"Baby, can you get her? Thinkin' she needs to hear all of this now so Syn don't gotta repeat any of it."

"Good idea," Autumn said, heading over to the door and pulling a coat off a hook. She shrugged it on and glanced at Syn. "I'll be back in a flash."

After the door closed behind her, the apartment became so quiet she could hear her heart beating in her ears.

"Brother, after this shit gets straightened out, we're gonna talk," Sig said to Dodge.

"Yeah, you're right, we are," Dodge agreed.

The tension between them clung in the air. And it was her fault. "I don't want to cause a problem between you two."

"Ain't no problem," Dodge assured her with a slight squeeze to her neck.

"No, there is and Sig is right. Just because—"

Her thought was interrupted when the door opened again. Two people and the winter chill followed Autumn back inside.

Syn blinked at the man with her. He looked like a Viking with the way his head was shaved clean on both sides and his long hair on the top was braided down the center from his forehead past his collar. His eyes were observant, but intense, as he took in the scene.

The woman with him was a tall, curvy blonde, maybe mid- to late-thirties, and carried a swaddled baby in her arms. The infant made a sound that shot a sharp pain from Syn's heart and radiated through her.

It had been about five years since she saw Maya. Five fucking years she'd been blocked from seeing her own damn daughter.

She only hoped the people now in this apartment could help her right that wrong. With strong allies at her back, she might have a better chance than on her own.

From beside her, Dodge said, "That's Deacon and his ol' lady, Reese. This is Syn, Sig's sister."

Both Deacon and Reese glanced at each other with confusion, then back at Syn.

"You got a sister, Sig?" Deacon asked. "Since when?"

"Since that cunt mother of ours squirted her out twenty-three years ago," Sig answered, shaking his head. "That shit ain't important right now. Need Reese to hear this fuckery. Need her expertise. The rest can wait."

That was very true.

"You're an attorney?" Syn asked the very put-together, older woman named Reese. For a new mom, she did not look exhausted or harried, but instead looked like she had her shit together. Just her demeanor oozed organized and no-nonsense. That could mean the child she held might not be her first.

"Baby, gimme my boy," Deacon said, holding out his hands to Reese, "so you can deal with whatever this is and not worry about him distractin' you."

Reese nodded and handed over the sleepy baby to his

father, then turned back to Syn, her expression all business. "I'm a civil litigator."

"That's a lawyer, right?" She had no idea the difference between a litigator and a lawyer or if there even was one.

"Yes, but—"

"Maybe you can help—"

"She had a baby, the people who adopted Syn took that baby and won't give her back." Sig's interruption was thick with impatience.

Reese shook her head as if to clear it. "What? When? That one sentence isn't going to cut it, Sig." She turned to Syn. "How old is this baby?"

"She's not a baby anymore."

Reese frowned and her head tilted like she already knew she wouldn't like the answer when she asked, "How old is she?"

This was where things could quickly get derailed. This was the part Syn dreaded even though it couldn't be avoided. She took a breath, then on the exhale answered, "Nine."

Reese blinked and silence descended the room.

At least until Sig exploded. "Nine? For fuck's sake, had to have heard that wrong." He turned to Autumn. "She say *nine*? Is my hearin' fucked up?"

Autumn had covered her gaping mouth when Syn had said Maya's age and at Sig's question, she dropped it to answer, "Yes, that's what I heard. Oh my God."

"You don't look... How old are you?" Reese asked, completely ignoring the men's reaction.

Syn also did her best to ignore the wildfire burning around them and focus on what was important. "Twenty-three."

"That's..." Reese shook her head, clearly at a loss for words. Her reaction was one of many reasons she never told anyone she had a daughter. "That's..."

"Fucked up, is what the fuck that is," Deacon growled.

"Holy fuck," Dodge muttered. "Holy motherfuckin' fuck. You had to be… What? Fourteen when you had her?"

Syn nodded but concentrated on the attorney. Someone who might actually be able to help her.

"You were fourteen when you got pregnant?" Reese asked quickly as if she knew the room was on the verge of combusting.

Syn braced. "Thirteen."

A pin dropping could have been heard.

Reese soldiered on as if she wore a flak jacket. "And the boy's family?"

"Boy?" Syn asked. *Fuck.* She was hoping to avoid the inevitable.

"The boy… The baby's father. I'm assuming it was someone about your age?" Reese closed her eyes and whispered, "Please say it was. That you were two kids… who didn't know what you were doing and only made a mistake…"

Syn wasn't sure what to say. She didn't want to focus on that. She wanted to focus on getting Maya back. Nothing more. The past couldn't be changed but the future could. They needed to focus on the future.

Nothing could be done about the past. Besides get past it.

Talking about the details wasn't doing that, it was making her relive it.

She didn't want to do that. She didn't.

She couldn't.

"Does it matter who the father is?" Of course it did, but she wished to hell it didn't.

"Well, yes, it matters. Will he fight for custody? Or fight keeping you from getting it?"

"Can he?" Syn asked Reese, not expecting that worry to

be added to the rest of the pile. "I was only thirteen when I got pregnant. Isn't that a crime?"

Dodge went so solid beside her, she thought he turned into a concrete statue. His fingertips dug into her neck. She winced and jerked her head enough for him to realize how hard he was pressing and he loosened his fingers. But what he didn't do was remove them.

Reese's face paled. "It depends, I guess. It would depend on his age and on the age of consent in whatever state it was where you got…" Air hissed out of her.

"What fuckin' state allows thirteen-year-olds to get knocked up by a man?" Sig raged.

"None that I know of, Sig," Reese assured him, "but this is not something I specialize in. I would have to check…"

"Was this in West Virginia?" Autumn asked gently.

Syn nodded.

Dodge released her neck and pulled the cell phone out of his back pocket and began to type quickly. His face was dark and stormy. As bad as Sig's. He stared at his phone for a second, his eyes shifting across the screen and when he lifted his head, he gave Sig a look. "Sixteen."

"Well, fortunately—and I hate to use that word in this case—that might help us," Reese said.

"No," Syn said.

All eyes landed on her.

"Why not?"

"I was told not to say a word to anyone about how I got pregnant. If I did, they threatened to give Maya away to another family and swore I'd never see her again. I don't know if that was true or not since they lied about so many other things, but at the time I believed it. I knew if Sig could give me to some random family, they could do the same with Maya. It's a risk I didn't want to take and still don't. I don't want to lose track of her." She glanced at Sig. "Like us. Look how long it took for us to find each other again."

Her brother rubbed a tattooed hand over his mouth but said nothing.

"How did you get pregnant?" Dodge asked, his voice a dangerous rumble. "This guy wasn't a teenager, was he? He was a goddamn adult?"

Syn pressed her hands over her eyes. She didn't want to go down this fucking road. "It doesn't matter," she whispered.

"It fuckin' does!" Sig roared. "It's one thing for two teenagers to fuck up, it's another when a fuckin' adult man fucks a thirteen-year-old."

"Rape," Reese corrected him. "Not fucks. *Rapes.*"

Syn took a strained breath. This had been a mistake. She dropped her hands from her face and glanced up at Dodge. "I can't..." The words got caught in her throat and she cleared it, shook her head, met his eyes and said, "I can't. I have to go."

She began to turn and expected Dodge to stop her but it was Autumn calling out that stopped her instead. "No, wait! This is important, Syn. We can see how important getting Maya back is to you. That means it's important to us. We want to help in any way we can. Maybe," she glanced around, "the guys could leave us ladies alone for a little bit."

"Fuck that!" Sig snarled.

Reese rolled her eyes. "That might be best until I get all the details and figure out what we can do to help. You guys aren't helping by," she scratched her forehead, "well, being you. Is the situation bad? Yes. Are you helping make it easier? No. Deke, can you take Sig and Dodge next door with Dane. There's a bottle in the fridge if you need it."

Deacon stared at his ol' lady for a few seconds, then finally nodded. "Yeah. Let's give them some privacy."

"No." Sig and Dodge said at the same time.

"Yes," Reese insisted. "That's what's going to happen. Deke, take them next door."

Deacon grimaced at that order. "You heard her. Let's go."

"But I need to know—" Sig started.

"You will, just not right now," Reese assured him. "Let me try to wrap my head around what happened and what has to happen, then we'll get you up to speed. Okay? It's either that or she walks out because of the pressure you're putting on her and then we find out nothing and Maya won't get the help she needs. You get that?" She raised both eyebrows.

"Fuck," Sig muttered, scraping his fingers through his hair.

Dodge stepped in front of her and tipped his head down so she could only focus on his face. It was unreadable, but his body was tense. "Gonna be right next door, got it?"

Syn nodded.

"Wanna know everythin'," Dodge said.

"That will be up to her," Reese stated firmly. "Not you. Not Sig."

Sig opened his mouth and Autumn pleaded, "Sig."

Her brother's mouth snapped shut and he stared at his ol' lady for a second. He seemed to deflate a little before he nodded. "Not sure if I want you hearin' the details."

Syn wondered why he had that concern. Maybe it had to do with that look Syn had seen behind Autumn's eyes. That he worried whatever Syn might say could be a trigger for her.

"This shit starts botherin' you, come next door." Sig turned to Reese. "You see it, you send her next door, you got me?"

Reese nodded. "Yes."

"Don't make me fuckin' regret this," Sig said over his shoulder as he followed Dodge and Deacon out the front door of the apartment.

"Oh God," Reese whispered. "These men. They love us

so intensely that sometimes their emotions get in the way of clear-headed thinking. They overreact before they think."

"I'm not sure if they're overreacting in this case," Autumn murmured.

Syn sighed. "Sorry. I didn't mean to cause any of this by asking for help."

"No. You're doing the right thing. I'm just glad Trip wasn't here. This would have turned into a war-time type of interrogation." She released a single dry, stilted laugh. "Okay, let's sit down. Red, can you grab Syn a glass of water?"

Autumn nodded and headed around the counter and into the kitchenette while Syn and Reese got settled on the sectional.

"So... First thing first. I don't do family law, but since you can't afford one, I'll do what I can. If I have to reach out to a colleague, I will."

"I can't afford—"

"At no cost to you. We'll figure it out. Money isn't important here, getting your daughter back is. And you're family. I have no doubt that Trip will get the club to help fund whatever is needed since he's big on family. But hopefully it doesn't have to get to that. If we can handle this on our own, that's what we'll do. But we *will* be getting your daughter back. As a mother, I promise you that."

Autumn stepped up to the couch and handed Syn a glass of ice water, then took a seat across from them. "If we can't get this solved legally, I'm afraid these guys will take drastic measures. We want to avoid that if possible."

"Agreed," Reese said. "However, I need more details so we know what steps we need to take."

Syn's fingers clutched the glass but she couldn't drink yet. Even taking a small sip might feel like drowning.

"First off, this family that has Maya, do they have legal custody?"

"They told me they have guardianship, so I'm not sure what that means in terms of actual custody."

"You didn't sign anything right?" Reese asked. "You didn't sign over your rights as her mother?"

"No."

"The father... I'm sorry but we need to know this if we get into some sort of legal battle. How old was he?"

"I don't know exactly."

"Did you know him?"

Syn nodded. "Yes, his brother."

"Whose brother?"

"The man who was supposed to be my adoptive father. It was his brother."

Reese wrapped a hand around her forehead and breathed, "Okay. Can you guess how old he was?"

"In his thirties, for sure. I don't know exactly."

"And... And..." Her green eyes flicked to Autumn sitting on the couch. "And you didn't want him to... touch you, right?"

Syn had to unclench her teeth to answer. "No."

"Did your adoptive parents—I'll call them that for now since I don't know what else to call them. Did they know he raped you? I mean, do they know he was the one who got you pregnant and that he's Maya's biological father?"

Syn forced a "Yes," up her closed throat.

"Did they have any part... Jesus, I'm so sorry I have to ask these questions. Did they have any part in what happened to you? Or did they find out after the fact?"

"I'm not sure. It happened whenever they asked him to babysit me and their son, who was a couple of years older than me. Sam would wait until their son went to bed, then... then..."

Reese shook her head and held up her hand. "I don't need to know the details if you don't want to share them. I get the picture." Once again, her gaze slid over to

Autumn, who sat quietly with her hands clasped tightly together in her lap. After a second, Reese turned back to Syn. "Okay." She blew out a breath. "Here's what I'm thinking… We could do this the legal way but if we do, everything that happened to you will be exposed. I'm afraid that if they fight you for custody it could be a long, drawn-out battle. Worse, they could hide her where no one can find her."

That couldn't happen. "I just want Maya back. I don't give a shit about what he did to me. That can't be erased." She'd lived with it for ten years as it was. It wasn't something she wanted to dwell upon and allow it to eat away at her for the rest of her life.

"I know, but what if he's doing this to other girls?"

Syn closed her eyes. Reese was right. Or it could've just been her because she was convenient and Sam knew his brother would never turn him in. Syn learned the hard way they would protect him over Syn.

To them blood was thicker than water. Syn being the dirty dish water.

"I know you wanted the guys out of here, Reese, but maybe it's best if they hear this," Autumn said. "They might need to get involved."

Reese stared up at the ceiling and, after a few moments, finally dropped her head. "They'll put themselves at risk. You know that. You know how they are."

"I know how they are," Autumn confirmed. "But, I hate to say it, it might be for the best. If a legal battle will delay Syn getting her daughter back and if Maya stays in that house that welcomes and protects a child molester…"

"Damn it," Reese whispered harshly as she pulled a cell phone out of the fleece vest she wore and sent a text. "Before they barge in here… What's going on between you and Dodge? I'm not sure how he's involved in all of this."

"We…" She let that hang, unsure on how to tell them

she and Dodge only spent one night together and suddenly he was all up in her business and trying to take charge.

Reese lifted a hand to stop her. "That's all you had to say. I can see it in your face and hear it in that single word. We know what it's like to get involved with these men. It can be intense and overwhelming. If you don't want him involved, just say so. It would only take one word to Trip."

Syn shook her head. "No. You don't need to do that. He hasn't pressured me to do anything. He's been nothing but helpful. I... like him." She did. Something about him anchored her feet to the ground instead of her floating help-lessly, struggling to get a foothold.

"The way he's acting around you, it seems he *likes* you, too." Autumn rolled her lips inward.

"These guys are *not* easy, but take it from me, they're worth it," Reese admitted. "Deacon opened up a whole new world for me that I didn't realize I was missing out on because I was so hyper-focused on my career. My sister was right, I might've worked myself to death and never got a chance to enjoy life along the way."

"Now look at you two," Autumn said with a soft smile. "And now you have Dane..."

"I had no plans to have children and, yes, now look at me. I now have two."

"Dane and Reilly?" Autumn asked, her brow furrowed.

She shook her head. "Dane and Deacon."

The two women laughed and for a moment, it was great to hear some easy laughter. It was true that it soothed the soul. She hadn't laughed in a long time, so Syn breathed theirs in like oxygen to keep from drowning in the depths of darkness.

Not even thirty seconds after that laughter died off, the three men were bulldozing their way back in, immediately surveying the scene. Sig did a visual inspection of Autumn, while Dodge did the same with her.

"Keep your shit together, you hear me?" Reese warned them. "Any of you get crazy, I will not hesitate to kick you back out. Sig?"

Sig's jaw shifted but he nodded.

"Dodge?"

Dodge nodded, too.

"Red thinks we should forego the legal way to handle this. And you know what, for once I agree with that route. It'll take too long and it sounds like we need to get Maya out of that situation as soon as possible. So—Jesus, I can't believe I'm saying this—we're going to do it the Fury way."

All the men stared at her like she had grown a third head.

"Say that again?" Deacon asked, bouncing up and down while patting the diapered butt of a now very awake baby.

"You heard me. I'm not repeating it."

"Damn," he whispered. "When you get bossy like that..." He grinned but it quickly disappeared when Reese shot him a "not now" look.

"Okay," Deacon's ol' lady started. "Here's what I suggest. For insurance, we need to grab the DNA of Maya, Syn and the father. This way if any questions come up down the line, we have absolute proof that Syn is Maya's mother. We'll also have proof who Maya's father is. That's proof we can use for leverage since Maya was conceived during the," she grimaced, "assault of a child."

The air began to vibrate.

"Keep it together," Reese warned the men again. "I already feel the temp rising in here. We need to think clearly and logically on this." She took a breath and addressed Syn. "Will they want that info exposed? That this man," she grimaced again, "touched a child and got her pregnant?" Reese shook her head. "I doubt that. Even if it came out, we would file for custody and win that case, Syn, using that evidence. I have no doubt about that."

"What if the fucker fights her for custody?" Dodge growled. "Hasn't that happened before? A rapist has fought for custody?"

"If he does, we'll expose what he did and he'll go to jail and automatically lose custody, anyway. At least I hope I'm right. The justice system is a little flawed—"

"A little?" Sig yelled.

Reese ignored his outburst and kept going, "I think if we need to threaten him with that, he'll go away quietly."

"Do we want that fucker to go away quietly?" Deacon asked with one eyebrow cocked and gleam in his eyes.

Sig's eyes narrowed. "Fuck that. That motherfucker's gonna go away, but fuck if it'll be quietly."

Chapter Nineteen

WHILE SYN WAS EXCITED to hear that something was going to be done, worry also ate at her.

She didn't want her problem to be the reason any of them did more time. Her brother had a home now and a woman who very clearly loved him. Deacon had a wife and baby. Or she assumed that Reese was his wife. Though, she didn't see any wedding rings on their fingers.

And Dodge… Would he be willing to sacrifice his freedom for her? A woman he hardly knew?

It didn't make sense.

"I don't want you to think I didn't try to do it the right way. I wanted to prove to them that I could take care of her. And I did take care of her every damn day until I turned seventeen. At that point I moved out, hoping we'd only be separated temporarily, and got a job and a shitty little one room apartment. But none of that was good enough for them to let her leave with me. I couldn't afford day care. I couldn't afford more than the rent. I couldn't afford shit. I then mistakenly thought they'd give her to me when I turned eighteen. Again, they refused and that's when they made up shit to get the restraining order. So, everything I did was for nothing. None of it was good enough."

Nothing she had done was good enough. And it never would be. They never had any intention of returning her daughter. They wanted to keep Maya for themselves.

Maybe they thought by keeping her, the truth about Sam would never get out. By keeping her, it was their insurance policy and used Maya as a tool to control Syn. To keep her mouth shut. What was crazy was Cara and Lyle Danzig had actually been decent parents to Syn. Until that first time Sam Danzig walked into her dark bedroom.

Then the second.

And the third.

Sam threatened her by saying if she said a word about what he was doing, what he did, no one would believe her and her "parents" would kick her out onto the streets. He said time after time that blood was thicker than water. He reminded her that Syn wasn't blood to them. Sam was. She was just a "silly" child who would be considered a trouble-maker and a liar. Who would believe a child over an adult? No one.

He also said her parents would be angry with her for causing problems. For lying about Sam and trying to get him in trouble. For trying to break their family apart. They would put the blame on her instead of where it belonged.

She closed her eyes and suddenly felt that larger-than-life hand covering her mouth. Smothering her, making her struggle for breath. The endless stabbing, sharp pains as if her insides were being torn apart.

The heavy weight crushing her. The drops of sweat dripping on her face and mixing with her hot tears. The low grunts. And that final thrust always accompanied by a long groan and followed by panting, his hot breath assaulting her skin.

After what seemed like forever, he'd collapse on her and

pat her head, telling her she was a "good girl" and that good girls took good care of their uncles.

Good girls took good care of their uncles.

He wasn't her uncle. He wasn't anything but a massive piece of shit who needed to be flushed down a toilet and sent down into the sewer where he belonged.

Once her "parents" figured out she was pregnant, it was too late to do anything about it. They forced her to tell them who she had "slept" with like it had been her choice. They wanted the family of the "boy" who "did this to her" to pay child support.

Funny that.

When she told them who it was, they didn't believe her at first. They called her a liar.

They even accused her of seducing Sam.

As if she would want a thirty-something-year-old man stabbing her insides hard enough to cause her to bleed and have debilitating cramps, while he sweated on and suffocated her to keep her quiet. In the end, eventually getting her pregnant.

Sam's fucking excuse? He didn't realize she was old enough to get pregnant.

He didn't realize she was old enough to get pregnant. Like that would have made a difference.

She was already five months pregnant when they discovered it. They immediately moved and removed her from public school to homeschool her. To hide her pregnancy. To cover up what Sam had done.

She lost all respect for the family that had taken her in once they claimed Maya as theirs. Once they let Sam get away with what he did.

Did his visits stop once the truth came out? Yes. Was he forbidden from babysitting Syn ever again? Yes.

But by then the damage had already been done. They did nothing to right that wrong. Not a damn thing.

They only made things worse when they took what didn't belong to them.

The couch sank beside her and warm, long fingers once again wrapped around the back of her neck, squeezing. Reminding her she didn't have to deal with this alone any longer. She would have people on her side for once.

But this whole discussion was exactly why she hadn't wanted to talk about this and why she only wanted to concentrate on getting Maya back. She did not want to fall back to the bottom of that deep, dark well.

"They still live in the same place?" Dodge asked.

"I'm pretty sure they do. Every once in a while, I go back and try to see her. It's been a few months, but the last time we were in the area, I had Rex drive the skoolie there. I begged them to let me see her. They slammed the door in my face and threatened to call the cops on me for violating the restraining order." She had forced herself to remain on her feet instead of collapsing and wailing like she really wanted to do.

Not only would it do no good, the guys would've witnessed it and demanded she tell them what happened and why.

"The guys know?" Dodge asked next.

She shook her head. "No, I made an excuse each time. I was afraid they'd want to break up the band so I could get another job. But they don't realize... Right now, my music is all I have. It's the only thing keeping the cracks in my soul from widening to the point where I'd just disintegrate into nothing. I'd become dust in the wind."

He cupped her face and turned it to face him. Once their gazes locked, he said, "You got us now, Syn. You now got a whole damn army behind you."

"We're gonna get her back," Sig stated. "That's for fuckin' sure. And that fucker's gonna pay. They all will."

"Sig," Autumn breathed.

"No one does that shit to my sister and gets the fuck away with it. No one, Red. My niece is comin' home."

My niece is comin' home.

"Wait… I… This isn't home," she said quickly. "We can't stay here. We need to travel to book gigs… I—"

"Listen," Dodge started, holding her chin and her gaze. "That's not what we need to concentrate on right now. That shit will all get figured out in the end. Right now, we need to get Maya. Agreed?"

She got what he was inferring but wasn't saying out loud. She wanted to argue but, yes, now was not the time. The priority was to get Maya back and then she needed to have a sit down with the band and discuss how they'd handle things from there.

They had a say. The band might have her name but it wasn't all about her. They'd been there for each other for a few years now and she wasn't going to abandon that family even though she found her brother and his Fury family.

Her narrow world was getting wider. She hoped to hell that was a good thing. She needed something good in her life besides her music.

She glanced down at the M she had tattooed on the webbing of her right hand. She rubbed her left thumb back and forth across it. She saw that reminder of her daughter whenever she gripped the microphone on stage. She saw it whenever she ate or drank. She stared at that reminder every damn day. A reminder of what she was fighting for. A reminder to never give up.

Everyone in that apartment right then, Sig's brotherhood and their ol' ladies might be what they needed. Becoming a part of Sig's life might give her and Maya some roots.

She could only hope. Something she'd clung to since the day she walked out the door to create a life for her daughter so she could finally get her back. That hope had been stepped on and crushed many times over the years. But now…

Now…

Dodge's deep rumbling voice drew her back. "All right. We're done here for now. Let's come up with a solid plan. This ain't Hillbilly Hill we're dealin' with, Sig. Nobody gives a fuck about what happens to the Shirleys except the Shirleys. Someone might give a fuck about these mother-fuckers."

Syn had no idea who the Shirleys were and what Hill-billy Hill was. She wasn't even sure if she needed to know.

"We wanna get Trip involved?" Sig asked.

"We got a choice?" Deacon asked.

"Nope," Dodge answered him. "We need to get a quick meet together and discuss how this is gonna be handled. We'll probably need more than the three of us. Thinkin' if we end up doin' this on our own and not tellin' Trip 'til afterward, he's gonna be fuckin' pissed."

Deacon nodded. "Yeah, thinkin' that's for the best. Plus, if we need the Grumpy Green Giant and Jet, we could have them help, too."

"Do you think Rook will be okay with getting Jet involved?" Reese asked, rising from the couch and taking the mewing baby from Deacon's arms.

Deacon's lips twitched. "D'you think Jet gives a shit what that asshole says? Think he needs a tit, babe."

"Yes, both my tits and I are very aware of that, thank you," Reese answered him.

"Fuck, I miss—"

"Sig!" Autumn yelled, cutting off Syn's brother.

Eyebrows rose throughout the room and Autumn's face became as red as her hair. She pressed a hand to her cheek and gave Sig a look that spoke volumes.

"Whatever," he muttered.

Syn wondered what that was about. Maybe it was best she didn't know since it involved her sibling.

Dodge snorted next to Syn. "Okay, then. Yeah, let's get somethin' set up with the brotherhood. Or at least with Trip and let him decide who all's gonna be involved with this. The Shirleys are just gonna have to wait for now. They ain't an immediate threat."

"Trip ain't gonna like that but he'll agree with it. And we still got the prospects takin' turns up there keepin' their fingers on those inbreds' pulse," Deacon said.

"It'd be better if my fingers were snappin' their fuckin' necks," Sig said.

"Wish it was that easy," Deacon muttered. "But we know it ain't." He put a hand on the small of Reese's back. "Okay, my kid needs to eat. Talk to Trip."

"The sooner we can get a plan together, the sooner we can execute it," Dodge said.

"Agreed," Sig said. "Think he's up at the house. Gonna go talk to him and let the rest of you know. Yeah?"

"Yeah," Deacon and Dodge answered in unison.

After Deacon and Reese left and went back next door with their fussy son, she and Dodge stood.

"You got an extra coat for her?" Dodge asked Autumn. "What's she's wearin' ain't warm enough for this weather and you seem to be close in size."

"Dodge…" Syn started.

"I think I do. Let me check." She disappeared down the short hallway to a room at the back.

"You didn't need to do that," Syn hissed.

"She won't mind and you can return it when we get you somethin' warm. One thing you'll learn about this club is everyone sticks together. Includin' the sisterhood."

"I don't belong to the sisterhood," she reminded him.

"The fuck you don't," Sig answered before Dodge could. He stepped in front of her. When he did, Dodge actually moved closer, standing behind her like a brick wall. Sig glanced up at him and then gave him a slight nod but Dodge didn't move away. He remained standing at her back.

Why Dodge felt the need to do that, she didn't know. A lot of undertones existed between the group she didn't understand.

"Thought I did you right. Guess I did you wrong. Gonna make it up to you. Got that?" her brother asked.

Syn nodded and whispered, "And I'm sorry for blaming you. You did the best you could at the time. I can't blame you for losing me just like I shouldn't blame myself for losing Maya."

"You ain't the only one sorry," he muttered, then surprised her by pulling her into his arms.

The hug was awkward and stiff between them, but it was a start.

For over five damn years she drowned in frustration and helplessness. Trying not to think about it too often so she could continue on and keep working toward a future where she hoped that she and Maya would be reunited.

Maybe after tonight that frustration and helplessness would end. Maybe tonight would be the turning point she'd been searching for. She hoped to hell that was true.

She also hoped the people now surrounding her would be the army needed at her back like Dodge said.

She shouldn't get her hopes up. Not yet. She still had a long road ahead.

But at least that road was now paved with good intentions.

Even better, she wasn't going to travel it alone.

———

"How soon do you think we can go and get her?"

"We?" Dodge asked as they headed back toward the

skoolie through the snowy winter night. She now wore a warm coat Autumn let her borrow.

Her brother's ol' lady had hugged her, too, on their way out the door. Hers was warm and encompassing, unlike Sig's. And Syn had done her best not to let tears fall while they did it.

Years of tears had gotten her nowhere. Only action would.

And if Dodge thought she wasn't going with them when they went to get Maya back, he would have a huge fight on his hands. "Yes, *we*."

"Don't know. How 'bout you go back to the bus and get your guys up to speed with whatever you wanna tell them, while I head over to the house to talk with Sig and Trip?"

"Then you'll come tell me what the plan is?" She was struggling to keep up with him since her shorter legs were no match for his much longer ones. For some reason, he seemed to be in a rush.

"Not sure if a plan will be made in Trip's kitchen or we'll have to get everyone together first. But yeah, will come get you after."

"I didn't say come get me."

"Heard what you said. You also heard what I said."

Damn. She put on the brakes. Why did his bossiness both thrill and annoy her?

Several long strides later, Dodge also stopped and glanced over his shoulder at her. "Problem?" he asked with a cocked eyebrow.

"Yes. I appreciate everything you've done and everything you plan on doing…"

"But?" he prodded, turning to face her. The falling snow creating a lace curtain between them. It was much heavier now than earlier and seemed to be quickly turning into a winter storm.

"But I'm not sure what to do with this."

He closed the gap between them, tipping his face down to hers. She stared at the snowflakes caught on his thick, black eyelashes and watched as they melted to drops of water.

She wanted to touch them with the tip of her tongue.

"Do with what?"

She shook herself mentally. "With this." She waved her hand in the narrow gap he'd left between them.

"Just what the fuck d'you need to figure out?"

"Why you're coming to *get* me instead of coming to *talk* to me after you're done with Sig and Trip."

"Shouldn't be any fuckin' confusion."

"Dodge. If I wasn't fucking confused, I wouldn't be bringing it up."

THAT ATTITUDE WAS BACK.

Dodge stood staring at her as her tongue swept over her bottom lip in the cold, in the dark, with the storm picking up around them at a quick pace.

At least she now had a fucking decent coat on her back.

"No confusion. You're gonna continue headin' to the bus, talk to your guys while I go talk to mine. When I'm done, gonna pick you up in my truck. Be ready."

"For?"

"What the fuck d'you mean 'for?' You purposely tryin' to misunderstand?"

She lifted her chin and that fire was back. The one that had been doused while in Sig's apartment. He didn't know what all had been said after he'd gone next door to Deacon's place, but one thing was for sure, he aimed to find out. Maybe not all of it tonight, but he would hear it all eventually.

"No, what I'm trying to understand is why you're picking me up."

"Fuck, woman. If I gotta spell it the fuck out, I will." He stepped close enough to go boot toe to boot toe with her. "So, listen carefully, only gonna say this once."

Her eyebrows rose so high they almost touched the cat-eared hood she had pulled up and over her head. The coat she borrowed from Red had been large enough so she could wear her beloved hoodie underneath it.

"Yes, I need you to spell it out."

"You know it's fuckin' snowin', right?"

She put her hand out, tipped her head toward the fat flakes landing on her open palm. "You think that's what this is falling from the sky?"

All he saw was that she needed gloves.

"Think you need a goddamn spankin', that's what I think."

Her eyes narrowed, but those lips parted and even in only the distant light from above The Barn's front door he could see her cheeks had darkened.

Fuck yeah.

A shuddered hiss escaped that mouth he wanted to do so much to.

"You ain't shiverin' 'cause you're cold, are you?" He closed the tiny gap between them and drove his hands inside her hood and into her hair, tipping her face up as he dropped his.

He claimed that mouth. Right there, standing where anyone could see them, and he didn't give a fuck. He drove his tongue deep, sweeping every corner. Tasting her. Feeling her soft lips against his.

He wanted those lips wrapped around his cock. He hadn't had that yet. But tonight…

Tonight, it was going to happen. He fantasized about it every time he'd laid in his bed with her sultry voice in his ear as they talked.

But none of that would happen until he got her back to

his place. They needed to wrap up what was going on and get back there. Especially with how fast the snow was falling.

He swallowed her groan and kissed her hard enough to make her do it one more time. When he broke the kiss, he pressed his beanie covered forehead to hers.

For a second, they simply breathed. The opaque fog caused by their rapid panting creating a cocoon around them.

"Listen carefully, Syn," he warned softly, once he didn't sound like he'd just finished a hundred-meter sprint.

She nodded but not enough to break their contact.

"Want you." That part was obvious. But what he said next even surprised himself. "Not a one night fuckin' fling, either." *Fuck it,* he might as well keep going. "Want you in my bed. Wanna teach you shit. Wanna explore shit with you. Want to know every fuckin' inch of you. Hope you want the same."

She pulled away and stared up at him. "You mean like permanently in your bed? Or just for the next few days until we get Maya back?"

"You weren't listenin'."

"I heard you, Dodge, but... I have a daughter."

"No shit."

"I mean..."

"What the fuck does that got to do with anythin'?"

"I want to start a life with her. Make up for the time we've missed. The band... My music..."

"Got all that. You sayin' there ain't room in that life for anyone else?"

"Are you being serious right now?"

She tried to step back, but he grabbed her wrists and held her there. "You think I'm fuckin' with you?"

"We hardly know each other."

"That's easily solved. Wanna know every fuckin' minute of your life. Wanna know your hopes and fuckin' dreams.

Wanna know what scares you. What'll make you purr, make you come, make you laugh. Or even just smile. Wanna hear my name on your lips when you come all over me, when you need somethin' or even when you don't need a damn thing."

"Dodge..." she breathed.

"Yeah, baby, just like that."

"But—"

"This ain't a negotiation, either, so don't think it is."

"What if I don't want you the same way?"

"If you don't, gonna see that as a challenge. But if you say you don't, also gonna call you a fuckin' liar. Those nights on the phone with me. Those texts every day. You think I lay around talkin' on the fuckin' phone like a horny fourteen-year-old virgin with just anyone? I've never done that before with anyone. Not even at fourteen. So, that should tell you something, Syn. And you're a fuckin' liar if you didn't look forward to them as much as I did." He leaned closer, pulled her hood away from her ear and put his mouth to it. "Didn't you?"

When she whispered, "Yes," relief flooded him and soaked him to his very core.

Why he wanted this woman more than any other he'd been with, he didn't know. He didn't understand it at all.

Maybe he wasn't meant to. It was possible he was only meant to accept it and not question what—or who—the universe put in his path. "Say it again, Syn, louder this time."

A shudder went through her and he fought to keep from grinning at her reaction.

"Yes," she just about shouted. "Yes, I looked forward to them, to hearing your voice. To your messages. I looked forward to knowing someone actually cared. So, I'm not going to lie, the answer was, and still is, yes." As he went to straighten, she grabbed his collar and kept him there. "I also look forward to later. I look forward to trying anything and everything you can teach me. I'm willing to learn it all. And I want to learn it all with you."

Jesus fuck. His dick was now a steel pipe in his jeans and throbbing as badly as a stubbed pinky toe.

If that conversation he needed to have with Sig and Trip wasn't so damn important, he'd drag her by her hair back to his truck, go find a dark spot and fuck the shit out of her. After he made her lay across his lap, totally fucking naked as he marked her ass with his palm.

For fuck's sake, he couldn't go talk to his brothers with a raging hard-on over Syn. With those fantasies swirling around his brain. With that anticipation. With his fingers itching to mark that perfectly pale skin.

"For however long it lasts," she added, bringing those thoughts to a screeching halt.

He straightened. "No, Syn. Told you this ain't a negotiation. Here's the thing… Once you're mine, you're mine. Ain't gonna be no time limit on that. You get me?"

He took a step back and said nothing as she blinked up at him.

He expected more attitude from her. He sure as fuck didn't expect compliance.

But that was what he got when she whispered, "Yes, I get you."

He wasn't sure what was hotter or what made him harder. Her being agreeable or when she argued.

"Now, wanna get the fuck outta here, but Maya comes first, yeah? So, gonna go take a minute to talk to my brothers and see what we're gonna do next. Then I'm takin' you back to my place for your first lesson. You up for that tonight?" If she wasn't, he'd understand. They had plenty of time to explore new things. To figure out her likes and dislikes. What she was comfortable with and what she wasn't. To show her what sex could be instead of only what she'd experienced in the past.

When she nodded, he shook his head. "No, need to hear it, Syn. You up for that?" he asked again, wanting her to be sure.

"Yes."

Thank fuck. "Now, before you head over to the bus, want your mouth again. From here on out, your mouth is mine and I want it before we go our separate ways. Every time, Syn, no exceptions. We'll make this lesson number one. It's an easy one but important." Every time she kissed him either in public, or even private, it would remind her who she belonged to.

It would also remind him she was his to take care of. To provide all her needs.

But… she wouldn't only be his, he would be hers, too.

He would make sure to be clear about that.

If she gave him everything, he'd do the same in return.

He stood in place and made her come to him. When she did, he snaked his arms around her, pulled her against him and planted both palms on her ass, wishing like fuck they were back in his apartment and his hands were on her bare skin instead.

Business first, pleasure later.

The anticipation might kill him but it would be worth it.

When she got up on her tiptoes and brushed her lips over his, he didn't move. When she pressed them harder against his, he opened his mouth enough to let her tongue inside. It tentatively touched his. The second time their tongues touched, she was more confident.

After the third time, he took over and kissed her until they were both out of breath again.

Good thing he had pulled on boxers, otherwise he might have a fucking wet spot on the front of his jeans from the steady stream of precum leaking from him. "If we weren't in the middle of a damn snow squall, I might fuck you under the pavilion there."

"Sig…"

"Gonna make somethin' clear with him, too. He's gonna have to get used to seein' you with me."

"Not like that," she exclaimed, making him grin.

"Right, not like that," he agreed with regret. He smacked her ass. "All right. Let me go figure out a game plan."

The relief on her face was clear as fucking day. He only hoped they were successful and it didn't turn out to be a clusterfuck.

"Before we leave, can we get some food and take it out to the guys?"

Dodge nodded. "Yeah. I'll check with Trip about givin' them access to the kitchen, the bar, the showers and the rest inside."

"Will he let them stay in the bunkhouse, instead?"

"Don't know, baby, but I can ask." That might be a tall order when it came to Trip.

"Be convincing."

His lips twitched at her demand. "Got it. Head to the bus and get warm. Be back in a bit."

Maybe the prez would let the guys share the bunkroom with Scar, Castle and Bones now that Dozer and Woody had moved into their own rooms. At least until they hit the road again.

If it was up to Dodge, and most likely Sig, when they hit the road again, it would be without their lead singer.

However, that wasn't the issue they needed to deal with first. They needed to get her daughter back. He couldn't imagine Syn would want to travel in a damn half-broken-down bus with her nine-year-old. Maya needed to go to school and have a stable home.

She also needed to bond with her real mother again.

Syn had been hardly scraping by. Having a kid with her would make her nomad lifestyle even tougher.

She really needed to put down roots. At least for Maya. And there was no better place for that to happen than right in Manning Grove. *Hell*, right on this very fucking farm.

As he headed toward the farmhouse, he took a quick glance over his shoulder to see she had reached the bus and was already climbing inside.

It was crazy how hard it was for him to walk away from her at that moment, even though he knew he'd see her again soon.

How a petite powerhouse, with a smoky voice that had sucked him in and refused to spit him back out, so quickly turned his life upside down and made him question the future he thought he'd already figured out.

If he was honest with himself, he wasn't hating the prospect of Syn being a permanent fixture in his life. As he strode through the snow, he realized, if he looked hard enough, lately he'd actually been hating all the nameless, faceless pussy that came in and out of his bed like one of those rotating doors.

Life was goddamn strange. He wouldn't deny the intense pull he had toward Syn or pretend it didn't exist.

Fuck no, he planned to ride it out and see where it took them.

That meant he also needed to pull Sig aside and tell Syn's brother his intentions. That might take a little more convincing than it had with Syn herself. But he was up for that challenge, too.

He'd make damn sure that was one challenge he wouldn't lose.

Chapter Twenty

As the snow piled up, they got back to his place before the roads became impassable. In fact, a few times it got a little hairy.

The town kept Main Street as clear as possible but after salting the roads, they usually waited to plow the back roads and side streets once the storm was over. Especially when storms blew in as fast as the current one. And the alleys? They were the last to be cleared every damn time. Luckily, with his Power Wagon's four-wheel-drive and knobby tires, his beast got through most shit.

Micah and Dozer had actually shut the bar down early because of the treacherous conditions. Nobody but a couple of diehard regulars who lived within walking distance had remained. Everyone else who drove to drink was smart enough to leave before having to be kicked out.

After walking in the rear door, he automatically went to double-check the front entrance to make sure it was locked. Then he took Syn upstairs with the duffle bag he told her to pack with whatever necessities she'd need for the next two days.

If the snow didn't let up soon, he had a feeling they'd be

holed up at Crazy Pete's for at least a day or so. If he had to be stuck at the bar, he wasn't going to bitch about being stuck there with Syn.

The first thing he did was strip her down, get them both into the shower and show her the kind of care he'd give her after their "lessons." He did this by washing not only her hair, but every inch of her body. Afterward, he wrapped her in a towel and dried her off before doing the same for himself.

If she gave herself to him, he would do whatever was needed to show his appreciation of that gift. Including spoiling her.

To be completely upfront, he told her he would expect certain things from her, but in turn, she could expect the same from him. Surprisingly, she seemed to be okay with the terms he laid out.

While it would be a partnership, he warned her that he would have the ultimate say.

Some women didn't like that—he couldn't imagine a woman like Reese or even Stella agreeing to those terms—and he expected some pushback from Syn.

He promised never to hurt her and always take care of her needs first. He also promised to listen and if she had concerns, she was encouraged to voice them. Respect was a two-way street.

Their relationship would be a give and take. An ebb and flow.

If she gave herself completely to him, he would give her everything in return. Anything she wanted, he would do his best to fulfill those wants and needs.

One of those needs was getting Maya back. On the trip from the farm to Pete's he gave her the lowdown on the plan he, Sig and Trip came up with.

Trip had called Shade while they stood there in the kitchen of the farmhouse discussing options, thinking he was the best man to help in this situation. Once the low-key Fury member heard the necessary details, he agreed to accompany Dodge and Sig on this very important mission.

The man knew how to move quietly and efficiently use a knife to kill, unlike Sig who'd simply hack off a man's dick and leave a huge mess behind for someone else to clean up.

Somehow Shade also knew how to break into a house and disable its alarm system without alerting the residents. Skills that might be needed in this case.

Of course, Sig's plan wasn't to quietly take out the man named Sam Danzig. Danzig might also not be the only one hauled in the back of the van across the border to Pennsylvania and the cremation furnaces at Tioga Pet Services. Then a few hours later, after being placed in the Easy Bake oven, placed into a bucket or box until the snow in the fields was gone. One of the far fields being their final resting place.

Ashes to ashes, dust to dust, you wanna fuck with children, teach you a lesson we must.

Another option would make their disappearance look like an accident. But that would take more planning and precision than just going in and getting the job done.

Dodge liked the shock and awe version better. Get in, get out. No fucking around.

He assured Syn as soon as the snow storm blew through and the roads were passable, they'd head south to West Virginia and collect her daughter.

Not unexpectedly, she insisted on going along. Dodge didn't like it. Knew Sig and Shade would hate it, but she made a compelling case.

Maya was nine. Her life as she knew it was about to be turned upside down. She would need a familiar face when men she didn't know busted in, retrieved her and took her away from the only family she knew.

It was going to be confusing and scary. With Syn there, Dodge hoped that would be minimized.

"She gonna remember you?" Dodge had asked her, keeping his eyes on the road as he carefully maneuvered through the snow drifting across their path.

"She should. It's been a few years since I was allowed to see her but I raised her until I left at seventeen. I only left to establish a household so I could get her out of that house and away from Sam, just in case he tried the same thing with her. That was my greatest fear even though he knew Maya was his biological child. I was worried that wouldn't make a difference."

She had buried her face in her hands for a few seconds and it was obvious that she was beating herself up for that decision. She shouldn't. She had only been seventeen and a child herself. She thought she was doing what was best for her child. It turned out to be a mistake.

Dodge didn't push her to continue. He waited until she was ready to do so on her own. He wanted to reach out and touch her, to comfort her, but, with as bad as the roads were, he had to maintain two hands on the wheel except for when he had to shift. Even then, his truck had gotten a little squirrelly.

"After that, they only allowed me supervised visits until I turned eighteen. They said those were the terms of the guardianship. I'm sure that was a lie and now I'm thinking a court-appointed guardianship never existed. Why would they lie to me like that?"

The pain and sadness in her voice made him want to punch his fucking windshield. He and Sig would most likely fight over who got to take out Sam Danzig and maybe even her adoptive parents, he now knew were named Cara and Lyle.

"'Cause those fuckers had their own agenda, Syn. People are goddamn fucked in the head. They go outta their way to hurt others without good cause and they don't give a fuckin' shit. They're selfish and goddamn cruel. They'll step on others to get the shit they want for themselves. Do a single bid in prison and you'll see shit that'll color your world a whole lot differently."

He didn't want to go into the distrust that had seeped into his blood and bones during all of his time inside. She already had that running through her body, too. He'd seen it the first night she walked into Crazy Pete's. Now that he knew some of the backstory, he didn't blame her for keeping her guard up.

He'd lived that life for a long time himself. He'd only started dropping his walls once he found his home in Manning Grove among the Fury brotherhood. But he'd kept that guard up with every woman that had crossed his path.

Until Syn.

The second he dropped it he knew it had been a mistake because she had gotten under his skin and he was unable to escape her hold.

Maybe it had been a mistake at first, but now? He no longer wanted to scrape her free.

That was the reason he spilled his fucking guts to her outside earlier and in front of The Barn.

That was the reason she was now in his truck heading back to his apartment.

That was the reason she would be in his bed for good, if he had any say in the matter.

That was also the reason he would give up the endless parade of women in exchange for only one. Something he never expected to ever do. He'd been ducking and dodging any serious relationships his whole life.

Many of his brothers had also given up that pussy parade when they found their ol' ladies. That one person worth giving up everything else for. The one they didn't want to risk losing. The one that…

Just. Fucking. Fit.

But telling that to Syn at this point would overwhelm her. Because, *for fuck's sake*, it overwhelmed him.

Who would have thought a very young, moody, petite woman wearing a cat-eared hoodie with a spellbinding voice would walk into his life and change it forever as if it was fucking witchcraft.

Certainly not him.

He had dragged himself back to their conversation. "You were eighteen when you last saw her."

That thought got his blood boiling. Those assholes cutting off a child from her mother pissed him the fuck off. Her adoptive "parents" were just as much pieces of shit as the man whose unwelcomed sperm created Maya.

His fingers strangled the truck's steering wheel with the urge to do the same to those motherfuckers' throats.

Every goddamn one of them.

He couldn't imagine being a thirteen-year-old girl and not only dealing with some thirty-something motherfucker forcing himself on her but having to bear the child of her very own goddamn rapist. That alone caused an unhealthy fury to burn inside him. Then add on that the family, who was supposed to love her and treat her like their own daughter, steals that very fucking child.

He blew out a breath and had to unclench his teeth before he ground them to the roots. He forced himself to contain his simmering rage since he didn't want to stress Syn out more than she already was.

But, if it was up to him, they'd all breathe their last breath soon. Every single fucking one of them. Syn had mentioned an older brother. How much older than her, Dodge didn't know or care, but he had to be at least in his mid-twenties.

He might be an adult but did they want to leave him without both parents? Did Dodge or Sig give a fuck enough to allow the mother to live? Sig wouldn't. Dodge shouldn't, either.

Syn's adoptive "mother," Cara, had been evil enough to go along with keeping Syn from Maya. She really deserved no pass.

"It's been five years," she whispered. "I'm sure she's grown so much since I last saw her."

He had taken his eyes off the road for a split second to stare at the woman on the far side of the bench seat, staring out the passenger window. Her cat-eared hood was again pulled up over her head. She wore that damn thing as if it was a shield. Like it had magical powers and when she wore it up, she became invisible.

At that very fucking moment, he realized she would never be invisible to him. No matter how hard she tried to retreat into herself. To hide that mix of emotions that had to be swirling around inside her.

He also decided right then and there that they'd take two vehicles to West Virginia. He didn't want Maya or Syn riding in the same van along with the dead body of a child rapist. One body at the minimum. Again, if it was up to him, there would be three piled in that van.

While they waited for the storm to move on, Deacon would do a little digging to find Sam Danzig's address and they'd hit that fucker's place first. Then they'd go retrieve Maya and deal with Syn's adoptive parents.

But they still had a couple of days before they could head out. In that time, they could solidify their plan. Of course, Trip wanted this extraction to be neat and not messy. He also made it clear he did not want whatever they did in West Virginia splashing on the Fury in any way.

None of them would wear their colors and if shit went sideways, they were to keep the club's name out of their mouth. They would use the new van purchased for the crematorium that didn't have the business name plastered on the side yet.

In fact, Trip said maybe they shouldn't mark up that van at all for cases such as this. He told Shade to have Cassie look into buying large removable magnets instead. This way it could be used when they needed to go incognito.

Dodge didn't expect any different from the club's president. On the surface, Trip wanted the Fury to stay "clean." What happened below the surface was a whole different fucking story.

When shit needed to get done, it got done in any way it needed to.

Like with the wannabe militia, the Shirley Clan, and their Guardians of Freedumb bullshit sovereign nation.

Like with Reilly's abusive ex-boyfriend, Billy.

Like with whatever circumstance brought Jude into Shade and Chelle's life.

One way or another, the Fury did what the Fury needed to do. Trip just preferred they do it not in such a reckless manner.

Unfortunately, sometimes that couldn't be helped.

Like Sig totally losing his mind and doing the nightmare-causing shit he did to Vernon Shirley.

Sig could not lose his mind on this one. Dodge hoped to fuck the man would keep his shit together and concentrate on executing the plan so they could get the fuck out of West Virginia before they got caught.

While the goal was to get Maya, it also was to do it in a way no one ended up wearing metal bracelets.

In the meantime, they had a couple of days to wait and work on that plan. He was going to spend that time with Syn. Before Maya came home.

Yeah, *home*. Because whether Syn wanted to see it or not, Manning Grove would now be home for her and her daughter.

If she thought otherwise, she would lose that fight.

However, right now, they weren't fighting about shit. What they were about to do was as far from fighting as they could get.

He was sitting naked on the edge of his bed, his dick a steel rod rising from his lap, while an equally naked Syn stood between his thighs. While he didn't know what it was before, he now realized the small, very faded, horizontal scar on her lower belly was from a C-section.

He couldn't imagine having to be sliced open to bring a child, one a product of your rape, into the world. Even more mind-blowing was still wanting and loving that child even when you were too young to bear or raise it. Still wanting and loving that child even though she might remind Syn for the rest of her life how her daughter came to be.

Wanting and loving that child even as if she'd been planned instead of forced upon her.

They all had supported Red's decision. It had been the best decision for everyone involved, especially for Levi. Sig's ol' lady had zero regrets for wanting the best life for that baby. She was selfless enough to know in their situation it wouldn't be with her and Sig.

Just like Dodge wasn't bothered by the state taking away his sibling from his drug-addicted mother. His hope was that decision had given the child a chance to have a better life.

Sig had done the same with Syn. His goal was to save his baby sister from horrible circumstances. Only he had no idea his good intentions would turn bad.

Now he'd have to live with that outcome along with all the other issues the man already dealt with. But maybe getting Maya back, bringing her into the Fury family, would help.

But that wasn't what Dodge should be concentrating on right now. Not when Syn stood in front of him, unashamedly naked and clearly ready for him.

When her fingers slid along his beard-covered jawline, he glanced up and saw her studying his face with her bottom lip tucked between her teeth.

Fuck.

"Don't know all the details about what happened to you back then and you don't gotta tell me. Willin' to listen if you do. But, here's the thing... Need to know if anythin' I do bothers you the very second it does, you get me? If there's even a question, raise it. Ain't gonna get mad. Ain't ever gonna force you to do somethin' you don't wanna do. There's plenty of other shit we can do instead that will get the same result."

He held onto her hips to keep her right where she stood while he made that clear. He wouldn't do anything that made her uncomfortable unless she wanted to push her boundaries.

Now knowing what he knew, when he wanted to try something new, either to her or even the both of them, he would start slow, not assume shit, and then build from there.

No matter how much something turned him the fuck on, if it didn't do the same for Syn, he would avoid it.

Give and take.

There was a time to be firm and dominant, but also a time to be soft and understanding.

He wanted her to enjoy his version of vanilla spice. He wanted her to sip that spice, savor it and then ask for seconds. If she was comfortable with whatever they tried, he'd increase the spice until they found what worked for them both.

Ebb and flow.

He'd seen how it worked for Deacon and Reese, who were total opposites. For them, their push and pull worked perfectly. Another example of complete opposites were Ozzy, who could be overbearing, and his introverted ol' lady,

Shay. It turned out Shay's personality was exactly what the club secretary needed for balance.

Dodge tended to be overbearing, too, especially when it came to sex. He preferred women who could handle his aggressiveness in bed.

He hoped like fuck Syn could handle him. He didn't want to dial himself down to the point he never got what he needed. Sig had to turn off a lot of shit to be with Red and sometimes it showed. Sig was willing to do what it took to be with Red, even if it was a sacrifice for him.

Dodge just hoped it never backfired. Red was the type of woman who wouldn't be able to live with herself if it did.

He pushed thoughts of Syn's brother out of his head and focused on Syn, instead.

Leaning forward, he pulled a peaked nipple into his mouth, sucking it as deeply as he could until his molars scraped the very tip. He continued to hold onto her firmly, not letting her pull away. If she didn't like what he was doing, she needed to speak up. He wasn't going to guess.

He'd stressed that to her when they had taken that shower together. And reminded her again when he slowly unwrapped the towel as she stood in front of him.

When he released her nipple, it was shiny and slightly swollen, but while he sucked it, her fingers had slid into his hair, gripping it firmly. She didn't free his hair when he pulled back slightly and looked up into her face. Her eyes were unfocused and her lips parted slightly.

He found that her having tits on the smaller side allowed him to take almost the whole thing into his mouth. He liked that. Much more than he expected.

More than a handful's a waste.

That saying wasn't quite true, but what Syn had was perfect for her size. And that mouthful was tasty as fuck.

He tugged one of her hands free from his hair and

wrapped her fingers around his hard-on, showing her what he wanted her to do.

As she stroked him slowly, he brushed the back of his fingers down her flushed cheek, then curled them firmly around the delicate column of her throat.

Breath play had always turned him the fuck on. She hadn't seemed to mind it the other night, but he also hadn't pushed it too far. Now, he didn't know if it might fuck with her head.

"Need to know if my hand on your throat's gonna trigger you. This is why I keep bringin' up communication. It's gonna be key with most of the shit we do." More like most of the shit he *wanted* to do.

"It didn't the other night."

"Good to know."

"Do you want to know why?" she asked, still stroking him but picking up the pace a little. He tried to concentrate on what they were discussing and not on what she was doing with her hand. But when she squeezed him tightly, his hips jumped. She did it again like she was trying to squeeze the last bit of toothpaste out of the tube.

He wasn't mad about it at all.

He forced his brain to function so he could ask, "'Cause you're into it?" Like her, her hands were petite, but the one jerking him still packed a fucking punch.

"Well, that. Surprisingly. But it's not the only reason."

He kept one hand on her throat and used the other to drag his thumb across her bottom lip before dipping it inside. One corner of his mouth curled up when the tip of her tongue touched the tip of his thumb. "Tell me," he whispered, his dick flexing within her fingers.

Her words sounded like they'd been drenched in honey when she said, "Because I trust you."

I trust you.

Fuck. Those three words meant more to him than she'd

ever know. To him they were almost the same as saying she loves him. He knew she didn't. They hadn't spent enough time together for that to develop.

To love someone completely, you had to trust them. So, it could be the first step toward something solid between them. A seed that could potentially grow into something more.

He could only fucking hope.

That realization shocked the shit out of him.

"Yeah, baby, trust and communication's gonna go hand-in-hand."

Releasing her throat, he turned her in place, breaking her grip so he wouldn't just blow his load in her hand.

He swept both hands down the silky-smooth skin of her back until he reached her ass. Cupping both cheeks, he squeezed and marveled how well they fit in his palms, just like her tit did in his mouth. Like she was made for him.

He considered himself an artist and her ass a fresh canvas. "Wanna mark your ass, Syn, but ain't gonna do it 'til you're ready. So, when you are, need you to tell me."

She trembled slightly under his touch but it was the catch in her throat that spoke to him the loudest.

"If there are toys, techniques or positions you wanna try, you just need to say the word. Nothin' is off the table. Not a damn thing. Even if it's somethin' you wanna try on me, all you gotta do is ask. You trustin' me means I gotta trust you, too."

"Do you?" Like her body, her question had a slight shake to it.

Keeping a grip on her ass, he tucked both thumbs into her crease and parted her there. He wanted to taste her in places she hadn't been tasted yet. "Yeah."

Every piece of her now belonged to him. She might not understand that yet, but she would.

He fell back onto the bed, tipped his head up slightly

and held out his hand. "Hop on, baby, wanna take you for a ride."

She turned and without any hesitation climbed on the bed and up his body, sliding her warm, damp pussy along his skin.

When she got to this chest, he said, "Face away from me."

As soon as she turned and sat on his chest, he separated those tight cheeks again, running a finger down the seam and around her even tighter hole.

"Off my chest and on my face."

She rose on her knees and shuffled backward until she hovered over his mouth. His mouth watered at the sight of her glistening pussy and the scent of her arousal filled his nostrils.

"Spread yourself. No, not there… That's it… there." He tentatively touched the rim of her anus with the tip of his tongue. "Come down to me, baby. That's it… Let go now."

He grabbed her hips and pulled her down so he had full access to that part of her. He licked and nibbled and kissed both there and her pussy until it was dripping what to him tasted like nectar. It smeared all over his beard, on his lips. His nose. He didn't give a fuck. He wanted more.

He alternated eating her ass and her pussy. After a few moments of simply spoiling her, he planted his hand on the center of her back and pushed her down. His dick was aching, his balls pulled tight and a string of precum hung precariously.

That was, until she caught it on the tip of her tongue.

A noise came from deep within her and he jerked when she grabbed the root of his cock and wrapped her hot, little mouth around the head. Her tongue swirled around the crown and he got so caught up in it, he had frozen with one of her folds in his mouth.

Fuuuuuuck.

It was awkward because she didn't know what the fuck she was doing, but he didn't care. Especially when she released his dick with a wet pop, then her little tongue darted out and licked up his length.

Holy fuck.

He'd had some really good head before and he'd had some really bad head, too. This was somewhere in the middle. But if this was her first time, he assumed it was, he could work with that.

He would enjoy showing her just what he liked.

But right now was not the time. Instead, he let her do what came naturally and he continued on his own trek to bring her to orgasm.

"Talk to me, baby," Dodge murmured into her ear as his hips flexed with each pump. This man knew how to hit all the right spots. He knew how to move, what to say and definitely how to bring her to orgasm.

"Keep going," she whispered.

"Yeah, that's a given," he said with slight amusement in his voice. "Meant with everythin' else."

"You're good."

"That's a given, too." He actually snorted.

"You don't have to get cocky about it," she chided him. Though, he really had every right to get cocky with his skills and about giving her the two very intense orgasms she'd already had.

He was now working on giving her a third.

Syn knew he was holding back, especially after he repeated himself over and over about what his plans were and how she needed to communicate with him.

She appreciated that. In her limited experience, she never had a man tell her that. For those men, it had been all about getting themselves to the end and not the journey getting there. She saw that now.

Dodge also made her realize why sex hadn't been so important to her.

Now… On only her second night with him, she could see why some people were obsessed with sex. Once you were with the right partner, things could change. And change quickly.

She had been missing out.

Not just with sex. But life in general.

Once she got Maya back, she would have to reevaluate her future and her goals.

Knowing she'd soon be reunited with her daughter gave her a sense of peace she hadn't had in a long time.

She just hoped like hell it went smoothly. She wasn't sure she could take any more heartbreak when it came to losing what she valued the most in life. Her daughter.

She might have been very young when she had Maya, but even so, the connection she felt when that little human was placed in her arms had been intense.

Especially after hearing her first soft cry. And during the bonding that occurred when she nursed her daughter.

The instinct to love and protect her had overwhelmed Syn.

That instinct hadn't been hampered by how that baby came about. It didn't matter who her biological father was. Nothing mattered except for Maya.

She closed her eyes for a second. A little over two weeks ago she had walked into a bar with her life in shambles and feeling like her life was no longer in her control.

Now her hope had returned stronger than ever.

A lot of that had to do with the man whose damp cheek was pressed to hers and whose warm breath swept over her heated skin, making every inch of her break out in goosebumps.

Simply looking at him made her heart flip upside down. In a good way. It also warmed her from head to toe. He heated her to her very core.

He made her think everything would turn out all right. That he'd be there for her every step of the way and support her when she needed it.

A sense of security she'd never had.

She didn't want to ever let go of that feeling. She hoped she never had to.

It was crazy. All of it was just plain crazy. She knew it and didn't care. It might be crazy but it felt right.

It seemed to be the same way for him.

He made it clear that he wanted her and not just in his bed tonight. He still wanted her knowing what happened to her and even after finding out she had a nine-year-old child.

"Promised you a third. I'm waitin' on you so I can get mine."

She opened her eyes and looked directly into his dark brown ones. She slowly blew out a breath.

"Thank you," she whispered.

His eyebrows pulled together. "For what?"

"For everything."

"Didn't do everythin' yet."

She cupped his cheek. "I know. But just knowing you want to give me everything…" She swallowed past the tightness in her throat. The tightness wasn't from his hand—he'd kept his grip super loose tonight—it was from those rising emotions she'd kept tamped deep down inside.

She couldn't believe it hadn't even been twelve hours since Rex drove their skoolie back onto that farm. So much had happened since then.

So much was about to happen.

Including another orgasm.

He promised her a third, he delivered on that promise.

Chapter Twenty-One

He was asleep on his stomach, snoring softly, with one arm thrown heavily over her waist. Most likely so he'd wake up if she tried to escape the bed.

But she didn't want to escape. Right now, she was perfectly fine with where she was.

They'd been snowed in for two days. During that time, her emotions had flip-flopped back and forth.

While she was anxious to go get Maya, she was also content to spend some alone time with Dodge. Being stuck at Pete's, temporarily shut down due to the storm, meant she didn't have to share him with anyone.

That would quickly change once they retrieved her daughter because it might be a while before Syn let Maya get farther away from her than within hearing distance.

She had no idea where they'd end up living. Or how she'd manage raising her when The Synners hit the road.

Because they would need to hit the road again. And soon. It was her only source of income, even as bad as it was.

Even if they played regularly at Pete's, it wouldn't be

enough to live on. Or pay rent. Or buy Maya school clothes and supplies.

Once Maya was back in her possession, so many arrangements would need to be made. It was too much to think about all at once. All of it was so damn overwhelming.

When she'd begin to fret, Dodge would ask her what was bothering her and she didn't hesitate to tell him.

He had insisted she always be open with him and he'd do the same. Better yet, he wanted to work out problems together instead of her trying to do it by herself in her head.

What they hadn't discussed was her staying in Manning Grove. She guessed he was waiting to team up with Sig to help convince her.

He didn't have to say it, she could feel it. He already acted as though she would settle in and stay. Even if that happened eventually, she had a daughter to think about and there was no way they could live in a studio apartment above a bar.

She and Maya would need to get their own place somewhere. Her daughter would need to go to school.

Syn also needed to have a serious conversation with her band members. Everything she decided would affect them, too. They'd been with her for years and she would never turn her back on them.

Even though she'd been singing ever since she could remember, it wasn't until she started piano lessons that she discovered her intense love of music and how naturally it came to her. She was told she had an "ear" for it and a voice to make audiences sit up and pay attention.

Those piano lessons quickly stopped because they ended up being too expensive for her adoptive parents. But by then she'd learned the basics, including how to read music. It wasn't until she hooked up with Eddie, Rex and Nico, a fledging band searching for a lead singer, that she learned to play guitar and drums. Nico had also taught her more about the keyboard than her piano teacher ever had.

Because they didn't have enough money to do anything, in their downtime or in the skoolie while traveling between gigs, Syn absorbed everything her bandmates taught her. While on the road, she practiced constantly and became decent with every instrument packed away under the bus.

She owed them so much for that, too, and another reason why she owed them her loyalty.

She twisted under Dodge's heavy arm to study the club colors tattooed onto his back, wondering if her brother had the same thing done to his.

To do something so permanently, Dodge had to be serious about belonging to the Fury. People didn't mark their bodies like that for something that was a fleeting hobby.

It proved the club was a huge part of his life.

The MC was a huge part of Sig's life, too. But then it turned out that Sig had a brother unrelated to Syn, the Fury's very own president.

In one of their long phone conversations in the middle of the night, Dodge had told her the story about how he became a part of the club after his last stint in prison and also why Trip resurrected an MC that had previously been obliterated.

Trip's reason for rebuilding wasn't to revisit the past, but to fix its mistakes. To help and connect the people who were affected by those mistakes. To make something whole from all those broken pieces.

Syn understood that. She wanted that, too.

To fix and strengthen her relationship with Sig.

To get her daughter.

And to finally live her life the way she wanted to live it.

Even live that life with Dodge.

He seemed to want that, but she couldn't wrap her head

around why, since they hadn't spent a lot of time together. At least not long enough to make any decisions about a possible "forever."

It was way too soon for that, wasn't it?

She slipped from under his arm and moved to straddle his waist. He had a nice back. Strong and lean. Though, it now bore scratches in several places.

If she pulled the sheet off from where it had caught on his ass, she'd find her scratches marking him there, too. If he rolled over, she'd see her handiwork on his chest and neck. Down his belly and over his hips.

His hellcat.

That was what he'd called her several times in the past two days.

My hellcat was what he'd whisper in her ear.

He made it clear she was his.

She belonged to him.

At first she thought it was just something he was saying, some sort of turn-on for him, then she realized he truly believed it.

He was claiming her. He wanted to totally possess her.

Well, if he was doing that, she was doing the same.

Dodge now belonged to her, too. He was hers.

She'd made many mistakes in her twenty-three years, she only hoped she wasn't making another one with Dodge. The problem with mistakes was that you usually didn't know you were making one until it was too late…

Like when she thought leaving her adoptive parents' house and establishing her own would be a good thing. Instead, it backfired. It handed control of Maya over to her "parents" and took it away from Syn. Opposite of her intentions.

Now here she was again, letting Dodge take control.

Only this time if things went wrong, she hoped she'd have Sig and maybe even Trip at her back.

She leaned over and slowly traced each line and curve of his huge Fury tattoo with the tip of her tongue. The snoring stopped, his breathing changed and his muscles twitched along her path. When she was done, she planted a kiss in the middle of the club's colors, right in the center of the skull.

If the man was loyal to his club, loyal to his brotherhood, enough to get that tattoo, then she had no doubt he could be loyal to her.

That would be a requirement for her to be his.

Her life would need to remain steady to raise her daughter. She had the next nine years to make up for the last nine before Maya would be old enough to travel her own path.

Husky laughter escaped her as he twisted and trapped her beneath him. He dragged his rough, wiry beard across her cheek before taking her mouth. When he was done with it, he drilled his elbows into the mattress and went nose to nose with her.

"These past two days have shown me you got a little freak inside you, baby. You just need to ask her to come out to play."

She shook her head. "*You* need to ask her."

Dodge fisted her hair in both hands and pulled her head back far enough to arch her throat. He dragged his lips along her pounding pulse and then dipped his tongue in the hollow. "Ain't gonna ask, baby, gonna demand it. You ready for that?"

Was she?

He shifted enough to nip one breast before moving to do the same to the other. He knew how to give her just enough pain to enhance the pleasure.

He was opening up a whole new world for her. One that was completely unexpected. One she looked forward to expanding.

Everything wrong in her world was slowly being righted.

Now, they just needed to get Maya.

Then life would be one step closer to perfect.

———

THEY BROUGHT Deacon along to drive the rented cage they'd use to haul Syn and Maya back to Pennsylvania. They removed the rear license plate from the new crematorium van and slapped on an old, expired plate from the junkyard behind Dutch's Garage.

They left their cuts at home. They also left their guns there, too, since crossing two state lines with them wasn't smart. Instead, they all strapped on knives in case they needed them.

During the long drive south, Dodge ordered Syn to stay in the cage no matter fucking what. Unless she was told otherwise. He told Deacon to make sure she listened. She was there only to comfort Maya after everything went down. To assure her daughter she was safe.

And, of course, to reunite with her.

Syn was not to get involved. She was not to witness anything else that happened. His brothers all agreed with him on those points. *Thank fuck.*

Deacon parked the rented cage in the parking lot of a strip mall a mile away and was to wait there until they got word that Dodge, Sig and Shade had dealt with Sam Danzig and were en route to Syn's adoptive parents' home.

The bounty hunter was to enter the neighborhood from a different direction and park the cage down the block from the target house. They didn't want the two vehicles connected in any way by any witnesses.

It would make for a cleaner getaway.

Shade insisted he should enter the first location by himself so he could do what he did best and leave behind no evidence but a body.

It would be quick and quiet.

However, that wasn't what Sig or Dodge wanted.

It took some convincing but eventually Shade relented. Even though, reluctantly.

Deacon also reminded them that they needed to grab DNA of Danzig before they turned him to ash. For insurance purposes, like Reese had said.

Hopefully they would never need it. But better to have it than not even if it never saw the light of day.

On the ride from the parking lot to Sam Danzig's house, they went back and forth over killing the bastard right there and hauling his ass home to Manning Grove to dispose of it or keeping him alive and making him pay before putting him out of his misery.

The second was a lot riskier than the first.

But, *for fuck's sake,* it would also be a hell of a lot more satisfying.

Dodge recognized the look on Sig's face, and in his eyes, as he advocated for the second. Syn's brother ignored Shade when he kept pushing for the first.

Dodge was torn. He just wanted to take care of business and get them all the fuck out of there without getting caught. He also wanted Maya safe.

That was his main goal. But vengeance pulled at him, too.

Making Sam, and even Syn's adoptive parents, suffer the very deserved consequences for their actions. Sam for what he did to Syn. Her "parents" for letting it happen, then taking a bad situation and making it worse.

Fuck them all. They all needed to pay.

No matter what, he needed to keep his shit together. And both Shade and Dodge needed to keep a handle on Sig.

Out of the four of them, he was the loose thread that could totally unravel and fuck up the whole mission.

In the dark of night, they moved quickly and quietly through the backyards of the cookie-cutter houses. Since they all looked alike from the rear, they had to be careful and make sure they broke into the right one.

Shade made a sound that sounded like a stray cat's meow from up ahead in the dark. Dodge couldn't see him or Sig in the shadows.

Dodge kept moving, staying low and sticking close to bushes and sheds or any cover he could find. When he finally got to where Shade and Sig waited, they had their backs pressed to the siding of a house that had no lights on inside at all.

Good.

The fucker was hopefully asleep in his bed and wouldn't know what hit him until it was too late.

"No security system," Shade whispered. "Gloves on?"

Both Sig and Dodge raised their hands to show that they were gloved up to avoid leaving prints behind.

Shade gave a quick nod, stepped up to the back door and pulled a lock pick set out of his back pocket. Within seconds, a soft click of the deadbolt could be heard. He gave them a chin lift and slowly opened the door. All of them held their breath, hoping the door didn't creak.

Thank fuck it didn't.

The three filed into the dark house and what looked like a kitchen from 1950. The sink was full of dishes, the table piled high with who fucking knew what and one of the cabinets had a broken door hanging from its hinges.

Dodge also noticed a few empty liquor bottles strewn across the counter and on top of the overflowing garbage.

Shade tipped his black beanie-covered head toward the hallway right off the kitchen, but then put up his hand to stop Sig and Dodge from following him. He quietly worked his way down the dark hallway, peeking into open doorways as he went. At the end of the short hallway, he stopped, stared and made the hand signal for them to follow.

They did.

Dodge also peeked in the doorways as he moved to make sure no one else was in the house besides the target.

Shade tipped his head toward the open doorway of the bedroom they were standing right outside of, lifted his hand, put three fingers up and counted them down. Three... Two... One... They moved.

Dodge went to the sleeping fucker's head and slapped both hands over the man's mouth. Shade grabbed his wrists and Sig sat on his legs.

That was when the struggle ensued.

Dodge smothered the yells as Sig quickly duct taped the man's ankles together to keep from fighting them. When he was done, Sig helped Shade wrap the gray tape around the fucker's wrists, pinning them together. Once Danzig was completely hobbled and helpless, Dodge released his mouth.

"Hey!" the man who smelled of stale booze screamed. "What the hell is this?"

Dodge held out his hand and the roll of duct tape was slapped onto his palm. He ripped off a large strip, said, "Sorry, couldn't hear you, asshole. What?" and covered Sam's flapping gums with the tape. "Sit him up," he then ordered.

Sig and Shade pulled the man to a seated position and Dodge used way too much tape when he wrapped it several times around the motherfucker's head, securing the man's mouth.

"That was too fuckin' easy," Sig growled.

"It ain't over, yet, brother," Shade reminded him. "Now we gotta get him outta the house and into the van without gettin' spotted."

Shade pulled a black nylon bag from his pocket and tugged it over the wide-eyed Danzig's head. Even with the tape covering his mouth, they could still hear his muffled screams.

Too bad, so fuckin' sad.

Shade said, "Gonna pull the van 'round back. Let's get him to the back door."

The three of them hauled the child rapist, squirming and trying to fight, through the small house, not giving a fuck when his head bounced off the walls and corners, and into the kitchen. They dumped him onto the linoleum floor in a loud thump.

Sig gave him a boot to the ribs for good measure.

Shade slipped out of the back door while Sig and Dodge shared a glance, then both looked down at the man who had stolen Syn's virginity, stolen her innocence, and gotten her pregnant when she was only thirteen fucking years old.

Man. No, that motherfucker wasn't a man. He wasn't even human.

Men protected women and children. *Men* protected the vulnerable. *Monsters* hurt them. A subhuman species that needed to be exterminated.

Like the fucker on the floor at his feet.

Dodge squatted down next to the squirming piece of shit. "You got a long ride ahead of you to think about all your shitty life choices. If you don't know what the fuck this is about, promise you'll be clued in by the end."

He stood and met Sig's suddenly soulless eyes as Shade reappeared at the back door.

Within five minutes, they had the fucker loaded up in the back of the van, wrapped in tarps and hidden amongst various car parts from Dutch's junkyard so anyone peering in the front windows wouldn't see anything suspicious.

Danzig wasn't a dead body yet. If it was up to Sig, it would take him a while to become one.

But that would have to wait. First, they were off to their next destination.

———

ENTERING Cara and Lyle Danzig's house went as smoothly as the first. The only difference was that Deacon parked the rental down the street, told Syn to wait there until they texted her and then joined them.

They figured there would be a minimum of two adults in that house. Possibly three if the older son still lived at home.

Shade went in, did a quick sweep of the house and came back outside. He held up two fingers.

"Maya in there?" Dodge asked quietly.

"Yeah, sleepin'," the younger brother answered under his breath.

Dodge nodded. "Think we need to get her out first, get her to Syn and then go back in and handle the rest."

"How I wanna handle it might take a while," Sig whispered in a bone-chilling, deadly tone.

"Ain't gonna happen, brother," Deacon told him. "Too fuckin' risky. We're gonna stick to the plan."

"They need to learn a lesson," Sig reminded Deke.

"Yeah, we're gonna give them a lesson, but not the way you want it," Dodge said. "Let's not be stupid. We need to get the fuck outta this state ASAP. Especially with the cargo we're haulin'."

Even in the dark, Dodge could see Sig's jaw shift sharply.

"Just gotta leave behind a clear message," Dodge said. "The one we agreed on."

"Didn't agree to that," Sig growled softly.

"The fuck you didn't," Deacon hissed.

Shade sighed and everyone shut up. "Gonna blow this before we even get inside?"

Dodge swore all of them took a collective breath, then blew out the stupid so they could focus.

"Now, let's do it like we planned," Deacon said. "Ready?"

They all nodded.

Once Shade quickly picked the lock to the rear door, they all followed him inside. Being a two-story, they figured all the bedrooms were up on the second floor and that was the direction Shade led them.

At the top of the steps, Shade pointed to one room with a closed door, then put his open hand up and out in front of his waist, indicating that was the room Maya was in.

He then pointed down the hall to another room with the door closed and held two fingers up again.

Everyone nodded in understanding.

Once Deacon, Sig and Shade quietly moved toward the room where the adults were, Dodge headed toward Maya's room.

He took a last glance down the hallway, waited for his three brothers to disappear inside, then quickly entered Syn's daughter's room.

Thank fuck it had a nightlight so he could somewhat see her under the covers with one arm flung over her head.

He had no idea how to wake her without scaring the shit out of her. Or, worse, having her scream.

He also wanted to avoid giving her nightmares for the rest of her life.

After sitting on the edge of the bed, he softly said her name.

The little girl stirred but didn't wake.

"Maya," he whispered again and shook her shoulder gently. "Maya, I brought your mom to see you."

Maya's eyes flashed open and when she spotted Dodge, they went wide. *Fuck.*

"Don't yell. I'm here with your mom. I promise. I'm not here to hurt you," he assured her quickly.

The girl's breath shuddered as she stared at him.

He quickly continued, keeping one ear open to whatever could be happening down the hall. So far, he wasn't hearing shit. That was a good sign. "My name's Dodge. I'm a friend of your mother. She's waitin' for you outside."

"No, she isn't." Even through the shake of her voice, Maya's attitude was unmistakable and much like Syn's.

"She is. I promise. She came to get you. She loves you and wants you to come with her. You wanna see her? Know it's been a long time. Bet you miss her."

Maya nodded, her bottom lip tucked between her teeth.

Even in the dark, Dodge could see how much she looked like Syn, too. Thank fuck she didn't look like that soon-to-be-dead motherfucker.

"You talk funny."

"Yeah, don't have an accent like you."

"No, that's not it."

Dodge pressed his lips together for a second, waited until the urge to laugh passed, then asked, "You wanna come with me?"

Maya shook her head. "I'm not supposed to go with strangers."

Dodge blew out a breath. *Shit.* That was normally a good thing, but not so much in this case. "Okay. That's true, you shouldn't. How 'bout if your mom comes in here and gets you, instead?"

Maya tilted her head and pushed herself to a seat. "Is it really my mom?"

"Yeah, it's really her, baby girl. She's been tryin' to get you back. She really misses you, too. She has a broken heart right now only seein' you will fix."

He grimaced. *Christ,* that sounded like something a kidnapper would say to lure a child into their fucking perv van.

He pulled his cell phone out of his back pocket. "Maya,

I'm gonna text her. While we wait, can you gather your most important things?"

"I'm leaving?"

He shot off a quick text to Syn and reminded her to stick to the shadows while approaching the house. "Yeah. You're goin' with your mom."

"My mom lives here."

Fuck. He shook his head. "Your real mom." He pulled up a picture of Syn and turned his cell phone toward her. "Remember her?"

Maya grabbed the phone from him and stared at it. After a second, she nodded.

"She remembers you, too, since you're all she thinks about. She's comin' now, so I need you to get whatever you wanna take with you. Yeah? Like anythin' special to you. A stuffed animal or a favorite shirt. We can't take everythin' but we can take a few things. Also need you to get dressed. Put on warm clothes and a coat."

"But where are my parents?" she asked as she pulled her legs out from under the covers.

Now was not the time to correct her about who her parents were. Now was the time to get her the fuck out of this house. "They're busy talkin' to my friends."

"Why?"

"'Cause they... My friends are gettin' permission from them for you to go with your mom."

"They said they didn't want me to go with her. That I had to live here. If I saw her, I was supposed to run and hide, call the police or scream for help. They said she wanted to hurt me."

Jesus Christ. "I know, baby girl, but they... changed their minds. Your mom don't wanna hurt you. I promise. They now believe it's best you live with your real mom and she's been workin' real hard to bring you home."

"This is home," Maya insisted. If she'd been anything

like Daisy, a stomp of her foot would've accompanied her words.

"Your home is with your mom." *Fuck!* He had no idea if what he was saying would fuck her up, but he didn't know how else to handle a kid.

He had no experience with children except for limited dealings with Judge and Cassie's girl. He felt goddamn helpless in this situation. It hit him then, if Syn remained in his life, he would need to learn.

But then, so would Syn. Raising Maya would be a learning experience for both of them.

Luckily, they'd have plenty of help.

It takes a village…

Your kids are my kids. My kids are your kids.

We're a fuckin' family. We step in when it's needed.

That was a good reason why Syn needed to remain in Manning Grove.

Family and support.

Not to mention, him.

A gasp had his head spin toward the open door. Syn stood clinging to the door frame with one hand and the other clamped over her mouth.

"Need you to pack some of her stuff and take her out to the car," Dodge instructed Syn slowly and calmly, giving her a look that said a lot more than his words. "Gonna drive you two back. Deke will go with Sig and Shade once we're done here."

Syn nodded, the nightlight reflecting off her shiny eyes.

"Hit the switch there, baby, and pack some of her stuff. Get her changed into something warmer than her pajamas. Yeah? And find her a coat."

She nodded again but remained frozen where she stood.

He could see it. The struggle to keep her shit together. She wanted to break down right there. Totally fall the fuck apart.

He didn't blame her, but she had to wait. And right now, it might freak out her daughter.

Syn flipped the light switch, giving the room a soft glow, then slowly dropped her shaking hand from her mouth. "Maya—" Her daughter's name got caught in her throat.

That right there closed up Dodge's.

After taking a step inside the room, she closed the door behind her and stared at the little girl who now stood next to Dodge.

Syn reached out her hand. "Maya. Come here, baby."

Dodge glanced down and saw Syn's daughter frozen in place, her eyes wide but as shiny as Syn's. The conflict on her face couldn't be missed as she stared at Syn's extended hand.

"I'm not going to hurt you." Syn's words were as thick as tar.

And so were Maya's. "That's not what they said."

"I know, baby, but it's not true. None of us are going to hurt you. But you need to come with me."

"They said you left me."

"I didn't. I promise I didn't. I'm here now. I tried to get you sooner, but…" Syn shook her head, then took the few steps separating her and Maya before dropping to her knees at her daughter's feet. "I've missed you so much, baby. I want to hug you. Will you let me?"

That question was like a knife to Dodge's heart. "Gotta wrap this up, Syn," he reminded her softly.

Her dark eyes hit his and she nodded. But before she could get to her feet, Maya rushed her and almost knocked her back onto her ass. Syn's arms automatically wrapped around her daughter and squeezed her tight.

Then the fucking tears started.

Dodge had to turn away. He began to rummage through a dresser, tossing some underwear and socks onto the bed.

He grabbed a couple of sweatshirts and sweaters from another drawer, adding them to the pile.

He risked a glance over his shoulder to see Syn brushing the hair off Maya's forehead and kissing her there. Then she hugged her tightly again as both continued to cry.

"I missed you, Mommy. I," Maya's voice broke, "missed you."

Jesus fuck. If that didn't rip his fucking heart out…

"I know, baby. I'm so sorry. I'm so damn sorry. I wish I could've been there for you all this time. I wanted to be, I swear." Her voice was filled with tears.

"Y-you l-left m-me." Maya's face was planted in Syn's borrowed coat and her body jerked with each sob.

"They wouldn't let me…" Syn shook her head and sniffled. "It doesn't matter. We're together now. You're coming with us. Everything's going to be okay."

"You promise?"

Syn leaned back and nodded. "I promise. Dodge and your uncle Sig are here to take us to our new home, where we're going to finally be together again. Do you want that?"

Maya nodded, wiping at her runny nose and sniffling.

Christ on a fuckin' cracker, Maya could be Syn's younger sister.

Maya was only a foot shorter than Syn, if that. She might have Syn's looks but she would have her biological father's height. She would be taller than Syn even before she was done growing.

He gave them another few minutes by digging through Maya's closet and pulling out some things he thought the little girl might need. At least until they bought her new stuff.

He found a small pink suitcase buried at the bottom of her closet, tossed it on the bed, unzipped it and began stuffing it full with the pile he made. He threw two sets of shoes on top and dropped a pair of snow boots on the floor near a pair of jeans and another sweatshirt he laid out on the mattress.

Syn needed to get Maya dressed and get her the hell out of there.

"Syn, gotta long drive home. We gotta go." Again, he made sure his tone reflected their urgency but hopefully not enough for Maya to pick up on it.

"Okay," Syn said with another sniffle, wiping at Maya's tear-stained face and then her own. "Is there anything you really want to bring with you?"

"All my stuff," Maya answered.

Of course.

Dodge cleared the thick from his own throat. "You can't take everythin', baby girl. Just grab the most important." He moved over to Syn, grabbed her arm and pulled her a few steps away from her daughter. He dropped his head and put his mouth to her ear, keeping his voice low. "Get her shit, and get her the fuck outta here. We'll get whatever she needs once we get back home. You see any pigs, you go. You take Maya and head back, you hear me? If that happens, get the fuck out of West Virginia as fast as possible. Don't fuckin' wait for us and don't stop unless it's absolutely necessary. Then head to the farm and directly to Trip. Tell me you hear what I'm sayin'."

She sniffled and nodded.

Dodge closed his eyes for a second to repack his shit tight. When he opened them he said, "Go. We'll be out shortly. Keep it together, Syn. For her."

Syn nodded again on a hiccup-sob he could see she was doing her best to suppress.

He tipped her chin up with his thumb. "Gonna go check on the guys. You got less than five to get her dressed and out to the car. Make sure you take her directly outside. No good-byes, if you get what I'm sayin'."

Syn nodded once more. This time he nodded, too, hopefully in a way that assured her that everything would be all right.

Dodge gave them one last glance, stepped out into the hall and closed the bedroom door behind him.

Then he took long, determined strides down the hallway to the master bedroom. When he got there, he closed that door, too.

Chapter Twenty-Two

"What if they try to get her back?" Syn asked. He was sitting on a stool at the bar and she was sandwiched in between his muscular thighs, leaning into him.

He swallowed his mouthful of the Jack Daniels Sinatra Select he kept hidden for himself behind the bar and set the glass back down.

Her pale, drawn face was turned up to his and he hated seeing the dark circles under her eyes. But outside the bar a new day was already breaking.

Both of them were exhausted from everything that went down and the long trip home.

A lot of tears were shed in that rental. That alone had to be draining on the girls. It had been draining on him, too, since he struggled the whole drive back to Manning Grove with keeping his own shit together.

After Maya passed out from exhaustion on the couch upstairs, he and Syn had gone back downstairs to the empty bar to discuss shit.

Like the couch, Maya living in the skoolie wasn't going to work, either, whether Syn thought differently or not.

They needed to have a serious conversation about where

things would go from here. Maya sleeping on his couch was okay for a few days, but not permanently. The apartment was already cramped and had no bedrooms, so them all living together in it wouldn't work. Maya deserved privacy as much as Syn and Dodge did.

He wiped his hand over his mouth. "They do, they're gonna regret it. We also got Reese on our side and she's a fuckin' Pitbull." He'd normally say Cujo, Rook's Chihuahua, but he didn't know if she'd remember the little shit from the garage. "Believe me, she can argue someone to death."

When Dodge had walked into the Danzig's master bedroom, Lyle Danzig had been curled into a ball on the floor.

He was way past begging for mercy, crying or even whimpering.

Shade and Deacon stood guard by the man's wife, making sure Cara Danzig didn't intervene with the lesson Sig taught her husband and Syn's *former* adoptive father.

The VP's knuckles looked like ground meat and blood was splattered everywhere Dodge could see. Including Sig's clothes and face.

"Syn get her out?" Deke asked him.

"Workin' on it. We'll keep these motherfuckers occupied 'til she does."

"How long?" Shade asked next, flicking his eyes toward Sig and raising one eyebrow.

Dodge saw the same as Shade. Sig was currently lost in his own head, standing over a man he'd beaten close to death using only his fists. By the blood on his boots, maybe he'd gotten in a good shot or two with those steel tips, too.

Dodge scratched the back of his neck. "Let's give 'em five. Gotta get her dressed and finish packin' some shit." He glanced at the motionless ball of bloody flesh and red-stained pajamas. "He still breathin'?"

Shade shrugged casually, most likely because he couldn't give a shit if the man was or wasn't.

Dodge glanced at Syn's *former* adoptive mother, who sat frozen with fear on the bed, staring at her husband with tears streaming down her cheeks. He had a hard time mustering up any sympathy for the woman who didn't give a flying fuck about her supposed "daughter."

The one she accepted into her home as an infant to raise, protect and love.

The only feeling he had toward her was disgust, disappointment and the urge to punch her right in the fucking throat. He curbed that urge since he didn't hit women, even when they were total pieces of shit and deserved it.

Dodge stepped up to the bed and got into her face. "Those tears? How many d'you think Syn shed for her daughter?"

"She doesn't deserve her."

Dodge's fingers curled into his palms. "And you do?"

"We gave her a good life. Syn can't give her nearly what we can."

"You kept Syn, and then Maya, in a house where a child rapist had access. You didn't give a shit about that?"

"Sam made a mistake. As soon as we found out, he never did it again."

Dodge wanted to laugh at what she said, even though it wasn't funny but totally fucking absurd. He and Shade shot each other a glance. The other man was good at hiding his expressions, but Dodge could see it in his eyes. He'd like to slice the bitch's throat.

Shade wasn't the only one.

Dodge turned his attention back to the woman. "How many times did that sick motherfucker come over to this house after he knocked up a thirteen-year-old?"

Cara Danzig blinked. "He assured us he'd never touch her again."

"And you believed a fuckin' child molester?"

The woman's mouth gaped open. "Did he?"

"You don't fuckin' know?" Dodge just about roared. Maya could still be in the house, he needed to keep himself under control.

"If she says he did, she's lying," the woman hissed.

"Just like you lied to her about Maya's legal guardianship?"

Cara's mouth snapped shut.

"That's what I fuckin' thought." He swallowed the fiery ball of anger back down his throat. "You didn't do shit. You didn't report it. You didn't have that motherfucker arrested. Worse, you allowed him in this house with two vulnerable girls. So there's no misunderstandin'... Gonna only say this once so listen fuckin' carefully..." He had his nose almost pressed against hers and held that bitch's eyes when he growled, "Maya belongs to Syn. You do anythin' to try and take back a child that does not fuckin' belong to you, we *will* come back down here for another visit. One that he," he tipped his head toward the bloody balled-up mess on the floor, "and you will enjoy a lot less than this one. You got me?"

"You can't take Maya."

"Sure we can. And we are." He straightened. "Heed my warnin', you cunt, or next time you'll be on the floor with him."

Shade and Deacon ended up having to pull Sig away from Danzig and haul him out of the room. Once they hit the frigid air outside, Sig snapped out of his fucked-up trance.

Dodge hadn't seen him like that since that night on Hillbilly Hill when they went to get his ol' lady back from the inbred goat fuckers who stole her.

Shade voiced a concern over Sig removing his gloves to

beat the fuck out of Danzig and the likelihood of leaving DNA behind.

"Don't give a fuck," was Sig's only response.

"You end up back behind bars, Red will give a fuck," Dodge reminded him.

"Hopefully they ain't stupid enough to call the pigs," Shade said as they moved back toward the van and the rental where Syn and Maya waited.

Dodge stopped at the van. "Gonna take them back to Pete's. You got this?" He jerked his chin up at the van.

"We got this," Shade assured him. "Nobody's gonna have to worry about that motherfucker again. Only one way to deal with a man who's got a thing for children…"

Dodge didn't need to hear the rest, he knew his brothers would finish handling the problem. Instead, he turned on his heel, climbed behind the rental's wheel and took his girls home.

And now here they were. Home but not *home*. Because living above Crazy Pete's wasn't going to fucking work. He'd need to huddle up with Trip since the prez would want someone living above the bar full-time. Dodge would recommend Woody or Dozer, but it could no longer be him.

He'd need to make some other arrangements, too. The sooner the better for everyone involved.

"You want, you and Maya can move into the motel temporarily."

"I need to hit the road. The band is my livelihood. Money is required to raise a child."

Dodge blew air out of his nose. He didn't want to argue. But if he had to, he would. "Syn…"

"I'm a singer, Dodge. That's what I do."

"Know it and you're a fuckin' good one. Not sayin' you shouldn't keep singin', sayin' you need to settle here and use Manning Grove as home base. You got people here to help you with Maya. Someone's gonna have to be with her when you do a gig. Draggin' her from bar to bar ain't gonna work. We also need to get her enrolled in school."

"We," she repeated.

"Yeah, *we*, Syn. *We*. Wanna be here for you. And her, too."

"But your apartment…"

"Yeah. Know it." He drew his thumbnail across his eyebrow. "Need to figure out somethin' else."

"Hold on… Are you talking about moving from upstairs?"

"What other choice I got?"

Syn blinked. "Dodge," she breathed. "You're not going to turn your life upside down for us."

"Ain't gonna be upside down and it's for all of us. You get that?"

"But—"

"Ain't no 'buts.' It's gonna take a bit to figure shit out, but it'll get figured out."

"But—"

"Just fuckin' said no 'buts.' Too tired to argue, Syn. Also ain't in the mood. All I wanna do is climb into bed with you and sleep for the next fuckin' week. Promise we'll figure shit out. For you and Maya. For us. For your band."

She released a weary sigh. "I'll need to sit down with the guys and figure out the future for The Synners. But, I'm telling you now, I'm not giving up my career or my dream. I will make it work one way or another."

While he loved her determination, she needed to realize that she no longer had to do everything on her own. She had real family now. Not just her fellow band members.

"Just need a good manager. One who won't bullshit you."

"We can't afford a manager, otherwise, we'd have one."

"You can't afford not to have the right manager, Syn. You're never gonna play any decent venues or make any decent scratch without the right one. You'll just continue to book shitholes that pay squat and take advantage of you. You need to play for somethin' other than fuckin' tips." He slid his knuckles down the soft, ivory skin of her cheek. "Listen, I might know the right one. Gonna make some calls this week and see if I can't hook you up with Dirty Deeds' manager. The lead singer's a member of one of our ally clubs, the Dirty Angels, and they played at Trip and Stel's weddin'. They fuckin' kicked ass. But be prepared, he might hand you some hard truths you gotta be ready to hear. Like about your bandmates. Especially when it comes to who will help you move forward and who will hold you back."

Her lips turned down at the corners. "I don't want to break up my band. I owe them more than you know."

"I get that. But sometimes hard decisions gotta be made. You wanna be serious about your music, then you need to make serious business decisions. Like raisin' Maya, it ain't gonna be easy."

"What do you know about either?"

"Truth? I don't. But I've booked enough bands in this joint now, that I got enough of an education on the subject just by servin' them drinks and listenin'. When I'm bored I've asked questions. Look, it can't hurt to contact him."

"And if he's not interested?"

"Then he ain't interested. We'll find someone else. Like I said, we'll figure shit out. With that and with everythin' else, too. Just gonna take a little time and patience."

What he didn't have patience for was getting Syn under him again, even as dog-tired as he was.

She cupped his face in her hands and pressed her forehead to his. "I don't know how to thank you," she whispered.

"Got an idea," he whispered back with a grin.

She straightened, cocking her head. "What?"

He shook his. "Soon as I get a chance, gonna show you.

But not tonight. And, so you know, it ain't what you think." He grabbed his glass of whiskey and downed the rest of it. Then he wrapped his arms around her and settled his palms on her ass, giving those amazing, firm cheeks a gentle squeeze. "You too tired for a quick game of pool? Thinkin' a good game will get our minds off what happened last night and what will happen in the future. Even if for a little while. Then we can head up and pass out."

She shrugged. "It depends on how aggressive the game gets."

"Baby, this game's gonna be slow and easy." He didn't have the energy to do much else.

"Well, I could use a little practice."

When she brushed her thumb over his bottom lip, he grabbed it with his teeth and bit down gently.

After he released it, he said, "Yeah, gonna keep it simple. When we got more time, more privacy and more energy, gonna teach you more complicated shots."

She leaned in again, murmuring, "I look forward to that, too," against his lips.

Fuck yeah, so did he.

―――――

THE RUMBLE of a diesel engine shook the windows of the temporary housing that had been set up on the farm. It was one of the mobile homes Reilly had purchased for Shelter from the Storm. Along with the temporary trailer, they'd had temporary utilities installed on a lot next to Rook and Jet's. The row of homes just on the other side of the tree line near the barn and the sheds was growing.

As soon as spring came, they'd break ground on that lot and have a modular home built on a foundation.

At least that was the plan. He'd been kind of vague about the details with Syn because he wanted to surprise her. Plus, things were still new with them and he hadn't wanted to push her. Things were also still getting smoothed out between her and Maya.

Mother and daughter were building their relationship. Syn and Sig were rebuilding theirs. And Syn was figuring out her place within the club's sisterhood.

A sisterhood that, of course, welcomed her with open arms because that was how fucking awesome those women were. And another reason why any of the Fury members would go to war for them.

It had been a bit difficult these last few weeks because, until they signed a contract with the manager of Dirty Deeds, The Synners had been taking gigs wherever and whenever they could.

Even against Dodge's approval. He didn't like some of the sketchy places they played. He'd had a serious sit-down with Rex, Eddie and Nico about that when Syn wasn't around.

They were his eyes and ears when the band was on the road.

"That your mom?" Dodge called out to Maya.

"Yes!" he heard her yell from the living room. He grinned at the excitement in her voice.

He wouldn't lie, he was feeling a little bit of that himself.

"How 'bout you put on your coat and go talk to the guys for a little bit while I speak with your mom about somethin'. Get them to play you a song so you can practice your singin'."

"Okay!"

Even from the master bedroom, he could hear Maya scrambling to pull on her boots and shrug on a coat. He'd quickly discovered nine-year-olds were not quiet. Maya wasn't quite as bad as Daisy but close enough. Maya's attitude was about a level five on a scale of one to ten compared to Daisy's level five-hundred on that same damn scale.

Even so, he was thankful Red liked to spend time with Maya so it would give him a break. Especially when Syn was gone overnight. Though for now, it was never more than one overnight a week. That was something he put his foot down about, especially since he didn't want her taking Maya along with her to those bars. The rest of the gigs she was scoring were within driving distance.

Having a kid was all new to him and took some getting used to. Especially a girl child who was chatty as fuck, unlike her mother. Syn tended to save her voice for the stage.

Maya liked to share every thought that popped into her head, whether it should be shared or not.

"Tell your mom to come in here right away," he yelled right before the door slammed shut.

Jesus. Kids didn't know how to close fucking doors like normal people, either.

He grinned.

In truth, Maya was a good kid.

Things were slowly falling into place.

How the fuck did he go from a bachelor living above a bar a couple of months ago, to now having a woman and a kid?

He didn't know. But here they were.

Truthfully, he wouldn't change a damn thing.

Well, he would… And things *were* about to change. Again.

For the better.

Syn appeared in the bedroom doorway, her face scrubbed clean of her stage makeup and her hair pulled up and out of her face into a ponytail. She was a picture of innocence and, makeup-free, looked way too fucking young for him.

But he was done caring about that. Age didn't matter. What they had between them did.

"How'd it go?"

She shrugged, crossed her arms over her chest and leaned a hip against the door frame. "It went all right."

"The manager paid you, right?"

She nodded. "Six hundred. In cash, too."

"Good."

She had told him the story of the bar owner in Scranton stiffing them. He and a couple of his brothers gave that bar owner a visit in the early hours one morning and collected what the band was owed. Dodge would also make sure that never happened again. Syn now knew to call him if anyone ever tried that bullshit with her again.

Nobody but him would ever tell his woman to get on her knees. Not if they wanted to keep breathing.

He dropped his voice an octave lower and ordered, "Close the door."

After a quick glance over her shoulder, she whispered, "We don't have time for that right now."

"Know it. Just close the damn door."

Heat flamed in her cheeks and he could see the tips of her nipples harden through the Eurythmics long-sleeved T-shirt she wore, making it very obvious she wasn't wearing a damn bra. In reality she didn't need the support, but he preferred she wear one in public for the exact reason he was staring at.

They'd had that discussion. Apparently, he'd have to have it with her again.

Just not right now.

Syn rolled her eyes, stepped into the bedroom and closed the door. "Am I in trouble?"

Dodge cocked an eyebrow at the game they had started playing on a regular basis. It was a fucking fun one. "You do somethin' to deserve me markin' up that perfect ass of yours?" He tipped his head toward her chest.

"I don't know."

She knew. She definitely fucking knew. "You don't know or you don't wanna say?"

She pursed her lips and donned a mask of innocence. She brushed both of her palms over her peaked nipples. "I might have forgotten something."

"Yeah, you did. C'mere."

Her eyes sparkled and her lips parted as she stepped closer. As soon as he'd heard the bus pull up, he had moved to sit on the hardback chair he kept in their room. They got a lot of use out of it when Maya wasn't around.

Syn's dark eyes flicked to the belt he purposely kept draped over the back of it. Dodge shook his head slightly.

He spread his thighs wider, pointed to the floor between his feet and ordered, "On your knees."

Dodge watched her throat slowly roll. No, not *her* throat. *His.*

He owned every piece of her.

In turn, she owned every piece of him. Every fucking piece. Including the heart that beat in his chest.

His dick was throbbing in his jeans as she licked her lips and slowly lowered to her knees.

This wasn't playtime, though.

This was serious.

She tipped her head down, as well as her eyes, and waited.

He could see her tremble slightly in anticipation and excitement. That made his dick turn to steel.

Ain't playtime. Focus.

He reached behind his back, grabbed the small box he'd tucked there and held it above his lap in line with her lowered gaze.

"Look," he said, giving her permission to raise her eyes.

"What's that?" she asked when her face lifted to his.

"A gift."

Confusion filled her eyes. "For what?"

He shook his head.

"For me?"

"Anybody else in this room?"

She narrowed her eyes on him, but smiled. "No."

"Then, guess it's for you. So, you better open it. Otherwise, Maya will find it and think it's for her."

"I don't need any gifts, Dodge. You've already given me so much."

"Open it up first. Then you can decide if you wanna refuse it."

She took the box from his fingers and lifted the hinged lid. Inside were two keys.

A tiny brass one and a larger metal alloy one.

She shot him a funny look. "Keys to your heart?"

He snorted. "Sorry, baby, ain't that romantic. But if that's what you want to think, you can."

She lifted and dropped one shoulder. "Then, what are they for?"

He plucked the larger silver key from the box and held it up. "This one will be for our house."

"Our house?"

"Yeah, told you this place is only temporary since the trailer belongs to Shelter from the Storm. We need somethin' more permanent. A foundation. For the house. For us. For Maya."

Syn's dark eyebrows knitted together. "Where's this house?"

"Nowhere yet. But this lot's ours." One of the perks of belonging and being loyal to the Fury.

"It is?"

"Yeah, and come spring—once a construction crew can

break ground—we're gettin' a house built on it. You up for that?"

"For the three of us?"

"Yeah. And maybe a cat or dog for Maya. We'll see. Let's get the house first. *If* you want that. You haven't said yes, yet."

"Yes," she breathed. "Hell yes. It'll be perfect."

"Nothin' in life's perfect, we both know that, but it'll be a step in that direction."

She glanced down at the lone key that remained in the open box. She pulled it out and held it up between them. "What's this one for?"

"That one's just as important as," he lifted the house key up, "this one." He dropped it back into the box. He took the tiny brass key from her fingers, then reached behind his back again and brought out the gift bag he'd been hiding there. He held it out to her. "Open it."

"It's not my birthday."

"No shit. In case you missed it, that wasn't a request, it was an order. Open it."

She shot him a bratty smirk, then parted the blood red tissue paper that peeked out of the top of the black gift bag.

She dug her hand deep into the bag and paused. Her brow dropped low and she slowly pulled out the circle of black leather.

Seeing it in her fingers just about did him in.

Ain't playtime. Not yet.

The smooth collar was only about an inch wide and instead of an O-ring at the front, the ring was shaped like the outline of a cat head. A circle with cat ears. Just like her cat-eared sweatshirt she loved so damn much.

She stared at it. "I don't understand."

"You will." As he rose from the chair, he pulled her to her feet. "Turn around."

She only hesitated for the slightest bit, then she did as he demanded.

His dick flexed impatiently in his jeans. It would have to wait.

"Lift up your hair."

She moved her ponytail out of the way, exposing the delicate column of her neck.

"Don't move," he warned in the voice he used when it *was* playtime.

He leaned in and pressed a kiss to the base of her neck, then straightened. After unbuckling the collar, he put it around her neck the same as he would a gold necklace with a diamond pendant.

To him this was a fuck of a lot better than any diamond or gold. He hoped she thought so, too. He pulled a tiny brass padlock out of the front pocket of his jeans and secured the collar around her neck. He made sure it fit snugly but not tight enough where it would irritate her skin.

"Like a fuckin' bra, you're to wear that whenever you're in public. Or, otherwise, when I tell you to. When you're on the farm or here at home, and we're not usin' it in play, then you don't gotta wear it unless you wanna. But you will *always* wear it on stage. Can't fuckin' wait to see you wearin' my collar under the lights while you sing, knowing you belong to me. Some people will recognize what it is, a lot more won't. If someone asks you about it, you tell them what you want. But you will always tell them you're taken. You got that?"

"Yes."

Using her hips, he turned her around and brushed his lips over hers. Then he took a step back and held out his hand, turned it over and opened it. On his palm laid the tiny brass key.

She stared at it in confusion.

"Take it. This one's yours. This way you can remove that collar any time you'd like. I never want you to think that you're stuck with me or that you're not free to leave at any time. But if you fuckin' do leave, it'll only happen once. You get me?"

She nodded, her eyes just as heated as her cheeks. "Yes."

"I'm in it for the duration, Syn. I hope to fuck you are, too."

She took the key from his palm, wrapped her fingers around it, and squeezed it tight. "I am." She then surprised him by grabbing his hand, lifting it and turning it palm up. She held out her fist, opened it and dropped the key back onto his palm. "I won't need this key."

Jesus fuck.

"You know what that means, right?" he asked her.

"Yes."

He raised an eyebrow. "You sure?"

"Yes. Are you?"

"Nothin' I want more, Syn. Okay, I'm wrong, there is."

"What's that?"

"Want you to be happy."

"I am," she whispered, a smile flirting with her lips.

"Also want you to feel secure."

"I do. And…"

"And?"

"I also feel very loved."

A strange pressure expanded in his chest and then exploded, almost dropping him to his knees.

No, it wasn't strange. He knew exactly what it was.

She brushed her fingers over the shiny black leather encircling her neck. "I love it. It's perfect for *us*. Thank you for expanding my world."

"Thank you for acceptin' me into yours."

Epilogue

A FULL TANK

Dodge kept an eye on Syn and Maya as they walked ahead with Red through the Super Walmart parking lot. Sig was walking next to him, doing the same thing.

Maya needed some more clothes, as well as some stuff for school.

He and Sig both hated shopping and would rather jam splinters under their damn fingernails but the fuck if they were letting the ladies go alone. The only problem was, the women had been doing a lot of shopping lately.

Nine-year-olds seemed to need a lot of shit.

Once inside the store, he would remind Syn that she better get everything Maya needed today because the hell if he was doing this again in a couple of days.

Suddenly, Sig slowed down to a crawl and called out, "Yo."

Dodge stopped and glanced over his shoulder at the VP. "What?"

He turned back to keep an eye on the women as they continued through the busy parking lot, unaware of what was going on between their men.

Sig stepped up to him and growled, "What the fuck's on her neck? You put a leash on my sister?"

Christ. He forgot that Sig hadn't seen Syn collared yet. Like they'd discussed when he gave it to her, she hadn't worn it on the farm and, if it wasn't for getting strong-armed into going shopping today, Syn's brother might not have seen it for a long time.

But here they were.

Now Sig knew. And, no surprise, the man knew that it was more than a decorative choker.

"I haven't yet."

Sig stared at him. "But you plan on it?"

What he planned on doing with Syn was none of Sig's fucking business. Brother or not.

"That collar's no different than the tattoos Trip and Stella got on their ring fingers. No different from the cut Red wears with your name on the back statin' very fuckin' clearly who she belongs to. Same shit, different execution."

Sig's beard-covered jaw shifted as it always did when his temper began to spike. "Ain't the same."

Dodge didn't give a fuck about the man's temper and leaned closer to say, "Prove otherwise."

"You think you own her, is that right?"

Dodge wasn't going to answer that question because Sig already knew the answer and would just have to fucking deal with it.

However, Sig wasn't done making his unwanted opinion known. "We don't do that shit here, brother. You officially want her to be your property, you claim her at the table like the rest of us did. That's the way of our world. You've been a part of it long enough. Don't act like you don't know."

"I know, and who said I wouldn't? Know what you're into, Sig. Just 'cause you no longer do it, don't mean you don't think about it. Well, same with me. It's been a long time since I found the right partner."

Sig's nostrils flared and his jaw jutted out. Dodge had no doubt the man was grinding his teeth to control his temper. What he used to do with women used to help with that. Now he no longer had that outlet.

The man struggled—some days worse than others—but he lived with it. For one reason and one reason only.

Red.

"We wanna do this here in the parkin' lot? In front of Maya and our women?"

In truth, Sig couldn't say a damn word because that collar wasn't much different than wearing a "property of" cut.

When Sig didn't respond, Dodge continued, "You know she's happy now, right? You've seen it. That's all you should be worried about. Along with makin' sure she remains that way and that her and Maya are taken care of."

Sig's jaw visibly unclenched and he yelled out to the women, "Red, wait up. Don't go any further."

The women were about to cross the travel lane that separated the parking spots and the curb to the store's entrance.

The three turned to face them, but waited. Neither Dodge or Sig wanted them to disappear from their view.

"Now," Dodge started, "we done talkin' about this? Or you wanna waste more time on shit you got no control over?"

"Do it the right way."

"Already claimed her, brother, but I'll do it at the table, too. Don't got a problem with that. But like that fuckin' collar, she needs to want it, too."

Sig blew a harsh breath out of his nostrils, sounding like an aggravated bull, shook his head and began to move again.

Thank fuck.

Dodge followed the VP and once they reached the

women, he said, "Let's just get the shit you need and get the fuck outta here. Know I said it before, but sayin' it again… I hate shoppin'."

"You didn't have to come along," Syn told him.

"Yeah, we did. First, you know why. Second, who's gonna help you two with all the damn shit you need to get? Remember what I said? Make this trip count. So we don't gotta keep repeatin' it."

"We're quite capable of handling stuff. If not, we could get someone inside the store to help."

Dodge's eyes narrowed on Syn and she shot him a bratty smile. He lifted an eyebrow in warning and her smile got even bigger. He then gave her a look that clearly told her that she was playing with fire and she gave him one back that said she knew it and didn't give a fuck.

Sig's snort interrupted their silent conversation. "Help? Here? They don't even got enough people to work the fuckin' registers. They ain't carryin' shit for you."

"Ears, Sig," Red reminded him, tipping her eyes down to Maya.

Dodge chuckled. He didn't bother to attempt to curb his cursing around Syn's daughter, it was pointless. Living on the farm, being a part of the club, it was impossible to keep their language G-rated.

Daisy was even younger than Maya and could already curse like a fucking trucker. Judge and Cassie tried to fix that problem but realized it was a losing battle. They did make it clear she was not to curse at school or around any of her friends.

So far, Daisy hadn't been hauled off to the school pokey, so she must be following that rule. It probably helped that Shade's ol' lady, Chelle, worked at the same elementary school and stepped in when needed.

The air around them shifted sharply when Red went stock still and turned ghost white, every freckle suddenly standing out on her fair skin. Her hazel eyes widened and her pupils dilated as she stared past Dodge to something beyond him in the parking lot.

What the fuck?

But it was when she slapped a hand on Sig's forearm and dug her nails deep into his skin that Sig and him went on high alert and the hairs on the back of his neck stood.

"What the fuck, baby? What's wrong?" Sig asked her, already starting to unravel.

They both spun to look at where her gaze was glued.

Sig's lip pulled up in a snarl and Dodge finally spotted what he did.

A dark fifteen-passenger van with dark-tinted windows was parked at the far end of the lot. The same kind of van the Shirleys drove.

Dodge's heart began to thump at what he was seeing. Women and children.

Fuck.

"Those motherfuckers," Sig growled. "They got the fuckin' balls to come to town in the daylight."

"Think that's the Shirleys?" Dodge asked, checking out the van and the people milling around it.

The women wore homemade prairie dresses, the only difference between them were the fabric patterns. Their hair was all up in a similar style, too.

The people outside the van sort of reminded him of the Shirleys but something was also off about them. They could be a van load of local Mennonites who looked similar enough to the Shirleys to spook Red. However, none of them wore "sin-sifters" on their heads like the local Mennonites did.

No, something was definitely off with whoever they were.

Red shook her head, but didn't pull her eyes from the van or the group unloading from it. "They're not the

Shirleys. But they're a branch of the Guardians of Freedom."

"How d'you know?" Sig asked sharply, his body going stiff as a board.

"Because," she took a shuddered breath, "that's my mother." She turned troubled eyes up to her ol' man. "Sig, that's my *mother*. What's she doing here? Why is she here? Is she with *them*?"

Of course she was. Because life couldn't go smoothly even for a few damn months. If it wasn't one thing, it was something else fucking shit up.

"Why isn't she in Ohio?" Red asked, panic filling her eyes and her voice.

"God-fuckin'-damnit," Sig roared, yanking Red out of view.

Dodge put a hand on a confused Syn's back. "Hold Maya's hand and get behind that truck."

"What's going on?" Syn asked while she did what she was told.

"Mom, what's wrong?" The fear in Maya's voice was apparent.

And hearing it pissed him the fuck off. "Just some people who ain't very nice and who we wanna avoid," Dodge said quickly, trying to keep his voice calm and level.

"Dodge!" Syn said sharply.

He didn't know what else to fucking say. Anyone involved in that bullshit sovereign nation could be dangerous. Any of them could be a threat.

Only, he had no idea why some of the Ohio clan was here in Pennsylvania.

Unless they were there to help repopulate Hillbilly Hill.

Could it be?

Was that how they'd grow their numbers again? Bring in women and children from other clans?

Fuck. Fuck. Fuck.

It wasn't hard to pick out Red's mother. Her hair was the same fiery color as Sig's ol' lady. Even pulled back in a tight bun, it turned to fire when the sun hit it.

"Whose kid she holdin'?" Dodge asked.

"My guess is hers. But my half-brother would be about five by now. That baby she's holding only looks about a year old."

Just then a redheaded boy about five climbed out of the van and stood next to Red's mother. Then the woman leaned into the van and helped a third kid climb down. That boy seemed to be a couple of years younger than the oldest one.

"Oh my God, Sig," Red whispered, one hand clamped over her forehead, the other still drilling into Sig's arm. "Oh my God. Tell me this isn't happening. Do you think they're here looking for me? It looks like she had two more children after Ezrah. Why? Why would she do that to innocent children?"

Forget the children, why the fuck would the woman do what she did to her own adult daughter?

Because the woman and Red's stepfather were completely fucked in the head. They had given Red to the Shirleys to be used as one of their breeders. To bring fresh blood to the inbred hillbilly clan. Her own damn mother had caused the biggest nightmare of Red's life. One that scarred her deeply. One she'd never fully recover from.

Sig had originally talked about going to Ohio to exact revenge for Red, but never did. Dodge wondered if his ol' lady talked him out of it. Sig was probably regretting that about now.

"No, baby, they don't know where you are," Sig assured her. "They wouldn't know to look for you here."

Dodge hoped he was fucking right.

"How do you know that? How do you know? They're

the ones who sent me here in the first place." Her voice had raised even higher.

If Red retreated into her dark space, Sig would lose his shit. And in the middle of Walmart's parking lot was not the place to have a meltdown. It would catch people's attention. Including the group near that van.

"Let's get the fuck outta here," Dodge suggested. "Start walkin' toward the truck, Syn. Hold Maya's hand and do not let go. You get me?"

"Yes."

Thank fuck she knew better than to be stubborn right now. He normally loved when she acted like a brat so he could teach her a lesson. It was one way they played.

But now was not the time. None of this was a game. All of it was serious.

Sig steered Red in the same direction they headed, keeping a firm grip on her. "Don't do anythin' to draw attention to us," he warned and then said to Red, "You ain't steppin' off that farm unless I'm with you. Syn, same with you. You go nowhere without one of us."

Red nodded as she walked. Dodge noticed Syn did not.

"This shit's got to end," Sig growled, taking longer strides. "Don't care what we gotta do. Don't care how we gotta do it. But this is gonna end once and for all."

Dodge agreed with all of that. He glanced down at his own responsibilities. The two people he had to protect.

He felt it down to his very fucking soul. He now understood why Trip was so protective of Stella. Sig of Red. Judge of Cassie and Daisy. Along with all the rest of his brothers who had women and children. Or had babies still in bellies.

A protective wolf was growing deep inside him, itching to escape, ready to growl, bite and snap the neck of anyone who tried to do Syn or Maya harm.

So, like Sig, Dodge didn't care how they had to do it, but

he'd help make sure it got done. He'd do anything to protect the family that now belonged to him.

Once they got home, he would make it clear to Syn how important Sig's order was and he'd explain why. He only wanted to avoid doing it in front of Maya. He had mentioned the Shirleys briefly, just enough to make sure she was aware they were trouble but not enough to make her worry about sending Maya to school. He didn't want his woman living in fear, but, unfortunately, he would now have to go into details.

Ugly fucking details to make sure she understood.

He only hoped those details didn't change her mind about staying in Manning Grove.

He'd also assure her he'd do anything to keep her and Maya safe, even blow up that damn mountain himself.

If that landed him back behind bars, so fucking be it.

As long as the people he loved and cared for were safe, that would be a sacrifice he'd be willing to make.

———

Don't expect change if you're not willing to sacrifice.

———

Sign up for Jeanne's newsletter to learn about her upcoming releases, sales and more! https://www. authorjeannestjames.com

———

You never know where the road may lead you. Or who you'll find along the way…

When Whip comes across a disabled motorcycle at the foot of *the* mountain—the one that's nothing but bad news—he hopes the stranded rider is nothing more than just that. Someone who needs help.
And not a trap. Or an undercover fed.

When her motorcycle breaks down on a deserted road, Fallon Murphy's caught off guard by the mechanic with the sexy smirk who comes to her rescue.
After shedding her restrictive corporate chains, she's now living life on her own terms. She no longer answers to anyone for anything.
Like most bikers, her motto is "live free, ride free."
But that's where her and Whip's similarities end.

The saying is "opposites attract," but Whip tried that once before. It didn't work out.
Fallon's not only far out of his league, they couldn't be more opposite. Even so, he isn't easily deterred.

However, to his surprise, Fallon has her own plans and isn't shy about going after what she wants.

Meanwhile, trouble on that mountain is brewing, and no one is safe.
His MC stands at a crossroads, and it's time for the Fury to take action once and for all.
No more excuses.
No more quarter.
No mercy given.
Especially from the one who goes by that name.

**Turn the page to read the prologue of
Blood & Bones: Whip**

Blood & Bones: Whip

PROLOGUE
Losing Forever

"P-pap! Pap!" Whip inhaled another big breath as he sprinted across the yard and up the porch steps. "P-pap!"

Just as he reached for the screen door, it swung open and his grandfather stood blocking his way. "Why are you out here wailing like a Tom cat who's following the scent of a cat in heat?"

"H-he's b-back!"

His grandfather's wrinkled brow pulled low. "Who?"

"H-him."

"Use your damn words, Whip. Just saying 'him' doesn't work, remember? Form your words and say them clearly."

He was trying. He'd been better about it. Until now. "D-dad."

The old man's spine snapped straight and his cloudy eyes narrowed. "The hell he is."

"Y-yes. He's…" Whip gulped another mouthful of air. "He's h-here."

His pap stepped out onto the wood porch that needed a

fresh coat of paint and let the wooden screen door slam behind him, making Whip jump and glance over his shoulder.

The screen door also needed a paint job, but Pap said he was getting too old to do that kind of "shit" and that Whip's mom needed to find herself a worthwhile man to do work around the house and help raise Whip. Instead of the one that she was currently married to, who also happened to be Pap's youngest son.

Blood or not, Pap said both his sons were useless pieces of shit. That was how he actually said it, too. He stated loudly and often that he wished he never had either one.

He also said the only good thing that came out of having those wastes of skin were his grandkids and his daughters-in-law. Whip, Whip's mom, his Aunt Jennie and his two cousins were the only ones left on Earth who made his life worth living.

Whip loved his pap.

Much more than his father. Or his uncle.

Pap called them low-life losers. A lot. Especially when stuff needed to be done around the house or bills needed to be paid and neither of them were anywhere to be found.

Pap said his Uncle Scott, who always insisted on being called Spider instead, was too busy running around on his motorcycle and getting into trouble with the law. While Whip's father was too busy getting himself in trouble with other women.

Whip didn't know why since his dad had a perfectly good one here at home. Maybe if he was a little nicer to Whip's mom, Pap would actually let him stay.

But his dad was never nice.

Not ever.

Not to his mom, not to Pap and not to Whip, either.

Whip actually hated his father. He was mean. Especially when he was drinking.

He had no idea why his mother married him. Whip asked her that once and she said he wasn't like this when she met him. Pap said Whip's dad wasn't a "mean son-of-a-bitch" until his drinking got out of control.

"B-bet he's… h-he's here for m-money again, P-pap."

"Wouldn't be surprised," Pap grumbled. He turned and pulled open the screen door. "Get inside and go find your mother. Warn her that your daddy's here and tell her to bring me my shotgun. The one that's loaded near my bed. I'm going to handle this."

Whip didn't like Pap's tone. It was the one he got when he was annoyed, like when the Steelers lost and he shouted that he was "done" with that "damn team." Sometimes he even threw things at the TV.

"P-pap…"

His grandfather shot him a frown and pointed inside. "Go do what I told you. And don't come back out 'til I tell you, neither. You understand, boy?"

Whip nodded.

"Go!" Pap barked.

Whip went.

"M-mom!" he screamed while running through the house.

"Why are you running?" she asked as she peered around the door from the laundry room. "You sound like a stampeding herd of buffalo." She must be folding clothes again. She was always folding clothes.

"D-dad's b-back."

He wasn't sure if she was frowning at that news or because of his stutter. It had been a while since he'd done it. The doctor said he had finally outgrown it.

Now it was back.

Just like his dad.

"P-pap said g-get his shotgun."

She blinked in confusion. "What?"

"Sh-shotgun."

She rushed out of the laundry room, her eyes wide. "No! I'm not getting his shotgun! Where is he?"

"Out… s-side."

"Where's your father?"

"Outside, t-too."

"Where?" she asked, rushing down the hallway with Whip on her heels.

"P-pap wants his sh-sh-shotgun."

"I'm not giving him his damn shotgun!" she yelled, sounding irritated.

Whip slammed on the brakes and stared at his mother's retreating back as she continued toward the front door. A second later, he heard the screen door slam hard.

Whip turned, ran back to his pap's room and spotted the shotgun leaning against the wall near the head of his bed.

He wasn't allowed to touch it. Not unless Pap was teaching him how to shoot it. Sometimes they did that out in the woods using targets. If he touched it now, he might get in trouble.

But Pap wanted it.

Pap was the man of the house.

Pap would protect them. He promised he always would. He said he would make up for his useless nut seeds. Whatever that meant.

The long gun was awkward but not too heavy for him to run down the hallway with it. When he got to the front door, he heard raised voices outside.

Pap was arguing with Whip's dad.

His dad sounded drunk. Again.

He shoved the screen door open with his shoulder and hurried out onto the porch.

"Let me pass, old man. I live here, too." Bobby Byrne's words were running together and he stunk like beer, even from where Whip stood.

"Get the hell out of here. You're no longer welcome here. Told you that last time," his pap yelled. "Tonya, you were supposed to bring me my damn shotgun!"

His pap liked to curse. A lot.

He also said he was ornery. Whip agreed once he learned what ornery meant.

"What are you going to do, old man? Shoot your own flesh and blood?" Whip's father shouted, his questions slurred, his face red and his bloodshot eyes narrowed.

Whip didn't like when his face got red like that. It always meant trouble. And not "good trouble" like his pap called Whip.

"If I have to," Pap answered, his face now red, too. He glanced at Whip and held out his hand. "Bring that here, Whip."

"Don't you fucking dare, boy," his father yelled.

"Tyler, take that back inside," his mother ordered, also yelling.

Why was she standing so close to his father? She was within fist range. Didn't she realize that?

"M-Mom!" he warned.

Pap turned on his heels and climbed the steps up to the porch, the hitch in his step worse than normal. Probably because of the arthritis his grandfather complained about often.

He rubbed his hip with one hand and held out his other, the knuckles also knobby from arthritis. "Give it here, Whip, and go back inside."

Whip shook his head.

"Get inside. Now!" Pap shouted at him, grabbing the shotgun out of Whip's hands and pointing toward the door.

His grandfather rarely yelled at him like that. Whip pressed his lips together and rushed inside. He stood just to the side of the door so he could see and hear what was happening, but not be spotted.

He didn't want to get grounded. He hated when he was grounded because he wasn't allowed to stay up late or play with his friends.

He watched Pap work his way slowly down the steps, putting the shotgun up to his shoulder and pointing the double barrels at Whip's father. "Get out of the way, Tonya. If he doesn't want to leave on his own, I'm going to help him decide otherwise."

Whip's mom stepped in front of her husband, her palms out in front of her. "No, Daniel, he's not worth going to jail for."

"Didn't think you were smart, woman, guess I was wrong," Bobby Byrne said. "He isn't going to shoot me. The old man's nothing but hot air."

"Don't try me, son," Pap warned, taking a step closer with the shotgun still raised. "Tonya, get the hell out of the way. Doing this to protect you and Whip."

"This isn't how to go about it, Daniel."

"Yeah, listen to my wife," his dad sneered, then shoved her out of the way. Whip almost rushed back outside when she stumbled.

A noise bubbled up from the back of Whip's throat when his dad rushed his grandfather. Before the old man could pull the trigger, he got knocked to the ground. Bobby Byrne kicked the shotgun out of reach, hauled Pap up by the collar of his flannel shirt, then hauled off and punched Whip's grandfather right in the face.

His pap fell back to the ground in a heap.

"P-pap!" Whip screamed.

"That's what you get for trying to keep me away from my wife and kid, old man. They're not yours, they're mine."

Whip pushed the screen door open, ran out and down the steps. He sprinted up to his father as he was leaning over to grab Pap again. Whip launched himself onto his father's back and hooked an arm around his neck, choking him as hard as he could. "L-leave him a-a-alone!"

At eight, he wasn't nearly as strong as his father, not even when the man was drunk.

"Get the fuck off me, boy!"

"L-leave us a-alone!" he screamed as he pounded his father on the back.

A hand clamped painfully around his arm and suddenly he was flying through the air. He hit the ground hard enough to lose his breath and see stars.

"Tyler!" His mom's panicked scream filled his ringing ears.

Whip shook it off, pushed to his feet, growled and rushed his father again. When he got there, his father backhanded him so hard across the face, he fell backwards and landed on his ass.

He sat with one hand on his throbbing cheek, waiting for the darkness closing in to pass.

"You said he stopped s-s-s-tuttering!"

Whip tried to blink away the pain in his head.

"He did. Now he only does it when you're around, Bobby."

"You're blaming me for the kid being s-s-stupid?"

"It's all your fault," she screamed, getting in his face. "And stop making fun of him!"

She shouldn't be that close to him. He would hurt her next. "M-mom!"

His father grabbed his mother by the neck and flung her sideways. As soon as she landed on the concrete sidewalk with a cry, he grabbed her hair, yanked her up and backhanded her, too.

"Don't blame me for your fuck-up!" Whip's father shouted.

"M-mom!" Whip cried out, unable to pull his eyes from

his parents to see where his grandfather was or if he was hurt.

"You're his damn mother, you caused this." He slapped her again. It was so loud, even Whip could feel the sting.

When she fell to the ground crying, Whip was able to get to his feet again and rush him. "G-get off of her!"

It was like hitting a wall. Two large hands shoved him and he fell backwards, landing next to his mother, scraping his palms on the concrete when he tried to break his fall this time.

"Goddamn defective kid. Starting to doubt whether you came from my loins."

"You want to talk about defective? Have you looked in the damn mirror, jackass?" his pap yelled.

Whip glanced in the direction of where the voice came from and saw his grandfather now standing and wiping away the blood trickling from his mouth. He also saw his grandfather had the shotgun in his hand again. But it was pointed to the ground since Whip and his mother were too close to Bobby Byrne.

They might end up full of buckshot if his grandfather pulled the trigger now.

"He stutters for attention. He does it on purpose. Haven't figured that out yet, old man? He needs it beaten out of him, not babied."

"I know more than you about your own damn son. I take care of them, not you, you useless piece of shit. Wish we never had you."

Whip's father snarled, "Too late, old man."

"I brought you into this damn world and I can take you out, Bobby."

"Do it, old man. Fucking do it. It's nothing but an empty threat."

Pap raised the shotgun.

Whip curled into a ball on the ground, making himself as small of a target as possible.

As soon as he heard his father begin to move, Whip peeked from between his fingers.

Pap had his finger on the trigger. Whip had been taught never to put his finger on the trigger until he was ready to pull it. He ducked his head again, covered his ears and squeezed his eyes shut.

Then his chest exploded as the shotgun went off.

Warm drops splattered his face, his hands, his arms…

None of what his mother was screaming made any sense to Whip. Maybe he wasn't supposed to understand it or maybe it was because his ears were ringing and he could only hear his own thumping heartbeat.

He didn't know and it didn't matter. None of that mattered right now.

Whip forced his eyes open. His father was somehow still on his feet, still moving toward Pap, but now with an arm held across his stomach where the buckshot had hit him and where he was bleeding. His eyes were wide but still held determination. Still remained focused on Pap.

How was he alive or even upright? His shirt was shredded, and so was the now exposed flesh underneath.

He glanced at his pap, who looked like he was in shock himself.

"P-pap!" he screamed in warning as his father closed in on his grandfather.

Did Pap hear him? Or were his ears ringing, too?

Why wasn't he moving? Why was he staring at the shotgun instead of his approaching son?

"P-pap!"

When his grandfather finally lifted his head, his face was so pale and drawn, his eyes empty, but by then, it was too late.

Whip's father yanked the shotgun out of Pap's hand.

"Pap!" Whip screamed as his father lifted the long gun high into the air and slammed the butt right into Pap's forehead.

It was almost like one of those action movies when things moved in slow motion. Whip watched his grandfather crumble where he stood and land into a motionless heap.

A gaping hole, gushing blood, was dead center in his forehead.

That was when Bobby Byrne fell over, landing on top of his own father.

Whip knew right then that his pap was dead. So was his father.

And during it all, his mother continued to scream.

Get Blood & Bones: Whip here: All Retailers

If You Enjoyed This Book

Thank you for reading Blood & Bones: Dodge. If you enjoyed Dodge and Syn's story, please consider leaving a review at your favorite retailer and/or Goodreads to let other readers know. Reviews are always appreciated and just a few words can help an independent author like me tremendously!

Want to read a sample of my work? Download a sampler book here: BookHip.com/MTQQKK

———

**Sign up for Jeanne's newsletter: http://www. jeannestjames.com/newslettersignup
Join her FB readers' group for the inside scoop: https://www.facebook.com/groups/ JeannesReviewCrew/**

Also by Jeanne St. James

Find my complete reading order here:

https://www.jeannestjames.com/reading-order

**Buy direct from the author here: https://
jeannestjamesauthor.com**

Standalone Books:

Made Maleen: A Modern Twist on a Fairy Tale

Damaged

Rip Cord: The Complete Trilogy

Everything About You (A Second Chance Gay Romance)

Reigniting Chase (An M/M Standalone)

Brothers in Blue Series

A four-book series based around three brothers who are small-town
cops and former Marines

The Dare Ménage Series

A six-book MMF, interracial ménage series

The Obsessed Novellas

A collection of five standalone BDSM novellas

Down & Dirty: Dirty Angels MC®

A ten-book motorcycle club series

Guts & Glory: In the Shadows Security

A six-book former special forces series

(A spin-off of the Dirty Angels MC)

<u>Blood & Bones: Blood Fury MC®</u>

A twelve-book motorcycle club series

<u>Motorcycle Club Crossovers:</u>

<u>Crossing the Line: A DAMC/Blue Avengers MC Crossover</u>

<u>Magnum: A Dark Knights MC/Dirty Angels MC Crossover</u>

Crash: A Dirty Angels MC/Blood Fury MC Crossover

Romeo: A Dark Knights MC/Blood Fury MC Crossover

Beyond the Badge: Blue Avengers MC™

A six-book law enforcement/motorcycle club series

<u>Double D Ranch</u>

A six-book MMF ménage series

<u>COMING SOON!</u>

Property of Stone (Kings of Anarchy MC: Pennsylvania)

Dirty Angels MC®: The Next Generation

WRITING AS J.J. MASTERS:

The Royal Alpha Series

A five-book gay mpreg shifter series

About the Author

JEANNE ST. JAMES is a USA Today, Amazon and international bestselling romance author who loves writing about strong women and alpha males. She was only thirteen when she first started writing and her first published piece was an erotic short story in Playgirl magazine. She then went on to publish her first romance novel in 2009. She is now an author of almost 70 contemporary romances. She writes M/F, M/M, and M/M/F ménages, including inter-racial romance. She also writes M/M paranormal romance under the name: J.J. Masters.

Want to read a sample of her work? Download a sampler book here: BookHip.com/MTQQKK

Buy ebooks and audiobooks directly from the author here: https://jeannestjamesauthor.com

www.jeannestjames.com

Newsletter: https://www.authorjeannestjames.com/
Jeanne's Down & Dirty Book Crew: https://www.facebook.com/groups/JeannesReviewCrew/

facebook.com/JeanneStJamesAuthor

instagram.com/JeanneStJames

bookbub.com/authors/jeanne-st-james

goodreads.com/JeanneStJames

Get a FREE Sampler Book

This book contains the first chapter of a variety of my books. This will give you a taste of the type of books I write and if you enjoy the first chapter, I hope you'll be interested in reading the rest of the book.

Each book I list in the sampler will include the description of the book, the genre, and the first chapter, along with links to find out more. I hope you find a book you will enjoy curling up with!

Get it here: BookHip.com/MTQQKK